I0824769

# *SONG OF THE SALTINGS*

ALSO BY

*RACHAEL KING*

*The Grimmelings*

*Secrets at Red Rocks*

RACHAEL KING

# SONG OF THE SALTINGS

Margaret K. McElderry Books
New York Amsterdam/Antwerp London
Toronto Sydney/Melbourne New Delhi

MARGARET K. McELDERRY BOOKS
An imprint of Simon & Schuster Children's Publishing Division
1230 Avenue of the Americas, New York, New York 10020

Jacket design by Sonia Chaghatzbanian

Interior design by Irene Metaxatos
The text for this book was set in Adobe Garamond Pro.
Manufactured in the United States of America
First Edition
10 9 8 7 6 5 4 3 2 1
CIP data for this book is available from the Library of Congress.
ISBN 9781665984331
ISBN 9781665984348 (ebook)

*For my sister*

*Harriet,*

*with love*

*The river in me is black.*

*I am the god, the beast that leaves no prints,*

*the pounce of wind on the sea, that place*

*where the lake darkens*

*and the surface breaks. I went,*

*taking the shape of water.*

—ROBIN ROBERTSON

# *SONG OF THE SALTINGS*

# PROLOGUE

THE ISLAND OF BRACK. *Brack.* Even the name lingers on your tongue like the musty taste of stagnant water. You can feel it in the air as you breathe, thick and heavy. It's an island of salt marshes, of bogs and heather, the rocky earth blackened with peat.

To the east, the village lies quiet, nestled near the sea like a collection of weathered bones: whitewashed stone houses with thatched roofs and cobblestone streets worn smooth by the wheels of horse-drawn carts. It's orderly enough, if you don't look too closely. Above the village, a solemn gray house, with its windows like mournful eyes, watches over the forbidden cliffs. They say too many folk have fallen to their deaths there, where great sea stacks stand tall while the ocean roils around them.

There's something else. The earth trembles there; it thrums and groans, as though the island itself were alive. The sea's roar mixes with a deep rumble, a sound like the island's bones shifting, or the Glimm turning in its sleep. It vibrates in your chest and hums in your ears. The island, breathing.

But out here, beyond the village, the moors are wide open spaces where the wind howls at you all year long, and the ground wants to suck at your boots with every step. Where makeshift stone huts shelter lonely shepherds, where barrows house the bones of the ancient dead, and the lights from the bog lure weary nighttime travelers to their death.

One step off the path, and the earth could swallow you whole.

Me? I've been here a thousand years, if you believe the village drinking songs, the children's skipping rhymes. *Stay away from Jenny of the bog*, they say; *she'll grab you in your sleep*. They ride past on their horses, herding their sheep, keeping carefully to the marked path, lest they wander off and fall in the bog. *My bog.*

I live on the frogs and the birds that come too close, the fish in the stream. The odd sheep. The villagers will tell you I eat children. But it was not *me* who offered children to the Glimm. It was *them*. I hear the souls of those children. Of my child.

I watched them, every three years, life after life—couldn't tear my eyes away, though it hurt—until the day when everything changed.

The procession came before dawn: masked minstrels playing bone flutes, the Council in black, proud as ever. How I hate the very sight of their faces. Different faces over the years, but always that same haughty expression. Square jaws, fine-boned hands on the reins of their fine-boned horses.

In the center: a girl on a nut-brown pony, pale and still, with a crown of blackthorn on her head. Her parents walked beside her, stricken and silent. Her brother skipped ahead with streamers colorful in the torchlight.

Down to the saltings they went, to the shadow of the standing stone cast by the rising sun. The girl was blindfolded. She did not cry. She was quiet, as if she already knew.

The sacrifice would be made. The blight would be avoided for another cycle.

But this year, things would be different.

The girl would survive. She didn't know it then, but her fate was tied to the island. The Glimm's breath on her face, hot as fever, would haunt her forever. She would not escape its pull.

The island has shifted since that day, and it will shift again. I can feel it in my bones, in the mud, in the peat. The song of the saltings hums louder now, as if calling for something more. At night the noise in my body is unbearable. I tore my clothes to rags long ago; now I wear only mud and weeds. My skin has hardened, toughened in the bog like leather. I should be dead.

*But here I am.*

I see the cave in the mountains, and I know what is inside. I know what makes the island hum, especially near the cliffs.

I know the Glimm.

But does the Glimm know me?

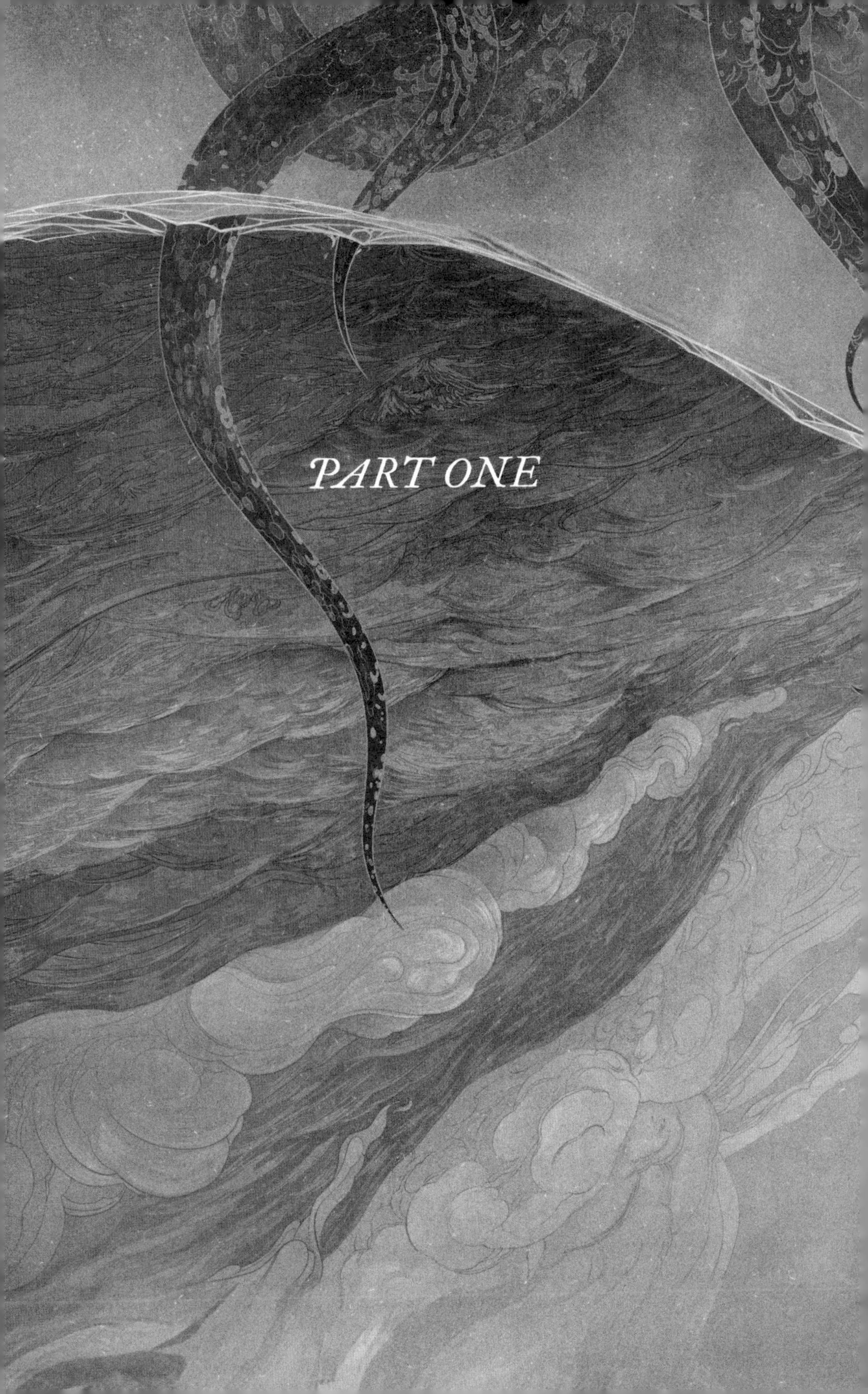

# PART ONE

# I

**THE DEAD MARE** lies just a few feet away. A hooded crow has settled on a nearby stone, watching with interest. Lotta looks up as the needle-sharp cry of a wheeling buzzard pierces the damp air overhead.

"Chancers," she says. She'll need to come back to the moors with men to bury the horse later—if the birds don't strip it dry before they get there.

She takes the glass bottle from her satchel and jumps from the dapple-gray gelding's back. She doesn't bother tethering it. It'll stay with her no matter what.

The skewbald mare on the ground could be asleep except for the flies that have settled in its eyes, and on its brown-and-white patchwork hide. Lotta doesn't have much time. The colostrum—the thick, rich first milk that will give the orphaned foal its much-needed nutrients—will dry up within a few hours of death. Lotta can't be sure how long the horse lay there before she found its foal and galloped with it back to the stables.

She rolls up the sleeves of her shirt and kneels on the moist ground, feeling the muddy coldness seep through her trousers into her skin. She reaches for the swollen teat, places the bottle beneath it, and squeezes.

Nothing.

She curses. “Ah, for Glimm’s sake.”

She tries again, with the other teat this time.

There’s a pause, then a popping sensation, and thick yellow liquid oozes into the bottle. *Got you.*

It doesn’t take long to get all that’s on offer—not much, but it’s better than nothing. If they’re lucky, one of the other broodmares will accept the foal.

As she slips the stoppered bottle into her shoulder satchel, then rolls her sleeves back down, the gray horse throws its head up, its neck stiff. Its ears prick forward, and it lets out a crying whinny.

It’s answered by another, beyond the barrow, the burial chamber to the west of the village. This call is high and terrified. Another escaped horse, wandering the treacherous peat bogs.

Lotta leaps onto the gray’s back and urges it into a canter.

The distance is farther than she expects, across the rolling moorland. The light is fading fast. Soon it will be too dark to see the way home, and she nearly turns back, but then she hears the horse cry out again, weaker this time. The figure of a man waits in the gloaming. A black mare with a mane the color of the surrounding heather stands up to its chest in murky water, trembling with exhaustion, eyes rimmed white. Its rider—not a man, but a boy her own age, no more than sixteen or seventeen, with dark, sweat-matted curls—stands frozen on the edge of the bog, dragging on the reins.

“Help,” he calls. “She’s stuck.” His thick eyebrows are clamped in determination.

Lotta doesn’t hesitate. She vaults from the gray’s back and plunges into the bog.

At first, the ground seems firm, but then it starts to move beneath her in slow pulses, like lungs filled with thick, peaty air. Each step makes a slurping sound as she sinks deeper. The cold reaches her ankles, soaking through the leather of her boots, but she doesn't stop—she has to keep moving if she wants to keep them.

"Careful!" The boy's pale face shines in the gloom. "The Glimm!"

Water swirls around Lotta's calves as the bog tries to grab her and hold on, but she won't let it.

"Have you ever seen the Glimm this far inland?" she says, scowling. "No."

There's no time for superstition, nor rumors, not even those based on truth.

"Jenny, then. I hear she comes up from below."

Lotta ignores him. She closes her eyes and imagines herself as light as air. She's always had a knack for it, and she has no idea how or why. Many have disappeared into the bog and never come out; she doesn't know why it favors her, why she alone can move through it freely.

The horse tries to heave away from her at first, but every panicked move creates a sucking sound and sinks it farther into the water.

"Stop tugging on her," she says to the boy. He releases the reins.

She approaches from the side and moves to the horse's head. It's a large animal, with a broad, convex nose and a white star beneath its forelock. Its neck is as thick and solid as a standing stone. Lotta murmurs sweet nothings, just noises, but they seem to do the trick.

The horse's body stills and it blows on her offered hand.

"What can we do?" The boy's voice is raised in panic. "We can't lose her; she's all we got."

The horse senses his agitation. It begins to shudder, a small earthquake rippling across its shoulder. Behind Lotta, the gray gelding shudders in sympathy. Just being near another horse with an elevated heart rate is sending shocks through its body; it could give in to its instinct, turn and flee. But it stands its ground.

"You can start by getting a long, sturdy rope."

"But it's too far. And I can't go back without her."

He's right. There's no time to wait for a rope. "Move away, then," she says. "You're only making it worse."

"She's my horse," he says. "I'm not leaving her."

"Do you want my help, or no? You'll have to trust me."

The boy opens his mouth as if to argue but closes it again and nods. He backs off and sits on a stone a safe distance away, arms folded tightly, eyes never leaving his horse—or Lotta.

She brings her attention back to the animal. Then she calls down into the thick, oily water.

She sings for the bog to set the horse free.

# 2

"IT'S A MIRACLE," says the boy.

The giant mare—now caked in mud and smelling like death—stands with its head bowed and its muzzle stuck into the boy's palm.

"If that's what you want to call it," replies Lotta. She's trying to keep her voice offhand, but the truth is that *she's* not even sure what to call it. The song has been visiting her dreams lately, bubbling up from some place deep in her body, and when it came to her in the bog, rising from the depths, she knew she had to let it out. She couldn't have stopped it, even if she'd tried. It felt as certain to her as the knowledge that she needed air to breathe, or that the ocean and the Glimm exist: The bog would hear her song and release the horse. And as the first note left her throat, she felt an answering hum from below.

She shivers at the memory. She should change the subject. "What's your name?"

"Moss," he says. "This is Hannah. Thank you. I mean it. I thought she were a goner. My mam would've killed me. Hannah's all we got."

"Well, Moss, maybe think twice about bringing your horse out this way."

He doesn't seem to have heard her. He's busy running his hands over the horse's legs, checking for injury, lifting her feathered, plate-sized hooves. At least he cares enough for that.

"How can I repay you?" he asks, pausing where he's bent over to look up at her. His face is nearly gone now, in the gloom. "We don't have much, but we could give you somewhere to rest for the night if you need it? Feed you my mam's turnip stew, which is better than it sounds."

She ignores him. "I'll ride back with you and lead the way. My one knows where it's going."

"Back where?" he asks.

"To the village, of course."

He draws in a breath and takes a step back.

She narrows her eyes. Come to think of it, she doesn't recognize him. "You're not from the village, are you? What are you? One of the bird hunters?"

He shakes his head, and it dawns on her. He's moved away so she doesn't smell him. Peat smoke. Those folk all live in blackhouses, with no chimneys, just a thatched roof for letting the smoke out. She's not been in one, but she's heard about it. A fire right in the middle of the house, its sour stink coating the walls and the clothes of the people who sit around it.

"You're one of them. A hideling."

The boy stands up straight and lays a hand on the big horse's neck.

"And what of it?" he asks. "Aren't we allowed out on the moors either? Where are we supposed to go, then? Stay in our little hamlet?"

"You do what you want," says Lotta. She pauses before she takes a flying leap onto the gray's back and her feet find the stirrups without looking. "I'm surprised to see you out here—I thought you'd be afraid of the dark. Oh, wait . . . it's the light that you're scared of, isn't it? You can probably see in the dark. No wonder you look so sickly."

"I get by," says the boy, Moss.

Stupid name. Like something that grows in the dark, away from sunlight.

"You're her," he says suddenly. "You're she. The girl who survived. Lotta."

A familiar weight drops into her stomach. How can he tell? She's never met him, although she has seen the hidelings and their families slope into the village to trade their peat. The parents nudge their children and point at her when they think she isn't looking. But she can always see them. Cowards, the lot of them.

"I have to go," she says. "I've got a newborn foal needs feeding. Get home safe, little hideling," she says, but she can't keep the scorn from her voice. It's going to be slow going getting home now, thanks to him.

He hesitates, then yells after her. "Don't call me that. It's not my fault! I didn't ask to be hid. None of us did. We don't deserve to be punished so."

"Well, some of us didn't get to hide," she says. "You look after that horse, Moss. It deserves better. And now I know what you mean when you said it was all you got."

She gives the gray its head and it sets off at a jog, while she tries to forget what just happened—the bog, the horse, the song—and concentrates on the task ahead: getting back to the Manor House's stables, where she left the colt with Dougie, the inexperienced young groom.

She skirts around the village, relieved to see empty fields and streets as everyone has gone inside to light fires and fill bellies as best they can. It's been a particularly hard winter, and everyone is looking forward to the spring lottery in less than a week, when the Glimm will be satisfied and crops will once again thrive. Everyone, that is, but Lotta, who can feel it creeping toward her, claws extended.

She is the girl who survived the sacrifice; nothing she can do or say will change it. Wherever she goes on the island, people try to touch her for luck, and she feels their eyes all over her as she slips past: on her back, in her hair. It doesn't help that she refuses to wear dresses anymore. Not for her, the heavy skirts of the island women; tweed trousers held up with braces and a thick woolen shirt are best for tending and exercising the horses. So folk always know it's her sloping up an alley, her cap pulled down over her eyes and her thick chestnut plait down her back.

That morning, when she saddled the roan pony for Daphne—her master's granddaughter, and her only friend—Lotta's cheeks were still burning from another humiliating encounter in the village. Old Biddy Jackson had sliced off a lock of Lotta's hair in the bakery and tried to hide it, jutting her square chin when Lotta turned around to glare at her.

"It's only because they admire you," said Daphne. "You should take some time to appreciate it."

But Lotta doesn't appreciate it. She can't. She wants to be left alone to get on with her job. Tending the horses for the next lottery. The next sacrifice.

"You wouldn't understand," she had growled at Daphne. "You were never meant for the killing. You're the special one, not me."

"Pishposh," said Daphne, as she stood idly by, waiting for Lotta to finish. Glimm forbid she should ever pick up a brush herself and dirty her hands. "I'm only special because of who my grandfather is. Where's the pride in that?"

"And I'm only special because of a silly pony!" Lotta tugged at the stirrup leathers a little too roughly. "The Glimm was confused by her. She saved my life."

Hazel. Her pony. Her best friend. Taken.

Her own life spared.

*

The road up to the Manor House is lined with lanterns, hung on tall poles to light the way. Beyond, Lotta can hear the waves crashing against the cliffs. She gallops the last half mile, fear that the foal will die swelling in her heart before she checks herself. *It's only a horse*, she thinks. *Only a horse.*

The foal is tucked into straw, wrapped in a blanket, its tiny chest rising and falling like a bellows. The stable boy, Dougie, sits beside it, blinking slowly.

"You were gone ages," he says, wobbling to his feet. "Did you get it?"

Lotta pulls the bottle from her satchel. The thick, creamy colostrum slides around inside.

Dougie lets out a low whistle. "I didn't think you'd get any."

"Barely did," she admits. "But it's something. Do you have it?"

He hands her the hollow cow's horn. It's warm to the touch. She slowly pours the precious liquid, careful not to spill a drop.

She crouches beside the foal and places the horn by its head, gently tapping the tip against its mouth. After a few seconds, it opens its mouth and she slips it in the corner, over its tongue. It begins to suck.

Relief warms her chest.

Dougie sits again, watching her in silence. She can feel his uncertainty around her, like anything he says might make her bark at him the way she did when she'd first arrived with the foal in her arms. She'd ordered him to get fresh straw, then a blanket. The boy did as he was told, and soon returned with the blanket, which he lay carefully over the foal's quivering body.

"Where'd you find him?" he asked.

"It's the skewbald mare's. I found them together, out on the moors. The mare must have escaped. It never did like being confined."

His eyes widened. "Not Bessie? But she wasn't due for—"

"And yet here we are," she snapped, sharper than she'd intended.

His next words were almost inaudible. "What should we do? Feed him? Should I fetch some cow's milk?"

"No, not yet," Lotta said, more gently this time. "Wait here with her. Keep her warm. I'll be back."

That was how she'd found herself on the moors, with that boy.

"Do you ever hear a song inside you?" she asks Dougie now. "That just has to come out?"

"Only the song my gran used to sing. She hummed it when storms came in. Said it was for keeping bones still under the barrows." He whistles a few notes. The foal's ears flicker. It opens its eyes and stares into Lotta's.

"Why are you so good with them?" Dougie asks. "Like you're his mam."

She doesn't answer. "You take over," she says instead. "I need to get the gray to bed." She stretches her legs and stands, holding the foal's head gently for Dougie to assume the position.

The gelding, which has stood waiting patiently outside the stall door, follows her now, nudging her.

"That horse loves you, you know," calls Dougie.

"Nonsense," says Lotta. "It's just well trained."

"Why do you call him an 'it'?"

Lotta pauses and spins on her toes. Her boot grinds into the dirt floor.

"Because it's an 'it.'" She sighs. "You can't get attached to animals; they're not people. I have to go."

She leads the gray toward its stall, but she hears Dougie addressing the foal in his arms. "She don't much like people, neither, little one."

"I like people!" she calls behind her, but she's met by silence. He wouldn't understand. He's too young to really know about what happened before.

# 3

"**THE STATE OF HER!** Honestly, Moss, how many times have I told you it's dangerous out on the moors? You could have been killed."

His mother stands with her arms folded, waiting for an answer, but Moss has nothing to say. How can he explain what just happened to their horse? To him? By the time they got home he was shivering with cold and shock.

Mam gives up waiting for an answer and goes back into the house, slamming the door behind her. He finishes wiping Hannah down in silence, then leaves her to roam freely in the yard with a blanket on her back, a full hay net, and fresh water in the trough. *That horse works too hard*, he thinks. *We work her too hard.*

After he'd finished stacking the peat that evening, he had only wanted to take her out for a break, for an easy canter on the moors, maybe down to the beach for a gallop if there was time. When he had fetched the rope bridle and was using the mounting stone to reach the horse's bare, wide back, Mam had come out of the house.

"Don't be late, Moss Smith," she said, drying her hands on her skirt. "And don't tire her out too badly. There's a big load of peat to pull to the market tomorrow."

Moss caught the weariness in her voice. She never applied the same care to herself. He's started to notice the veins in her hands and forearms, twined like knotted serpents. Her wrist bones are sharper than he's ever seen, and her small, pinched lips have almost disappeared under her pointed nose.

"It's all right, Mam," he promised. "I won't ask her to do anything she doesn't want to."

They passed the makeshift blackhouses of the other so-called hidelings—Moss and the others prefer "exiles"—evenly spaced out on the moor, some with peat smoke filtering up through the low thatched roofs. The nearest house, the one that belongs to his friend Sadie and her mother and brother, has a hole in it. He knows the rain gets in. He must keep his promise to help them patch it.

Moss never tires of feeling the wind on his face, hearing the undersong of the moors. In the dull afternoons, he doesn't have to cover his eyes or squint; they only water a little. Though he doesn't remember most of them, those years being kept inside, in the dark, have taken their toll on his body. Even now, he still can't go outside on cloudless days; thankfully, there aren't many. His pale skin burns easily. He's always been small for his age, though that is changing, finally. He can already see that his brother, Stone, will be as tall as he is before he's twelve.

The evenings are his domain. His eyes are sharper in the dark than most and he loves nothing more than wandering on the moors while everyone else is asleep. Some nights, the sky glows in green shimmers: a gift from the Glimm to show his love for his people. On nights like that Moss imagines he can hear the serpent deep beneath the island, turning in its sleep. And further, that he can hear the other serpents in the mist that guard the island, billowing the oceans, lifting their voices to the Lights. Nothing gets in, but nothing gets out, either. There must be other islands out there in the vast sea, on the other side of the mist, all with their own Glimm and their own guardians, but he can never know.

Hannah wanted to run this evening, and he crouched low as she thundered into a gallop, hares scattering from the path. Up there the terrain is drier, harder, and a path was made long ago across the moors that avoids the softest ground. It hadn't rained for a while, so the ponds and boggy patches weren't in unexpected places.

As the lowering sun streaked the dark clouds with gold, he slowed Hannah to a walk, letting the familiar wind sing in his ears. The watery cries of distant curlews, readying for the night, lulled him. That was his first mistake.

There was an explosion of air beside them and Hannah shied, leaping sideways as a waterbird squawked away. Moss teetered on her back and fell, landing heavily in the heather. A pain shot through his hip, and he set his teeth against it. *Ow.*

He climbed to his feet and moved toward Hannah but stopped when he realized that she was standing up to her knees in black water.

"Come on then, old girl." He reached forward and grabbed her reins, which trailed in the brackish puddle.

But Hannah didn't move. She heaved a sigh instead.

"Come on." He clicked his tongue and tugged on the reins. Her head craned forward but her body stayed put.

Panic seized him by the throat. He'd heard of horses being lost in the bog. Of sinking so far that only their nostrils were visible before they too disappeared. He's always believed it's the Glimm being greedy—taking a horse for itself despite the yearly offerings. Johnno Flynn told him a pony had to have its throat cut once, to put it out of its misery, and the image haunted Moss's dreams for months.

Hannah must have sensed his agitation. She lowered her head, and Moss saw her shoulder muscles ripple. Then she threw her head back, and he saw the whites of her eyes. She grunted.

"Come on, girl," he said, dragging on the reins, but this only made matters worse. His scalp prickled and his shirt stuck to his back, soaked in the sweat that had sprung up between his shoulder blades. A rook alighted on a nearby rock to watch with interest, its beak shiny and black, half open, as if calculating how to swallow Hannah whole once the bog was finished with her.

"Get outta here!" Moss shouted at it in desperation.

Just then, he heard thudding hooves in the distance. Someone was coming. They were saved. The sun had fallen below the Black Mountains to the northwest, and the moor was washed in gloom. On a normal day it would be just how he liked it, but now it seemed a bad portent.

The hooves stopped some distance away.

"Hey!" he called. "Over here!" But the breeze was blowing in the wrong direction, back toward the hamlet, and there was no answering call. He couldn't see anything on the undulating terrain.

He realized with a sickening lurch in his gut that Hannah was sinking. The water was up to her chest now. Unwelcome images crashed into his head: coming home without her, his mother and Stone meeting him, weeping. How would they carry the peat to town with no horse? How would they survive? The Council would never give them another—and if they did, they'd be in debt for the rest of their lives. *More* in debt.

But he forgot all that when he glanced at Hannah, whose black neck was now flecked with foam. All that mattered was the horse now, getting her free. In this instant she'd become all he'd ever known.

A high whinny pierced the gloaming. Hannah answered, and then there was the sound of hooves again, coming closer. Then a girl with thick auburn hair flying, cantering toward them on the back of a fine dapple-gray horse.

When he at last comes inside—cold, stiff, his hip aching—Mam is banging around the cooking area. She's left him a steaming bowl of turnip stew on the table, with a hunk of bread beside it, so she can't be too angry with him.

But he can't eat. He sits down at the table and pushes the stew away. A lump of rock is growing ever larger and harder in his belly. He can still hear the girl's voice in his head.

*You're one of them.*

The look on her face.

*A hideling.*

Like it meant he was less than her, less than anyone. Like he chose it. But he hadn't. None of them had. The parents chose. The ones who couldn't bear to see their children's names drawn in the lottery.

And back then, everyone believed the Glimm demanded a child. That unless it was a child that was offered—not an adult, not a sheep, not a chicken or a cow, but a child—the Glimm would curse them all, the crops would fail and babies would be born dead or sick. Famine and disease would spread through the island, leaving only a few survivors to rebuild. Lore dictated it, and the lore was based on hundreds, perhaps *thousands* of years of the island's history. There were burial chambers all over the island, filled with bones of those who had defied the lore in the past.

But then the girl, Lotta, was chosen, and the Glimm took her pony instead, and nothing happened. No curse. No pestilence, no disease; in fact, the crops were especially hearty that year. Just the right amount of rain fell, and there was more sun than usual.

The Glimm, it seemed, wanted horses. So horses, conceded the Council, it would receive. And so, the hidden children had emerged, blinking into the light, from cellars and cupboards, pale and thin. But alive. Safe.

*Hidelings.*

Moss pulls the side of his trousers down and sees the swollen red mark that is darkening on his hip.

"What is it? Are you hurt?" There is fear in his mother's voice, and it irritates him suddenly, so much that he bangs his fist on the table.

"I'm fine!" he says, louder than he meant to. Then, "What are you looking at?" His little brother, Stone, who has stuck his head out the curtain of the bed, fixes him with a sleepy eye. His startled face withdraws in a blink.

Mam sits down at the table opposite him.

"Mossy." Her voice is wheedling.

He can't look at her.

"Talk to me."

Fine. He will talk. "I met that girl on the moors."

"Which girl?"

"The girl. Lotta. The one who survived."

Mam doesn't say anything, only turns her face to stare into the stinking peat fire.

"Aren't you going to say something?" he asks.

She spreads her hands. "What do you want me to say?"

"Aren't you curious? Even a bit?"

"Well, what happened?" She sounds like she did when he was a child, when he'd come to her with skinned knees.

"She rescued Hannah. Hannah was stuck in the bog."

Mam sucks a breath in through her teeth.

"For the love of Glimm, Mossy. What were you thinking? You know there's no coming out of the bog. She's all we got."

"I know that, Mam, d'you think I don't know that?"

"Tell me."

"She just appeared, on a gray horse. Royalty, it were. It must have been the Council's horse. Never seen a day of peat work in its life."

Mam nods. "She looks after Judge Hawthorne's horses. And the horses for the Glimm. It's an important job. Then what happened?"

"Hannah were stuck good, but, Mam, she got in the water with her. She started singing."

"To Hannah? To calm her, like?"

"I don't know. I swear she were singing to the bog itself. Or maybe to the Glimm."

He closes his eyes and listens for the haunting melody in his memories. But it's gone, like the edges of a dream. Her voice, low and murky, full of a yearning like he's never heard. "And then the next moment, Hannah gives a great heave and steps out of the bog as calm as you like, covered in stinking mud but not hurt. I checked," he says quickly when his mother raises her eyebrows at him.

Mam says nothing, and they sit in silence for a moment. But the rock is still swelling in his belly, growing hot as coals now.

"She's special, that girl," Mam says at last. "Well, what were she like?"

"She were horrible. Superior." He still stings from the way her whole demeanor changed when she realized who he was. What he was.

"She's a special girl," she says again. "We owe her a lot. We owe her Hannah's life. Your life, maybe."

"My life? Do we really?"

"Without what happened, you might have been next in the lottery, Moss, you know that."

"Except I wouldn't have been, would I? If she'd been taken by the Glimm, I'd still be hiding out in the cellar, wouldn't I? Like a coward."

"Stop."

Like a coward. Like a cheat. That's what people say. As if hiding from death is some kind of betrayal. As if he'd chosen it, when all he'd done was sit quiet in the dark, year after year, while the rest of the island gambled their children in a bloody lottery. And now everyone calls them hidelings and treats them like vermin: shunned, spat on, barred from school and Temple, barred from everything that makes a life worth living. Cheaters of the Glimm, unworthy of its love.

"If you hadn't hidden me, we'd be respectable members of society," Moss says. "We'd have enough food to eat. We'd have salt. And oil. Not this slop." He shoves the bowl so hard it flies off the end of the table and shatters on the dirt floor. "We'd have slate for a floor instead of this. And a chimney. Mam, we'd have a chimney. Da would be the village blacksmith still, and I'd be helping him, learning a skill more than just cutting bleedin' peat!"

The mention of his father—dead from a broken heart after his livelihood was taken away—is too much.

"And you might be dead!" Mam jumps up, knocking her chair over in the blast, and puts her hands on her hips.

This, he's not expecting.

"You can bleedin' well build a chimney," she says, flinging out an arm. "There's the mountain! We've got a cart, and a horse. You go gather and cut the stone yourself, ungrateful boy."

She throws the rag she's holding onto the table and walks out into the night, her head grazing the doorway.

Moss can't remember the last time he's seen her angry.

"You've done it now," comes Stone's voice from the bed. "Gone and made her mad, you goose."

"Shut it!" yells Moss. But he's already feeling deflated. How can Stone possibly know how he feels? He was born into this house, doesn't know any different, never met their father, not really. He doesn't know what they've lost. What they could have had if his parents hadn't hidden Moss, condemned him forever to be a hideling. A coward.

Condemned him forever to be nothing better than a smear of peat on the boot of Lotta Salter.

# 4

***She stands,*** *waist-deep, in the bog. There's no horse here, no boy. Just Lotta and the silent moors in the last light.*

*The humming starts beneath her feet. It rises up through the mud and the water until the surface of the bog is shimmering.*

*A note comes to her, then another.*

*The song aches through her body, building and building.*

*She opens her mouth and sets it free.*

Lotta wakes with a thick head. The last notes of the dream die away before her memory can grab hold of them.

She throws off her covers and lies there for a moment before dragging herself out of bed. This small, spartan room above the stables has been her home since the Judge's son-in-law, Councillor Lewis, came to offer her an apprenticeship three years ago.

After the killing, when her pony was taken, it took a long time for her to understand what had happened. Her ma had prepared her thoroughly for the life beyond with stories, passed down like family heirlooms, of a place green and lush, with great forests of tall trees, and land as far as the eye can see; with the most colorful birds imaginable, and huge animals that roam free in mountains—not just sheep and goats, which she knew, but bears and wolves and foxes and lions and tigers, mythical beasts that only exist in stories. There would be food aplenty, with vast fields of wheat and barley and corn. There would be all manner of sweet and delicious fruit growing in the temperate climate.

Her parents promised her that almost no time would pass before they would all join her, one by one, in the life after. She remembers her mother smoothing her hair, voice trembling as she promised: "You'll see your granny soon. She's waiting with Winnie by the garden gate. Just follow the Glimm's path." Even her big brother, Marten, had been jealous. Granny had died of a sore chest the previous winter, and their cat, Winnie, had gone with her.

Lotta had understood that she would leave the island, never to return. That she was very important and that she would ensure the survival of everyone else on the island, not just her family. It was a true honor to be chosen in the lottery.

She would be with the Glimm, cradled by its love.

She would never be hungry, or cold. Or lonely.

Later, she came to understand this: She also would have been dead. And now her pony was dead, and she had to live with the people who had done nothing to prevent either loss.

Councillor Lewis came when she was just thirteen. Word had spread of her uncanny knack with animals, horses in particular. She had gone willingly, because she could no longer live with a family who had sent her, without a fight, to her death.

Her parents had let her go, saying they hoped she'd have a better life in the care of the Manor House, now that they had a new baby to look after. But as Lotta was helped into a fine carriage, her mother's legs gave way, her face etched with grief, and she had to be supported by her father.

In the quiet darkness of the carriage, Lotta had looked away.

Now breakfast is a hunk of bread held between her teeth while she dresses. Her only trousers are filthy and stink of bog water. She was so exhausted last night from the day's trials—the skewbald mare, the black horse caught in the bog, the effort it took to free it—that she threw them on the floor and fell into bed.

The song had bubbled up like blood from a wound, and afterward she was spent, shaken. And then, there was that boy, with the strange dark eyes and ghost-pale skin. She'd never met a hideling child up close. That sour smell. His pleading with her—*I didn't ask to be hid.* She supposed that part was true. *He* hadn't asked for it, but his family had, and now he was paying the price.

Perhaps she'd been too hard on him.

Lotta throws on her one long skirt, which drapes heavily around her legs. Ugh. How do girls walk in these, let alone run, and work, and ride? Her comb snags on her curls, before she shrugs and tosses it back in a drawer. Already the horses below are banging on their stall doors for their breakfast; they've heard her moving around above them.

Dougie has already started filling the hay nets and can't hide his smugness at beating her to it.

"Afternoon, Lotta," he says, with his cheeky grin.

Lotta jabs him in the ribs, making him squeal, which in turn startles the dun gelding he's tending to.

"Mornin', Dougie," she says. "Lots to do today. Have you checked on the foal?"

"Fed and sleeping like a baby."

Lotta grabs at a piece of straw in his hair. "Did you sleep here?"

He blushes under his dirty cheeks. "I had to. I couldn't leave it, not after everything it's been through. I were only keeping it warm."

Lotta smiles, startling him with an unfamiliar expression. "You're a good boy, Dougie. You probably saved its life. Have you eaten?"

He nods. "Beth brought me something from the kitchen."

"Good. Daphne and Roderick are both riding today. Get those horses groomed and tacked up, quick as you can."

She dumps her trousers in a bucket with some soap and stirs it with a stick. They'll have to soak and wait to be hung out to dry.

Before long, the sound of high laughter carries across the yard. Daphne always announces herself this way. Life is a lark for a girl like her, no worries on her shoulders.

"All right, Dougie, Lotta? Got those nags ready for us?" Roderick is all blond hair and big, healthy teeth. The badge of the Council's kin. Daphne is already standing in front of her pony—Wheatie, she calls it, for its light brown hide—kissing its nose. She wears fine knitted gloves and clutches a leather whip. Her pale hair is caught up in a net at the nape of her neck, her head topped with a glossy hat, made from material like the coat of a black cat. Where she has got it from, Lotta can't fathom; she wouldn't put it past her friend to skin a cat, however.

"Psst, Roddy."

Lotta's brother, Marten, beckons Roderick from one of the empty stalls. How did he get in there without her noticing? Has he been there since daybreak, or did he sneak past when her back was turned?

Roderick pokes his head out of the stable doors and does a thorough check.

"Keep an eye out, will you, girls?" He winks at Lotta and Daphne before ducking into the stall and closing the door firmly.

Daphne rolls her eyes. "They'll get caught one of these days," she says. She's speaking to Lotta, but her eyes are on Wheatie as she strokes his forelock over and over.

"Is that so bad?" says Lotta.

Daphne finally looks at her.

"You know it is. Marten will be dismissed. Roddy will be paired up with one of the Councillors' daughters. Marten will have to find a boy his own class to canoodle with."

"The Council doesn't seem to mind that *we're* friends," Lotta points out.

"Pfft, you're different and you know it. And it's not like we're in love. We're just companions."

"What if it were me and Roddy? What then?"

"I'd say you're dreaming, my girl! Redirect your fancies elsewhere!"

Lotta blushes. "You know that's not what I meant! What if it's Henry Gray or Maxwell Stirling? A mere salt farmer's daughter with their precious Council offspring?"

Daphne snorts. "You're not a *mere* anything, and you know it. You're probably right, though. Being the miracle stable girl doesn't buy you marriage rites. It's still against the lore. You'll just have to find yourself a plain old village boy."

The stall door bangs open, and the boys roll out, flushed and smiling. Just in time. Through a small dirty window, Gregory, the head gardener, appears, striding across the yard, huge shoulders swinging and a determined look on his generously whiskered face.

"Get out there, now!" says Lotta, and Marten, despite being two years older, obeys like a chastised child. They both might work for Councillor Lewis, but Lotta ranks higher.

"There you are!" Gregory's great booming voice reaches them inside. Roderick suppresses a laugh and Lotta shoots daggers at him with her eyes.

"It's not funny," she warns.

As if to back her up, Gregory continues the tongue-lashing. "Late again, young Salter, and your work not finished from yesterday. You'll lose this job if you don't step it up, so help me Glimm, I mean it this time."

He grabs Marten by the arm, but Marten shakes him off.

"All right, old man, I'm coming! No need for the roughhousing." He casts a glance back toward the window where the others are assembled, watching. He gives a wink, and a grimace, then continues on his way.

"Stupid old codger," spits Roderick. "I should get my father to dock his pay for insolence."

"He's right, though," says Lotta. "You're too much of a distraction for Marten. You'll get him in trouble, and he'll be the one that cops it, not you."

"Hark at you," says Roderick, "a lowly stable hand, telling a Councillor's son what to do."

"Shut it, Roddy," says Daphne. "You know she's right. And she's not just any old stable hand. You wouldn't be riding that stallion if it weren't for her taming him for you. He'd have trampled on your head months ago. She's a miracle worker is what she is, our Lottie. Dougie's a stable hand, but Lotta's the horse *master*."

**She smells the salt** on the wind today. It buffets her up the road, threatening to take her cap, which she clamps down on her head. Beside her, on the cobbled street, horses and carts are jammed nose to wheel, laden with wares for the morning market. They're going to be late. She's grateful now for leaving the old stable pony tethered outside the village; it's quicker to walk.

"Get a move on!" yells a man in the cart beside her, shaking his whip.

The woman in the cart in front turns and leers. "You shut up, Pete. Everybody knows your eggs are black inside and your turnips are moldy!" She laughs. Her teeth are a sickly yellow.

Pete—*Stormy Pete*, they call him, on account of all his bluster—goes red in the face as he glowers at her and mumbles something, but he soon redirects his ire at another woman, on foot this time, who is weaving her way between the carts with a great heavy basket of peat bricks on her back. She wears a leather strap across her forehead to stop herself from falling backward from the weight. She puffs with the effort, her thick eyebrows clamped in concentration.

"Oi!" shouts Pete. "Get in line like everyone else!" He flicks his whip at her. He doesn't make contact, but the woman flinches away, and as she does so, her step falters and she trips. That lifts Stormy Pete's mood, and he roars with laughter.

The woman sprawls on the ground and just as Lotta decides to help her, a few men jump down from their carts, or lope from the path into the street. They bend to pick up the spilled bricks of peat.

Lotta is so distracted she doesn't see her family until she's almost on top of them—no time to duck into the butcher's shop.

"Lottie!"

A tumble of rags launches itself at her, scrambling up her legs to jump into her arms. She embraces the squirming figure of her little brother, Wolf, and drinks in the sweet scent of his grubby little neck.

"Hello, Wolfie, my darling. My favorite person in the world."

He goes limp for a moment, enjoying the closeness, but is soon thrumming with excitement. He corkscrews himself around in Lotta's arms to look behind him. "Look, Ma, it's Lottie!" She can hear the huge grin in his voice.

Her mother and father are unavoidable. If she keeps walking, she'll have to crash through them—with all the carts on one side, and the butcher's on the other, there's no room for any of them to step around each other. She catches sight of the woman with the peat lifting herself off the ground. Her basket is empty. Lotta just manages to see the men who she thought were helping swagger off with armloads of the stuff, whistling and laughing. One frees a hand and claps another on the back. The woman was likely there to trade the peats for food, and now she'll go hungry. But she's a hideling mother, surely. She must be used to it.

*I didn't ask to be hid. We don't deserve to be punished so.*

The hideling's words are getting under her skin.

"Nice to see you, Lotta." Her mother, Shona, brings Lotta's attention back. She has a hesitant look on her face, like she doesn't know whether to embrace her daughter or turn and flee. "You look nice in a skirt. Keeping well?"

Lotta's father stands stiffly beside Shona, his cap off his head and twisting in his hands like dough.

"Fine thanks," she says.

Wolf plays with the scarf around her neck. "When you coming home?"

"Yes," says Shona. "When? Lottie, you're welcome anytime, you know that, love." She takes a step forward and her hand begins to lift toward her daughter. But Lotta anticipates it and flinches away, saying nothing.

"What about just for a meal? After Temple. Your da's going to butcher one of the old ewes soon, aren't you, Allen?" She looks at him for help. Allen clears his throat.

"That's right, love. It's been a hard winter, but only four days until the lottery, and then the Glimm will provide." He looks down. "Thanks to you, love, and your work with the horses."

Lotta's face hardens. She's tried to stay neutral, but her father has gone and ruined it. She's been pushing the upcoming lottery from her thoughts. She thrusts Wolf into her mother's arms, which are weaker than Lotta's and soon give way. Wolf lets out a squeal as he drops the short distance to the ground.

The silence stretches until her mother fills it. "Well, have you seen Marten, at least?"

Lotta nods. She's seen her older brother, all right. He hangs around the stables too much now, trying to be near Roderick, pretending to help out, when he should be doing the job he's paid for, tending to the Judge's garden. "He's fine, too," she says. "Look, I've got to—" She gestures in front of her, as if it's obvious what her business is, on market morning.

"All right, love," Shona says softly. "You know where to find us." Her voice drops to a whisper. "And you know how much it means to Wolfie to see you. Think of him if nothing else."

Her words hit their mark. Lotta glances at Wolf. His cheeks are ruddy with the wind, and a small estuary of snot makes its home in the dent above his top lip. She reminds herself that everything she's been through is for him. It's kept him safe. He's the best thing worth living for right now. She reaches out and touches his cool cheek. He giggles and turns into it, tickled, and the cold moon inside her cracks and shifts.

The carts ahead have finally started to move. Moss wishes he'd brought some water with him, or his father's book of poems to read while he waits.

It's a rare morning that he's in the town for market with Mam. Usually, the light is too much for him and the familiar pounding in his head starts up before they even reach the main street. But today is a blessed dull day, the sky a uniform gray, not threatening rain, just biding its time.

Mam has gone ahead with a basket of peat bricks to deliver directly to Jemima the baker, the only villager who pays them with real coins and shows them any kindness. Moss and Stone wait with Hannah and the cart, the one that's shared by all the families in the hamlet. The exiles—he won't call them hidelings—have to wait at the back, and it's not until everybody else has set up their stalls, and the best of the flour, vegetables, tools, and bags of salt—a luxury they go without—have been picked over that they are allowed to trade. There's always a market for peat, though. Trees are scarce on Brack, and wood is precious, used for making things, not burning. Except by the Council. They can burn as much wood as they like. Moss imagines they have enormous fireplaces, with great chimneys that carry the smoke out of their houses to drift up into the sky.

Paper is also scarce. Moss doesn't know where Da's poetry book came from, but he suspects it somehow made its way from the Judge's library to Da's pocket when he was blacksmithing for him. Rumor has it that the Judge has a whole room lined with them, with spines of red and gold. What Moss wouldn't give to have the knowledge contained in those pages.

Two girls jump skip ropes beside them, chanting:

*Jenny Green went out one night,*
*Boots unlaced and eyes too bright.*
*Followed cries that weren't her kin,*
*Stepped where ground gives way to skin.*
*Now she hums beneath the moss,*
*Silver hair and lips like frost.*
*Say her name near dusk or rain,*
*Never make it home again.*

"That's a new one," says Stone. "Not as bloodthirsty as one I heard the other day, where Jenny tears off your skin and wears it like a suit."

Moss shudders. He's had nightmares about the bog witch Jenny since he was small. Being unable to resist her call, being swallowed by the bog. The feel of cold mud filling his nostrils and closing over his head haunts him for days after.

"Come on, Hannah." Moss clicks his tongue. He's relieved to get away from the girls, who have started eyeing them menacingly as they chant. "Away we go."

Hannah braces and the cart lurches unsteadily on its uneven wheels. Behind him, Stone laughs.

"What you laughing at?" asks Moss.

"Nothing! Just lost my balance, is all. Hey look, there's Mam."

Mam's face is a thundercloud. Her hair has come loose from its ties, and . . . is that a limp?

Moss brings Hannah to a halt and jumps to the ground. "What is it? What's happened?"

"It's nothing," she says, though it clearly is something. "I need to go back to the bakery on the way past to deliver Jemima's peat."

"What happened to your basketful?" He helps her up onto the cart and follows after. She's quiet while he settles into his seat and takes up the reins again. "Mam?"

"I lost it," she says. The pinched look on her face says *Don't ask me any more questions.*

Moss can guess. For so long he has accepted the way they're treated in the village. Only allowed in on market days, when folk need something from them. Not allowed to go to the village school along with all the other children. They'd throw stones at him anyway, just as they do when he crosses their path on the moors or on the streets.

Forbidden to attend Temple.

He has taken small pleasures in his life all the same: the sound of the skylark knitting the air as it climbs; the wind on his face as he rides Hannah; the feel of the Hanging Rock warm against his back as he lies watching the clouds make familiar shapes on summer evenings. His mother's voice as she sings while she cooks or tells them stories around the fire. His poems, his bone flute.

But this he cannot stand. The way his mother is scorned. She's rubbing at her wrist, twisting it as though testing some pain inside, and he knows she has fallen, or come to harm.

"Who did this?" he demands.

"Leave it, Mossy. Just keep your head down. It's better that way."

Why is it better? He still holds the residue of anger from the night before. She brought this on them—she and Moss's father. But Da is no longer around to fix his feelings upon.

Moss remembers his words to Lotta Salter yesterday: *I didn't ask to be hid.*

The rock that took root in his gut is still there. He knows it will stay there until he does something to improve their situation.

Stone nudges his back. "Look, it's her!"

Moss doesn't need to ask who he means. Lotta is striding with purpose down the path beside the road, her tweed cap pulled low, and a parcel tied with string under her arm. Her skirt looks wrong on her somehow; she seemed more at ease in the trousers she wore last evening.

"Hush," says Moss. He doesn't know whether he wants her to look up or not, but soon he has no choice in the matter.

"Greetings to you on this fine day, Miss Salter."

Moss could punch his brother in the face if it would only shut him up. He turns his collar up and sinks into his seat, but it's too late. Lotta's head snaps toward them. She takes in Hannah, and her gaze flicks immediately to Moss, seeing straight into him, inflaming the rock in his gut.

He looks back, taking in her freckled face, her broad, strong shoulders, and her hair—thick and oily. He imagines it smells of berries and flowers, and the soap with which she washes her horses. He dares to lift his hand from the reins to wave, but she's already gone. Is that an acceleration in her gait he detects? As she passes a group of people, they all turn to stare at her, and she acknowledges them no more than she has acknowledged this family of hidelings.

"Stone," he says through gritted teeth, "I swear I will kill you one of these days."

"Haughty, in't she?" says his brother, and Moss does not, cannot, argue, but he saw something else in her face.

Loneliness. But also, a flicker of recognition. An acknowledgment that he exists.

"Come now, Stone," says Mam. "What makes you think she'd be any different from the rest of them? Don't try to talk to folk; it's not safe to draw attention. We need to do our business and go."

But Moss knows that Lotta is different from the rest of them, and somehow, he means to prove it.

"How can you stand it, Mam? There has to be something more. There has to be a way. Look at you!" He gestures to her wrist, which is starting to swell. "How can you work when they push you down and steal your wares?"

"That's not what happened," she protests, but she hides her arm under her shawl all the same.

"Leave her alone," says Stone. "Bully."

"Fine," he says. "But if you don't do something, maybe I will."

His mother is quiet for a moment and there is nothing but the sound of the groaning of the wheels and Hannah's hooves on the cobbles.

"I've never heard you speak like this before last night, Mossy," says Mam at last. "What's got into you? You've never said so much as a harsh word to me. You've always been content with your lot. I've done my best for us all."

"What's got into him?" pipes up Stone. "Miss Lotta Salter is what."

"That's it!" Moss turns and lunges for Stone, who leaps backward, knocking the haul of peat against the back gate of the cart, which gives way. He tumbles out the back, along with a good portion of their load. Hannah, sensing trouble, comes to a halt.

"Moss!" says Mam. "People are looking! Go and help him put the load back and let's get on our way."

Nobody rushes forward to help or to steal the peat. The street is nearly empty now, with everyone at the market, save for a couple of kids, kicking a leather ball against a wall. They only stand and laugh.

"He don't deserve my help. You do it!" He tosses the reins into her lap and jumps off the cart. Stone is on his feet, unhurt, and throwing peats back into the cart haphazardly. Many of them are broken and crumbled, and Moss knows those ones will be coming back on the cart for them to use at home because they won't be able to trade them. He feels a stab of guilt, but he's in motion now and resolute. He sets off on the long walk home.

# 6

**The morning air** is crisp, and the stable yard is quiet except for the soft snorts and shifting hooves of the horses. Lotta moves steadily among them, checking bridles and tightening girths, her hands sure and practiced. Dougie is saddling the bay mare—the same one that had returned alone that terrible day a year ago, when the head groom died. Ever since then, Lotta has trained the horses herself.

Philip, the head groom, used to pass her a brush without a word, nod once if she'd done well, and sometimes leave her a heel of bread and cheese wrapped in cloth on the tack room bench. She'd never known if he even liked her, or thought she'd done a good job, but he always gave her the colts no one else could settle and never once took the lunge rein from her hands.

It was Lotta who found him, after he was thrown and struck his head on a rock—alerted when the bay mare he was exercising returned to the stables, broken reins trailing. She avoids that path now.

She tries not to dwell any longer on what she saw that day. There's work to be done, and the Council won't wait.

Lotta glances toward Dougie, who catches her eye and gives a small nod. They work in easy rhythm, the familiarity of the morning routine grounding her. Each horse is calm and responsive to her, and she knows every twitch of an ear or flick of a tail.

"The gray, the gray!" Daphne comes bounding over, her long skirts swishing noisily.

"It's too fiery for you," says Lotta.

"Pishposh," says Daphne. "He *will* be mine one day! You're doing a wonderful job with him. I mean, I love Wheatie, but he's getting too small for me, and isn't so . . ." Her hand flashes out to touch the gelding's nose, but it snorts and pins its ears back.

"Move slower or you'll startle it!" Lotta shakes her head as she reluctantly shortens the stirrups for Daphne, who fiddles with the buttons of her too-tight tweed jacket while she waits. Lotta expects them to explode off her chest at any moment under the pressure. It's the fashion, she supposes, among the Council daughters. What would she know?

"I know he's your favorite," says Daphne as Lotta helps her mount.

"I don't have favorites," Lotta snaps back. She can't afford to.

"I'll be kind, I promise. Look, I'll leave my whip behind." She hands it to Lotta, who takes it.

"Gentle hands," says Lotta, looking up at her. "Use your seat. And your voice. It'll listen to you."

"If you're not careful," Daphne teases, "I'll give him a name and then he'll be mine!" She turns its head and it moves away. Lotta twists the whip in her hands.

The Council riders begin to gather near the gates, their cloaks misted with dew. They all live up here, slightly apart from the village below, within the walled grounds of the Manor House, which dominates the horizon. Beyond it lie the eastern cliffs, where nobody, not even bird hunters, are allowed to go. Lotta hears the crash of the waves at night and tastes the salt on the wind. She longs to go close and dare to peer over the edge. But it's forbidden.

Lotta steps back, wipes each hand on her worn trousers, and watches as they mount, their faces set with purpose, and ride out for the village. Judge Hawthorne leads the parade, followed by six other men, dressed in black with wide-brimmed hats shadowing their faces. Daphne and Roddy ride side by side behind their father, Councillor Lewis, Roddy on his black stallion. Daphne turns back and gives Lotta a cheerful wave, which Lotta doesn't dare to return. As the Judge's only grandchildren, her friends hold special status that shouldn't be tainted on Temple day.

The other Council families ride in carriages prepared by their own grooms. Dougie and Lotta follow at a distance on foot, along with Marten and Gregory, and the rest of the Manor House staff. She has no choice: everyone in the village must attend Temple, even her. Lotta can't help feeling proud of the way the villagers who line the cobbled streets stand in awe of the Council horses, of the way they lift their feet and arch their necks. Blacks, chestnuts, and grays, most of them, tall and leggy. Their shoes on the cobblestones ring like music.

As usual, Lotta waits until everyone has filed in before taking her place at the back of the Temple. The air is close in here. Nobody dares turn around and stare at her except for the smallest children, but once she's contorted her face into the meanest expression she can, they shimmy back to the front and never look at her again.

Marten has joined her family a few rows ahead; she's managed to avoid them. Dougie—whose da died two winters back—is with his mother and younger siblings.

At the front of the Temple, the six Council members sit up high, facing the congregation, their faces solemn. She spots Marten craning his neck to catch a glimpse of Roddy among the other Council sons at the front—those who are old enough freshly shaved, and all of them trussed up in tight neckbands, with pink cheeks and clean blond hair. Marten is no doubt willing him to turn around. But Roddy is reserved today and stares resolutely forward, his normally proud shoulders slightly caved.

Daphne has joined her friends, the daughters of Councillors Gray and Stirling; they've been comparing brooches and hairnets. It's a social occasion for them, unlike the slow torture it is for Lotta at the back. She just wants to be out on the moors again. Maybe ride past the hidelings' hamlet and see what that Moss boy is up to.

The Judge emerges from the room at the front, adjusting his black robes. He pauses beneath the great archway above the altar that twists and curls into the shape of a serpent. According to local history, the Temple has stood for hundreds, maybe thousands of years. Made from stone, with high vaulted ceilings, it has room for the whole village. Carved into the stones, and at the end of the wooden pews: more patterns of a serpent, intricately entwined with reeds and flames.

Judge Hawthorne closes his eyes and makes the sign of the serpent across his chest—a sideways letter S—and kisses the end of his finger as he opens his eyes and raises them to the arch.

The room falls silent.

Judge Hawthorne steps up to his podium. He tilts his head back so that he's forced to look down his sharp nose at the congregation. Above, his eyebrows have a life of their own, giving him a perpetually surprised look. His great gray muttonchops wobble as he speaks: "May the light of the Glimm fall upon you, good people of Brack."

The congregation lifts their voices as one in answer: *"And upon you, as bright as the sun."*

He nods, satisfied.

"It's been a harsh winter, we know. But the lottery is this week. The horses are ready to make their sacrifice, as am I."

Lotta crosses her arms. He always acts like the horses are his, as if sacrificing them is a personal loss, when he sees them as no more than livestock. She doesn't know, but she suspects he would never enter the precious Council horses in the lottery any more than he entered the Councillors' children, who were exempt. It's usually the island ponies whose numbers come up and that get sent to sacrifice, and it's often those too old or weak to work. But they say the Glimm guides the Judge's hand when he draws the numbers, so perhaps the Glimm is more merciful than it seems.

The Judge begins his sermon, and Lotta finds herself nodding off. It's always the same. Be courteous to your neighbor, know your place, go without so that the Council may thrive and enact the Glimm's will.

"And you, Robert Shilling? What will you go without this week?"

Robert gets to his feet. The neck that sticks out of his collar is as thin as a stick of rhubarb already. Lotta isn't sure he should be going without, not with the heavy work he has to do as a stonemason.

He clears his throat. "This week, we will go without eggs. We give them gladly to the Council."

Hawthorne nods and Robert sits down. Lotta sees his wife elbow him sharply, clearly wishing he'd thought of something a little less nutritious.

"And you, Biddy Jackson, what will you go without?"

Biddy leaps to her feet. It's been some weeks since she's been called upon to declare her offering publicly, and she isn't going to waste the opportunity. "Why, this week, Judge Hawthorne, my husband and I will go without our coats and without the blankets on our beds. We gladly give them up to keep the Council warm. There's snow coming. I can feel it in my knees!"

Judge Hawthorne's nose twitches. Surely the last thing he wants is Biddy and Shaun Jackson's threadbare coats and blankets. He sighs. "Very well," he says. "You can deliver them to the stables tomorrow."

A snicker runs through the room, and Biddy glances around

nervously. She catches Lotta's eye before she can look away, and her face lights up. It seems to satisfy her somehow, that Lotta will be in charge of distributing the blankets, even if it's to animals instead of to the precious, pristine Council.

A few more offerings are made before Hawthorne's face grows grave.

"There is something we need to discuss as a community. Constance Giver has brought it to my attention. But perhaps it's best that Constance inform you herself."

He beckons to the front row, and the island's chief midwife gets to her feet. She looks so old, thinks Lotta. Her hair is all white now under her bonnet, and she's developed a stoop like a mushroom. She has the look of one who carries an island's worth of pain on her shoulders. She's been around for so long nobody knows how old she is, but she's the oldest living person on the island—well, not as old as Jenny Green, who they say has been here since the beginning of time. If she even exists, that is. Lotta's never seen her, but others claim to have been chased out of a bog by her.

Constance delivered Lotta's ma and da. She delivered Lotta, and Marten before her, and Wolf after. She saved Wolf's life when he was born with the cord wrapped around his neck and was blue in the face. She called him as fierce and determined as a wolf to stay alive, and the name stuck, even though wolves on the island died out long ago and only exist in stories now.

Constance's voice rings out loud and true. "We lost another babe today. Young Eleanor's first. The poor thing was stillborn."

The room sighs collectively.

"A baby girl she was. There was nothing we could do."

"But that's not all, is it, Constance?" says the Judge.

Constance looks at him, her lips a tight line. She shakes her head and turns back to address the room. She points to the second row. "Stand up, dear," she says, not unkindly, but with a note of command in her voice.

A young woman stands up, holding a sleeping baby in her arms. It's tiny, no bigger than a loaf of bread.

"Show them," says Constance.

The face of the woman, Hildie—Lotta recognizes her as the butcher's daughter—glows hot as anything. But she does as she's told. She unbundles her sleeping baby and holds her aloft. At first, Lotta isn't sure what they're all looking at, and others raise themselves in their seats, straining to see. Then the murmur swells. A dark red mark curls across the baby's chest, the shape of a sideways S, no bigger than a worm.

"The Glimm!" cries a child.

Hands go to mouths. Gasps. Murmurs. Hildie hastily rebundles the child and sits down. The baby has hardly stirred.

Constance holds up her hands for silence. "The babe is otherwise strong and healthy, so maybe the Glimm has marked her merely as a warning, or a sign that this child will be spared. Because have you not noticed? Children are falling ill more often. Those twins who died last summer, from catching a cold, Glimm rest their souls. Agatha Crow's little boy, Joe—his heart beats so fast in his chest sometimes he has to lie down. What kind of toll would that take on a young boy? He'll have used up all his heartbeats by the time he's eleven years old.

"It's not just the children being born; it's all the ones who aren't being born. All the miscarriages, all the eager young couples who can't seem to get pregnant no matter how hard they try. It's getting harder and harder. Soon there'll be no children left to grow old."

A frightened murmur breaks out. A man's voice calls from the back. "What do you think is causing it, Constance?"

"I have my suspicions," she says. "Most likely—"

"The Glimm!" calls a man. "It's right there on the babby's chest! What does it want?"

"Thank you, Constance," says the Judge. "You can sit down now."

He gives her a warning look before going on.

"It is foretold in the Book that one day the Glimm will become dissatisfied again. That our crops will fail, that our animals will start to die. Why, only the other day my prize mare was found dead on the moors, picked over by crows and buzzards!"

Lotta starts. Where is he going with this? He hardly cared for the mare, let alone *prized* it. It was an island horse, a workhorse. It isn't the animals or children that disturb her—a tiny birthmark is no curse—but the way he twists their fates into prophecy.

Farmer Evans jumps to his feet. "My ewe miscarried a lamb the other day. Only it weren't any normal lamb. It had two heads!"

A murmur of disgust goes around the building.

Biddy Jackson isn't going to let the action pass her by. She calls out, "My cat was killed by a giant rat! It had red eyes and fangs as sharp as pins. I saw it with my own two eyes!"

Judge Hawthorne is nodding along, eyes shining. He leans forward, with hands gripping the pulpit like claws, his shoulders up around his ears so he resembles a vulture perched in a dead tree. He glares around the room. "We knew this day would come!" he cries. "The Glimm is hungry again! Horses alone will not do to counter the sins of the people!"

More murmuring breaks out.

"Silence!" Spittle flies from the Judge's mouth—Lotta can see it from where she sits.

People start to turn in their seats, their eyes searching her out. Her gut gives a shudder. Where is this leading?

"The lottery is in three days." This time his voice is low, calm, measured. "The Council will meet to decide what the right course of action is."

As the congregation lets the words sink in, the giant doors blast open, and Lotta jumps. It appears that everyone else has the same thought: that the Glimm itself has decided to make an appearance.

But it isn't the Glimm.

It's a woman, standing still in the doorway, letting the cold, gray day in. The breeze is a relief.

The Judge glares at her. "Go away. You are not welcome here."

The woman walks in anyway, taking a determined step over the threshold. Lotta sees only her profile, her dark hair tied back carelessly, some of it falling over her ears. Her hands make fists at her sides, as if to give herself strength to keep going. She walks up the aisle, then stops halfway.

"Please," she says.

"I said leave." The Judge points one bony finger coldly past her to the gathering mist outside.

To Lotta's surprise, the woman sinks to her knees. She brings her hands together as if to pray. "Please," she repeats, more forcefully this time.

"Let her speak!" Lotta startles herself as much as she does those around her.

The Judge glares at her but nods curtly.

The woman speaks. "I'm begging you now, Judge Hawthorne. Please. We've been exiled for too long now. We're starving. We're freezing. We're dying."

Lotta realizes why she looks familiar. It's the same woman who fell in the street yesterday and was treated badly by the villagers. She feels a twang of guilt. Lotta could have helped her but then her mother and father were upon her, and she forgot about her.

Now she's struck by the darkness of the woman's hair, her bony wrists, and the large eyes that remind her of the boy she met on the moors. She saw him again yesterday with that big horse hooked up to the shabby cart. What was his name? Moss. He'd had the same pleading look when he'd called after her on the moors. *I didn't ask to be hid.*

"We've learned our lesson. You must let us back now." The woman pauses to look around at every single pair of eyes fixed on her, and stops on Daphne's father, Councillor Lewis. "Amos? We love the Glimm as much as any of you. We was wrong to try to hide from it. But enough now. Enough."

Councillor Lewis looks away, scowling. Angry to have been singled out. Lotta sees Daphne and Roddy exchange confused glances, but they say nothing.

Mutterings rise like a horde of moths.

The Judge holds up a hand for silence. Without speaking, and with a look on his face as though his mouth has filled with saliva, he nods to two men in the front row—today's henchmen, Proctor and Harris, huge and muscled like bulls—who stride toward her and lift her under the arms like she weighs no more than a curlew feather. They drag her backward toward the door.

"You'll be sorry!" she yells, which only agitates the congregation further. They rise in a chorus of shouting and hissing, telling her to

*get out!*

*get out, woman!*

*and shut up while you're at it.*

The woman kicks uselessly at the space in front of her while her worn-out boots make a track of mud to the exit.

She catches Lotta's eye, and her face opens with recognition.

"Lotta Salter! You helped us once. Please, help us now!"

She screams as the men throw her out and slam the doors behind her.

Lotta shudders. All faces have turned to look at her—appalled, curious, suspicious. She meets the Judge's steely gaze and sets her jaw. Trouble is coming. The lottery is the least of it.

She vows to slip out early and check on the woman, to make sure she isn't seriously hurt, but when the communion begins, and she opens the door a crack, the square is empty.

# 7

**Mam took Hannah** into the village this morning but wouldn't say why, so there is no work for Moss today. Yesterday, she'd come back from market grim-faced and cold, barely able to look him in the eye. Stone had also given him the silent treatment, but Moss didn't care. It was a respite from his brother's inane chatter.

Moss is supposed to sleep on brighter days, to protect his sensitive eyes, and work at night, but Stone likes nothing more than to sneak into the sleeping area, climb on the bed they share, and stare at Moss as he sleeps, breathing thickly through his wet nostrils until Moss wakes up, turns over, kicks out at him, and jams the pillow over his head, which is exactly what he did today. Moss has since escaped to his special spot—the smooth, flat rock that juts from the hillside overlooking the moors—to get away from him.

Moss was nine years old when he saw his first spring flowers, his first raven. The beauty of the world floored him; it still does. The years he was kept inside, in the dimness, the quiet, have not only made his eyes sensitive to light, they have surely enhanced his senses. The wind is music in his ears. In summer the scent of meadowsweet and thyme wafts over the moors like fine perfume. Every day brings something new to look at—the land is alive, and he revels in it. When he puts his ear to the rock, he hears the thrum of the island, maybe of the Glimm itself, of the power it holds. They say it controls everything, that only the upcoming sacrifice can usher in the spring and bring an end to the relentless cold and damp and hunger, to ensure crops will be bountiful.

In the winter, the animals live in a byre under the same roof as their people; it's the only way to keep them all warm enough. At Moss's place, Hannah, the sheep, and the goat munch their hay knee-deep in straw at one end of the house, while Sadie's family owns a strong, hairy cow with a sweet nature and horns like turned up bars. They swap wool, and sometimes meat, for milk to drink and to churn butter. Stone used to fall asleep leaning up against the ewe, cuddling her for warmth, until Mam had to pluck him off so she could shear her. "She's got enough wool for everyone, pet, don't be greedy." Mam sits up into the night, spinning, and they fall asleep to the wheel gently whirring, the sound like the hoverflies they catch in summer. There's only one loom for the whole of the hamlet, and women and men take turns weaving their meager supply of wool into cloth.

By now, spring should have started to come on its own ahead of the sacrifice to the Glimm, out here on the moors at least. Moss used to lose himself staring at the small white blackthorn flowers and the bluebells, but everything is resolutely brown. The distant Black Mountains have turned mauve in the dying day.

He can't stop thinking about Lotta. He sees her shape in the clouds. He sees her in the wind that lifts the wings of the skylark, in the striped buzzard's feather that spirals down to earth, to be caught by a net of heather.

He feels sure that she holds the key to ending the suffering they endure, but how? She seems as much of an outsider as he is. She is a folk hero, given special privileges, yes, but also held apart by her difference. He detects, in the way the villagers regard her, a quiet fear.

They are right to fear her. He just doesn't yet know why.

But what is he to her? Nothing. A hideling.

Ugh, Stone is right. Lotta Salter has come over him, that's what.

He would never be accepted in her world. Not that she is a part of it herself. She is to the village what the moon is to the earth. Perhaps they aren't so different. He was hidden from the sacrifice; she was spared. He would give anything to have joined in the lottery with the rest of the children, to be one of them. He isn't afraid of dying. He is more afraid of living a life of cruelty and hardship, which is what he realizes this is, though it isn't all bad. At least he has friends in the hamlet he can talk to and tell anything.

Does Lotta get lonely? He wants to ride across the moor with her on the back of the beautiful gray gelding. To put his arms around her waist and feel her hair in his face, buffeted by the gurling wind.

"There you are, Moss Smith! Been looking everywhere for you, you nit!" Sadie drops her cloth bag and flops down beside him. "I need to show you what I got from the market yesterday."

She draws out a small carved wooden box.

Sadie has a knack for blending in. It's as though she's still hiding in her parents' broom cupboard, invisible to the world. She slips unnoticed into the straw of a cart, the stacks of peat, melts into the gray of the stone shops and buildings. Her hair is the color of dried mud, her skin pale and forgettable. People look right through her, only realizing they've seen a girl when she's already passed. They turn to check again, but by then she's vanished into shadow, and they doubt their own eyes.

There is no way Sadie bought this, or traded for it. Moss knows all her secrets.

"See," she says, pressing the box into his hand. "It's magic. You look."

He puts his fingernail beneath the clasp.

"Gentle," she says. "Slow."

"I know." Moss can tell she is wanting to draw out his wonder, his pleasure, and for that he is grateful.

The music escapes as soon as the box springs open a crack. A tinkling melody, one he recognizes that his mam taught him on the bone flute. A tune that tells of horses running free. He opens it fully.

A gray horse, rearing onto its hind legs, turns in time to the music.

"In't she beautiful?" breathes Sadie.

She is. But this isn't a mare. This is one of the Judge's finest horses. This is the gray gelding trained and ridden by Lotta Salter.

"I know this horse," he says gently.

Sadie looks at him sharply. "What do you mean, you goose? It's new. How could you know it?"

"It's Lotta's horse."

Sadie says nothing.

"I know it," says Moss again.

Sadie surprises him by slamming the lid shut, narrowly missing his fingers. "What would you know, Moss Smith? If you knows so much, what's he called? What's his name?"

"He doesn't have a name."

"Aha! You're making things up. All horses owned by people have names. Your Hannah. Our Pumpkin. Anyway," she continues, "you don't know that girl. She's nobody's friend. She's far too high-and-mighty for the likes of us."

Moss knows she is right. "Let's get a move on," he says, standing and brushing down his threadbare trousers. He catches a glimpse of his exposed ankles. Maybe he's growing at last.

"Race you!" Sadie streaks off ahead of him, her dirty hair flying behind her, the bag thumping her back.

When he gets home, puffing—well behind Sadie, who jumped and waved at him in triumph before heading home for her own dinner—he's pulled up short by the sight of a strange horse in the yard with

Hannah. Not just any shaggy island pony. A Council horse. It stands placidly tethered to a hook with the water bucket and some straw at its feet. It has kicked the bucket over and valuable fresh water soaks into the dirt.

For a few precious moments, Moss thinks that it must be Lotta, come to visit him. But when he opens the door, he finds a man standing in the middle of the room, and Mam standing not far from him. They stop talking and turn to look at Moss. Stone is nowhere to be seen; Mam must have sent him out to dig potatoes for dinner.

The man's black hat nearly touches the low thatched ceiling. He is broad-shouldered, with a heavy cloak. His face is lined with age, but his sharp gray eyes look past Moss, like they're measuring him.

"What's this?" Moss says, feeling bold. He won't be bowing to a Councillor, not today. "You all right, Mam?"

She nods but her face is pinched and pale. "This is Councillor Lewis. He's only just arrived. This is my son, Moss."

The Councillor looks Moss up and down, then turns back to Mam.

"We've got trouble," he says.

He is far too comfortable here, like he knows this place, like he knows *them*.

"What do you mean?" Moss can't keep the challenge from his voice. He glances at his mother, who stands rigid near the fire, her expression unreadable.

"Sit down, Moss," she says quietly. There's a tightness to her voice that makes him falter. "Please."

He sits, and she does the same. The Councillor remains standing, a heavy presence in the small house.

"You've got a problem, Heather," he says, and Moss starts at the sound of his mother's name, which he hardly ever hears in the hamlet, let alone from the village, from a *Councillor*. "Your horse. She's going to be named in the lottery."

Moss looks at his mother. Surely not. But she's not jumping to her feet, not flinging her chair aside, not screaming at the man to leave. Instead, she bows her head and curls her hands into fists on her lap. Moss sees that it's up to him to speak.

"No . . ." His voice cracks. "That can't be right. She can't be in the lottery. She's not—"

"Aye," Lewis interrupts. "She is. The Council has decided. She's been selected to be sacrificed to the Glimm."

"But the lottery's not for days! And it's always the horses that are bred especially! Not working horses!" Moss's head spins. His first thought is to reject it; his heart refuses to believe it. He's known Hannah since she was just a foal, grown strong alongside their work. She's their livelihood, the one thing that keeps them from going under.

"No," he says resolutely. "They can't take her. She's ours. We've earned her."

Mam holds out a hand to him, but he will not take it. "Moss," she whispers. "You know the rules. No one can question the lottery."

"No!" Moss is on his feet now, and the Councillor flinches, closes his eyes as though waiting for a small child to finish its tantrum. He sways slightly, as if in a breeze, and opens them again. His face is cold.

"I don't care about the rules," says Moss. He turns to Mam. "We don't have to give her up. They can't take her!"

"Sit down!" Lewis bellows.

Moss stumbles back at the force of his voice and does as he is told.

"This is my fault, Moss. I'm so sorry," says Mam.

"What do you mean?"

But it's Lewis who answers. "Your mother thought it fitting to pay a visit to the Temple today, to address the congregation."

Moss's head swims. It is forbidden for exiles to set foot in the Temple. She knows that. "Mam?"

Mam nods slowly. "Mossy, I thought I was doing the right thing for you. For us."

"What did you say to them?"

"I asked them to let us back into the village."

"Mam. They would never!"

"I had to try. For you. And for Stone. You deserve better. It's not you who should be punished for what I did. What we did, your father and me." She glances at Lewis, whose presence fills the room like a black thundercloud.

"But . . ." Moss has to think, to check all that he knows about the lore. This can't be right. "The lottery isn't for three days. They can't *choose* a horse before that. It has to be random. It's the lore."

The Councillor says nothing.

Mam says nothing.

"You're not taking her," he says again, with a steadiness in his voice that makes Mam blink. "You'll have to kill me first."

Lewis's eyes narrow, and for a moment, Moss thinks he sees a flicker of sympathy in the older man's gaze. But it's gone in an instant, replaced by a cold, calculating indifference.

"That can be arranged, certainly. But you don't get a choice in this, boy," he says. "The Judge has spoken. The Glimm's will is done, whether you like it or not."

The words hit Moss like a blow to the chest. The very ground beneath him seems to shift, as if the rules of the world have suddenly changed in ways he can't understand, certainly can't control. His pulse roars in his ears.

His mother's eyes are wide with sorrow, regret, but also something else—something darker.

*She knew.*

She knew something like this would happen, and she did it anyway. Not a single word to him about what she planned to do.

"She's all we got," Moss whispers. "Why? Why didn't you tell me what you was doing?"

But Mam doesn't answer. She can't.

"Is it really the Glimm's will, Councillor Lewis?" The rock in Moss's belly is back, making him despair, but also making him bold. “Or is it the Council’s?”

Lewis turns on his heel and opens the door. As he steps through it, he calls over his shoulder. “They’ll come in two days to take her. I would not repeat what you have heard here. Nor what you just said to me, young hideling, about killing you to save the horse. It just may come to pass.”

And with that, he is gone, the door banging behind him.

# 8

**ASKING A MARE** that has lost its own foal to adopt another is never easy—sometimes impossible—and for a moment Lotta is sure she's failed.

"Come on, please," she whispers in its ear, then hums a few notes as the foal instinctively reaches under the belly mouth first, seeking out the teat. Lotta's nostrils are filled with the sharp scent of the mare's own excrement, smeared on the colt to convince its new mother that they are kin. Lotta braces for a kick to the foal's head but it doesn't come. Instead, with Lotta's hand on its neck, and encouraging sounds, the mare soon relaxes, and the milk flows. Lotta exhales in relief.

Both foals were born too early. Lotta's heard murmurs of others on the island foaling too soon, of mares disoriented on the moors, losing their way, some falling into bogs like the hideling horse did. She can't be there to save them all.

The island ponies are made of sturdier, more placid stuff than the flighty, fine-boned Council horses. They are bred to work the farms and pull the carts, and now, to be offered to the Glimm.

Only the hidelings have to earn their horses. That boy was right the other night: Had they lost their mare, they wouldn't have been allowed another. Not until they had earned it again. The Council, and the villagers, will ensure the hidelings never forget what they did. Will they eventually die out there? The only thing the villagers will care about is having to go back to cutting their own peat.

Standing in the outer paddock, watching the colt and its new mother, Lotta remembers what the Judge had said in Temple yesterday: *Why, only the other day my prize mare was found dead on the moors.* What was he playing at? That horse was no more his prize mare than Lotta was his own daughter.

The villagers have been on edge ever since. Now Lotta thinks she hears whispers on the wind—the same kind directed at her this morning as she walked up the road. But when she turns to scan this paddock and the one beyond, she sees only the horses, upwards of forty of them now, of all sizes: some the height of a child, with shaggy coats and quick teeth; others tall and sturdy, like Hannah. Coats of patchwork brown and black. Most of them are grazing the short grass or dozing.

She feels folks' grim stares on the back of her neck as she passes. She knows they're scared, as they always are just before the sacrifice. The fear is always the same. What if it doesn't work this time? What if the Glimm wreaks revenge on the island for depriving it of the life force of a child?

But always, the Glimm takes the horse; spring arrives, the crops grow and the bounty returns.

Things are different this year; she can feel it. It's not just the problems with the babies, with the animals, with the hungry bellies. The wind should be warmer now, should carry the sweet smell of new growth, but instead it carries the chill scent of damp and mud, stronger than ever. And something rotten.

The lottery draws ever closer.

Back in the stable, she gives Roderick's recently returned black stallion a drink of water and brushes it down. Dougie leans in the stall doorway, his eyes bright.

"Such a looker, that one," he says. "One day maybe I can ride him." He steals a hopeful glance at Lotta and she can't help but smile.

"Maybe one day, little flea," she says.

"Hey!" He goes to protest but then stops and turns his head toward the window, at the clattering of hooves in the yard. "Glimm! It's his lordship himself. I'm gone!" He scampers off down to the far end of the stable, no doubt to lock himself in a stall until the danger has passed.

Councillor Lewis stalks in and removes his hat, whip still in his other hand.

"Where's that boy of yours, Lotta? I expect him to take my horse from me when I arrive, not make me chase you both around the stables."

Dougie must have heard. He slinks back and swipes his cap from his head, leaving his ginger hair sticking up in surprise.

"Here, sir. Sorry, sir." He runs outside and is soon back, leading Lewis's bay gelding in to untack it.

Lewis waits for Dougie to pass and turns back to Lotta.

"I need you to make room for a new horse," he says. "It'll be joining the lottery nags. But first I need you to keep it in here. I don't want it jumping the wall like that skewbald mare did."

"Where's it come from, then?" asks Lotta.

"Don't ask questions, girl, just make sure there's a free stall for it when it arrives tomorrow. I'm sending my men to collect it. It's quite a large animal, so will need one of your roomier stalls." He sizes up the stallion that stands, dozing, with one back hoof balanced on its tip. "This one'll do. Roderick will cope. Put this one in another stall and turn a horse out into the field. It won't be for long."

"And the Judge?" says Lotta. "Does he know of this plan?"

"He does." Lewis slaps his riding whip impatiently against his leg.

"Do you have any more questions, or can I trust you will do as I have asked?"

Lotta bites her tongue, but nods.

"Good." He moves closer to her, and Lotta takes an instinctive step back. "Another thing. How do you know Heather Smith?" Lotta must look confused, because he adds, "The hideling woman in the Temple yesterday."

She puts her hands in her pockets to hide their trembling. "I . . . I don't know her."

"Don't lie to me, girl. She said, with the Glimm as her witness, that you helped her. What did you do?"

"I didn't help her, not really. I . . . I helped a hideling boy. His name was Moss. His horse was stuck in the bog."

Lewis ponders this for a moment. "Another one," he says quietly.

"It's all right," she says. "I freed it."

His eyes lock on hers. "How?"

Lotta shrugs, as if it was nothing. "I don't know, I just calmed it down and together we pulled it out."

Again, he pauses, absorbing her words. "They were lucky, then."

"Yes. They would have lost their only horse."

His eyes narrow. "And what do you, of all people, care if a hideling loses a horse?"

"What do you mean?"

"You were chosen in the lottery. Those families who hid their children, they shrank the odds. You might have escaped."

"I *did* escape," she says, matter-of-fact. What she doesn't say, though she wants to, so much: *And you might have put your own children into the lottery and improved the odds for us all.*

"Well, the family is going to pay now. The horse that is coming tomorrow, you will recognize it. It belongs to them."

"But that's—"

"Highly irregular? Yes, it is. But the Judge has ordered it. He won't have the hidelings thinking they can barge into our sacred Temple, making demands. It's time for them to pay their tithe."

Lotta's cheeks start to burn. What is he saying?

The Councillor puts his hat back on and turns to leave. "Or at least, for them to experience the lottery. They can have the nag back when it's finished."

"If they lose that horse," she says, "how will they get by?"

Lewis turns back. "That is not my problem. Or the Council's."

"Will you give them another in return?"

"You know we will not. Now stop asking questions."

"But that is deliberately cruel."

Lewis glances over his shoulder, then takes one long stride toward her. She has nowhere to go. He has her pinned against the stall door. She can see the white hairs that are starting to invade his light brown muttonchops. His gray eyes are rimmed with red. She braces herself for a blasting. Or a whipping.

Lewis leans in close. "I'm only going to say this once, Lotta Salter." He speaks very slowly and softly. His breath smells of tobacco. "If you know what's good for you, you'll stay away from the hidelings."

She can't meet his eye and looks over his shoulder, waiting for Dougie to pop out of the far stall at any moment.

"You've enjoyed special privileges because of what happened to you, and don't forget it. You get paid more than most of the staff here. But you're only still here because the Judge doesn't trust you and wants to keep you close. He is watching you. So, this is a reminder. A warning. Keep your head down, or you might find yourself living with the hidelings."

He straightens his back, adjusts his hat. For a moment, his eyes soften.

"You're important to my daughter. I'll keep that in mind. But the Judge . . ."

He steps back, releasing her.

"Don't cross him. I'm telling you for your own good."

Then he turns and strides out, pulling his cloak close against the night air.

~

After Lewis has gone, and Dougie has left for his dinner, Lotta is still shaken by the encounter. She's always suspected that she is here not because of her skill with the horses, but because of what happened to her—because she survived. The Judge is probably right to be suspicious of her. After all, no other child has ever returned from the sacrifice. Of course he wants to know why. What makes her tick. If she does have some kind of bond with the Glimm, that would make her dangerous, because only the Judge is supposed to have that honor. The Glimm speaks through him, conveys its will through him, and when he dies, it will be Roderick, his only male heir, who will inherit that privilege.

A shadow slips into the stable. "Has he gone?" When Daphne comes closer, she looks as though she's been crying. Her nose is pink and runny.

"What's wrong with you?" asks Lotta.

"Let's go upstairs," says Daphne.

Lotta follows her up the wooden staircase to her room. Daphne collapses onto the bed, while Lotta hovers in the middle of the room, unsure what to say.

"Do you want tea?" she asks eventually. She's not accustomed to visitors. Daphne shakes her head and blows her nose into a rag she's produced from the pocket of her deep blue skirt. Lotta sits on the hard chair by her tiny table and waits for her to speak.

"I don't know how to tell you this," says Daphne. "There's gossip in the village. After what happened at Temple yesterday, some of the villagers met last night to talk about it all. About the baby. The Glimm, the hideling mother. You."

"How do you know this?"

Daphne isn't usually one to mingle with the villagers.

"Beth said it as she was dressing me this morning. Well, she said something, and I made her tell me."

"What? What did she say?"

"Oh, it was only when I mentioned your name. You know her, she worships you, normally. But she just went quiet at first, and gripped my hair too tight, and brushed it too hard, so I asked her what was wrong. She just said that maybe I shouldn't see you, and that was it. So I held her by the wrist and wouldn't let her go until she told me what she meant."

Lotta is appalled and intrigued in equal measure. Would it be so bad if Beth no longer squeaked and ran away whenever Lotta entered the Manor House, pretending to flick dirt away with her feather duster but staring staring staring until Lotta had to leave?

"And?"

"She said she'd been to a meeting in the tavern that her father organized. They were swapping stories of failed crops. You saw at the market, didn't you? Everything was so depleted. And the potatoes were green, and the oats blighted and full of weevils. Disgusting." She screwed up her nose as if someone was trying to force her to eat some at that very moment.

"What's that got to do with me?"

"Don't you see, Lottie? They're terrified. And they're saying it's all because of you—all those poor dead babies, the miscarriages. They say it's because you survived the Glimm and broke the pact, and now it's angry."

Lotta lets the news sink in. She narrows her eyes. "Let them say that to my face."

A sudden blirt of wind rattles the window and Daphne jumps. "You don't mean that."

"I bleedin' do." She stands.

"Where are you going?" asks Daphne, her voice fearful.

"It's been ever so long since I went to the tavern for dinner. Care to join me?"

# 9

**OUTSIDE, THE WIND** shakes the stables, bringing with it rain that stings Lotta's face. Daphne shrieks and pulls her shawl up over her head.

"I'm not going anywhere in this, and you shouldn't either!"

She makes a break for the house, where the windows emit an inviting glow. Out here, the rain has slicked the cobblestones to an oily black.

"Suit yourself!" Lotta calls after her, as Daphne disappears into the night. She's not going to let a bit of wind and rain distract her from her mission.

As she's leaving the stable yard, about to shut the tall wooden gate to the road, it is pulled from her hands.

"Where are you going? I've been looking for you!" Marten holds the gate open and beckons her to come back inside.

"I'm for the tavern," she says. "Come with me. I'm buying."

Marten looks up at the sky, frowning, then back at her. His face tells her he thinks she's either brave or crazy.

"I'm taking the shortcut on foot," she says. "It's quicker than saddling up a horse."

He nods and joins her on the road, pulling the gate shut behind him. "I were just thinking I couldn't stand another night of Mrs. Frost's servants' slop. You'd think with all its plenty the Council could spare something better for the people who slave their arses off for them. What's up with you?" He's caught the look on Lotta's face, which she knows must be as tight as her gut. Her jaw is starting to ache with it.

"I'll tell you at the inn!" She has raised her voice to compete with the wind and clamped her hand down on her cap to keep it from flying away like a startled grouse.

They stride briskly down the road, arms around each other for support, before cutting across a field—weaving in the wind—and into the small thicket of elder trees that stands between the Manor House and the village. On the high street, a tattered shop awning comes loose and flaps its merry way up the road ahead of them before becoming snagged on an abandoned cart.

"At least it's blowing us toward supper, not away from it!" Marten yells.

They bring a huge gust of wind into the inn with them, which snuffs several candles and knocks over a nearby empty cup. It smashes to the ground. The curtains flutter and the flames in the fireplace leap but do not extinguish. The door slams behind them.

The band stops playing and, along with the whole room, stares stony-faced at Lotta and Marten. Lotta can't help glaring back at Stormy Pete, the wretch, and his wife, fish-faced Rona, whose mouth is opening and closing.

Marten, of course, is oblivious to the hostility oozing toward them like a tide across the saltings.

"Woo!" he says. "Bit windy out there, lads!"

She shouldn't have brought him; she realizes that now. This is her fight, not his, and he doesn't deserve to have her supposed curse rub off on him in the eyes of the village. But it's too late. Marten is walking to the bar, rubbing his hands and blowing on them, tossing his sodden hair from his eyes.

"Evening, Maggie," he says to the innkeeper, a woman who rarely smiles but is as warmhearted as they come in this dreary village. Usually. "Sorry about that cup, I'll pick it up for you just as soon as I've ordered, if that's all right with you."

"What'll it be, Marten?"

Lotta knows Maggie is avoiding looking her way. She's staring too intently into Marten's eyes, and he recoils slightly.

"An ale for myself, and a ginger wine for my little sister, thanks. And two of your finest meals. She's paying."

Maggie just nods and then directs her eyes at the ale pump instead.

As Lotta passes her on the way to a table in the farthest corner, she can't help herself. "Light of the Glimm upon you, Maggie."

Maggie scowls into the now-full mug and sets it on the counter in front of Marten. "And with you," she mumbles.

Lotta stops and turns. *"As bright as the sun."*

There's a pause and once again Lotta feels all eyes in the room upon her. The band has not yet started up again and she knows that everyone is listening.

Maggie relents, begrudgingly. "As bright as the sun."

Lotta continues on her way and sits down. The corner is dark enough that she feels a little safer. The room turns away from her and she removes her soaked shawl.

The band starts up again: bone flute and fiddle, with pretty young Alice Turner, wearing a scarf woven with mangy pheasant feathers and a drooping silk flower in her hair, singing. It's a slow, mournful tune that Lotta knows very well.

*Oh, sing me a song of the saltings*
*Where all of our power lies*

*Where he'll come each year, on the first day of spring,*
*To show his love for us all*

*For we must give so he will give*
*And painful though it may be*
*We'll all be together, at the end of the day*
*And he will love us all*

"What was that about?" Marten slides onto the opposite bench and puts her drink in front of her.

Lotta checks for spit floating on the surface—nothing would surprise her tonight, but it's clear—and takes a sip. The warmth of the ginger stings her throat and slides down into her belly, doing nothing to quell the fire already there. She can barely keep the knot of rage in her chest contained.

As if in answer, the wind throws hailstones against the small window beside them.

"Hail now!" declares Marten. "If it gets much worse, Maggie will have to have a lock-in and we'll have to drink and sing and dance all night."

A voice blasts across the room as the song finishes.

"That's hail, that is! Our crops will take another beating tonight. It's almost as if we're being punished." There are murmurs of agreement, but this time, nobody turns to give Lotta an accusing stare, which unsettles her even more than if they'd all glared at her. That is telling in itself. They think she's somehow responsible for the weather now.

"Lottie? Talk to me. What is it?"

"It's nothing," she says. "I'm just hungry." She waves his concerns away with her free hand, while taking a larger than usual gulp of wine. At least with the villagers giving her the cold shoulder rather than confronting her head on, Marten is less likely to notice. Her stomach rumbles obligingly, backing up her lie. She hopes dinner won't be too long away.

"Good, then, because I need to tell you something."

*Not him too.* She lifts her shoulders and drops them with a sigh. "What have you heard?"

"Heard? What?" He takes a draw of his ale, which leaves a slug of foam on his upper lip. He wipes it away with his sleeve and puts his cup down. "It's Roddy. Roddy and me."

She groans. She knew something was going to go awry with those two. "Glimm, you haven't been caught, have you? Marten, I told you that you were being too bold. Gregory nearly let you go the other day. You have to be more careful."

"It's not that." His face has grown somber in the candlelight.

Lotta waits for him to go on. It takes a lot to steal the light from Marten's eyes.

"Roddy thinks he's about to be betrothed. To Meg what's-her-name. The Councillor's daughter."

"Gray? Aren't they cousins? That seems grim even for them. Didn't they play together as children?"

"No, she's adopted. From Farmer Jack. They're not related by blood. She didn't go to live with the Grays until she were thirteen. Her family gave her willingly, for all that bounty."

One of them. The Council sometimes adopts children into their ranks, so they don't keep marrying each other. And there's payment. Lotta forgets sometimes that her own family's life also would have had such comforts if she'd gone to her death. Compensation, for giving up their child for the greater good. Like the Jacks, the Salters would have had a new cart, a larder that was never empty. She wonders if they regret her survival sometimes.

"What am I going to do?" says Marten. "I'm losing him, Lottie."

Lotta puts her hand on his arm. "You knew this day would come."

"I thought somehow this might be different."

"Well, what did he say?"

"That's the worst part. He just said he had no choice. His *duty*, he said. He said I wouldn't understand the pressure on him, that I can marry who I like. I can marry for love." He snorts. "But I can't, can I? Because it's him I love. And I can't bleedin' well marry him." He takes a last, long draw of his beer and slams the cup down. Lotta is glad for the music drowning it out, and for the fact that Marten's back is to the room, so the others can't see his misery.

"Here you go." Maggie appears beside the table and sets down two plates, with roast mutton, mashed swede, gravy, and boiled kale, but doesn't linger for a chat as usual. Marten doesn't seem to notice. Lotta's mouth starts to water. It's been too long since she's had much more than a hunk of bread, a wedge of cheese, and a carrot or a turnip, which she has lifted from the horses' supply. She's long given up dining with the Manor House's servants, whose stares bruise her. She seizes her fork and digs in.

"I'm sorry," she mutters through a mouthful of mash. "Maybe they won't go through with it. Or maybe it'll just be a sham, and you can carry on in some way. But you knew it couldn't last as it was."

"So you've said." Marten also picks up his fork and shoves a mouthful of kale into his gob. He barely chews it before swallowing. "You wouldn't know what it's like. Have you ever loved someone?"

Lotta thinks about the people who matter to her. Marten. Wolf. Her parents? *Next thought, please.* Daphne, though she isn't sure Daphne would show loyalty to her over the Council and the lore any more than Roderick would. No, love isn't the right word for how she feels about her friend.

"You know I haven't," is all she says. "What will you do?"

"Da could use me back on the salt farm. I don't think I can stay here and see Roddy every day." He puts down his knife and fork, suddenly too teared up to eat.

"I'll miss you."

"You can come home once in a while, you know. It won't hurt."

Lotta says nothing. She's given up trying to explain it to him.

"What about Wolf? And me? *We* didn't send you off to sacrifice, you know."

"I know that." Another blast of wind rattles the window. In the soft glow of the candle, fat raindrops cluster tightly together as they hit the glass.

"Well?" asks Marten. "Are we never to see you?"

"You can come and visit me anytime. Or we can meet up anywhere, go for a ride on the moors. I can tell you how Roddy is."

"Don't," he says. "I couldn't bear it."

"Well," she says. "It may not happen. You said he only *thinks* he is to be engaged. Maybe he's mistaken. Maybe he loves you too much for that to happen."

"I'm not even sure he does." His face collapses in dejection.

A sudden gale sweeps the room; one of the men has opened the door and is trying to leave. He's blown backward and falls into a table. It takes two more men to close the door, pushing down the bar to secure it.

Marten has turned to watch. "Looks like another lock-in. Hunker down, sister. Another drink? I'll buy this time." He must be feeling reckless; the price of two drinks is half his week's pay.

"I can't stay here," she says. "Can you not see what's happening?"

"What do you mean?"

"The way they all look at me. The way Maggie was with me. They think I'm the cause of their dead sheep and cattle, their failed crops."

"But they *always* stare at you, Lotta. You're the girl who survived. They've always been a bit scared of you, sure. But they look at you with respect."

"You call that respect?" Lotta flicks her jaw out, indicating over Marten's shoulder.

He turns, then quickly turns back when he is greeted with the glowers of several of the men. Even Alice Turner, who usually blushes around him, looking up at him through her eyelashes, seems to glare, her coal black eyes reflecting the burning embers of the fire.

"Holy Glimm. What's got into them?"

"Temple the other day, remember? The Judge hinting at something. I have a bad feeling."

"But you're their prize groom. The great Lotta Salter."

"They've got a funny way of showing it." She pushes her now-empty plate aside. The wind is still howling, louder even than the music. In fact, the musicians give up: There's no point, in this racket.

Marten whistles, but his face is crinkled with worry. "That's going to be a mess to clean up tomorrow in the garden. Gregory will throw his rag. He'll probably find some way to blame me."

"Or me," says Lotta with a grimace. "Didn't you hear them before? They think the Glimm is mad and it's my fault."

"Rise above it, Lottie. You're better than them."

"Don't. I'm not."

"You're a lot to live up to, you know? Even though I'm bleedin' two years older than you, I'm always Lotta's brother. They adore you. At least, they did. Maybe this is my chance to come out from under your shadow." His grin is welcome after his misery.

"Did you believe all that stuff they fed us back then?" asks Lotta. "About the better place we all go to? That I was lucky? You said that to me, you know."

"Said what?"

"That I was lucky. Do you believe in that place?"

Marten looks shocked. "Of course I do. It doesn't mean I wanted to go right at that very moment. But I reckon if it had been me chosen for the lottery, I'd have been excited. Honored, you know."

Lotta is silent, turning this over. It makes her feel ill, truth be told. She washes the taste of the mutton from her mouth with the last of the ginger wine to calm her stomach. She suddenly remembers what she said to Daphne, the whole reason she came here. *Let them say that to my face.*

"What if that's what they want us to feel? Honored. What if . . ." The thought is too unformed. "Never mind."

Out of the corner of her eye, she sees something flying toward them. She ducks, but it crashes onto the ground behind Marten, who leaps to his feet, alert. A broken beer cup lies on the floor.

"Who threw that?" he yells to the room.

For the first time all night, nobody is glaring at them or even looking with half interest. The whole tavern has their eyes turned resolutely away from them, looking at the floor, the ceiling, out the window, at each other—everywhere except toward their corner.

Maggie appears at their table. "Now then, Marten. We'll have no trouble." She has a shovel and a brush and bends to sweep up the pieces. She's fast because she has to do it often, Lotta senses.

"Why don't you tell that lot?" says Marten, twisting on his bench, gesturing to the room.

"I've got a lock-in on my hands. It's not safe to go out there." She looks pointedly at Lotta. "We've got hours to go and need to keep things civil, like."

"You'll have an inn full of drunkards on your hands, you mean, Maggie," says Lotta. "Rather it were you than me."

Maggie's lips are a thin line. "Yes, well," is all she says, before hurrying away to dispose of the mess.

"I've had enough of this." Lotta stands and throws her napkin down on the table.

"What are you doing?" asks Marten, grabbing her wrist. She shakes him off. She won't be stopped now. It's like a force that's been building inside her all night.

"You all got something to say to me?" she yells. Every sham conversation comes to a halt. Bodies stiffen. Drinks freeze halfway to faces. Only a few people turn to look at her: Stormy Pete, of course, and Biddy Jackson's man, Shaun. Butcher John. She never did like him, even though he's always trying to give her extra chops. It never feels out of the goodness of his heart but something more obsequious. Appeasing. Like if he is good to the girl who survived, the Glimm will somehow reward him in the After. Well, there'll be no free chops anymore.

"Come on, ya cowards! I knows you've been talking about me. Let's have it."

It's fish-faced Rona who speaks first. "Lotta Salter, I don't know what kind of curse you've put on me, but my bread won't rise, and my hens won't lay."

Curse? On her *chickens*?

"Who else?" says Lotta. "What else have I done?"

"This storm will ruin my new crops," says a farmer she recognizes as her parents' neighbor, Ted. "The village relies on me. We'll starve."

Then it's Butcher John's turn to speak. "There were maggots on my legs of mutton this morning."

Lotta laughs. "Maybe you should be more careful with how you keep your meat, John. Stop letting it go rotten enough to attract the flies. For Glimm's sake."

There's an audible gasp.

"You'll not take the Glimm's name in vain in my inn," says Maggie, in a low, menacing voice.

Lotta laughs, disbelieving and bitter. "You all do it! We all do it! This isn't Temple, you know, it's a tavern for drunks and bastards."

Now they all look at each other. Did she just insult them? Too right she did.

An almighty *CRACK* sounds above their heads and one or two women shriek.

"It's only thunder," says Lotta. "What are you all so afraid of?"

"The Glimm!" It's the butcher again. "You saw my wee grand-babby the other day. That birthmark. This can only be the work of the Glimm."

"Well, if it's the Glimm, why are you blaming me?" She thumps her fist against her chest.

"It's hungry!" says Rona, and she looks to Pete to back her up.

"Too right," he says. "It's mad and it's taking it out on all of us."

A chorus of agreement ripples around the room.

"You should have been sacrificed that day!" A woman's voice, hoarse, but full of fire.

Lotta takes a step back. "Who said that?"

Nobody speaks. Seemingly from nowhere, John the butcher has produced one of his knives, and is testing the tip with one finger. He draws it away and a bead of blood slips to the stone floor. He makes eye contact with Lotta and holds it as he puts his finger in his mouth.

Still nobody speaks. The rain drums on the roof, finding crevices in the thatch. A stream of water gurgles onto Pete and Rona's table, and into Alice Turner's hair. She screams and hits at her head, dislodging the flower, which falls into her drink.

Lotta turns to Marten. "Come on, let's go home."

"But the storm," he says.

"You think you're safer in here?"

He takes her point and gathers his coat, handing Lotta her shawl. Lotta throws coins onto the table. "That should more than cover it, Maggie. Have a nice night, won't you? *May the light of the Glimm be upon you all.*"

This time, nobody responds to her call. All eyes are on them as they cross the room, and Marten helps Lotta wrestle the bar off the door as the storm thumps to get in.

Lotta throws it open, and raises her arm to her face, expecting a blast of wind and rain—or worse, ice-cold hail—but it does not come.

Instead, she is met with a cold silence. Beyond the threshold, the world has become suddenly still.

# 10

HE WAKES, his chest cold and slick with sweat. He listens to the quiet morning, to Stone snuffling in his sleep and to his mother's softer breathing. A clatter as one of the animals kicks over an empty bucket with purpose.

Last night, they just managed to bring Hannah, along with the goat and their only ewe, into the byre before the storm exploded: wind, rain, hail, thunder—the lot. Moss thought the roof might blow off; it was a huge effort to keep the fire going when water dripped into it with a sizzle.

The smoke was unbearable. Stone got into Mam's bed, coughing more deeply than ever, while Moss turned his back on them both, his shoulders around his ears and his fists jammed into his armpits. He didn't know if he'd be able to sleep anyway. The visit from Lewis swirled around his head, as it had done all day as he worked, buffeting inside him.

Mam had just given up after Lewis left, slumped into her chair, her face burning with shame and sorrow. After a time, she'd sluggishly gone about preparing a basic supper.

"We have to hide her," Moss had said.

"No, Mossy."

"You hid me!"

"*Moss.* Hannah is much bigger than you, and she doesn't understand."

"I didn't understand, neither."

Silence. Mam's jaw pulsed. She ground her teeth, her eyes fixed on peeling turnips. Finally she looked up at him.

"There are consequences to such things, Moss. We had a very real reason for taking the risks we did. You can't understand the agony we went through."

"So tell me."

"It's more complicated than you think."

"So. Tell. Me."

Mam stared at him, hard. He could see something momentous turning over in her mind. He could feel it like a physical wall rising between them.

"Hark at you," scoffed Stone, breaking the tension. "You been stomping around the place since you met that girl, mad as a goose at Mam for hiding you, now you want to do the same for Hannah."

Moss said nothing; Stone was right. How he hated it when Stone was right. What good would hiding her do? She was too big. They couldn't put her to work if she was hiding. But the Council would have to take another horse—one of the island ponies that nobody would miss. What would be wrong with that?

During the storm, Hannah moved around the byre, giving agitated grunts at each vicious gust or rumble from the sky. There was no way they could take her.

*The Glimm's will be done.*

The lottery was a farce. And if the lottery for the horses was a farce, did that also mean the lottery for children was as well? But that would shake the very foundations of the island. Surely.

Then suddenly, the weather went quiet. It was eerie, wrong somehow. As if the Glimm had brought it down upon the island and then changed its mind.

Soon the house was filled with Stone's soft snores, and Moss was finally able to sleep.

He dreamed of Hannah: ploughing a field in the soft evening light, peat baskets swinging at her sides, her mane tangled with heather. He brushed her, spoke to her, led her through golden grass—until the ground beneath them began to suck at her hooves. He shouted, pulled, screamed for help. But this time, Lotta Salter did not appear. The Glimm rose instead, breath hot as fever, coiling like smoke around Hannah's trembling neck, and pulled her under with the sound of cracking bones.

The light has only just begun to pinch the horizon. It's his time. The before-light. While the world is bleary-eyed. He knows what he must do. Find Lotta and beg her to help save Hannah. She is their only hope.

He wraps a hunk of bread in a cloth and grabs a flask of stale water, careful not to wake his family.

Hannah is dozing in the byre. Moss slips the bridle on her. He opens the door and shoos the sheep and the goat outside, kicks some hay at them and leads Hannah to the mounting block. Before he jumps on, he strokes her forelock and presses his face to her neck. He inhales the scent of her: sweet hay, soon dominated by sour peat smoke.

*We're the same*, he thinks. *Sour-stinking hidelings, the both of us.*

The yard is littered with reeds from the roof, and thick with mud after the night's rain; his boots are caked in it. The peat stack has collapsed—all that drying gone to waste—and will need to be rebuilt. Nonetheless, he flings himself up onto Hannah's back and sets off for the moors. The light is dim, but Moss's vision is sharp. He takes a different path from the one where Hannah got stuck in the bog, passing the exiles' modest shared crops. He turns his gaze away from the carnage: delicate first shoots swamped, seaweed from the lazy beds strewn all around. He has more immediate things on his mind.

He regrets leaving his scarf behind and has only a thin kerchief knotted at his neck. His woolen jacket bares his wrists in the same way his trousers expose his ankles, and he can no longer button it up. Time to pass his clothes on to Stone and help Mam make him new ones—but when will she find the time? He thinks of his father's oversized jacket that Mam still wears every winter, cinched tight with a thick belt. By rights, he should have it, but he can't bear to take what's probably all she has left of her husband.

Small lakes and puddles on the moor have swollen with rain to brown, pungent oceans; the carcasses of a few drowned sheep within make him uneasy, but he doesn't stop. The *slub-slab* of Hannah's hooves fills his ears as she picks her way through mud; agonizingly slow going.

The moors stretch wide, the wind riffling through the grasses, carrying the scent of damp earth and peat. Moss's thoughts blur, but one image cuts through: Lotta, standing there, her voice low and haunting, singing to the bog. He remembers the way she looked at him, the way her eyes flicked over him like he was nothing more than a shadow on the wind.

After more than an hour, he reaches the edge of the village, where a group of women sits at an outdoor table, their bodies quick with movement. He recognizes the work they do: They're fulling the woolen cloth, soaking it in buckets of soapy water and then kneading it like bread to soften it ready to sew into garments. They sing as they work, and Moss slows to take in the beauty of their song, three-part harmonies soaring together. They have smiles on their faces, happy in their work. He feels a pang for what his mother has lost.

He listens, unnoticed, and strains to make out the words of the song. At first it sounds like a harmless nursery rhyme.

*Jonny's fallen and broken his toe*
*lift him up, lift him up*
*Jonny's fallen and broken his toe*
*lift him up and help him on*

*Jonny's fallen and broken his thumb*
*make him work, make him work*
*Jonny's fallen and broken his thumb*
*make him work, the work's not done*

The look of glee on the women's faces takes on a darker edge, and Moss feels a knot of discomfort forming inside. He starts to move Hannah away, and catches the eye of one of the women, a red-faced matron in a headscarf who nudges the younger woman beside her.

*Jonny's fallen and broken his neck*
*Lay him flat, in the creek*
*Poor young hideling's got no use*
*Let's leave him there to drown*

Moss puts his head down, but he feels their eyes on him. Their song grows louder as he passes, aiming for the road to the Manor House.

*Whoopsy Jonny, whoopsy Jonny*
*Jonny Jonny Jonny Jon,*
*Whoopsy Jonny, hideling Jonny*
*Let's leave him there to drown*

With every "whoopsy" they let out a high *whoop*, then they dissolve into shrieking laughter when they finish. Moss refuses to look back, even as he hears a voice call out to him: "Light of the Glimm upon you, hideling!"

He preferred it when they shunned him, wouldn't speak to him or look at him. For the first time he thinks of the island greeting as menacing, unnatural. For surely these women wish him no such light at all.

A cart piled with hay bales approaches, driven by a couple who spit at him as they pass. He flinches away, trying to control the bite of shame and anger. From the back, a young girl of no more than six or seven years old throws a stone, which strikes him on the shoulder. He turns, red-faced, to glare at her; she glares back, then draws her thumb slowly across her throat. Moss is shocked into averting his eyes again.

He leaves the village behind as the lane narrows and climbs steeply, opening suddenly onto a grassy plateau where the great Manor House sits, alone and proud, perched on the edge of the cliffs, tall windows like deadened eyes. It's surrounded by a matching stone wall that blends into the sky. The wind blows fiercely here, the salt tang of sea spray sharp in Moss's mouth. It feels like another world, far removed from the cramped, suspicious village below.

Moss avoids the grand entrance gates and instead makes for the stand of trees across a nearby paddock. What was he thinking, bringing Hannah here? They'll likely take her if they see her, and he'll have saved them the effort of coming to collect her. He makes extra sure to tether her safely in the trees, hidden from view, then heads for the side wall, where he finds the gate to the stables.

At first there's no movement inside, but then a young man appears, wheeling a barrow filled with long-handled tools: a rake and a shovel, perhaps. He's got auburn hair and a smooth, hopeful face under his gray cap. He pauses to put the barrow down and wipe his brow with his sleeve. Too late, Moss pulls back from the gate. He's been spotted.

Crunching footsteps come toward him.

"Is it something you're wanting?" His voice matches his face—smooth, lilting. Kind. He hasn't spotted what Moss is, then. But why should he, really? Apart from his paler-than-usual skin, Moss has the same kind of face as anyone.

Moss steps back into sight. This boy—a few years older than him, so a man maybe—is a servant, clearly. A smear of dirt licks his cheek, and his hands, which grip the gate, are filthy, with broken fingernails. Maybe he'll be helpful.

"I'm looking for Lotta Salter," Moss says. His voice comes out low and gravelly. He clears his throat. "She's the groom here, I think."

"I know who she is," says the man. "Don't you know me?"

Moss shakes his head. "No, sorry."

The boy looks him up and down, and Moss can see realization dawn on him. Of what he is. But instead of shouting at him, or turning him away, the boy looks over his shoulder, then unlatches the gate.

"I'm Marten," he says. "Who are you?"

"Moss."

"Well, Moss. You'd better come into the stables, quick, before you're seen. And you'd best tell me what a hideling wants with my little sister."

# II

**Moss doesn't know** how to reply as he slips through the open gate. He doesn't know how much he can trust Marten, even if he is Lotta's brother.

"You're all right," says Marten. "You can tell me when we get there."

As they approach the corner of the stables, Marten holds up a hand: *Wait.* He peers around the side of the building, then looks back at Moss and nods.

"All clear. We don't want the groundsman showing up, or worse, his Lordship."

Moss's stomach grinds at the thought of meeting a Councillor. No, not a Councillor—his Lordship, the *Judge.* He has a feeling the Judge would have him thrown to the Glimm on sight.

"I'm grateful," he murmurs, as Marten leads him past the stables, where he glimpses a young boy with a mischievous face grooming a chestnut horse, singing to it as he works. Moss doesn't dare listen out for the words after the fulling women's song.

The sun has burned off the low cloud now, and Moss's head is beginning to ache already. He closes his eyes as he walks, rolling them inside his head.

"Here you go."

They've arrived at a field bounded by a wooden fence; only the Judge would have a wooden fence for his horses—all those precious trees wasted—while Moss and his family have to make do building pens from rough stones. It's no ordinary field, either: The ground is covered, not in grass, or dirt, or mud, after last night's rain, but sand. A gleaming black horse trots—no, prances—in a wide circle, its neck arched and fine knees lifting high. He's seen this movement before, from a distance, as the Councillors have ridden through the village. The result is breathtaking, otherworldly, especially when there's a parade of them. It makes sense that Lotta is the person to have trained them to walk like this. She sits deep in the saddle, a look of concentration on her face, her body apparently still but no doubt sending subtle signals.

Marten doesn't call out to her. Perhaps he doesn't want to startle the horse. Instead, he waits for her to turn in their direction. As soon as she spots them, she murmurs something and the horse's posture relaxes; it falls back into a walk, stretching its neck out. Lotta scowls at Marten but then her gaze shifts to Moss and her face softens. She hides it by busying herself dismounting.

"You have a visitor," says Marten, his voice straining with curiosity.

"You shouldn't be here," says Lotta, lifting the reins over the horse's head. "You'll get all of us into trouble."

"Can we talk?" says Moss.

Lotta thinks for a moment. "You should go," she says to Marten. "I'll deal with this."

Marten sniffs, then turns to leave. Lotta waits until he has rounded the corner, then she starts walking. She doesn't need to tug on the reins; the horse follows her, ears pricked, eager to please. "Well, come on," she says. "It's safer inside the stable."

She leads both of them—Moss and the horse—into a stall, which she closes behind them.

"Everything good?" A young voice from outside, shuffling sounds of hooves on the cobblestones.

"It's fine, Dougie," Lotta calls back. "Take the mare and turn her out into the field for a spell."

"If you say so," says the boy, and leads the horse away.

The air is close in here. Moss is aware of every sound: the rustling of the straw, the sigh of the animal as Lotta removes its bridle, the blood in his ears as he realizes his heartbeat is escalating. She removes her cap; her hair is damp beneath it, a darker rust at the temples. Up close he can see every freckle scattered across her nose and cheeks.

"You're more comfortable in here," she says, not looking at him, focusing on the horse instead. "You're not squinting anymore. Does the light bother you?"

He ignores the question, unsure whether it's a trap or not—an apparent show of sensitivity and sympathy, or an excuse to torment him for being a hideling, brought up in darkness.

"Your brother," he says. "Will he tell someone I'm here?"

"Don't worry about him," she says. "He's none too happy with the Council right now. Or the villagers, come to that. He'll hold his tongue."

"That's good."

"Why are you here?"

Moss takes a deep breath and lets it out. He puts his hand on the stallion's warm neck for courage. "I need your help."

She surprises him by nodding. "I figured. But I'm not here to solve your problems, Moss."

His heart leaps. She knows his name.

"Please," he says. "It's our horse. It's our Hannah."

She takes a brush and begins working it over the horse's neck. "What of it?"

Is she avoiding his gaze?

"Please, Lotta," he says. "They've named her. They've decided she'll be the next one to be sacrificed. You can help. I know you can."

She stops brushing, her face wrinkled with confusion. "What do you mean, *named* her? She's only going into the lottery. Along with a lot of other horses. The odds aren't bad."

Moss's stomach lurches. "You knew?"

Her cheeks redden, a sight he was not expecting. Not from Lotta Salter. "One of the Councillors came to me yesterday," she says.

"Lewis?"

"How did you . . . never mind. He told me to make way for a new horse for the lottery, that he didn't want it out in the field. A big horse, he said."

"Hannah. It's what I told you. Didn't you ask why?"

"You think I can stand up to the Council on a whim?"

Moss shakes his head. He has no idea, really, what her part in this village is.

"I didn't ask him, but he found out I'd helped you in the bog, and he told me it was the same horse. That the Judge was sending a message to the hidelings after your ma barged in on Temple day."

It's Moss's turn to blush. What must she think of them?

"Well, with any luck," she goes on, "another horse will be drawn, and it'll be returned to you."

"You're not listening to me. There's no luck involved, can't you see? Hannah will be chosen in the lottery. She'll be sacrificed. We're ruined."

"But why?" she asks. "It makes no sense. The lottery is random. It has to be. It's the lore."

"Lewis told us Hannah's already been chosen."

"But that means . . ."

He lets it sink in, watches her face change as the truth dawns on her. Then he nods. "The lottery's a sham."

The stallion rumbles and paws the ground, sensing Lotta's escalating pulse. Its ears flatten and for a moment she thinks it will turn and bite Moss. He must sense it too, because he backs away to stand against the wall.

Her breathing is coming fast and shallow, and she strokes the horse's neck, calming them both, until it slows, but her hand still shakes.

The lottery is rigged? This changes everything.

She opens her eyes wide and stares at Moss, not sure if she can really trust him to be telling the truth. But why would he lie about something like that?

"Why come to me?" she asks, her voice measured. "What do you think I can do?"

"You helped before." His whisper is urgent now. "When Hannah were stuck in the bog. You saved her."

"I only got her out. That doesn't mean I have the answers you're looking for."

"But the song. You sang to the bog." His voice drops to a conspiratorial whisper. *"Like you knew it would listen."*

Lotta stiffens, her shoulders tensing. For a moment she sees it as clear as day. The bog. Hannah's hot, sweat-flecked body. The song, rising from her, pleading. The answering hum from below. He was a witness.

"What do you know about me?"

"Only what I've seen with my own eyes," he replies. "You know things. You know more than you let on." He takes a tentative step closer. The stallion has calmed down now and is reaching for its hay net.

"I know this village," she says. "I know the lies they tell, the stories they spread, the masks they wear. They fear anyone or anything they don't understand."

"Like me, you mean? Like the—" He pauses, and a look of pain comes over him. "Like the banished. The *hidelings*." His lips pinch defiantly.

*Don't call me that.*

"I'm sorry," she says.

"I'm not so different from you," he continues. "The Glimm surely knows it."

His dark eyes are so open and pleading she doesn't know whether to laugh or feel pity. "I hate to tell you this, but the Glimm doesn't care for you, any more than the Council does."

Moss recoils as if she's slapped him. "But the Glimm loves us all!"

"Your family shunned that love as soon as they hid you, you must know that! Why do you think you're not allowed at Temple?"

He looks at his feet, his cheeks burning.

"I'm sorry," she says quickly, berating herself. Why had she said that? "That was cruel. I didn't mean—"

"It's fine," he mutters. "I'll go. I shouldn't have come."

He turns to the stall door, but she stops him with a hand on his arm.

"Wait," she says. "Maybe we're not so different."

His cool forearm quivers under her touch, his jacket too short, exposing dark, downy hair. He looks at her expectantly.

She needs time to think. The lottery. How can they have already chosen a horse? And why Hannah? If it's punishment for Moss's mother daring to show her face in Temple, well, that calls everything into question. She needs to find out more.

Moss's gaze is hungry, desperate. Maybe he can help her answer some of those questions, this hideling boy with the dark curls, with the spotted kerchief around his neck.

"What do you want me to do, exactly?" she asks.

"You tend the horses. If Hannah's coming here, you could move her somewhere safe. Then they'll have to choose another horse. They have so many. They don't matter like Hannah does."

Lotta draws herself taller and puts a protective hand on the black stallion's rump. "You think these horses don't matter?"

"Well, do you? You barely look at them. Do you even give them names?"

She grits her teeth. Takes a breath. She needs to put it into words.

"Don't you see? All horses matter. I don't give them a name because . . . well, look at yours, at Hannah. You talk about her like she's a piece of farm equipment that you need to survive. But I can tell it's more than that. You care for her."

"She's family."

"Exactly. It's never easy, the lottery. The sacrifice." Every year is a wound in her side. "How could I stand it if I lost a family member every year?"

"So you keep your distance."

"To name something is to accept it has feelings."

"The horses care for you, whether you like it or not."

Lotta nods curtly, pressing her lips together. She doesn't need this boy pointing it out to her. She'd rather believe her system is working.

"You know how things run," he says. "The Council respects you. You could talk to them."

"You think I'm above the lore? That I can change it? I just keep my head down and if I'm lucky they leave me be. Well, they *did*." Can she trust him? She has nobody to talk to about this. Certainly not Daphne. And Marten is preoccupied. She decides to take a chance. "The villagers fear me. They used to think I had special favor with the Glimm and that's why I was spared."

"And do you?"

Lotta thinks of the songs that come to her in her dreams then abandon her. The ache she feels, the sighs that hum beneath the earth that nobody else hears.

"I was just lucky, that's all. But things are shifting. Can you feel it?"

"I'm not sure," he says.

"Now they think I've brought all the ills on the island. The sacrifice is supposed to keep the Glimm sated, so the island can prosper. They think I cheated somehow, and now it's angry. That I'm cursed and they're paying the price. Like the storm."

"The storm last night? Our crops are drowned."

Lotta nods wearily. "They'll tell you it was my fault." She's not entirely sure that it wasn't. It started when Daphne told her about the villagers' suspicions, and she felt the ire rising inside her, pressure building. Like the weather. The storm was eldritch, otherworldly. The way it ceased so suddenly. She and Marten had walked home in a daze. She can still feel the eyes of the villagers silently watching them leave.

"Even if I did . . . even if I could help you hide her, what then? Where would you go? What would you do?"

"I don't know." His voice is hollow. "I don't care where we go. I just can't lose her."

It's impossible. She knows it. He must know it too.

"I can't change the lore, Moss. The lottery's coming. The Glimm will take what it needs."

"No." His voice is shaking now. "That's not how it works. They've already chosen. Lewis told us. The lottery's a lie."

Lotta hears the scrape of a boot on the stone floor outside the door. She puts a finger to her lips. "Is that you, Dougie?"

There's a pause but she can sense him breathing. "It's me," he says. "Master Roderick and Marten want me to saddle up a couple of island horses. Is everything all right?"

"We're fine," she says through gritted teeth. "Go and get them from the field and saddle them in the yard." That will keep them all out of the way. Dougie's nosiness will get her punished one of these days. Though he *is* loyal, she reminds herself.

"You'll have to wait here out of sight until they've ridden out."

Moss nods but looks defeated. "I don't have anyone else. You're the only one who might be able to help."

"You're asking me to defy the Council," she says flatly. "To defy the Glimm."

He draws himself tall and locks his gaze on hers. "So will you help me or not?"

Lotta moves around to the horse's head. It nudges her pocket, smelling the carrots that were once there. She lifts its forelock away from its eyes and strokes the white star on its forehead. She's never noticed until now how it's like a spiral, like a coiled serpent.

"I will think about it," she says eventually. "But understand this: *Nobody* defies the Council, and especially the Glimm, without consequences. We might just need each other."

# 12

**It's the smell** that hits him first. Peat smoke, wafting across the moors. Thick, sour. The sky has turned an ominous gray, clouds pressing down on the landscape. Hannah grunts underneath him as he kicks her into a canter.

He passes Sadie's house first and is aghast at the chaos there. The cart lies on its side; Sadie's brother and mother are pushing uselessly, trying to heave it upright. Their chickens flap around the yard. Straw is strewn everywhere. The front door of their blackhouse is hanging off its hinges. Sadie is raking peat bricks into a pile from a smashed stack. At the sound of Hannah's hooves she looks up and drops the rake. Her face is red and tear-streaked as she runs toward him.

"There you are! Where you been? They've been on a rampage looking for you and for Hannah. They thought we was hiding her!"

Moss's blood runs cold. He hears a scream in the distance, toward his house. Sadie hears it too, and alarm spreads across her face.

"Are you hurt, Sadie? Did they hurt you?"

She shakes her head. "You should go. They might be doing worse over at your place. Go!"

It's not just Sadie's house. Other houses show the same chaos, debris spread around, a peat stack on fire, sparks threatening the thatched roof of the Flynns' house. Young Johnno Flynn is up there throwing water on the reeds to protect it. His mother, Margo, weeps over a sheep with its throat cut. Her husband and daughter stand silently beside her, glaring at Moss as he rides past. This is his fault. The Council has been dying to punish the exiled folk all this time, and now he's given them an excuse.

The scream. He's sure it was Mam.

He pulls Hannah up sharply at the sight in his yard. Six horses are tethered to the wall outside, and within, five tall, silent figures stand like stones in a circle. Their faces are covered by masks, roughly hewn from sackcloth, wonky holes torn in them for their eyes, dark and flat, to peer from. The masks, tied close around the neck, mark them unmistakably as the Council's enforcers, the thugs sent when things need to be done swiftly and without question. The masks don't only make them anonymous; they erase any sense of humanity to be appealed to by those they come to collect from.

Mam is on her knees in front of one of them, bent over, clutching her stomach. Stone is also on his knees, but his neck is in the grip of one of these monsters, his arm twisted behind him.

Smoke pours from their smoldering peat stack as well, and Moss can also see pieces of wood burning—the vandals have fed their makeshift gate to the fire, some of the only wood they own. The goat and sheep have escaped but Moss isn't worried about them; they'll not go far and will return home when their bellies need feeding.

"Let them go!" Moss shouts. "It's me you want. It's Hannah. Here she is. You can take her." He dismounts.

Mam looks up and her stoic face collapses. It says everything. *Where have you been?* And *How could you?*

A cloaked figure steps out from the shadow of the house. Lewis? No, this man is not as tall, not as imposing. He wears the same hat—a Councillor, then. His face is grave, but Moss knows that he is enjoying himself; why else would he have inflicted such cruelty on them?

"So, hideling," he says. "You decided to come back. That is very wise of you."

"I only went to the village. I weren't gone long."

"And yet your family here couldn't tell me where you were," he said. "So I had every reason to believe you'd tried to hide your animal to prevent us from taking her, and they couldn't prove me wrong. As if we would tolerate that from hidelings, after all you've done." He spits on the ground in front of Moss.

Stone cries out as the man holding him throws him roughly forward. Mam reaches for Stone and he goes to her, helping her to her feet. Moss can't bear to see the betrayed look in their eyes. He can tell Mam is about to ask him why he'd gone to the village without telling her, but he shakes his head quickly and she stays silent.

"Well, I'm here now. I'm not going nowhere."

"Take her," the Councillor says to one of his henchmen, who steps forward and picks up Hannah's trailing reins. He jerks on them and she backs away instinctively with a sharp squeal.

"Hold her!" the Councillor barks. More of the masked men come forward, surrounding her. One produces a stick and waves it in her face, threatening to strike her across the nose. Her fear only makes her struggle more.

"Wait!" Moss cries. "You don't have to do that. She's placid as a lamb. Let me calm her—you're only making it harder for yourselves." It's not them he's worried about. If Hannah is calm, she is safe.

The Councillor nods and the men retreat. Moss goes to her, places a hand on her foam-flecked, shaking neck. "I'm sorry, old girl," he whispers in her ear. "It can't be helped." As he strokes her, the trembling subsides. He lays his face against her mane. "You've been such a good horse, you know that?" Hannah shifts from hoof to hoof. She gives a rumbling whinny.

Suddenly, Mam and Stone are beside him. Moss takes a step back and lets them close. Hannah lowers her head so that Stone can throw his arms around her neck and sob. Mam strokes her nose, tears forming and then falling from her eyes.

"I'm so sorry, Mam," Moss murmurs. "But all is not lost, I promise."

She looks at him sharply. "What did you do?" she hisses.

"Enough," says the Councillor, too far away to have heard. "We'll take her now." He signals to the men again. One comes forward and takes the reins. He's learned his lesson and tugs on them gently, so Hannah—dear, trusting Hannah—follows.

"Wait!" calls Stone. "She likes turnips. Here." He reaches into his pocket and pulls out a morsel, which he offers to the masked man. The man stares at it a moment, before shrugging and taking it from him to put in his own pocket.

What would the man say, if he were allowed? It's as though all their tongues have been cut out; their silence is unsettling, uncanny. It makes them far more terrifying.

The men mount their horses. The Councillor's is a fine chestnut; Moss recognizes its arched neck and high-stepping gait as Lotta's work, and a note of hope begins to hum in his ears. She will help them. She has to.

Hannah resists at first, tries to look back at them, her eyes wide with confusion. Moss sees a glimpse of her as a foal, when she first came to them, tripping over her own too-large feet, glaring at them indignantly. How he had gained her trust with gentle hands.

She receives a whip to the rump and then she is gone, on her way.

The Councillor wheels around. "We'll see you after the lottery, hidelings. Who knows? Maybe your horse will be spared and returned to you. The Glimm will decide."

The insult, *hidelings*, is the last straw; a wildness rises in him. "Or maybe the lottery is rigged," says Moss. "And the Council is corrupt and full of liars."

"Moss!" Mam grabs his arm and pulls him back, too late: The Councillor plunges his horse forward and strikes Moss across the face with his whip. It burns like fire on his cheek.

"Blasphemer!" The man spits. "You can forget about ever seeing this animal again, regardless of the outcome. And you'd better watch your tongue in future." And with that, they are gone, and Hannah with them.

"What have you done?" Mam cries. "You've made things so much worse, Moss."

Moss is clutching his face and brings his hand away. Blood.

Stone sits on the ground, his face in his knees, sobbing. He won't look at Moss.

"I'm sorry," Moss says. "I don't know what I was thinking. I just saw red. They can't treat us this way. It's unfair."

"We can't think about that now," says Mam. "We need to get this cleaned up. And what of our neighbors? Those men went looking for you all over the hamlet. I dread to think what damage they've done, and what they'll all think of us."

"It's not good, Mam."

"Then we need to forget about our own troubles and go and help them first, or we'll be outcasts from our home as well as the village, and then where will we be?"

"I'll fix this somehow, Mam."

"How, Moss? How will you fix it?"

"I don't know."

He will find a way. He must.

# 13

**SHE SITS AT** the small table in her room, warming her hands on a mug of steaming tea. Outside, the heavy cloak of black cloud is braided with gold as the sun sets, a sign of the gentle nor'wester. The clouds will slowly drift and churn but there'll be no more rain, no storm tonight. She's still shaken by the conviction that it was her mood alone that caused the weather last night. And even more so by her conversation with Moss.

The lottery. A sham.

It will be drawn tomorrow night—she doesn't have long to work out what to do. Is he asking too much of her? She's already been warned by Councillor Lewis to keep her head down. How much is she willing to risk for someone like Moss, really?

They'd been taught to hate the selfish hidelings. Many of the villagers had wanted to throw them off the cliffs and be done with them, to feed them to the creatures that circled the island, but the Council said there were too many of them, that *they might be useful one day.*

Useful for what? Harvesting peat? Or taking the blame?

She doesn't hate Moss.

She'd never met a hideling before, and he's *not* what she expected. She'd pictured them skulking about the place, as miserable as they deserved. But something stronger burned inside him. Determination. His face in the sparse light showed such desperate hope. His pale skin contrasted sharply with his dark hair and eyebrows, his deep red lips, probably chapped by the relentless cold and wind on the moors. Though they didn't look rough. They looked soft as butter.

A clattering outside, beyond the wall of the Manor grounds, distracts her from her thoughts. Hooves on the cobblestones. The bell at the gate sounds. Who can it be, this late? Dougie has already gone home for his supper. She doesn't know where Marten is. She hasn't seen him since he let Moss in this morning. There was something about going out riding with Roddy; she hopes they've made some peace. It must be them.

She pulls on her boots and jacket, then makes her way down the narrow staircase, gripping the walls to steady herself in the gloom.

"Come on, girl." It's square-faced Councillor Gray on his chestnut mare, which whinnies in pleasure when it sees her. "We can't stand out here all night."

Lotta swings the gate wide. Gray is not alone. He's got henchmen with him, dressed in their simple cotton smock shirts that gape at the neck, rough hessian cloaks around their shoulders.

She is shocked when she realizes that two of the silent figures on sturdy island horses are Marten and Roddy. She shoots Marten an incredulous look, but before she can say anything, he puts his finger to his lips, glancing at Gray's back. Roddy stifles a laugh with one gloved hand. He thinks it's a grand joke.

Gray nods to the other three men, who give Lotta filthy stares. She recognizes them as Eddie, the butcher's son; big Tommy Carter, who used to follow her around with moon eyes when they were young, desperate to be her friend, or more; and his brother, Ash. Now Tommy can't wait to escape her. They set off at a brisk trot.

Roddy is leading another horse, a heavyset, large animal, with a solid, curved nose and a large star. She recognizes it immediately.

Gray looks Lotta up and down with barely concealed contempt.

"You're expecting this animal? Councillor Lewis has informed you, I'm sure. You're to keep it inside the stable until the lottery."

"Yes," Lotta says simply.

"Well." He looks her up and down again as if expecting to find her wearing different shoes, perhaps, or a new hat. "I must be off home before it is so dark my mare breaks her leg." The Councillor's mare steps forward and nudges Lotta in the shoulder.

Lotta puts her hand on its nose. It was especially hard not to develop a soft spot for this one. In training, it used to steal Lotta's cap from her head, and the Manor cat took a shine to it and was frequently found curled on its back, sleeping, while the mare moved gently to not disturb her. Dougie nicknamed her Apple Pie, but she doubts very much that Councillor Gray would have allowed the name to stick.

Gray jerks the reins, pulling the mare's head away.

"Good work today, Roderick," he says, ignoring Marten. "I'll be sure to tell your father. It's good for you young ones to travel under cover with us, to learn how to deal with these hidelings. I trust you did learn something?"

"I did, sir, thank you. Very interesting." Roddy glances at Marten, whose return stare is brittle, then swings his leg behind him and drops heavily to the ground, kicking his poor mount on the way down. Thankfully he didn't take his stallion out on the moors. Roddy is reckless in the saddle. He sits heavily and uses his hands far too much; Lotta doesn't trust him not to ride into a thicket or a bog.

"I daresay you'll get your chance to lead such a party yourself before long," says Gray. "Once you're married to my lovely daughter."

Lotta can't look at Marten.

"I hope so, sir," says Roddy.

"You're dismissed, gardener," says Gray to Marten. "But help your sister, would you? We don't want her losing the hideling's horse because her back is turned while she puts those other nags out to pasture."

And with that, he is gone, back out through the gate and clattering up the road.

Lotta closes the gate behind him, then turns back to where Roddy and Marten stand in strained silence.

"What on *earth* have you two done?"

Roddy tosses his reins at Marten. "Oh, shut it, Lotta. I'm not going to be lectured by the likes of you. This was Council business. Which means it's none of yours."

"None of mine? Except I have to care for this horse. Do you know why it was taken?"

Roddy shrugs.

Marten stares at the ground. "It's for the lottery."

"Exactly. And this horse will be drawn in the lottery."

"Don't be daft," says Roddy. "You don't know that." He runs his gloved hand through his sand-colored hair and inspects it afterward. He shakes off whatever he finds there. "The lottery is chance. Only the Glimm knows which horse will be chosen."

Lotta pauses. How much can she trust Roddy, really? She should keep her mouth shut around the Council's kin. She can see that now. If she lets on that she knows about the plan cooked up by the Council to draw Hannah, to rig the lottery as punishment, they'll want to know how she knows.

"Well, it's just cruel, taking away an animal from people who have nothing."

Roddy whistles, low and long. "Hark at you, Miss High-and-Mighty. They're only hidelings, who cares what happens, right, Marten?" He turns to Marten now for support, and even in the dark evening Lotta can see her brother's cheeks fill with color.

"Yeah," Marten says quietly. "Maybe. But look, it's getting cold. You go home and I'll help Lotta get these lazy beasts to bed." He stares at the ground. It's almost as if he can't bring himself to look at his friend, his love. Lotta recognizes a broken heart when she sees one.

Roddy moves toward him, then stops. Lotta can see him turning an argument over in his mind. Marten waits in hopeful silence. But Roddy stands up straight suddenly and breaks into a benevolent smile.

"Very well." His voice has grown formal, awkward. "Thank you for your work today, Marten. It was good to have you there by my side."

He turns away. Marten mutters, "Your loyal servant."

Roddy has heard him; his body tenses, then his shoulders give out and he slouches away.

Lotta doesn't know where to start, so she says nothing that's really on her mind, barely keeping a lid on the simmering heat inside her.

"These horses are filthy."

"The moors were muddy from the storm," says Marten.

"Go and light some lanterns so we can see what we're doing. They're in the cupboard under the stairs."

Marten does as he's told, as though he is the younger sibling accepting orders. Lotta is left with the three horses, and she gives the workhorses a pat on the nose each, finds carrot pieces in her pocket for them. They'll need something more substantial after that ride. Marten emerges with the lanterns, casting a soft glow on his face. His eyes are puffy, like he's been rubbing them.

Hannah moves toward him, stretching out her nose.

"Look," says Lotta. "How can she trust you, after what you did?"

Marten puts his hand in his pocket and pulls out a gray lump. The horse lips it off his palm, then nods her head up and down as if in approval. "Turnip," he says. "The boy, Moss's brother, gave it to me. It's probably got his smell all over it." His face falls.

"You could have told them Moss was with me," says Lotta. "Why didn't you?"

"And get you in trouble?" He shakes his head. "You should have seen how they treated them, Lotta. What they did to the other hidelings when they couldn't find Moss or the horse."

"How could you, Marten?"

"You know I don't have any choice! I have to do what I'm told around here."

"You don't. You were talking of leaving this house anyway and going back to work with Da at the saltings." She turns her back on him and tethers the island horses. "I need to feed these two."

Marten follows her into the stable, where she lights the stove to heat the mash that has been soaking all day. "You know why I had to go."

"Roddy, I suppose. I can scarcely believe it. My brother. A thug for the Council."

"Don't," says Marten. "I didn't give your friend away, or you. I put my own self in danger."

Lotta stirs the pot. "Oh, how very *noble* of you. And he's not my friend."

"What did he want, then?"

"Isn't it obvious?" She glances outside at Hannah, waiting patiently where Marten has tied her.

Her brother's soft face puckers. "You need to be careful, Lottie. They don't muck about. I've seen what they do to people who stand in their way."

"Don't you worry about me. I know which side I'd rather be on. Now go and rub those horses down properly, while I finish up here."

That's it, then. She's made up her mind to help the hideling. The lottery is tomorrow night. She doesn't have much time.

# 14

**THE GLIMM CALLS** *to her with a song.*

*It calls her back to the saltings, to the place where she'd been tied to a standing stone all those years ago and left to die.*

*The melody is familiar to her because she's heard it before, again and again, in dreams she could never quite remember on waking. But now she knows. It's the same song she sang to the bog, to the island, to set Hannah free.*

*In her dream she moves through the moors, down to the salt flats, where the skeletons of salt-poisoned trees puncture the sky. She can't see the Glimm. But she feels its presence all around her.*

*She draws the melody up from the boggy ground and sings back like the chiming of a hundred bells.*

*A song of the saltings.*

*A sharp cry makes her look up. An eagle wheels through the churning sky above. She raises her arms and the eagle dives, bringing with it the clouds, which swirl down to envelop her. She curls her arms into her body, then pushes. The clouds and the eagle rush upward, dissolving into the sky. The ground rumbles beneath her feet.*

ꟸ

She wakes with the sound still groaning in her ears, heart hammering. For once, the dream doesn't disappear. She remembers every sound, every blackthorn flower, every barb of the eagle's feathers.

Lotta understands now, that it wasn't only the bog that she was singing to that day. She was singing to the Glimm. Because all of it—the island, the weather, the horse, and the eagle—is the Glimm. The cliffs, the mountains, the moors, and the bogs. All one.

Does this mean that she, Lotta—the girl who tames horses—is somehow one with it all as well? Or is the Glimm calling to her because she should have been sacrificed that day? Are the villagers right, that she is the reason the island is sick, that she's causing all its ills?

She throws on her clothes and goes outside to stand at the edge of the horses' field, where the great oak tree stands, split by the storm. She looks south.

Lotta hasn't been to the saltings for a long time and hasn't been home in years. Her family has worked the edges of the marshes for generations, collecting salt. They have always half feared that the Glimm, or something worse, would one day attack. But they have always been left in peace.

She's never laid eyes on the Glimm. Is this why she never sees it in her dreams? She's had no desire to witness the annual sacrifice, and she was blindfolded when she was its offering.

But she knows what it feels like to be near it. And she knows that the lottery is rigged.

It's time to find out what they know.

ꟸ

The white house sits quietly by the edge of the salt marshes, smoke drifting from the chimney. Beside it, chickens scratch freely in the earth; a cow and some goats are penned by a low stone wall, along with two horses and a much smaller pony—Wolf's. Lotta's heart gives a small flutter as she remembers Hazel, who was the same size, nuggety and tough, with a shaggy chestnut coat and a mane and tail the color and coarseness of straw. The cow lows. The sound carries easily in the still air, rare for this time of year, when Lotta is used to being gnawed by the wind coming off the sea.

A distant figure works the salt pools near the shore. Steam rises from the pans that boil the briny water captured from the spring tides. Soon, clean white salt crystals will crust on its surface, to be gathered and sold at market. At least, whatever the Council doesn't take for itself first will be sold. Marten will soon join her father there, she supposes, once he has left the Manor House.

Sheep wander freely across the marshes when the tide is out, cropping the seagrasses, turning their meat tender and tasty. They are bright white against the green of the marshes and the blue of the tide, reflecting the rare sunny sky. The skeleton trees remind her of guards.

The gray gelding comes to life beneath her as the horses in the pen call out to it. Lotta feels its bones shift as it lengthens its stride, ears pricked. It calls back.

A black dog appears from around the side of the house and starts barking, but even from here Lotta can see Teapot's tail wagging. His steps are creaky with age.

She is heartsick. How idyllic the house is that she grew up in, away from the town, away from the prying, vicious eyes and tongues of the villagers. She remembers the hours she spent in that yard, chasing the hens, or ambling down to the edge of the marsh with her father, and playing contentedly in the salty mud. The Glimm was so abstract to her then, just a word that threaded itself into everyday speech. She didn't know that just around the bay stood a stone where children who were to be taken were secured. Roped.

Lotta's first six years had been bliss, full of warmth and cuddles, games and laughter. She had given Teapot his name when he was a puppy, all roly-poly folds and clumsy paws. Before she'd had to go to school in the village and her education began. Before she knew her fate. If only Wolf could be forever suspended at the age he is now.

A figure emerges from the house: her mother, Shona, wiping her hands on her apron. A small shadow slips out beside her.

"Lottie!" Wolf streaks toward her, scattering chickens, with Teapot limping behind.

"Wait for me!" laughs their mother, catching up to Wolf and swinging him onto her back. Together they jog toward her like a two-headed beast.

Lotta dismounts just as Teapot is upon her, whining with joy, wiggling his hindquarters. She crouches down and rubs his ears, accepting a lick on the cheek. His muzzle is newly salted with white.

"Hello, Wolfie!" Still crouching, she grins as the boy wriggles down from his mother's back and runs to Lotta for a hug, elbowing Teapot out of the way. She holds him close, stomach churning.

"You came," says her mother, slightly breathless from the uphill trot.

"Is this your horse?" asks Wolf. His eyes are lit like candle flames.

"Sort of," says Lotta.

"Can I pat him?"

She clicks her fingers down by her thigh and the gelding lowers its head obediently.

Wolf gently strokes its nose, an expression of wonder on his face. "So beautiful," he breathes. "What's he called?"

"Oh, it doesn't really have a name."

"Why?" asks her brother.

"Come on, let's go to the house." Lotta guides him to one side and picks up the reins.

"I'll call him Salty," Wolf declares.

"Salty?" her mother chuckles. "That means cross, doesn't it? He looks anything but."

"I know, but he's salt-colored and—" He darts forward, tongue protruding, and licks the horse's shoulder. "He *tastes* like salt!" He wipes his mouth and makes spluttering noises.

Lotta laughs. "It's sweat, you nit. And now you got a hairy tongue!"

Wolf laughs as well and Lotta drinks in the sound like warm broth.

"I wish I'd known you were coming, love," says Shona. "I'd have made something for dinner."

"I'm not staying," says Lotta, as they walk back toward the house, Wolf skipping ahead with Teapot. "I have to talk to you about something. You and Da. It must be teatime?"

Shona nods. "There he is, look."

Lotta recognizes the pale coat of Dobbin, plodding toward them from the direction of the marsh. A swaying shape sits up high on the cart behind. Shona waves, and the figure lifts its hand high in the air, holding it there in salute for a good few seconds.

"He'll be so pleased to see you," says Shona.

"It's not a party," Lotta reminds her.

"But you'll have tea?"

Lotta hesitates.

"There's fresh soda bread," Shona adds.

Damn her. How can she resist?

"All right," she concedes. "Tea and bread."

Inside the house, the yeasty, comforting smell of bread almost overwhelms her. She reminds herself that this is no longer her home, though there's the yellow cloth on the table, still faintly dotted with her childhood blood from learning to darn; there is the stove with the kettle warming on it. There is the chimney, drawing the smell of peat out of the house. She'd always taken it for granted.

Wolf's wooden animals are arranged on the floor in conversation. They used to be hers, and Marten's before that. Da carved them himself out of the deadened trees that puncture the marsh. Wolf dives on them and brings her a horse with pride. The wood is bleached nearly white.

"Salty!" He shoves it into her hands, and she turns it over, putting on a show of admiring it.

The cart's wheels crunch on the ground by the house. "Whoa, Dobby," floats through the window.

The door bursts open and her father stands there, bringing with him the smell of the sea, the tang of seagrasses and salt. He bends to take off his sandy, muddy boots and casts them aside as he crosses the threshold.

"You came!" he declares, unable to keep the smile off his ruddy-cheeked face. He takes off his cap. His hair is grayer than before—thinner, too. His forehead has grown larger and his scalp shines through. "I in't butchered that ewe yet. You've taken us by surprise."

Shona bustles between them, her hands raised as if in a warning.

"Calm down, Allen. Give her room. She's only here for tea. She's got something to ask us."

"Oh, aye?" He lights up even more and Lotta remembers the day he gave her the wooden toys—the hopeful look on his face that she would love them as much as Marten had. Which of course she did.

She shouldn't have come. This is too painful.

"Sit." Her mother gestures to the chairs at the table. Wolf climbs onto Lotta's lap and twirls her plait in his fingers. Shona pours water into a teapot then sets down a slate with bread, removing the cloth as she does so. Lotta's tastebuds start to fire.

Allen, opposite her, clasps his hands together, fingers entwined.

"What's this about, love?"

"Ma," says Lotta. "Please stop." Her mother can never sit still, is always up and bustling around the kitchen while everyone else is eating. Shona nods, then slides into her chair, with one leg cocked to the side, ready to spring up again. She pours the tea into three cups while Allen slices the bread. The rasp of the knife is thick in the silence.

"I've come to ask you something. Ow!" Wolf has pulled too hard at her hair and her scalp stings like a bite. She grasps him roughly by the arms and lifts him to the ground. He looks shocked. *Please don't cry,* thinks Lotta. But she's too agitated to offer him words of apology, or comfort, except through gritted teeth.

But just as Wolf's wide eyes start to blur with tears, a giant slab of bread with butter and jam appears in front of his face, and the tears quickly recede.

"Take it outside, Wolfie, there's a good lad," says Shona, sensing what is to come. "We won't be long. Go and see how many eggs the chickens have laid. Don't come back until you've counted them all! You can leave the door open."

Lotta flicks her plait behind her back and takes a sip of tea to calm herself. She bites the bread and closes her eyes as she chews and swallows. Better.

Her parents' faces are full of concern.

There's a scraping sound at the door, and then a deep voice: "Hey, hey, what's going on here?"

Lotta's skin almost leaps off her body. She twists in her seat only to find Marten filling the doorway, wiping his boots.

"Don't do that," she snaps. "I thought you were a Councillor. Or a henchman. Which, I suppose, you are." Marten shoots her a filthy look and she juts her chin at him, undeterred.

Shona has taken the opportunity to jump up from her seat again. She pushes a chair toward Marten. "Just in time for tea. Did you see Wolf out there?"

"I did, but he were too busy with his head in the chicken coop to notice me. I didn't expect to see you here, Lottie. I looked for you before I left."

"You got the day off?" asks Shona, putting a slice of bread in front of him. Marten seizes it and tears a chunk off with his teeth.

"I've quit," he says through his mouthful.

"Oh, Marten!" says Shona. "Why?"

"Yes, why?" Allen's palms come up to lie flat on the table.

"I want to come back home, Ma. To work the salt flats with Da. I know you could use my help." He lifts his eyes to Lotta, then away. "I'm done with the Manor House."

So he regrets last night. Good. Or maybe it's just Roddy he regrets. Lotta can see her father turning Marten's words over in his mind. Extra help, yes. But also an extra mouth to feed.

"We'll have to talk about this later. Lotta has some pressing business."

Marten looks at Lotta quizzically, chewing with his mouth open.

It's time. The question has been burning a hole in her stomach all morning. "Why did the Glimm spare me?"

There's a silence around the table as her parents stare at her, confused, until her mother says, "I don't understand, Lottie. Why are you asking us this now? You know what happened. Hazel escaped and the Glimm took her instead of you."

"But what if there's more to it?" Lotta presses.

"What other reason would there be, love?"

"That's what I've come to ask you!" She's surprised to find tears prickling her eyes. "They're turning against me, Ma. The villagers. They think the winter's been so bad because of me. Because the Glimm is mad I wasn't taken."

"The Glimm made its choice," says Allen. "It released us from the sacrifice. It were clear."

"Was it clear though? Or was there something about me that meant that it wouldn't take me? Or couldn't?"

"You're being very cryptic, Lottie," says Ma. "What are you getting at?"

"Well, has any Salter ever been taken before?"

"Not in my lifetime," says her father. "But odds are they must have been at some time. We been here forever."

"So we've always been tied to the saltings."

"Well, yes, love. It's right there in our name."

Lotta goes quiet, trying to order her thoughts. She can't picture the Glimm in her mind, because she's *never seen it.*

"Have you ever seen the Glimm around this part of the salt marsh?"

"No, it's always left us alone, as far as I know," says her father. "My brother, Glimm rest his soul, came screaming in the door one day saying he'd seen it, but it were just a dead log, floating on the tide."

"But you've seen it. Around the bay. On the saltings."

"Yes, love. Of course we have. Every year, now," says Allen.

"I don't know where you're going with this," says Ma. "What you thinking?"

"Yes," says Marten, his mouth full of bread. "What?"

Lotta turns to him. She's not sure what she's trying to work out either. Her thoughts are slippery eels. "The other night, that storm. It came on so suddenly, right?"

"Like a flash," he agrees. "And stopped just as quick, when we left the inn."

"Not just when we left it," says Lotta. "When I *opened the door.* One second it was howling outside. The next it was still."

"I know. We said it on the way home—strange as anything. Like the storm let us go." Marten glances at his parents. "It was a lock-in. Folk were getting really nasty. Told Lotta she should have died."

Shona draws in a sharp breath and her face puckers.

"I've been having these dreams," Lotta says. "I hear this song. I think it's the Glimm. I think it's calling me back."

Another silence. For a moment Lotta thinks her mother is about to leap up again, to stoke the fire, to gather the dishes to be washed, anything to get away from the moment.

"You were different," says Shona. "After."

"Different how?"

"You were so mad at us—"

"Still am," says Lotta.

"—but there were something else about you. The animals behaved different around you—they was drawn to you. Sometimes, I swear, the weather changed, depending on your mood."

"That was just nonsense talk," says Allen.

"I know you never believed me." Shona is curt with him. She barely looks at him, just turns her gaze, both fretful and warm, on Lotta again. "But you moved through the world different. The bog never seemed to touch you. You could walk anywhere.

"It didn't help that the other children treated you odd. We had to keep you around home after that—they was always cutting off bits of your hair, stealing your gloves."

"We knew the Council would come for you eventually," says Allen. "They needed to keep a watch on you. They knew you were different too."

"And you went so willingly." Shona's eyes fill with tears. "We knew we'd lost you."

"You sent me to die," says Lotta.

"We did," says her father. "But it's more complicated than you can ever know."

Lotta rolls her eyes. This again. "So you've said," she says bitterly, slumping in her chair.

She turns to look out the open door, checking that Wolf—or an unexpected visitor—isn't about to walk in.

"Look, there's something up with the Council." She turns to Marten. "I need to know that what I'm saying doesn't leave these four walls. You can't tell Roddy, or anyone. If the Judge finds out what I know, it's all over for me."

*"Roddy."* He practically spits the name on the table. "I'm done talking to him. Don't you worry."

Her mother looks at him with curiosity but stifles it. She knows that now is not the time. "What is it?"

Lotta swallows. "You know I tend horses for the lottery. But they've confiscated a hideling horse to put in the draw for tonight. There's no chance about it—it *will* be drawn. The Council's already decided."

She pauses, waiting for a reaction. When none comes, she presses on. "The lottery. It's rigged."

Shona and Allen exchange a long, heavy look.

"Did you hear what she said?" Marten says.

Shona nods at her husband. She closes her eyes as Allen turns to face them. He spreads his hands wide.

"So now you know."

# 15

**For a moment,** Lotta can't speak. Her face grows hot, pulsing in time with her heart. *This* she was not expecting.

Beside her, Marten is pale with shock. He grips the table and looks back at Lotta, as if gauging to see if her reaction matches his.

"You *knew*?" Lotta asks finally.

Allen won't raise his gaze from the table. "It's always been the way." Shona takes his hand.

Lotta lets out a long, disbelieving breath. "Does everyone know? It's never been random?"

"Oh, I'm sure it often is," says her mother. "It keeps up the ritual. The festival. It's a much happier occasion than before . . ."

"When they used to take children," says Marten.

A cold finger trails down Lotta's spine. "And before?"

Allen moves his chair closer to Shona's so he can put a protective arm around her. "The islanders don't know this, or they refuse to see it. The Council's always used the lottery as punishment. But we didn't know, until . . . they used it against us. So no, everybody doesn't know. And you was never supposed to find out."

Lotta feels woozy. She can't speak.

"Back when you was both children," says Allen, "we stopped going to Temple. We disagreed with the way the Council was demanding all kinds of sacrifices from the islanders. Not just their children, not just the lottery. Every week at Temple we was madc to give up our food, our comforts. So they could have more. We kept you away, remember? We was determined you'd have a happy childhood, before you had to go to school. It's another reason why you was always so different to the other children. Your heart's always been so open. Well, it were."

Lotta's heart fractures. He's right. She's held it tightly shut for so long.

"One winter, eight years ago," Allen continues, "there were a famine, worse than ever. Livestock died in the cold. It were too freezing to gather salt; the market closed down. There weren't nothing to put salt on anyway, so there weren't nothing to trade for. The ground were frozen, and the stores of peat ran dry. Everybody tried to do the best for themselves, but folk was left with nothing but turnips."

"Like the hidelings now, you mean."

He ignores Lotta's comment. "Anything they had left were taken by the Council. People filed into the Temple every week like sheep and gave and gave until there were nothing left." He gulps.

Shona puts her hand on his knee. "They realized we weren't coming to Temple, so they marched down here and took the last of our livestock. Me and your da called a meeting and tried to convince the rest of the village to stop giving them so much. The Council got wind of it. The villagers were too loyal—"

"Too daft, more like," says Allen. "They all thought that one day they might be welcomed into the fold of the Council, or that their sons and daughters might marry into their lines and then they'd have access to the same privileges. As if that has ever happened."

Marten shifts in his seat and Lotta puts a hand on the back of his chair.

"Soon after," Allen continues, "the lottery were drawn, and it were you, Lottie. We knew then there weren't nothing random about it. The Glimm, if it controlled chance, were a cruel creature. But we know it weren't the Glimm. It were the Council."

The room has grown too hot suddenly. So many questions tumble in Lotta's head she has to make a wild grasp to catch one. What does this mean for everything she's understood about her family, about the islanders?

The silence is broken by a sob from Marten, his face in his hands. Shona tears her gaze from Lotta and reaches out a hand to him.

"Why didn't you tell us?" he asks.

"To protect you, of course," whispers Shona.

"But—" Marten heaves a shuddering sigh and begins again. "Lotta's been gone all these years, and you just let her go. You let me go and work there and all. For the Judge."

"But as long as the lottery was for horses, not children, she was safe. The Council respects her, however grudgingly. They think the Glimm spared her for a reason. Maybe they even fear her."

"So they keep her close." Marten is talking about Lotta as if she's not there.

"And you," Shona continues. "Well, you know we wanted you here, but you wouldn't listen."

"So," says Lotta. "Let me get this straight. You let the Council take me for sacrifice, even though you didn't believe in the lottery?"

"They'd have killed us all, Lottie. I'm so sorry."

"You don't know that."

"You've seen how the villagers follow them like drunk mice. They'd all have turned on us. They'd have dragged you down to the standing stone themselves. It were better you went willingly. It would've been so much more frightening for you otherwise."

"And those stories you fed us, about the land I would go to, that Gran would be there, and that you would join me soon?"

"That's what we was taught to believe. And part of us still wants to. But I don't know anymore, love. I just don't."

There's a roaring now, in Lotta's ears. Did challenging the Council make them strong, or were they weak for giving her up so easily?

Lotta stands up and draws herself tall. "We need to help that family. Hide the horse. *Something.*"

"Have you gone daft in the head?" Marten wipes his face with his sleeve.

"I don't understand," says her father. "What's that to do with us? With you?"

"That horse is all they've got. It'll ruin them."

"Since when have you been friends with any hidelings?" asks Ma.

"I'm not."

"We can't help you," says her mother. "It's too risky. Do you know what they'll do if they find out? Can't you help them by giving them one of the island ponies?"

Lotta gapes at her mother. How can she be so naive? "They're hidelings, Ma. They'll have to earn another. It could take years. They've nothing to earn with if they don't have a horse." A flash of a memory: Moss, his quiet pleading. His dark eyes swimming in the dim light of the stables. *She's family.*

"It's true," says Marten, his voice still miserable. "I've seen up close how the Council treats the hidelings. I know they're traitors, and we all think they deserve to be outcasts, but Ma, they're still people, like us."

"Tell them," says Lotta. "Tell them what you saw."

Marten relays what he saw with Roddy at the hideling hamlet. The destruction. The cruelty. Most of this is new to Lotta. He didn't tell her much last night. Shame is etched on his face.

A lump crushes her throat. Moss. He risked everything coming to her, and so many people paid the price. She jams a finger and thumb into her eyes, pinching away the tears that have formed there.

"We're sorry," says Allen, his arm still around Shona's shoulders. Their faces across from her are resigned. They won't defy the Council again.

"So you won't help me. Won't help the hidelings. This is your chance to make amends."

Shona looks at her with something like sorrow in her eyes, but there's a hardness to her expression too. "You don't understand, love," she whispers. "Sometimes fighting them just makes it worse."

The walls close in around Lotta as the weight of the past and the present threaten to overwhelm her. She can't stay here, not with this pain, not when there's work to be done. The roaring in her ears grows louder. She opens her mouth before she knows what she's going to say.

She utters one word. "Cowards."

Her mother's eyes widen with shock.

"Lottie!" says Marten. "Leave it."

She turns to her brother, simmering. "You just said so yourself—they're people too!"

"Yes," he says. "But we also have to look after our own." An edge of coldness has crept into his voice, where before there had been sorrow.

"Then you're part of the problem!" Hot tears spill onto Lotta's cheeks but she's sure it's not sadness that she's feeling. It's boiling rage. She grabs her chair and flings it to one side.

Her mother doesn't react; instead her eyes become sharp, and she turns her head to the side, alert. "What's that noise?"

The roaring has grown louder. It's not in Lotta's head. It's coming from outside, where Teapot sets up a frantic barking.

A high-pitched scream spins through the open door. *Wolf.* Before she can think, Lotta dives through the doorway, her family leaping to their feet behind her.

The yard is empty, save for the chicken, running in circles, flapping and squawking. There's a booming sound as Dobby, nose bag dangling, explodes from around the side of the house where Allen left him, and takes off at a gallop up the road, the cart clattering and bouncing behind him as if in pursuit. The animals in the pen, including the gray gelding, are agitated, trembling, their calls high-pitched.

"Wolf!" Lotta yells.

His scream comes again, from the side of the house. Lotta darts around the corner, Marten on her heels.

"What *is* that?" Marten gasps.

Wolf stands with his back to them looking out toward the salt flats. At first Lotta can't interpret what she's seeing. The bucolic view from earlier is gone, replaced by a surging wall of white. As they watch, it engulfs the sheep standing on the flats.

Wolf is frozen to the spot. All he can do is scream.

"It's a wave!" cries Lotta. She seizes her brother and throws him to Marten. Wolf wraps his legs around Marten's waist and buries his face in his shoulder, shrieking. Teapot runs circles around them with a piercing bark.

Her parents are upon them, but Lotta pushes them away. "Run, for Glimm's sake, run! Up the hill!"

"The animals," says her mother.

"There's no time, just go!"

She doesn't have time to fetch her horse, and as she runs, picking her mother up when she trips, she is filled with a certain dread that the animal will die, will be swept out to sea. All these years she has worked so hard to not care, and for nothing.

She can't help what she does next.

"Lotta!" her father cries as she veers away and runs back toward the animal pen. "What are you doing?"

She can't explain it. She knows only that the tide can't hurt her. The next moment the gray gelding leaps the wall and gallops to meet her.

"Good boy, Salty." She throws herself onto his back.

Dougie was right: Salty doesn't just trust her. He *loves* her. And now they need to trust each other. Instead of turning him away from the coming wave, she turns him toward it.

The wall of water moves slowly—unnaturally so. It should be upon her now, swirling around the house, scooping up the chickens, crashing over the wall of the pen to take the animals. The roar is deafening, and above it, gray clouds bubble and churn, just as they had in her dream. The crows that roost in the dead trees now carve rings in the sky above. Salty trembles beneath her, ears sharp, body tense.

The song begins low in Lotta's belly, rises through her chest, and bursts from her throat: three long notes and words she doesn't recognize. They feel ancient, as though they've always been a part of this place. She raises her arms and closes her eyes. All her instincts tell her to stay still, and to sing.

At first, she can barely hear her own voice above the din of the water but slowly, slowly, the sound of the wave begins to die down. The song is full of sorrow and regret but also longing. It's as though all her ancestors are with her, humming up from the depths of the earth. Tears wet her cheeks, salt her lips.

The water listens.

Still singing, Lotta opens her eyes to watch the wave roll back to where it came from. The salt marshes emerge in its wake. The sheep that grazed the flats have gone. Instead, hundreds of silver shapes dance on the sand. Her horse trots forward, as curious as Lotta, and the silver shapes soon become clear. Fish. An offering from the sea, the domain of sea monsters. No, not the sea. The Glimm.

She leans over and vomits onto the mud.

The sea could have killed her family, wiped out their livelihood at the very least. And it would have been her fault, just as the storm was—her anger manifested. It's as though the Glimm is listening and responding to her every mood. But why?

Lotta turns Salty and canters past the house, up the hill to her family.

They sit huddled on the ground, watching her. Dobby crops meager grass nearby. Teapot dashes forward and runs circles around them, barking madly, while Salty's ears flick with displeasure. Lotta dismounts, and stands before them, her knees shuddering. Or is it the ground beneath them?

Instead of running to her, the family rises slowly to their feet. Even Wolf is eyeing her with fear.

"I'm sorry," she says, and takes a step toward them.

Wolf flinches and moves to hide behind Allen. It crushes her heart.

"I'm sorry for not forgiving you," she says. "I understand, now, that you did what you had to."

Still they stare. Only Marten moves, turning this way and that, as if searching for something.

Lotta tries again to connect, to break their silence. "It's not you I should be angry with. It's the Council."

"But, Lotta . . . ," says her father.

She waits for him to go on. She takes another tentative step.

Allen looks at Shona and Marten, as if checking they all have the same thought on their minds. He opens his hands. "What *are* you?"

The question hangs between them. Lotta starts to cry. All the tension of the day, the horrors she confronted, and what they only narrowly escaped, erupt out of her.

"I don't know," she sobs. "I think . . . no, I'm sure. It's the Glimm. I don't remember what happened that day, only what you've told me. I only know that I felt different. And that it's not finished with me."

Wolf is the first to come forward to embrace her; of course he is. But he is quickly followed by her mother, then Allen, and finally, Marten.

"What does it want from me?" asks Lotta.

Nobody can answer, any more than she can.

"I need to find out. But I don't know how to. I don't even know where to start."

"Lotta . . ." Her mother speaks for the first time. "There's someone who might be able to help you. Someone who's been here longer than anyone. Who might understand the Glimm better than the rest of us."

"Who? Constance?" The midwife is the oldest person in the village.

Shona shakes her head. "Jenny."

"Jenny *Green*?" says Marten. "The bog witch? Ma, what are you talking about?"

"Marten, shush," says Lotta. She needs to think. It makes sense.

"Who's Jenny?" says Wolf, wide-eyed.

Lotta looks at his pale, tear-streaked face, then back at her mother. "You haven't told him about her?"

"There's plenty of time for that," says Shona. "He'll learn about her soon enough, from the other children when he gets to school."

Lotta puts a reassuring hand on Wolf's shoulder. "She's just someone people tell stories about. To keep them from wandering into the bog and getting lost. Nothing to worry about."

Wolf nods, seems satisfied.

"You really think I can find her?"

"My mother saw her once, and I believed her," says Shona. "And if anyone can find her, it's you. You just need to go north. She'll know the island better than anyone. But be careful."

Lotta nods. Finding Jenny can't be any more unlikely than a storm brought on by anger, or a wave that rolls backward. Or a song that sets a horse free.

"And the Council . . ." The anger stirs again, low in her belly. She looks up. The clouds have stilled; an eagle rides an invisible current above. "Something's not right," she says. "If they've done this to Moss and his family, who knows what they could do to any of us? I have to find out what else they're hiding."

She looks around at each of them in turn. "People still trust them. Still believe the Council speaks for the Glimm. But surely they don't. Not always. Maybe not ever."

"So what will you do?" Allen asks, his voice quiet, wary.

Lotta straightens. "I want people to see what the Council really is. I want to show them that the Glimm isn't theirs to control. That belief doesn't belong to them alone. If I can do that . . . if even one person sees through the lies . . ." She swallows. "Then maybe it'll be a start."

# 16

**THE WHOLE VILLAGE** has turned out for the lottery. The early evening is overcast as it so often is, with a fresh wind coming off the moors, lifting hair and jackets, tossing horses' manes into their eyes. Everyone is gathered around the pens, where the lottery horses jostle one another, each with a number painted on its rump in white or black, depending on the color of its coat. Children sit on the shoulders of their fathers; others elbow their way to the front, clutching sticky honeyed oatcakes and candied rhubarb, to get a good view. The air is filled with the delicious, warming scent of hot mead and potatoes roasting on coals. Jemima the baker has made a huge batch of scones, which she sells with the last of her crab apple jam for a coin or a kiss on the cheek, depending on the buyer.

Four bonfires mark out the corners of the village green, casting a warm glow over the scene. Bunting is strung along the edges of the pen, brightly dyed cloth cut into triangles that flap in the breeze.

A band strides around the perimeter of the gathering with a bone flute, a fiddle, and a drum, taking requests, making up silly songs about the villagers. Some brave couples even take to dancing, their feet kicking up mud that splatters their clothes.

Moss, watching from a distance, sees one girl slip and fall, then get up again, helpless with laughter, dirty as a pig, and just as happy in the muck. Or so it seems. There's tension in her laugh, like a piece of string about to snap. He's never seen such bounty, especially at this time of year. It can have only come from the Council, sharing their abundant supplies with the villagers for the festival. To keep them fed, happy, and drunk. His stomach betrays him by gurgling in response.

"Noisy lot, in't they? Not like our quiet hamlet," says Sadie at his shoulder, tearing at a piece of bread while her gaze travels wistfully to the oatcake cart. "Can you see her? Hannah, I mean?"

"No, it's impossible. The crowd's too thick." He looks around and spots a large rock nearby, worn smooth by village children using it for play, with handholds chiseled into it. "Wait here."

He jogs over and pulls himself up with little effort.

"Don't draw attention!" calls Sadie.

Moss shrugs. It's probably too late for that. He's already seen children stealing curious glances, their faces sour, tugging on their mothers' skirts and pointing him out.

From the top of the rock, he sees over the festivities. A platform has been built on the other side of the pen, and several figures in black sit on chairs, still and solemn. Behind them are more folk, set apart by their finely woven clothes as Councillor families. The young women and girls lean their elaborately styled heads together, shielding their conversations with gloved hands, while boys stand at the rear, watching the crowd, occasionally slapping each other on the back.

Moss scans the crowd for Lotta, but there's no sign of her. She's not among the officials, nor the villagers, nor anywhere near the pens that he can see. His chest tightens. What if something's happened to her? What if she's not here at all?

It's not difficult to find Hannah. She's a hand or two above the other horses, with the number 32 painted in white on her black rump. The band has circumnavigated the crowd now, and as it draws closer to the platform, a couple of the Councillors insert their fingers in their ears.

From his vantage point, the festivities take on a different tone. When people laugh, they open their mouths too wide, tip their heads too far back. Several of the children on shoulders are waving brightly colored scarves, with horse masks on their faces that verge on the grotesque. A father turns to reveal one of them as a boy with the number eleven pinned to the back of his jacket. A quick scan of the crowd shows more children, boys and girls, some with masks, or riding brooms, prancing like ponies, but all with numbers somewhere on their person.

"Sadie! Come up!"

Sadie looks around her, then scrambles up to be with him.

"Blimey," she says. "Look what we been missing all these years. Why don't they just pick a nag and be done with it? Surely the Glimm don't care which horse it gets."

"It's a ritual," he says. "Like how they all go to Temple once a week and have to give things up for the Council. The Glimm's supposed to guide the Judge's hand."

Or so he thought.

Sadie snorts. "That's stupid. What makes him so special?"

She speaks the truth, Moss knows now, and it chills him, but he's not ready to tell her what else he knows.

"It's a festival, a celebration," he says. "Mam said it used to be a solemn occasion because it meant someone's child would be taken."

"Well, I'm glad our Pumpkin's not in there." She looks at Moss. "Sorry. But she'll be all right. Hannah, I mean. She has to be."

Last night, Moss climbed onto the roof of Sadie's house and patched it up, even the hole that was already there before the attack, which he should have fixed ages ago. While everyone else was inside, exhausted, and the smell of lamb stew drifted up through the thatch, he lay on his back, wondering at the indifferent lights in the sky and crying silently. He'd scarpered before they could thank him, because he wasn't sure if they would, and it was too awkward.

This morning's sky was unbearably bright, and Moss had hidden inside with a headache, while Stone and Mam helped the other households continue to restore order. He hated himself then, but he was no good to anyone if he couldn't see. When the clouds rolled over, Sadie had arrived, greeting him like the friend he was, handing Mam a bowl of stew, and coaxing Moss outside. There she told him of her plan to get them to the lottery to bear witness. "Then you can bring Hannah home again," she said, "when the Glimm chooses a different horse." Moss didn't reply.

She persuaded her brother, Art, to take them in the cart with their chestnut Pumpkin pulling, but he left them to walk the last mile. "I'm not going near that lot," he said. "Not after what they did to us. Stay safe, you two. Keep out of sight." Sadie laughed at him then, because telling her to keep out of sight was like telling rain to be wet—it was in her nature. "You're not going to do anything stupid are you?" Art looked at Moss. "Like trying to steal Hannah back? We'll all pay for that."

"I won't," he promised. A part of him couldn't believe Hannah wasn't already back home safely. He had been sure that Lotta was going to intervene, somehow, to help them.

"Not your savior, then?" taunted Sadie. "Just an ordinary girl. Who'd have thought?"

---

Lotta sticks to the shadows of the Council's platform, shielded from their gaze as well as from the crowd, while she keeps an eye on the horses. The energy of the villagers—already restless from the music and too much mead—seethes around her. It's more raucous than she remembers lottery day being. It's messy and loud, and jittery under the surface, as though the island knows something's coming.

Dougie walks among the horses, painting the last of the numbers on their rumps: 42. That's a lot of horses brought here for nothing, to support this sham of a ceremony.

"There you are." Marten appears at her shoulder. He's dressed up for the occasion, with a waistcoat and a red kerchief. He's freshly shaven. He still smells of fish, but she doesn't have the heart to tell him.

"All done?" she asks.

"Yep. They're on their way. I rode ahead." He gestures to the hitching posts, where their father's bay horse is dozing, one back hoof balanced on its tip. "Have you seen Roddy?"

Lotta points upward, to indicate that Roddy is up there with the rest of them. Marten blushes, matching his kerchief.

"Is she up there too?"

"I wasn't looking hard enough, Marten. I imagine so, yes."

He steps out and looks up. He hesitates, then lifts his hand ever so slightly, fingers fanning. Then he curses and ducks back under the platform.

"He saw me," he says. "He even smiled at me. But then Meg came up beside him."

Lotta sighs. "I thought you were done with him?"

Marten covers his face. "I know, I know." His voice is muffled by his hands.

"Well, let's get out of here and go meet Ma and Da."

She puts her head down and pulls her cap low as she enters the crowd with Marten close behind. Almost immediately, someone spills their drink down her arm. She doesn't stop until she's forced to. A horse's skull suddenly lunges in front of her—hollow-eyed, jaw snapping, leering inches from her face. She barrels back, her heart hammering, and Marten catches her before she goes over.

A careening laugh rises from the skull, which wears a crown of blackthorn and willow, just as she had worn the day the Glimm was set to take her.

"Bog off!" shouts Marten.

The person wearing the skull is covered by a white sheet. Only a man's grubby hands are visible, holding the sticks the skull is attached to, working them up and down, making the mouth open and close in a grim imitation of speech: "You'll get yours, Lotta Salter!"

The ghost horse spins away, back into the revelers.

There's some kind of commotion in the crowd near the platform but it's too dense to see. From the corner of his eye, Moss sees a cart approaching, lit by the fire at the southern corner. A man and a woman sit on top with a small boy between them. They pull up between the rock and the crowd. The cart is laden with baskets. The man stands up and calls out.

"Come and see the miracle! A gift of the sea from the Glimm, for us all on this lottery day!"

That attracts Sadie's attention and she elbows Moss in the side.

"I can see it," he says.

The curious crowd begins to trickle over in the way sheep follow one another.

The man jumps down and moves to the back of the cart, where he reaches in and pulls out a parcel. "Fresh fish, for us all!" He hands it to the nearest person, a child in a horse mask. The boy pulls the mask off and sniffs tentatively at the package before it's snatched away by an adult, presumably his father.

This man unwraps it a little and his face lights up. He holds it up. "It's true! The light of the Glimm upon us!"

There's an answering line delivered with gusto. "As bright as the sun!"

"I've never tasted seafish before," says Sadie. "Only fresh. Is it true that it tastes of salt? On account of it being from the sea?"

“How did they get it?” Moss wonders aloud.

“From the Glimm! Does that mean we’re allowed some?”

“There’s no way that crowd’s letting us through.”

“You’re forgetting something, Mossy,” says Sadie, bringing her feet in beneath her. “I’m a ghost. Nobody can see me!”

Moss tries to grab her as she turns to shimmy down the rock face, but misses. “Don’t, Sadie! That in’t why we’re here.”

She stops halfway down and turns her face up to him. “It might not be why *you’re* here, but I’m not turning away from free food. You of all people should get that.”

Moss nods and lets her go. She’s right. She clocks on to someone and follows close behind them, blending into the crowd. Soon she is lost among them.

# 17

**Lotta and Marten** arrive at the edge of the crowd just as the cart approaches.

Lotta's pulse ticks in her ears as she scans the crowd, alert to any more trouble. Hopefully what is about to happen will appease them.

Allen and Shona sit upright, flanking Wolf, who bounces with excitement. Baskets made from woven reeds, damp and infused with the scent of the sea, fill the back of the cart.

This is the moment they'd agreed upon, carefully planned this afternoon before Lotta left to get the lottery horses ready for herding. After everything had finally broken open between them. Her parents hadn't hesitated long, just enough to admit their fear. But here they are, doing it anyway.

Her throat tightens with pride and dread.

Allen stands as the cart rolls to a stop. His clothes are damp and salt-stained, as though he's just walked out of the sea. He raises his arms and bellows: "Come and see the miracle! A gift of the sea from the Glimm, for us all on this lottery day!"

The band stumbles to a stop, their instruments sagging at their sides. The chatter picks up, excitement flocking people together.

A murmur rolls through the crowd, which is curious and hungry. Folk dive like crows drawn to a carcass. Allen reaches into a basket and pulls out a wrapped bundle, handing it to a child in a horse mask. The boy unwraps it slowly, reverently, before an adult snatches it away, holds it up to the sky, and declares:

"It's true! The light of the Glimm upon us!"

The response rolls back without hesitation: "As bright as the sun!"

Lotta steps forward, heart hammering. This is the plan: that the villagers would embrace the miracle. That they would believe, even if only for a moment, that the Glimm might choose to bless someone besides the Council.

That maybe Lotta and her family aren't tainted after all.

The crowd accept their gifts with rapturous faces and move away, letting others take their place. More people flock to see what the commotion is.

Not everyone is celebrating. A whisper goes through a tight knot of older villagers, who frown beneath their hats. Eyes flick to the platform, uncertain. A few people step back from the cart, looking suddenly afraid to be seen too close.

Lotta scans the platform. The Councillors are rising from their chairs. All of them. Even from here she can read their body language: stiff, sharp, not a single smile among them. Behind them, Daphne and Roddy and the other Council kin whisper to each other and point. Daphne catches sight of her and gives a quizzical look. Lotta spreads her hands wide and shrugs.

Judge Hawthorne leans over the front rail, face pinched. Beside him, Councillor Lewis has the big brass bell in hand. He looks to Hawthorne.

She knows what they are thinking. This is an unsanctioned miracle. Which means it's dangerous.

The Judge nods once. The bell begins to clang.

The crowd freezes in confusion. The cheer drains from their faces. Adults' gazes drop to the ground, and they fall into a tense silence, listening to the harsh sound of the bell cut through the village green. Only small children continue to cavort, but they are soon brought into line.

The bell stops and there is only the sound of the horses, alarmed by the noise, shuffling and calling. The bright sheen of the celebration darkens.

Lewis's deep voice rings out. "Take your places for the lottery! The lottery will now begin!"

There are confused mutterings all around. The Judge has not acknowledged the gift from the Glimm. Surely he is aware of it?

Lotta pushes forward through the crowd just as Wolf spots her and wriggles free from the cart. He runs into her arms.

"Shh," she whispers into his hair. "It's all right, I got you."

She pulls back and crouches before him, pressing a finger to her lips. He nods, wide-eyed. Behind him, Shona has stepped down from the cart. Allen's already looking toward the platform.

The bell begins to toll again, and the crowd moves forward. No more dancing. All eyes strained toward the Judge. Some are still passing the fish hand to hand.

Lotta draws her family close. They see him at the same time: the Councillor cutting a path through the villagers, black coat flaring in the wind.

She stands tall and intercepts him before he reaches her parents.

"Is there a problem?" Lotta asks, keeping her voice even, official.

Councillor Stirling—short and stocky as a bull with a face to match—doesn't answer her directly. His eyes flick over her shoulder to the cart.

"Lotta Salter." His voice is low and scathing. "Is this your family?"

“You know it is, Councillor. They’ve brought an offering. A gift from the sea. From the Glimm.”

He ignores her, looks over the cart, the remaining baskets of fish. She glances back and catches Shona’s subtle nod. Agreement. They’re sticking to the story. That’s all they can do now.

“We didn’t want to cause trouble,” Shona says. “Only to share the gift.”

A moment of silence.

“Here.” He hands Shona a piece of cloth. She takes it warily.

“What’s this?” says Allen.

Stirling nods toward Wolf. “For the little one. A number, remember? All the children wear them for the ceremony.”

Shona looks relieved and busies herself pinning the cloth to the back of Wolf’s jacket, but something in the Councillor’s eyes makes Lotta uneasy.

Stirling lifts his hand.

Lotta knows what that means but too late. Four masked enforcers appear from the edges of the crowd, sackcloth hoods over their heads, heavy boots thudding against the ground. Shona and Allen silently draw closer together, each with a protective hand on Wolf’s shoulders. Lotta’s stomach turns.

Without a word, the men descend on the cart and begin to unload the remaining baskets.

Lotta exhales. The confiscation is swift and silent. They’ve walked right into it.

A few villagers turn back, murmuring protests.

“Why’s the Council taking it?” says bold Jemima the baker.

“Weren’t it a gift?” says a man, balancing a boy in a horse mask on his shoulders.

“Taking what’s not yours!” This is met by jeers of agreement. More people have turned back to watch.

Stirling, glowering, stands his ground while the men shoulder the baskets and carry them off toward the platform. “Go back to your places, all of you, or you'll really have something to complain about!"

"They didn't bring it! Why should they have it?"

There are more questions, until someone barks at them to shut it. Two voices rise in heated argument and are immediately drowned out by another toll of the bell. Suddenly a cheer goes up; through the chaos, Lotta sees a henchman—his hood pulled off to reveal a red-faced Tommy Carter—clambering to his feet, while the contents of his basket are spirited away.

Stirling puts his finger close to Lotta's face.

"You won't get away with this, Lotta Salter," he spits, before walking off.

Behind Lotta, Wolf whimpers. She turns, gathers him again, and presses his head to her chest. She whispers a song—one her mother used to hum to her—but this time, there's no power in it. The words feel hollow.

She glances back up to the platform.

Hawthorne hasn't moved. He still grips the railing, eyes fixed in their direction.

And still, he has not acknowledged the gift.

It's clear: The Council doesn't want miracles unless they come from their own hand. They want control. And yet, she feels the shift in the crowd. She catches it in the sideways glances, the clenched jaws, the murmurs passed from hand to hand like the fish had been.

They won't forget this.

They've seen something unexpected and good, and they've seen it taken from them. Not by the Glimm; by the Council.

The plan has worked.

# 18

"**DID YOU CLOCK** all that?"

Moss jumps. "Don't sneak up on me like that!"

Sadie settles herself beside him, shaking her head. "The villagers are crazy. That's all there is to it."

Moss can't disagree. While the festival had been messy before, he gets the sense it was controlled mirth. Now it seems like chaos.

When Lotta had emerged by the fish cart, he'd understood that it was her family who had brought the gift, and the Council was not happy about it.

What is she playing at?

Beside him, Sadie unwraps the parcel in her hands. "In't it beautiful?"

The fish is pale and slick with cold, lying limp on a scrap of cloth. Its bright white belly merges with the dark silver of its back, but as Sadie turns it in wonder, its scales reflect other impossible colors—pinks and blues, like a sunset sky. Moss stares at it, then back toward Lotta's family. The men are gone, and the family is in a huddle. Lotta is smiling! She claps her father on the shoulder, then walks away in the direction of the platform.

Moss can scarcely believe it. Somehow, she's happy to see those thugs, even after the way the men treated his family and the other exiles. Disappointment seeps through him like cold water. He was a fool to expect help from someone so embedded with the Council.

"Look what else I got!" Sadie waves an oatcake partially wrapped in cloth in his face. It's crumbly and shiny as a slick of oil and Moss knows it will taste of the island's honey. His mouth waters. Then Sadie reaches into her coat pocket and pulls out a crumpled mask. "Ta-da. I got you something too."

He eyes it. The stiff paper muzzle is dented on one side, and the mane, made from scraps of wool and string, is half pulled loose. One of the ears is bent, giving it a lopsided, pathetic look.

"I figured if you want to skulk around, better to do it properly."

"You took this from a child, didn't you?"

She shrugs. "He dropped it. I found it." She brings the fish to her face and runs her tongue over it. Her face lights up in surprise. "Salty! Told you!"

Moss slips the mask over his head, flinching as it brushes the graze that bloomed on his face from the Councillor's whip. The world narrows. The inside smells of honey and someone else's stale breath. But it's a disguise. That's what matters.

"Ugh!" Sadie spits out a large, sticky chunk of oatcake, her face curdled. Moss lifts his mask to stare at it with her; it lies, congealed with spit, on the rock between them. From within the cloth still in her hand, an earwig emerges and crawls onto her wrist.

"Get it off!" Sadie hisses, flicking her hand sharply, sending the insect and the rest of the oatcake tumbling away. The mess lies on the rock, mottled and rotting like some foul wound.

"Disgusting!" Sadie kicks the whole lot over the edge. "Who makes oatcakes out of rotten bleedin' oats?"

"They must have seen you coming," says Moss. "Served you up a hideling surprise."

"Don't," says Sadie. She crosses her arms over her stomach, genuinely disturbed. "I hate this place. Let's go home. At least I got a fish."

Moss wishes he could go home. Wishes he'd never been forced here by circumstance. He is much happier out on the moors. The sweetness, the cheer of the festival, has all turned rotten. The oatcake is the least of it.

Sadie sits down and hugs her knees in disappointment, while Moss slips the mask back over his head.

"Wait here," he says. "Get low. Keep out of sight."

He slides down the rock, careful not to catch anyone's eye. The bell continues to toll. The crowd is silent. All eyes on the platform. On the Councillors.

He moves low, dodging behind backs, carts, the steaming mead barrel. He skirts the crowd until he's on the other side of the pen from the viewing rock, where Sadie is barely visible against the gray. *Good girl.* He doesn't know how she does it.

With the mask on, no one sees him, either. They see a shape they expect—a child in a mask—and he makes himself as small as possible, to feed the illusion. He's not much older than a child, really. He makes his way to the edge of the platform and pushes himself into the crowd, not caring if people give him hostile stares. From here, he can see both the horses in the pen, and, if he turns and cricks his neck, the Councillors' podium.

Lotta has emerged in the pen, walking among the horses, laying a hand on their necks and rumps, murmuring to them. There's a softness in her he hasn't seen before. He holds his breath as she approaches Hannah. The horse turns her head to greet her and makes a soft rumble. Lotta slips her hand into the pocket of her trousers and offers Hannah a gray lump. Turnip. As the mare munches on it with closed eyes, Moss's eyes prickle. Lotta lays her cheek on the horse's broad forehead.

Somehow, in such a short time, they have bonded. It's as clear as day to Moss. Hope lifts inside him.

There's a creak and footsteps as the Judge takes the podium. Up close, Moss can see that the Councillors are mere men. Their solemnity crumbles at the edges—creased brows, twitching lips. Lewis holds a black cloth bag, and the bell, which he sets down on the table beside him.

The Judge lifts up one hand. It is thick with heavy rings on almost every one of his fingers, which curl with age. He places his other palm on a book that sits on the podium. The Book. He's heard Mam talk about it—it contains the history of the island and the origin of the Glimm. There is only one, and it's kept under lock and key in the Temple.

"*Light of the Glimm be upon you*, good people of Brack." His voice rings out loud and clear. The wind has died with the light, and his words carry easily across the crowd.

The villagers' voices lift as one. *"And upon you, as bright as the sun."*

He raises his hand again, and the crowd falls silent.

"People of Brack!" The Judge's voice swings through the quiet, setting a tone of both reverence and warning. "The Glimm, in its infinite wisdom, has provided us with this blessing on this auspicious day, the day of the lottery. It has brought forth its gifts from the sea, offering us the fish that it is too dangerous for us to harvest. And so, we must accept this offering as a reminder of the strength of our bond with the Glimm, and the price of our continued survival."

He pauses, letting the words sink in, as stares fall on the fish, the remaining baskets of which are now on the platform at his feet. He's taken the bulk of it for the Council, Moss thinks. The fish will be rotten before they can cook it all.

"Remember," the Judge continues, "this fish comes at a cost. As all gifts from the Glimm do. It is through our service, our sacrifices, that we are allowed to receive such bounty. And so, we stand together, bound by our duty to this land, to the Glimm, and to the system that protects us."

Moss watches the scene unfold, his stomach tightening. His eyes flick to the fish again, their shimmering scales reflecting the firelight through the reeds of the baskets. He knows this isn't the Council's doing. The Judge is taking credit for something that has nothing to do with him or the Council. He's using it as a tool to reinforce his power. How do the people just stand there and let him?

"As you partake in this gift, remember what it symbolizes. Your place. Your duty. Your sacrifice. The Glimm watches, and we must remain worthy."

The crowd shifts uneasily. Some nod; others avert their gaze. But the weight of the Judge's words is clear: There is no such thing as a free gift in their world. The fish, like everything else, comes at a price. And that price will always be paid with obedience.

Moss steals a glance at Lotta, still standing beside Hannah. She has her head down, as if in prayer, but it gently shakes from side to side. She looks up suddenly, straight at him. Can she see him? Does she know it is him?

It's probably risky, but from his dark corner, he dares to lift the mask to reveal his face to her. Her expression doesn't change. Somehow, she knew it was him. He pulls the mask back down hastily, before anybody else clocks him.

The Judge goes on. "And now for the moment we are all here. The Glimm will decide, through the lottery, which horse will be this year's sacrifice. I have heard a rumor that bets have been placed on which number it will be. Let me remind you that gambling is a sin. Stormy Pete will return any coins to their owners, and we will say no more of it. The Glimm is clearly in a good mood on this day, and we don't want to spoil it."

There's a tumble of laughter through the crowd, and many a man is elbowed by his wife, or pulls his cap low. A huge red-faced fellow standing at the edge of the pen swipes his cap from his head and runs his sleeve over his forehead while the crowd jostles and jeers at him. Stormy Pete, Moss presumes.

Councillor Lewis clangs the bell again once, to bring order back to the crowd. Hannah shies at the sound, and another pony kicks her in the back leg for her trouble.

Lewis holds the bag up, high above his head. He nods to Judge Hawthorne, who nods to the people behind him. They must be getting to their feet. Moss can't see them, but he hears the shuffling of boots, the creak of the platform. He stares at the Judge hard as he raises his hand.

Moss smells fish, mixed in with horse manure and, underneath it, a sickly perfume drifting down from the platform. The crowd is utterly silent.

From so close, Moss sees a flash of white already in the Judge's fingers as he plunges them into the bag. He makes a show of stirring up the contents, expanding the moment. Then withdraws his hand and holds it out, palm open to Lewis, who nods. The Judge glances at it, then lifts it for all to see.

"Number thirty-two! The Glimm has chosen!"

A great cheer rises from the crowd.

Moss is knocked back by a surge of nausea. Not the Glimm. The *Judge.*

# 19

**THAT SEALS IT,** then. Not just Hannah's fate but the fact that Moss was right: The lottery is not drawn either by chance, or by the will of the Glimm. Lotta doesn't know exactly how the Judge did it, but she imagines he already had the number in his hand before he slipped it into the cloth bag. Her eyes find Moss. She knew it was him even before he showed his face—the too-short jacket, his slight build, and the kerchief knotted at his throat. He clutches the wooden frame of the platform. Suddenly he rips his mask off.

He mouths something to her.

*Happy now?*

He looks up at the Council above him and puts both hands on the frame tentatively, searching for a handhold. He's going to climb. She must act quickly.

"Not that horse!"

Her words make Moss hesitate. She shakes her head at him and mimes pulling the mask back on, but he stares at her defiantly.

Nobody else has heard her over the din, so she moves closer to the platform and yells again. "Not that horse!"

The Judge gazes down at her, blinking under his prodigious eyebrows. His lips are curled in a question. So her words still carry some weight. After all, she is the reason they're choosing a horse today, and not a child.

"What are you saying, girl?" he barks.

At the Judge's voice, the excited clamor dies down.

"Choose another horse," she calls, a challenge. "This horse is too valuable."

There's a murmuring from the crowd. "The Glimm has chosen!" comes a voice from somewhere.

Another comes from the side of the pen. "Where's the child?" Stormy Pete's wife, Rona, is turning her jealous face this way and that. "The chosen rider? Who's got number thirty-two?"

The crowd takes up the chant: "Thirty-*two*! Thirty-*two*!"

The Judge holds Lotta's gaze for a few more seconds, then beckons her forward so she can hear him over the chant. "That person is correct," he says. "You should know, Lotta Salter, that the Glimm deserves the very best. Especially after his bountiful gift from the sea."

"She wants to take the fish back!" Lotta recognizes the voice of Biddy Jackson, a thorn in her side. "Boo!"

This sets off a stream of booing in the crowd, but Lotta's sure most of them don't know what they're booing for. She stares around the pen at leering faces, all concentrated on her. Then the hissing starts.

Moss continues to watch her from the shadow of the platform. Waiting for her to prove herself. The hissing sound is unbearable. It drills into her head. The Judge just stares at her, gloating, and does nothing to silence the crowd.

"You're in no position to make demands, Lotta Salter," he says. "Have you forgotten you work for me? Know your place. The Glimm has already decided."

"Are you sure it was the Glimm who chose the horse?"

For a split second, she sees doubt flicker in the Judge's eyes, just a flicker. He glances at Councillor Lewis, whose jaw clenches. Judge Hawthorne straightens up, regaining his composure, and his expression hardens into stone. "You don't understand, girl," the Judge says, his tone quieter now, but sure of its authority. "This is about survival. This is about keeping the balance. The Glimm chooses what to take so it may give in return. We don't question it."

The crowd renews its jeering. Lotta catches her mother's eye. She's by the gate with Da, her hands clasped together, pleading with her. On Da's shoulders, Wolf is looking around, confused by the crowd insulting his sister. Moss has gone from his spot beneath the platform, and she has no idea where.

*Stay calm,* she thinks. If she lets her emotions gain momentum, who knows what will happen after this morning. If only they knew the power she held, they wouldn't be treating her like this.

She lets her shoulders, which have been pushed back defiantly, fold. "Very well," she says.

Let him think he's won.

A sharp pain strikes her lower back as a stone hits her, bouncing off and onto the ground with a dull thud. In the distance, a rumble of thunder.

"Enough!" calls the Judge, and she isn't sure if it's aimed at her or the wretch who threw the stone.

"If this is *truly* the will of the Glimm," says Lotta, "then who am I to question it?" She stares the Judge full in the face as she says it, and his lips twitch. Caught in a lie.

*Thirty-two!* *Thirty-two!*

*Thirty-two!*

The crowd has started up its chanting again and Lotta realizes with a sickening lurch that someone has opened the gate to the pen and is pushing her family into it. Wolf's face is a mix of terror and excitement. As Allen lowers him to the ground, Lotta gets a glimpse of the number pinned to the back of the jacket.

Thirty-two.

Of course it is.

She strides over to them. "How do you have this number?"

"Councillor Stirling," says her mother. "You was there. All the children got them. It's just random. The rider's part of the ritual. No harm will come to him."

The writhing in her stomach is trying to convince Lotta otherwise. "Nothing is random, Ma, remember?"

Her mother doesn't reply, just looks away with tight lips. This is a bad sign; they both know it—Lotta's just not sure why. But surely a turn around the pen on Hannah's back won't hurt?

Lotta unclenches her jaw to smile for Wolf, aware of the villagers crowded close to the low stone walls, watching her every move.

"It's all right, Wolfie, don't fret. Let's get you up on Hannah and complete this ceremony, shall we?" Wolf smiles back tentatively. Dougie appears beside her, leading Hannah. She now wears a rope halter, and puts her soft muzzle next to Lotta's ear, blowing warm air. Dougie is also bewildered, Lotta can tell, by what has just happened. She puts her arm around his shoulders and gives him a squeeze. An apology.

"This is Hannah," she says to Wolf. "You can pat her if you want."

Dougie makes a strangled noise and looks at her in confusion.

"Since when do the lottery nags have names?" A father holding the hand of a tear-stained young girl in a white dress sneers at her, clearly annoyed that his daughter wasn't chosen.

"Get on with it!" comes a voice. "It's getting cold!"

Wolf's feet dangle as Allen hoists him onto Hannah's broad back. Lotta takes the lead rope from Dougie and begins to lead them around the perimeter of the pen, slowly and deliberately.

Someone throws the first flower, a purple bloom so small and weather-beaten it's barely holding together, as the song starts up: Young Alice Turner is on the platform, with a bone flute player beside her, belting out the ceremonial song.

*Oh, sing me a song of the saltings*
*Where all of our power lies*

Lotta shudders. She last heard Alice sing the song at the tavern the other night.

*Where he'll come each year, on the first day of spring,*
*To show his love for us all*

More meager flowers follow: ashen snowdrops, a few scraggy dandelions with half their petals missing, sprigs of gorse blossoms, soft gray catkins. They arc miserably through the air and strike Wolf's legs, Hannah's flank, the ground.

Wolf holds on, eyes wide, staring straight ahead.

A ceremony. A celebration.

A substitution.

Once, it would have been Wolf earmarked for sacrifice, not Hannah. The number pinned to his back is the same as the number drawn by the Judge. No, not drawn. *Held up.* Deliberately. Bile rises in Lotta's throat. She can't help but think about her own lottery, and her newfound knowledge that her name was not chosen by chance. Back then, the children weren't present for the lottery.

There was no festival with candied rhubarb and music and colorful, flapping bunting.

Lotta realizes how much she has given this village. If it weren't for her, none of them would be here, half drunk, dancing and hauling away fresh fish, throwing flowers at a boy who is not destined to be killed.

Wolf sways slightly as the scraps fall around them like soft rain. The crowd—which only minutes ago was jeering at her—now cheers, obedient again. Nothing to see here. All is as it should be.

The mercurial mood is unsettling.

"So, is she special or not?"

Lotta overhears young Audrey Burns, who has been stealing glances at her ever since Lotta's parents arrived with the fish. Poor girl. It must be confusing; on the one hand, the villagers blame Lotta for all the ills that befall them, and on the other, here comes her family, delivering the bounty of the Glimm, only for the Council to confiscate most of it.

In some ways, Lotta has the villagers right where she wants them. Wary.

Lotta lifts Wolf—unhurt and glowing with pride—from Hannah's back with a final cheer from the crowd and stands with her family. Marten has joined them.

The bell rings again, drawing attention back to the platform.

"Very good," says the Judge. "The Glimm has spoken. The horse will be sacrificed at sunrise in five days' time. The Glimm will bless us once more."

There is a smattering of applause until the Judge holds up his hand for silence.

"One last announcement." He moves aside as Councillor Gray steps up beside him.

Gray clears his throat. "I'm happy to announce there will be a Council wedding this summer."

The villagers don't applaud. A wedding means a feast. For the Council. There's many who will go without to feed their hungry table.

Disconcerted, Gray continues. "My daughter, Meg, our precious gift from the Glimm, is betrothed to Roderick Lewis, future Judge of Brack."

Hawthorne nods his approval alongside them. Lewis beckons to Roddy and Meg to come to the front of the platform.

Beside Lotta, Marten trembles, suppressing sobs. "They call everything a bleedin' gift from the Glimm, just so they can take what they want," he says.

She finds his hand and squeezes it.

Down below the platform, Meg's other family look as though they have found honey under their tongues. Farmer Jack and his wife beam. Mrs. Jack is surely already picking out her best hat and coat in her mind. The only time villagers are allowed to attend a Council wedding is when they have given up a child to join the Council.

Dougie has started to round up the rest of the horses to return them to the paddock, and the crowds will soon drift away. He's brought Salty, all tacked up, so between them they can herd the ponies back to their field.

The last of the light is draining from the sky. The bonfires still burn brightly, sending up sparks like fireflies against the night air.

Lotta leans in close to her family, and whispers, "Don't be alarmed about what comes next. It will be all right."

They look back at her, clearly already alarmed.

It's now or never.

The bell rings for the last time.

"I draw this evening to a close." It's Lewis. The Judge sits on a chair, looking weary, aged. "Go well, good people of Brack. Enjoy your fish, if you have it, and don't forget to give thanks to the mighty Glimm."

As a half-hearted cheer rises from the crowd, Lotta pulls the pin from where it has been tucked inside her jacket.

"Sorry about this, old girl," she whispers, and drives it into Hannah's flank.

Moss is on the rock again, sobbing. Sadie rubs his back. Lotta has failed him. Hannah will be sacrificed. He nearly made a move. Nearly climbed that stupid tower and smacked the Judge in the face. He pictured himself jumping down, leaping onto Hannah's back, and taking off. Smashing through the gate and galloping out onto the moors. But where would he go?

Lotta stopped him doing anything reckless, but the Council tamped down her challenge so quickly he wonders why she even bothered. Then they brought that boy—her brother, clearly—forward, and Moss had to get away. As the light faded and the fires danced like devils, he watched from his lookout as Lotta paraded her brother around the pen on Hannah's back—on *his* horse—while the villagers threw flowers at them in some hollow performance of celebration.

"Let's go, Moss," says Sadie. "There in't nothing more we can do. Let's get home and get warm. We'll have to hurry, or Art'll be cross."

Moss presses his thumbs into his eye sockets to clear the tears just as a scream comes from the pen, followed by shouts. He jumps up in time to see a commotion. The horses are jostling, running and kicking at each other. Hannah rears and whinnies again; even from here he can sense her panic and her heart beating like a drum. She separates from the pack and takes off at a gallop toward the wall.

"No!" he shouts, clutching his throat. Hannah's not a jumper. She's too big and ungainly. She'll crash into the wall and kill or maim herself.

Sadie grabs Moss's wrist. "She's goin' over!"

They watch in wonder and terror as Hannah leaps the wall, knocking her back hooves on the way down and stumbling, nearly falling, but getting up again. Adults and children scatter as she bucks, catching the mead cart with her back hooves, sending it crashing like a barrow of bones to the ground. She's nothing more than a black silhouette against the bonfire as she puts her head down and bolts toward the rock where Moss and Sadie are standing. She's moving too fast for Moss to do anything, and while he calculates the height to the ground, Hannah is already past, away from the village, onto the moors, up the road that winds north toward the mountains.

The Judge is back on his feet. Moss can't see his expression from here, but he can imagine. He screams down into the pen. "Get after it, you stupid girl! This is your fault, and you will bring that horse back in time for the sacrifice, or Glimm help you!"

Lotta's voice is faint. "She'll be long gone by now. I'll be chasing her until dawn!"

Hawthorne's voice is lower, menacing, and Moss can't catch what he says, or Lotta's reply, but he catches the Judge's final words. "Very well. Just do it."

"I've got to go," Moss tells Sadie. "Don't wait for me. I'll be fine."

Sadie tries to grab him but she's too slow. He's already climbed down to the ground before she can open her mouth and say, "Be careful, you nit."

Moss pulls the horse mask from his pocket, slips it on, and runs for the pen. Lotta is there, throwing saddlebags on her gray gelding.

"There you are!" she says. "I thought you'd gone and this was all for nothing. Get out of sight and wait for me behind the big rock. You're coming with me."

"To get Hannah? But then what?"

She tightens her girth with a jerk and puts her hand on her horse's neck. She turns to him with the reflection of the fires burning in her eyes. "To find answers."

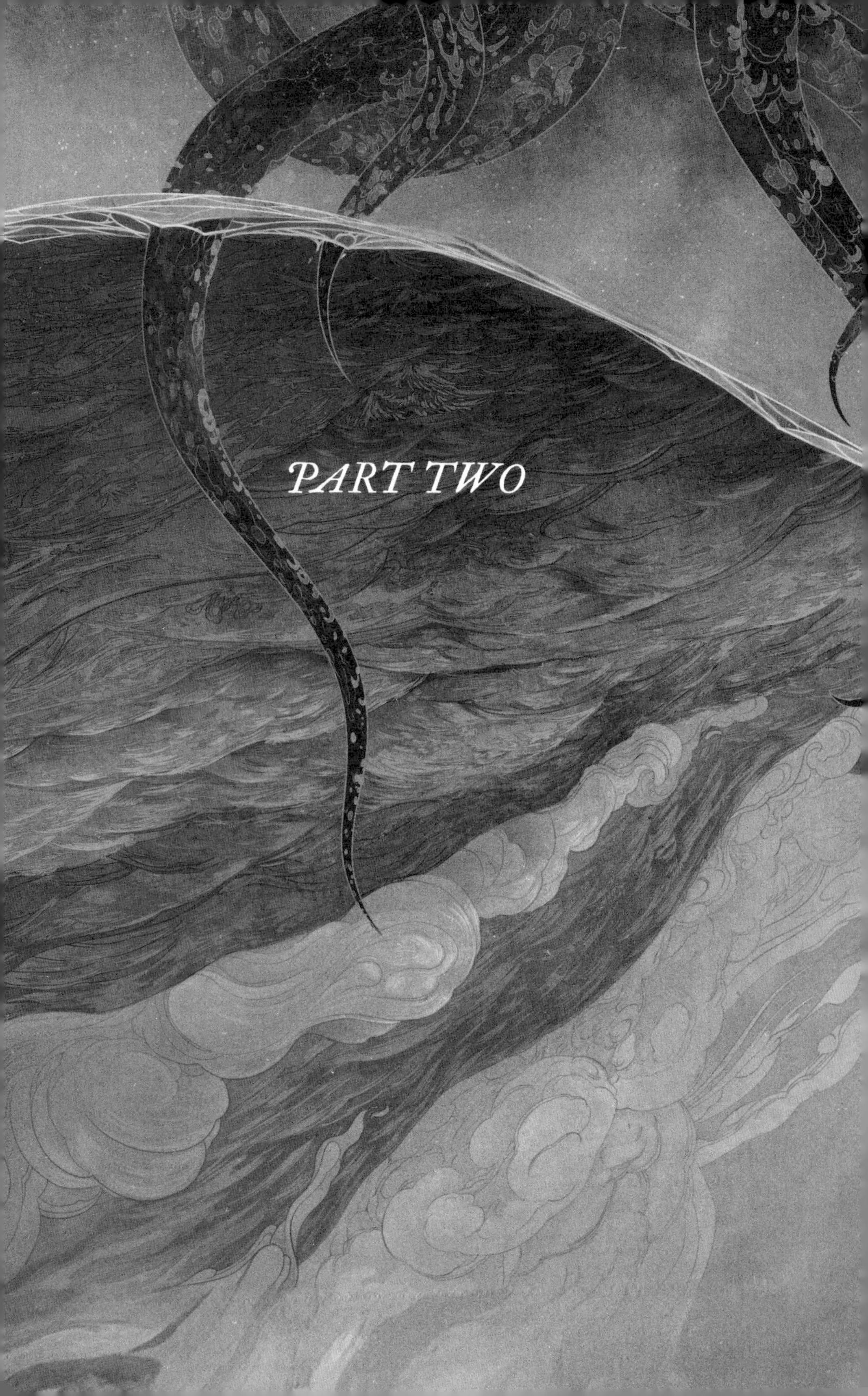

# PART TWO

# 20

"HOLD ON!" Lotta yells.

Moss tightens his arms around her waist. Her hair is in his face; it's not the sweet scent he foolishly imagined, but smoke and hay—sharp, earthy. The gray gelding stretches into a gallop, and the pounding of hooves on the dirt road north fills Moss's ears. Darkness envelops them as they leave the village, and its soft lantern glow, behind. He dares to let go and bring one hand to his face and sniff: oh, wonderful. He smells of fish and mud. He hopes she can't catch his odor with the biting wind in her face.

Salty, she called the gelding. Such a babyish name for such a fine horse—for a rider so serious, the weight of the world on her shoulders.

"Will she head for home?" Lotta shouts into the night. "That seems most likely."

"Hope not." His breath bounces back, warm, from her ear. "There's no way of getting there without crossing the bogs. Keep going. Maybe she's not gone far."

The moon hides behind the low cloud, its light diffused, smoothing out the shadows.

"There!" He points into the distance, where a smudge moves quickly against the brow of the hill.

"I can't see a thing in this light," says Lotta. "How can you see that?"

"I've got good eyesight. I'm used to working at night." He pauses. "And hiding in the shadows, remember?"

She says nothing but he can tell she is taking it in. Perhaps she feels guilty about the way she spoke to him, that first time they met.

What will they do if or when they catch Hannah? Lotta didn't stop to explain; she just tossed him a blanket, which he draped gratefully around his shoulders and fastened in place with his belt. She handed him a satchel—"Supplies," she said—and then offered him Salty's stirrup to step up onto the horse's back behind her. The horse feels uncannily narrow after riding Hannah, and he worries it won't take their combined weight. But it's easier to grip a smaller horse, and its gait is as smooth as a knife.

"Keep your eye on her," says Lotta. "We can't lose sight of her."

"Can we go faster?"

"No," says Lotta. "We're not going to catch her, not just yet."

Moss's hands are ice cold, and his sleeves too short. He tentatively tucks one inside Lotta's coat, grazing up against the knitted woolen tunic beneath. She doesn't react, so he tucks in the other one.

"Cold?" she asks. There's a hint of amusement in her voice. He quickly withdraws his hands, embarrassed.

"I don't mind," she says. "Can't have your hands freezing and falling off. We might need them later." To prove it, she tucks his hand back in. He concentrates on the warmth of her body, not the damp cold seeping into his feet, or the gnarly wind gnawing at his exposed ankles. If he gets out of this alive, he's going to ask Mam for Da's trousers and jacket to wear.

They streak through the night, Salty's hooves eating the distance. Moss's tailbone begins to ache. Why is Hannah still running? He can only think that she's been spooked by the sound of them in pursuit. They pass threadbare herds of sheep, their fleeces pale globs in the gloom, and stone huts sitting squat in the meager moonlight. Ahead of them lie the Black Mountains—the forbidden part of the island. Surely Hannah won't lead them that far?

Lotta slows Salty, bringing him steadily back to a walk. He is puffing, his coat beneath Moss's legs damp and hot.

"Listen," says Lotta. The only sounds are Salty's huffing and the squelch of his footfall. But then, something else. Running water.

"I knew the stream was around here somewhere." She elbows Moss lightly in the gut. "Get down."

He does as she says. Pain shoots through his cold, sleeping feet as he hits the ground, and he crouches to steady himself. Lotta swings herself down and says, "It's brutal sometimes, isn't it?"

Moss accepts a swig of water from her flask and then settles himself on a rock as she leads Salty in the dark toward the sound of the stream.

"I've never been this far north," he calls. "Have you?"

"Yes," she says. "The road forks west ahead. There's a camp by the western cliffs that hunts seabirds. I've taken them horses before, watched them work. Do you know them?"

Moss shakes his head but realizes she can't see him. "No," he says instead. "I've not been anywhere near the cliffs. Mam says it's not safe."

"What, is she worried you'll be blown away, little hideling?"

The word stings. He says nothing.

"They send children down with nothing but a rope around the waist," she goes on. "They steal the young birds right from the nests." There's a note of awe in her voice. Moss can't imagine ever being so brave. Maybe she's right to tease him. Hideling coward. But he still says nothing.

He hears her footfalls on the stones by the stream, a pop as she uncorks her flask to refill her bottle. And over the sounds, a small word. "Sorry."

Beyond the stream, bogland stretches for miles. He can't see it, but he senses it. Plenty of animals—people, too—have been lost to the island, as Hannah nearly was. At least she's had the sense to stay on the road this time.

His skin prickles with cold. The bog makes popping noises but there's something else. A moist, dragging sound. He feels watched, uneasy. The wind shifts slightly, and he catches a note of rotten meat that turns his stomach.

This is Jenny the bog witch's territory—the peat bogs that have spread over the center of the island, too treacherous to harvest. Mam says there were once green fields as far as the eye can see. Now everything is decaying. He thinks of the stories they were told as children: Jenny of the mire, who sang to you from beneath the duckweed, or mimicked the voice of someone you trusted. Who reached up from the soft places in the earth and pulled you under before you could cry out.

He used to remind himself they were just stories. Now he only hopes they're lies.

"What are we doing?" he asks when Lotta returns to the road. "I don't think we're going to catch Hannah like this. We're just driving her farther away."

Lotta tips her head back and drinks from her flask.

"Also," he continues, "Hannah's not fast. She's strong, sure. But she's a plodder. Surely we should have caught her by now."

He's been expecting to see her standing in the middle of the road, looking sheepish, or foraging beside it for turnips and grass. But she's still running.

Then it hits him.

"You're not trying to catch her. You're *herding* her."

He waits for her to answer while she tucks the flask back into her satchel, then finally turns to face him.

"If we catch her, we have to bring her home. And then we're right back where we started, and she'll be sacrificed, and all this will have been for nought."

Her face is unreadable in the dark.

"It's late," she says suddenly. "We should try to get some rest."

She busies herself fumbling in the dark to unbuckle Salty's girth. Moss moves to help her and she steps aside gratefully.

"I've got a lantern," she says.

"Save it." He finishes unbuckling and steps aside as she pulls the saddle off and sets it on a rock.

"So . . . were that your plan? Back there. To have Hannah jump the wall and bolt into the night? You stopped me from making a scene. I thought you'd have something firmer in mind."

"I bought us time," she says.

"And the fish? What were that for? Were it really a gift from the Glimm?" He's struggling to understand her. If she has a plan, it's erratic—not what he'd expected from someone so in control of herself.

"In a way, yes. I wanted to get people thinking that maybe the Judge isn't the only person the Glimm grants favors to. Even if just for a moment. And to try to buy some favor with the village." She gives a bitter laugh. "But the Council took most of it, and then took the credit for the miracle, as if they had always known it was coming and must be reciprocated. They think fast, I'll give them that." She spits on the ground as though the very thought of them leaves a bitter taste in her mouth. "I knew they'd intervene somehow. Taking the fish made them look petty and greedy. Which they are."

"So you're trying to turn the village against them. That's the plan."

"Not all at once. They're too suspicious of me for that." She piles the saddlebags next to the rock. "Just enough to make a crack. But we'll prove to them one way or another the lottery's a sham and the Judge doesn't speak for the Glimm."

"And your brother. That wasn't a coincidence, was it? They're on to you."

She goes quiet, and Moss doesn't push.

"So what now?"

Lotta doesn't answer right away. She takes a blanket and spreads it on the ground. "Now we take our time. Let Hannah run. Let the Council stew. We've sown a seed. People have started to wonder if the Glimm is really making all the choices, or if it's just Hawthorne pulling strings."

She sits on the blanket and motions for Moss to join her.

He lies back with his head on his hands, staring up at the clouds. "So no one knows what's real and what's show."

"Exactly." She picks up a pebble and tosses it into the dark. "And that will make the Judge nervous."

For a while, they sit in silence.

"You said we was going to find answers," he says.

She hesitates for a moment, then pulls straw out of a bag for a fire. She's really thought of everything. "We will," she says. "Just not all at once."

"That's not really an answer."

"I know," is all she says.

Why does he get the feeling she's not telling the whole story?

# 21

**The wind changes.** It crawls across the moor, low and wet. Lotta catches a shift in the air just as Moss lifts his head. She must have been sleeping; the small fire she lit has gone out, but the night still presses in around them.

They both lean against Salty's warm body. Lotta's trained him so well that he lay down like a tired child, or a dog in front of the hearth. The ground is hard and gritty beneath her hip, which is shot with pain when she sits up.

A high-pitched call keens through the air. Salty flinches, and makes an answering rumble, deep in his belly.

Moss is on his feet, reaching out for Lotta.

"That's Hannah, that is!" His hand shakes as he pulls her up.

They stand facing the wind, which dampens their cheeks and hair. Another whinny cuts through. Salty scrambles to his feet.

"Do you see that?" asks Moss.

She doesn't need night vision to see what he is looking at. Out on the bog ahead of them, two lights flicker, low to the ground. Blue-white, like candle flames.

"Who's there?" Moss calls. He rearranges his blanket around his shoulders and walks over the road. There's no answer. "Lotta," he whispers. "There's someone there. They've got Hannah."

"Wait," she says. "Be careful. I've heard of this, of lights in the bog. They're made by no human." A chill slips under her collar and she shudders.

"What do you mean?"

"Just . . . take care. Let me light a lantern."

Leaving their camp as it is, with her satchel and saddle propped against a rock, she leads Salty over to join Moss, holding the lantern to his face, which is creased and anxious. "Can you see a path through?" she asks.

Hannah calls again.

"I can," he says. "Stay close behind." He crosses the stream with two strides on flat stones and Lotta follows, letting Salty splash through the shallows.

The lights don't look dangerous at first, just strange. They hover ahead, bobbing like lanterns carried by unseen hands, gliding farther north into the bogland where the road fades and the moor softens into sponge and muck. Lotta's lantern creates a warmer glow that moves with them, lighting the ground beneath their feet. Moss walks slowly, testing for firmness with each step. Moonlight dances on the surface where water has pooled, great stretches of it. No, not moonlight.

"There's another," says Moss. "It's moving, like it wants us to follow. It's heading toward the others. And Hannah."

"Can we trust it?" Lotta asks.

"I don't know," breathes Moss. The wind hasn't followed them into the heart of the bog. It's almost as though it was sent just to wake them and is now holding its breath. The only sounds are the trickle of water and the suck of mud on their boots and on Salty's hooves as they move.

The lights weave like dragonflies darting through the air, drawing them farther from the road. Salty hesitates as the ground turns to peat and stunted grass, resisting Lotta's pull. Her nerves bristle at every sound. This is it. This is what she has come for.

"Moss, wait." She puts out a hand, but he shakes her off and says nothing, just continues on his way, determined.

Then they see her.

Hannah. Caught between the lights, wild-eyed, halfway across a crisscross of narrow turf paths. She's trembling, fetlock-deep in standing water, surrounded by mud and blackness. The bog stretches wide, sucking at her hooves. One step wrong and she could vanish. Forever.

"She's trapped," says Moss.

The two horses call to one another, just as they did the first day they met.

Lotta hands Salty's reins to Moss but keeps the lantern. "Stay there," she tells him, and goes in front, threading her way between the causeways. Moss would have sunk here. But she doesn't.

"Wait—Lotta. Look."

She holds the lantern high. There's something beneath the water. Pale shapes, drifting just under the surface. Faces. Too small.

Children.

Lotta gasps. She blinks, but they're still there. A dozen of them, maybe more. Faces half glimpsed, eyes open, skin like glass. They float in silence, watching. Then, just as quickly, they fade away and are gone.

"What in Glimm's name was that?" Moss asks. He's doubled over, his voice choked with tears.

"An illusion," says Lotta, as though she believes it. "Just like the lights are an illusion." Her heart is hammering in her chest. All those children. She refuses to believe they're real.

The lights scatter suddenly, retreating. The air goes still. Something moves among the cotton grass.

A figure, human-shaped, emerges from the vegetation and stops just outside the pool of lantern light. Lotta takes a hurried step back and reaches for Moss. He takes her arm; the warmth of him presses into her side.

The creature is hunched and ragged, its long hair matted with moss, its feet bare, skin the color of bog water. Its eyes, when it lifts its head, are startling: bright, and too human in the lantern light. It ignores them and starts to move toward Hannah with a heavy gait, dragging its feet through the mire. Its lips part, and a sound comes from its throat like bubbling mud.

"Get away from her!" Moss stares wildly at the ground near him. He spots a loose stone and bends to pick it up. He draws his arm back, ready to throw.

"Moss, no," says Lotta, grabbing his arm.

He looks at her in surprise. "Why not?" His eyes dart back to the hag, which crouches and freezes, eyes on him, ready to leap.

The wet sound again, then it coughs and spits a great gob of something into the mud. "You've come," it says. Its voice is cracked and papery. A woman's voice, striated with age and disuse. "Finally."

"Yes," says Lotta. "I—I didn't know you were expecting me."

Moss drops to his knees. He stares up at Lotta in disbelief, then back at the creature. "What are you?"

The woman blinks slowly. "Surely you know me, Moss Smith, as well as you know your own tongue. I'm the bog witch. The ghost that haunts the moors. I'm the mist that rolls over your fields and whispers in your ear as you sleep." Her gaze flicks toward Hannah, who hasn't moved. "I steal your animals. Your proud horses and terrified sheep."

Lotta takes Moss's hand and squeezes reassurance. He uses it to pull himself back up to standing. "You're Jenny," he says. "I didn't know if you were real or not."

"I'm real, all right."

"I . . . I didn't know you talked to people like this," he says.

Jenny tips her head back and laughs bitterly, showing teeth that are algae-coated and sharp. Just right for tearing flesh.

"How old are you?" asks Moss. "They say you're as old as the island itself. How do you survive?"

Jenny looks at the exhausted Hannah, stops herself too late.

"Don't even think about it," says Moss, his voice low with menace, as the horse stands in the wet mud, her head hanging. She's lost all her fight.

Jenny takes a step back and raises both hands. The fingers are long and tapered, with thick talons at the end of each. "Mudfish!" she says. "Eels. And frogs. And birds. Tasty ducks and curlews."

"Not horses?" questions Moss, suspiciously.

"Maybe the odd horse that has lost its way, if it's old and tired and stuck in the bog. It would be a shame for it to go to waste. Sheep too. And even a deer once." Her voice drops to a low mutter, as if talking to herself. "I don't know where *that* came from."

"And people?" Moss's voice is trembling now. Lotta lays a reassuring hand on his arm to bring him back to her. But Moss goes on. "Children? That's why our parents warned us about you, isn't it?"

Jenny spits something on the ground. It's a tiny bone, no bigger than a frog's. "Pishposh," she says.

Lotta starts. It's exactly the phrase that Daphne uses when she's dismissing something Lotta has said. It sounds strange and new out of the creature's mouth. As if it hasn't come from something inhuman, something as old as time itself.

She expects Jenny to go on, but her face has crumpled, and a low growl leaves her throat.

"I would *never* hurt a child," she says finally. "The islanders talk about me to keep children away from the treacherous bogs. Any fool can see that. It's nothing to do with me."

"But what was that illusion we saw?" asks Lotta. "The children's faces in the water. It looked so real."

"Oh, you saw that?" Jenny nods. "It's one of my tricks, to keep people away."

"What are they?"

"I carry them in here with me." She thumps her chest wetly with a curled fist. "All those children, lost. And for what?" She turns a finger on Lotta. "Not you, though. You were spared. You are the girl who survived."

Lotta jumps as Salty nudges her from behind. The lantern flickers. She wonders how long the candle will last. Her vision tunnels, blackness edging it like spreading mold.

Moss speaks first. "How do you know that?"

"I know everything," Jenny snaps.

Before Moss can open his mouth to speak, Lotta steps closer. "You lost your child to the Glimm, didn't you? To the sacrifice."

"Yes," the woman says. "A long time ago."

Silence. Even the horses have stilled.

"Freya was her name. They took her when she was six. They said the crops would fail if they didn't. I begged. I wept. We tried to run. They hunted us down and dragged us back to the village."

Moss looks sickened. Is that guilt in his eyes?

"Island lore says you're thousands of years old," Lotta says.

The woman smiles, faint and bitter. "I was twenty-four when they killed my daughter and tried to give me food and blankets and trinkets to take her place. Gifts from the Glimm, they said. I didn't want their bribes, though my husband took them greedily. They said if we had another child they could marry into the Council, and I told them no child of mine would marry such filth. So they made an example of me. They sent me into the bog. They thought they were killing me."

"They said you became part of it," says Lotta.

"It held me. Fed me. I forgot how to be anything but cold and wet and grieving. The Glimm held me too. Its song courses through my black veins, giving me strength. Giving me *life*."

Lotta's stomach tightens. "Its song?"

"You're seeking answers," says Jenny.

Moss turns to Lotta. "What does she mean?"

Lotta ignores him and doesn't take her eyes from Jenny. "Yes. But you've just left me with more questions."

"Ah, but the right questions can *lead* you to the answers."

Lotta knows she should be asking her about the sacrifice, the lottery, the Council. All the creeping feeling of unease that has been building—for her, and for Moss. He will want to know. They need to know what happens next, when they return to the village with Hannah. How they can face the Council.

"Ask me," says Jenny. A dare.

A rush of blood in her ears. Surely it's all connected. She needs to know. Her mother told her to find Jenny. This is why she has come. The questions bubble from deep within, like a spring. "What is the Glimm to me? Why do I feel it?"

Moss glances at her. His head tilts to the side, almost unseen.

She looks back. "You've seen it. That day we met. Hannah."

"You sang to her. Calmed her down."

"No, Moss. That wasn't it. There was much more. You said it yourself, that I sang to the bog like I knew it would listen. Well, I didn't know that. Not in my head, anyhow. It just happened."

Moss simply nods. He believes her. Because he's seen it with his own eyes.

Lotta turns back to Jenny. "Why do I feel it deep inside me? Calling to me? Is it because I escaped? Is it coming for me?"

Jenny moves toward her. She wades into the water between them and reaches out. "Come."

Moss puts a hand out in front of Lotta, a useless protection. "What are you doing? Don't touch her!"

But Lotta can't stop herself. She pushes the lantern she's holding into Moss's outstretched fingers and steps forward. She takes Jenny's hand—cold, clammy as mildew—and allows herself to be pulled into the freezing water. The ground gives beneath her weight; the mud wraps around her ankles like hands, gentle but insistent. She gasps at the slow, pulling hush, like breath against her skin.

Jenny beckons and Lotta allows herself to fall back, a slow-motion surrender. The icy water closes around her back and shoulders, cool and viscous. It kisses her collarbone, slips behind her ears, cradles her head. She exhales, long and steady.

Moss yells her name but is forced to hold Salty back as the gelding, confused, tries to follow Lotta, all senses alert. The sight of Lotta in the bog also seems to give Hannah a strange burst of energy; she takes a flying leap over the body of water between them to stand, trembling, beside Salty, who calls anxiously to his mistress. For a moment, Moss is pushed out of sight by the two horses.

And then Lotta is surrounded by the blue lights, and a song comes to her, up through the peat and the mud and the stinking bog. It rises through the soles of her feet, a low hum that vibrates up her spine. It presses into her chest and curls inside her ribs. The lights gather around her—cool flames brushing her cheeks, tickling her throat, stroking her arms like curious fingertips. She is held, completely.

She closes her eyes.

*The whole island is spread before her: the cliffs, battered by waves as high as a temple, where children hang from ropes and fall to the rocks below, clutching birds; the estuary, where her family has gathered salt for centuries; the village, with its weathered-bone houses and cobbled streets; the Manor House that looms above it all. Under the village, something stirs.*

*In the saltings, the standing stone waits.*

*It waits for her.*

*Now she stands beside it, a rope tied tightly around her waist. She cannot see anything except black. A blindfold. Music floats across the saltings, cacophonous, from a hapless band of musicians watching from the shore, along with the rest of the village. She can feel the black clouds pressing down.*

*Then, beneath the tuneless music, a bubbling, watery sound, a splash, a rush of water and the noise of bones clicking together like a stick brushed along a stone wall. The music stops suddenly.*

*She has been here before. She had forgotten. The terror returns in a rush. Her muscles give out and she slumps down, the rope cutting into her waist.*

*A wail from the shore. Mammy?*

*And then a blast of hot air on her face and a rumble like a wild boar. And with the breath, light. Coursing through her veins. A new song starts up, twisting inside the breath of the Glimm like a bedtime lullaby. A sweet melody soars from her belly to meet it, and she opens her mouth to set it free. She is at peace, no longer afraid.*

*A piercing whinny cuts through the air and the song stops. The air around her face goes cold, but the warmth of the song stays with her, pulsing around her heart.*

*She recognizes the sound. Hazel. There's a splashing of hooves through water, then on sand—a pause, and then a landing and a grunt. Hoofbeats come closer, and shouts from the shore.*

*Then an almighty roar, a squeal, and a huge splash.*

*Silence.*

In the bog, Lotta gasps and breathes in the moist air. It's all inside her. The saltings. The bog. Jenny. The Glimm. Lotta and the island are one. With a rush she travels up, up, up to the mountains. And inside the mountains, a cave.

# 22

**In the cold** dawn light, a thick mist has rolled across the bog.

With it, Moss smells decay and sodden earth. A wet, soaking rot seeps into his clothes, his lungs and bones.

For a while, Lotta has lain motionless in the bog, her hair fanning around her like waterweed, but now she starts to twitch.

"What have you done?" he shouts at Jenny. "Time to let her go!"

Jenny smiles and holds up a filthy hand. In her leathered face, her eyes look suddenly young and human. "*Wait,*" she says. "She's remembering."

Behind him, the horses shift restlessly. Salty lets out a low, troubled whinny.

Moss holds up the lantern and leans out as far as he dares, to stare at Lotta's face. Her eyelids pulse and flicker. "Come back, Lotta," he whispers. "Please. Don't leave me here with ghosts."

Suddenly she gasps for breath.

The mist rises from the marsh, enveloping her like a shroud. Her shoulders are shaking, and Moss can watch no longer.

"Enough!" He drops the lantern and surges forward into the muddy water.

The bog sucks at his boots. Panic seizes him as he loses his balance and falls. Waterweed and algae brush his skin, making him shudder. The water is warmer than it should be—thick and brown like gravy. Or blood.

He yelps. With a last leap he tries to reach Lotta and grab her unconscious form, but the bog resists; he sinks further. Jenny stands back, watching but not stopping him.

"Help us!" he shouts at her.

Jenny nods, and the bog releases him. His feet find solid ground, and he heaves himself upward, Lotta's limp, heavy form now cradled in his arms. He staggers onto the path and collapses, breathing hard.

The mist still swirls around her, reluctant to let her go.

"Lotta," he says, brushing wet curls from her brow. Her skin is pale, almost gray. He gently wipes away the mud and peat smeared on her cheek, and when she doesn't respond, he shakes her and calls her name again, louder. "Lotta!"

Her eyes flash open.

"Thank Glimm," he breathes.

She curls into him, her body trembling with the cold.

"I remember," she sobs. Heat rises from her face. Moss wraps her in his blanket and rubs at her arms and legs.

"What do you remember?" he asks.

"The Glimm," is all she says before her eyes flutter closed. Moss thinks she has fainted, or fallen asleep, and shakes her gently.

She opens her eyes again and locks her stare on him. "We've got to go to the mountains," she says. Her voice is clear, certain.

Jenny's voice bubbles across the surface of the water. "Good girl."

Then she sinks into the bog and is gone.

Lotta wouldn't say what happened to her in the water, just insisted that they gather their things, wrap themselves in the dry—thankfully—blankets, and journey to the Black Mountains, which now loom ahead of them, the shadowed backs of beasts against the sky.

*Follow the stream,* Lotta had said, when she woke up in a near trance. *It will take us to where we need to go.* So now, they plod beside each other in silence, their damp clothes spread across the horses' rumps in the hope they will dry in the new, gray daylight.

Moss sits bareback on Hannah, and she moves stiffly, stopping to graze at rocky patches of grass that sprout between the stream and the road, if you could call it that. It's uneven, rutted dirt and mud—slow going after last night. At least her back is soft and broad, unlike Salty's, and he can make do with a halter and rope.

Above them, a wheeling cry announces a white-tailed eagle. Moss watches it dip and glide on currents of air. The cliffs must be near, though he can't hear the sea, just the constant trickling of the stream to their left, showing them the way.

"What did she mean," Moss asks, breaking the stillness, "when she said she were expecting us?"

"She must have known I was looking for her."

"Why didn't you say you was looking? You never said that were part of your plan."

Lotta shifts in her saddle uncomfortably. "I didn't think you'd go along with it. I knew Hannah would lead us to her. I just didn't know she'd be waiting."

"Why would Hannah lead you to her?"

She looks at him pointedly.

"But she doesn't hunt horses," he says. "She said so."

"Unless they're old and tired and wander into the bog," says Lotta. "Or she lures them, with pretty lights."

"You think she were lying?"

"I think she can't deny her nature, as much as she wants to."

"All that talk last night, about not catching Hannah because then we'd have to bring her home. That weren't the whole truth of it, were it, if you knew she would lead you to Jenny?"

Still, the girl says nothing. The truth strikes him like a dagger in the gut.

"You used her as bait." He pulls Hannah to a stop. The mare doesn't mind and immediately starts cropping grass.

Lotta keeps moving.

"Lotta!" Moss shouts. Hannah's head launches upward, still munching.

Lotta turns Salty around. She sighs and starts back toward him.

"I had to. I'm sorry. I had to find answers."

"So it were never about saving Hannah? About helping us?"

"It was! Of course I wanted to help. If only you knew what I went through to try to help before the lottery." Her eyes take on a faraway look. She seems to be watching the eagle, now being bothered by a raven farther down the valley. They tumble together in the air, then separate.

Her attention comes back to Moss. "I needed to find Jenny and I needed an excuse to leave the village to do it. I didn't know where I would find her. But I thought a lost, scared animal would do a better job."

"How *could* you?" Moss's voice breaks in his throat.

"I knew she wouldn't hurt Hannah once I talked to her. That's why I didn't stop you from going into the bog, only told you to be careful. I suspected the lights would lead us there, but I wasn't sure."

"You don't get to decide what's safe," he says, surly. "You don't get to use people like that. Or animals."

"I needed answers, Moss; you wouldn't understand. I had no choice."

She's right. He doesn't understand. He really doesn't know her at all. The closeness he felt last night, with his hands inside her coat, is dissipating.

"There's always a choice," he says.

They stare at each other. Then Lotta turns away. "We need to keep moving. We want to get there before night."

"Why do you need me? I could just take Hannah now and go home."

Lotta sighs, exasperated. The sigh says *How can you be so dim?*

"You'd go right back into the arms of the Council, and who knows what they'll do to you? And to your family?" At the mention of Mam and Stone, Moss sags. She's right.

"Also, there's a cave, and whatever's in it is going to help us. I just know it is."

"How do you know?"

"I can't explain it right now. You'll just have to trust me."

The terrain is much steeper when they stop for a rest and some food by a waterfall that spills into an inviting pool. Lotta has packed enough for several days; if Moss had known this, he would have been more suspicious of her motives.

A shepherd's hut squats in the distance, its gray stone blending into the moor, but no smoke rises from its thatched roof, and no sheep graze nearby. The landscape is too harsh now for a flock, thinks Moss. Who knows how long it has stood there?

He sits on a rock while she moves around, seemingly unable to be still. She fusses over the horses, combing a dirty knot from Salty's mane, slipping Hannah a piece of turnip and putting her cheek to the horse's forehead as she munches.

"I can't believe she trusts you," he says. "Even after all that."

Lotta says nothing but lifts her face and brushes Hannah's forelock away from her white star, murmuring to her. He realizes what she is doing: offering Hannah a quiet apology.

Finally, she turns away with a last pat and joins Moss on the rock.

"Look," she says. "It's hard for me to explain, but I knew Hannah would be safe."

"I don't know how you can know that. She could have fallen in the bog."

"I'm sorry, Moss."

He can't accept her apology, not yet. He changes the subject.

"When you was in the bog, Jenny said you was remembering. What did you remember?"

She folds her arms, hugging herself. "The day of my sacrifice."

Moss feels like he's overstepped. Her face is grief-stricken.

"I'm sorry. You don't have to tell me. I can't imagine." There's that guilt again, gnawing at his gut.

She shakes her head. "It's all right. I've spent my whole life not knowing what happened that day except for what everyone told me. So I've always seen it from the outside in my head, you know? But Jenny showed it to me. At least, she showed me how to see it.

"I know now that when I was on that island in the saltings, and the Glimm came to take me, I felt its breath on my face. And it changed me. It changed my whole being. I think it must have done this with all the children it's taken. I wasn't afraid anymore. I felt the nerves and the tendons of the island, its beating heart. I became one with it, and with the Glimm. And then . . ."

She pauses, and Moss reaches up to wipe a tear from her cheek.

"Then my pony, Hazel, was there, and the Glimm took her instead."

"And you survived," says Moss. He never saw a sacrifice—didn't gather with his family and the rest of the villagers to witness the Glimm taking the children. The only time he remembered it happening, Mam and Da came back changed. Wrecked. He was six years old and can still remember the triangle of light cast down the cellar steps and feel his mother's wet cheek against his own as she crushed him into her. So he can only imagine what Lotta went through.

"I was forever changed by it," she says. "As all the children were.

They just didn't survive to know it. I was right. It has been calling me, but not how I thought. It's a part of me."

"When did you suspect?"

"When I was with my folks. I've always kept my head down, shut myself off. But that day I was so furious with them that I unknowingly called a giant wave from the sea. It nearly drowned them. I suppose it would have taken me, too. But as soon as I tried to save Salty, as soon as I realized how important he was to me, despite all my best efforts not to care, something shifted inside me. I just knew what to do. I stopped it."

He had always suspected she was different, just as he had suspected he was different too.

"I feel it sometimes," he says. "They say we don't deserve the Glimm's love, but I feel it. Not *connected* to it like you," he says quickly. "But when you've been kept in the quiet, in the dark, for so long, the world is different. Sharper. Sometimes I think I hear the Glimm sighing in its sleep. I see all its gifts that others don't."

"What do you mean?" Lotta asks.

He thinks for a moment. He points to the sky. "What do you see up there?"

She looks up. She turns her head, taking in the dull day. "Nothing. I saw an eagle before, but it's gone."

"How many colors do you see?"

"One. Gray."

He nods. "This is what I mean. You see a uniform gray. But I see more than that." He points to a patch above them. "See how there's not just one big cloud covering the sky? It's lots of different ones, all with their own color and texture. Look at that one. It's closer than the others. The wind's making it move like a herd of wild horses across the sky. It's darker than the ones behind it so it stands out, and it has curved edges and spirals, like a snail shell."

"Oh, yeah!" she says.

"And over there, toward the horizon." He points to the east.

"They're more like a solid wall, with golden feathers sprouting where the sun is touching them."

"Like flames," she says.

"Let's try something else. What do you see out there?" He gestures around them.

"The waterfall, of course—I'm not blind. It's so peaceful."

"And around us?"

"It's just the moor." She thinks for a moment, squints her eyes. "But if this is a test, I'll say I can also see some rocks, but it's hard to miss them when there's so many. And look, there! Birds!" A pair of hooded crows launch from the ground in the distance.

Moss laughs. "Where you see *just the moor*, I can see all the shades of black and brown, and the purple and white and yellow tinges of different flowers, and see that glint of light reflecting off the patch of bog water?"

"I see it."

"The color of the reflections is different depending on the time of day or the weather. Sometimes it's golden; sometimes pink, or black. The moors are alive with color and texture, not to mention . . ." He closes his eyes and inhales long and deep through his nose.

"It stinks," says Lotta and laughs. Moss joins her.

"I weren't going to say that. But it does have a lot of different smells. I can tell when animals are near, or if there's something dead that's rotting. Peat doesn't really have a smell until you burn it, but when it's wet, and muddy, it just smells of the island."

"Well, we all know what peat smells like when it's burning. Sour. It takes over everything." She swallows. "I'm sorry about what I said to you that day we met, about how you smelled of it."

Moss picks up the water flask from beside him and takes a drink. He wipes his sleeve across his mouth, unsure how to respond.

"I know you've been taught to hate us," he says. "But we've been punished enough."

"I agree. And I don't hate you." She takes his hand. "You can see that, can't you?"

He watches their hands entwine. She squeezes his palm, and then his fingers. Both hands are gray with grime, with black-rimmed nails. It's hard to see who owns which hand.

Finally, he looks into her eyes. "I can see that now," he says. "Yes. But it's hard for me to trust you."

"I know," she says.

The moment stretches between them, and for a long minute it's just the two of them, with nothing but the breeze on their cheeks and a distant skylark singing its way to the clouds.

Salty grunts and shakes himself, rattling the saddlebags, and Lotta tears her gaze away, removing her hand at the same time.

"I'll tell you," she says. "Nobody's ever said that to me before, that they can feel the Glimm. So I need to explain to you, and I think—I hope—you'll understand."

He almost doesn't dare to breathe, in case she changes her mind. But she continues.

"That night we met, when I sang to the bog, I felt like I'd been taken over. That song came up through my feet from inside the bog. I know now that it was the Glimm I was singing to. It was the Glimm that freed Hannah. That's how I knew it wouldn't let any harm come to her."

"You didn't seem surprised, though," he says, remembering her cool demeanor, her quick tongue.

"I told you, I was lying to myself. I think I have been for a long time. I hate that the villagers treat me differently. I just want to get on with doing my work with the horses. Live my life."

She twists a button on her coat, as if nervous of what she's about to say.

"But there was more. The weather. When I got mad, the weather came up suddenly. The villagers have been saying that I'm responsible for their crops being moldy, their babies being born wrong. I got angry, and the storm that came . . . I think I caused it."

"That storm, the night before I came to you?"

"Yes, the one that tore the tree down in the horses' field."

"It tore out our crops, too."

"The hail destroyed so much. It only made them blame me more. I see the way they watch me. Something's brewing and I don't like it. I heard them say I should have been taken that day, not spared."

Moss's head swims. He was right that she was special. "They've got it all wrong, though. They fear you. They know you got a special connection to the Glimm, which is why they've revered you for so long. Could it be . . ." He pauses, thinking for a moment. It's becoming clear. "The Council is threatened by you too. They're turning people against you. They're planning something and I think it's much bigger than just an exile's horse taken for the lottery. That were just about keeping Mam in her place. But they've slipped up. They've been betrayed by one of their own. He told us, by warning us, that the lottery is rigged. I'm not even sure if he meant to. And if this lottery is rigged, have they all been rigged?"

Lotta nods. "It's true. My parents told me."

He listens then, with every nerve in his body vibrating, as she tells him about her last visit to her parents. How she had asked them for help with Hannah and how it had all come out. Their resistance to the Council all those years ago, and Lotta's number coming up in the lottery.

"They was too scared to help us, because they've seen what happens when you challenge the Council," says Moss. "Is that where . . ." He's trying to make sense of everything that has happened since. "The fish."

"Yes. We framed it as a gift from the Glimm, and I suppose it was, really, though we lost some sheep as a price. They knew what they were doing when they gave Wolf the same number as Hannah. They let me parade him around on her back and never forget how close I came to death."

They sit side by side in silence, listening to the sounds of the day: Hannah's unshod hoof catching with a dull thud on a stone as she forages for grass; Salty's quiet breathing, and iron shoes crunching on the ground; the peal of the eagle, which is back, circling above as if watching what they'll do next; the quiet rustling of the heather, and the wind skating over the rocks.

Moss feels at home out here on the moors as much as he does in his own hamlet. He wishes they could stay in the moment and not face what is surely coming. Lotta stands suddenly. "Come on," she says. "We've dallied long enough. Let's get to those mountains."

# 23

**The bodies**—impossibly tall, their heads crowned with branches of bone—are tied with rope either side of the gate, which stretches high above Lotta and Moss like a dark waterfall. The flesh is long gone—whether to time or carrion birds, it's hard to say. Only a few patches of rotted cloth remain, hanging by threads. Lotta feels oddly calm, while under her, Salty trembles.

"What are they?" says Moss, the horror stiffening his voice. "What is this place?"

At the foot of the mountain pass, beside a small, dark lake, a natural wall is formed in the rock, and set within it, a giant gate formed of wood and iron. Lotta dismounts but holds on to her reins in case Salty decides to bolt. Moss joins her on the ground and together they examine the skeletons more closely.

"Look at this," says Moss, and gestures to the symbol carved over and over in the gate: the sign of the Glimm, the letter S lying on its side.

"And there," points out Lotta. On the foreheads of the two skulls, the same symbol. She recognizes the bones seemingly growing from their heads, sees a flash of a memory, standing in Judge Hawthorne's library in the Manor House. A fire leaps high in the grate, the heat intense on one cheek as she faces him. A rich red rug beneath her feet, covering wide wooden floorboards. The Judge is welcoming her, but his eyes bore into her like hot embers through snow.

Above the fireplace, an animal skull, with branches of bone sprouting from it, impossibly high for such a small head.

"What is it?" she dares to ask. His gaze follows hers.

"That, my child, is a stag—a male deer. A magnificent creature that was unfortunately hunted to extinction many years ago."

"What's the bones on its head?"

"They are called antlers. When the deer is alive, they're covered in lustrous velvet."

Lotta eyes the vivid curtains, almost the same shade as the rug. He sees and turns to look behind him.

"The curtains are very old as well."

"I'd like to see a stag," she dares to declare.

The Judge stands. He walks to the shelf where he keeps his books and pulls one down. It's bound in green leather, and shines in the firelight.

"You may look at this book if you like. It will show you many animals that are no longer with us, that died when the people before us were selfish and did not sacrifice their children to the Glimm."

"Or their horses?" asks Lotta.

"Nor their horses, it seems." His lips are a tight line on his face.

"They're deer horns," says Lotta, the memory giving her confidence. "Like the goats have. But bigger. Fixed to their skulls with leather straps, see? They're called antlers."

"Jenny mentioned a deer." Moss peers at the antlers, standing on his tiptoes as though that will help. "Do you think they carved the signs there when the folk was still alive? Did they pin them up there with horns strapped to them, left to die?" His face is pale, like he's going to be sick. "I don't like this. I've never seen human bones. It gives me a bad feeling."

"It's supposed to," says Lotta. "It's a warning. Whoever put these here doesn't want anyone going inside. It's *meant* to scare us."

"Well, it's bleedin' working." He lifts his shoulders to his ears and shudders. "We was always told the mountains were forbidden. I just didn't realize they was so serious about it."

He lifts the heavy ring on the gate and tries to turn it. "Locked."

"Why do you think the bodies are holding spears?" asks Lotta. The spearheads, carved in bone, point to the sky. "Do you think they're guarding it, even though they're dead?" It's her turn to shudder.

"I don't understand," says Moss. "We passed the quarry, so people have been going to the mountains forever—maybe they still do. There's always things to be built, stones to be carted back to the village for bridges and walls. Chimneys."

She almost doesn't catch the last word, he says it so quietly. "Not this far into them, though, not to the pass between them."

"What's on the other side of the pass?"

She shrugs. "The ocean. More cliffs. Just a guess."

"There must be *something* they don't want people to see in there."

They turn to look back the way they have come. From up here they can see so much of the island: the moors, the saltings, even the village. And beyond it, another forbidden frontier: the ocean. She's heard of people making wooden boats to escape the island and being taken by the creatures that encircle it. They say the ocean is bountiful, and the yield of fish from the wave was just a small glimpse. Life would be so different for the islanders if they could fish in boats on the sea.

She tries to look at the landscape through Moss's eyes, picking out the colors and the details, but she doesn't have the patience, not now.

"It's beautiful," he says simply.

They both turn and look up at the gate.

"So what do we do now?" Moss asks. "Turn back?"

"No." Lotta hands Salty's reins to Moss and goes right up to the gate. She examines the lock, then opens her satchel and takes out her knife.

"That's a big knife," says Moss.

Lotta ignores him and begins digging into the wood around the ring-shaped handle. It comes away in chunks, soft as the sphagnum moss that grows on the bog. She knocks with her knuckles in several different places on the wood and detects different density.

"I think we can break this." She raps again. "It's rotten."

"How? I pulled and it wouldn't budge."

"Luckily, there's someone here who is much stronger than you or me."

Moss's eyebrows rise. "Hannah?"

She nods. "I've got rope. She's used to pulling heavy loads."

Moss puts a protective hand on Hannah's neck. "I don't want her to get hurt. Not after everything."

"I won't let that happen," Lotta says, more confidently than she feels. She'll have to be so careful. Moss's trust is already as flimsy as the clothing on those skeletons.

After she persuades Moss to connect Hannah by rope to the ring, and has loosened it some more with her knife, the lock pops off like a cork from a bottle, with minimal strain from Hannah. It whistles through the air. Moss ducks just in time. The iron piece clatters to the ground behind him. The force of his movement tips him to the ground on his backside. He looks back at where the hunk of iron lies in the gate's shadow and can't help but laugh in relief.

Lotta holds out her hand to him. "Let's see what's on the other side, then, shall we?"

# 24

**The gate is stiff** and catches on the rocky ground, but Moss throws his shoulder behind it and Lotta joins him; working together they move it enough to get through.

"Should we close it after us?" asks Moss.

"Best do that," says Lotta. "We don't know what will get out, or in, if we don't. It won't be locked, though."

The terrain rises steeply; the loose scree slides beneath their boots as they lead the horses uphill. As they come to the top of a rise, Moss is in the lead. He gasps as he stares out in front of him.

"What?" says Lotta, trying to break into a jog while the shingle underfoot fights her with every step.

He turns to look at her and his face is etched with wonder. "You're not going to believe it."

It's the overwhelming sense of *green* that hits her first. Spread out below, with mountains rising on either side, is the pass. The stream they were following is a branch of a bigger river that furls down the mountain, splitting off to feed a high-country lake, which is a creamy blue. Here are stands of trees with bright leaves, and a meadow untouched by peat or bogs. The weather is different here, too, as if by passing through the gate they passed into a new climate.

It's too much for Moss. He covers his face with his hands.

"Are you all right?" asks Lotta. She's concerned—of course she is—but she also feels an inexplicable lightness, and excitement has raised the pitch of her voice.

Moss takes his hands away, but his eyes are squeezed shut, leaking tears. "The lake's too bright," he says. "It's all too vivid—it's already giving me a headache. Tell me what you can see."

Lotta stills, though her breathing is slightly labored after the steep climb.

"I'm trying to look through your eyes," she says. "But it's overwhelming, just like you said. Moss, there are animals here. I think they're deer. Their horns—their antlers, I mean—they're not as big as the ones on the gate, and they're all different sizes." She can see more details though, thanks to him—hides that are brown, shot with reds and black, some with a hint of white spots.

At the mention of the deer, Moss opens his eyes again. "I can't miss this," he mutters. "Pain be damned."

He takes it in through watering eyes. "It's like we've entered another world," he says.

Beside them, the horses stand rigid, ears pricked forward. Suddenly Hannah lets out a long, melodious whinny that wends its way down toward the lake.

To their surprise, it is answered. A shape comes charging out of the trees. A sturdy horse, a smaller version of Hannah, trots toward them, tail high. Then stops. It turns sideways and begins pacing back and forth, neck arched, nostrils flaring and blowing like bellows.

"He's beautiful," breathes Lotta. "What a fine fellow." A movement from the trees catches her eye and she points. "Look!"

More horses wander out of the forest, their curiosity piqued. Some of them have foals with them, wobbling on beanpole legs, or cantering to keep up with the herd, their tiny tails wriggling like eels.

"Come on," says Lotta. A clear path is cut into the hillside, so she mounts Salty and sends him down it. Moss follows suit. Their horses prance like colts, eager to meet the stallion, but it's wary of them.

"We'll need to ride around the herd," says Lotta. "We mustn't get between the stallion and the rest of them or who knows what he'll do to protect them."

With a wary eye on the leader, they skirt around the edge of the lake. The herd watches them go, while the deer scatter in alarm. In the cool gloom of the trees, Moss's face relaxes, as though his vision has cleared and the pounding behind his eyes has started to fade. They're engulfed by a clamor of insect and birdsong.

"How can something so noisy be so peaceful?" Lotta wonders.

The forest thins, and the path opens into a wide glade. In its center stands a circle of stones, tall and weathered. Inside the ring is a stag, knee-deep in golden grass. It lifts its head, watching them approach.

Lotta draws Salty to a stop. "Don't move," she murmurs.

Moss freezes, one hand on Hannah's mane.

The stag lowers its head, unthreatened by their presence. It stretches one foreleg out and rubs its nose on it. The huge antlers bob and sway. It turns and walks slowly to the edge of the stones, then turns again before crossing the circle's boundary. There, it pauses, looks back at them, then vanishes into the forest.

They dismount, drawn forward. The air inside the circle feels different. Cooler. Hushed. Lotta counts the stones: twelve. Each bears the same carved mark: the Glimm's sigil, the sideways S, some worn nearly smooth, others still sharply etched, as if time has moved differently for each stone.

In the middle, lying low and flat like a bed, is a thirteenth stone.

"What's this one?" Moss asks.

"It's an altar of sorts, maybe? There's one in the Temple. It's to make offerings."

"Offerings? Like a sacrifice?"

"No, they don't sacrifice people or animals in the Temple. It's where folk light candles and leave their offerings to the Council—food and blankets and the like. But I suppose this one could be anything. It looks ancient."

More carvings are visible here—not just the Glimm's mark, but other sigils: spirals, circles, wavy lines. One looks like a boat. Tiny bone fragments rest in a hollow at its center. Not human, Lotta thinks. Bird bones, perhaps. Offerings, as she thought.

"How old do you think it is?" Moss asks.

Lotta lays her hand on it. "Very."

"Then why's it still here? Why hasn't anyone come back to live here?"

Lotta doesn't answer. They walk on, following a thin path that leads uphill through bracken. It curls behind a rise, and there, nestled into the hillside, is a wide stone opening—a shallow cave mouth, framed by lichen-covered rocks.

"Should we leave the horses here?" Moss asks. "Tie them up?"

"Salty won't go anywhere," says Lotta.

"I don't want to lose Hannah again," he says.

"I don't think she'll leave Salty. Not now."

Moss nods but she can tell by the tight, stiff way he dismounts that he's uneasy. She knows she should be as well. This valley in the mountains, unseen from the rest of Brack, is otherworldly. It seems too good to be true.

Inside the cave, the air is damp; it smells of earth and something sweeter, like decayed fruit. Lotta lights the lamp, and they push through.

"Look," says Moss. "On the walls. It's getting lighter."

He's right. Beyond the shifting shadows cast by the lantern, the walls reflect a low gray light. They round a corner in a passage, and it is lighter still. Moss puts his hand on the walls. "This has been chiseled," he says. "Folk made this. And look, more carvings." His hands trace the serpent shape of the Glimm sigil and more wavy lines.

"What do they mean?" she asks. "Water? A river?"

Before Moss answers, they round another bend, and there at the end of the passageway, the cave opens out. They step into a large cavern with daylight falling through a hole in its soaring ceiling. At once, the air changes. It feels cooler here but charged, like the hush before music begins.

Moss whistles, long and low.

Lotta knows immediately what this place reminds her of.

"It's a temple," she says. "It's just like our Temple." She looks back at the passageway they have come through, and sure enough, a makeshift archway is carved and twisted into the shape of a serpent.

"I've never been in our Temple," says Moss. "I'm the unloved, remember?" There's no bitterness in his voice this time, and she thinks he might be making a joke.

Tall knuckles of stone topped with plants and vines rise around them, casting shadows. Tiny yellow stars drift in the air. Pollen. Moss sneezes.

"Come and look at these," he says, moving to the outer walls of the chamber, into the shadows. "Bring the lantern."

The walls are covered with drawings, alive with story.

The lantern's light catches a wide panel etched and painted in earth tones, reds and browns and faded blue. The Glimm's shape is unmistakable—long and sinuous, curling like a river, with feathered lines radiating out from its body.

The images are rough but clear. They show folk carrying offerings: bowls of fruit, cloths or blankets, small figures shaped like animals—carvings perhaps.

"What's that?" says Moss, touching one figure holding a bowl filled with tiny squares, daubed in faded white.

Lotta's heart leaps in recognition. "Salt crystals, I think."

"I thought the Glimm didn't take such offerings. Only horses."

"Or children," says Lotta.

The next panel makes Lotta cry out: the Glimm, with human figures beside it holding flutes, and drums decorated with spirals. People are gathered around fires on a shoreline, some with hands linked, feet mid-step. Lines curl from the creature's open mouth—a painted song that winds like ribbon through the air and around the dancers, drawing them all together. And on the Glimm's back: smaller figures.

"They're children, Moss. Riding on its back." Her fingers on the Glimm are blurred through tears. Moss puts his hand on her shoulder, bowing his head close to hers.

"That's what the lines in the passageway were, and on the stone altar. It's music. They made music for it," Lotta murmurs, astonished. "They danced with it. On the saltings, look." She recognizes the reeds of the saltings, the lines that form the waterways.

The standing stone.

"And it sang back." Moss points to the glowing lines that rise from the Glimm's mouth.

"It must've been so beautiful," she whispers. "A sound so big and strange you could feel it in your bones."

This isn't the terrifying figure from the Council's stories, punishing and monstrous. The islanders offer it fruit, and salt, and music.

"I don't understand," says Moss, his voice confused.

"That's because it goes against everything we've ever been told," says Lotta. "They lived with it. Celebrated it."

In the center of one scene, a stag stands tall, flanked by two kneeling people with bowed heads. The deer stands calmly within a ring of stones, antlers painted gold.

"They didn't sacrifice children, or horses. Deer, maybe, but it doesn't look like it." Lotta presses a hand to the stone, as if she can feel its rhythm.

Image after image shows deer running through green meadows, people walking beside them, hands outstretched. Small children riding on their backs. Figures weaving under tall trees. A world in harmony with deer, and with the Glimm at its center, not as a god or a monster, but as a part of life.

Lotta moves around the perimeter of the cave. The scenes shift along the wall, a progression. One shows a great fire, trees blackened, birds and deer fleeing into the distance. The Glimm twists upward, smaller now, drawn in jagged lines. The music is gone.

"I think it's a story," whispers Lotta. "What does it say?"

"I think there were a fire," says Moss. "A big one. It burned everything."

"Then they must have left the saltings," Lotta adds. "Look—" She points to the final drawing.

It shows a group of people walking away, small against a gray mountain backdrop. Their heads are bowed. In the sky above them, the Glimm's sigil hangs like a setting sun.

Then: barrows with bones laid in curling patterns inside them.

"So there was folk here once, who lived with the Glimm," says Moss. "And they wasn't afraid of it, not like us. So what changed?"

"The fire burned all the forests down there. Maybe it broke something," says Lotta.

"Maybe the Glimm changed."

Lotta runs a hand along one of the drawings—the circle of people around a fire.

"Or maybe we did," she says.

They stand together in silence. Behind them, the wind stirs faintly through the passageway and in it, just for a moment, Lotta thinks she hears something.

A low hum. A melody, half remembered.

# 25

OUTSIDE, THEY MOVE in silence, taking it all in, piecing it together.

As they walk beside the horses, Moss looks around him, at the place so different from everything he's known.

"Maybe this has only now regrown," he says. "Maybe it's taken this long."

Lotta doesn't answer. The scenes in the cave upset her more than she's letting on, he can tell.

The sun has abandoned the day, and the first sprinkling of stars speckle the sky. Dark shapes move in the distance; they startle another young stag, which leaps away from them, bracken and other undergrowth cracking beneath its hooves.

"We'll need to find somewhere to sleep," says Moss. "I'm dead tired."

"What about in the clearing? In the stone circle? There might be room for us both on the altar."

"That feels a bit . . . gruesome," says Moss.

"We could go back to the cave? Build a fire?" She peers onto the ground. "Plenty of wood."

Moss sighs and stretches his aching back. "I could just lie down right here, make a bracken bed. Cover up with a blanket."

The arrow lands with a sharp *thunk*, buried deep in the bark of a tree less than a hand's width from Lotta's face. She freezes. Moss stares at her, not quite believing what he's just seen.

"Move!" she growls, grabbing his hand. She pulls him behind the trunk of the tree. The horses lumber after them, too exposed. "Who's there?" calls Moss, desperately hoping they've just been mistaken for game by a friendly hunter. Somehow, he thinks that's unlikely.

There's an explosion of air above them as a flock of birds takes off, then the forest around them is silent again—no birdsong, no rustling leaves. Just the creak of leather as Lotta shifts beside him and takes out her big knife.

Then comes the voice.

"Don't run," it says, calm and low, from somewhere in the trees. "Next one won't miss."

A dark shape steps out of the undergrowth, bow still drawn. What little light there is left in the sky battles with the treetops to illuminate her. As she creeps closer, she comes into focus, with silver-streaked hair, plaited and pulled tight against her skull. Behind her, another figure emerges, masculine, with short hair and thick woolen trousers, an axe slung over one shoulder. Both wear layers of animal hide and old wool patched a hundred times over. Their faces are lined, not unkind, but wary.

"We saw the horseshoe prints," the second person says, and Moss is surprised to hear a woman's voice. "And you were too quiet to be Council." Her eyes narrow, scrutinizing them. "We don't like surprises."

"You're right that we're not with the Council," Lotta says quickly, her voice steadier than Moss feels. Yet she was the one who nearly took the arrow.

He can't leave her to brave them on her own. "We're from the village," he lies. It's safer this way.

The one with the axe narrows her eyes. "Nobody from the village comes here."

"We did," Lotta says. "We had to."

The other woman lowers her bow and arrow and murmurs something to her companion.

"Does the Council know you're here?"

Moss looks to Lotta and can see she's thinking the same thing. *Can we trust them?*

"No," says Lotta.

"And you've been to the cave?" Another glance between them. So much is unsaid.

"We have," says Moss.

There's a long pause. The tension crackles the air around them. What if this is the wrong answer, Moss thinks suddenly. Have these two even met anyone from the village here before? Then the axe woman grunts. "Come on, then. Let's talk somewhere warm."

Moss and Lotta stay close, alert to every movement the women make. Warm lamplight accompanies them through the forest to another clearing. The short-haired woman doesn't lower her axe until they're halfway across.

The stone cottage sits tucked among the silhouettes of fruit trees; the edges of an enormous vegetable crop are lit by the women's lantern as they pass. Moss recognizes the shapes of delicate frames waiting for peas to push through the soil, shoots of carrots and other seedlings lined up neatly, unscathed by harsh winds and hail. Beside the cottage, a henhouse emits contented croons, and a large pen corrals restless sheep. They turn the horses out here too with armfuls of hay.

Inside, with the fire crackling, Moss can't stop staring. There's so much wood—real, living wood. Planks with swirling grain, antlers strung above the door, shelves carved with curling leaves. Wooden creatures line the shelves: owls and sheep, and Glimm-like shapes with gentle curves. A lifetime's worth of woodwork. Through a wooden door he glimpses a solid bed frame, carved with twining flowers, a patchwork woolen blanket in bright colors thrown on top.

It's the most beautiful place Moss has ever seen. A life like this has to be made piece by piece, over years. His own house is gray and lifeless in comparison, though it's not without warmth. He sees his mother's face then, and he turns the thought away.

Thick deer hides cover the windows and the house smells of freshly cut pine, fire smoke, and drying herbs that hang from beams in the ceiling. Something sweet, too—jam, maybe. The hearth glows. A pot hangs above it, steam curling from beneath the lid. Moss realizes how hungry he is.

The silver-haired woman, who introduces herself as Fern, hands them bowls of stew. "Venison and carrot," she says. "Eat it while it's hot."

Her companion, Esther, with arched eyebrows and a no-nonsense face under her cropped gray hair, sees their uncertainty. "It's deer." She sits down heavily on a three-legged stool and regards them as they eat.

Moss's shoulders relax. It's hard to be on guard when you can feel warm food sliding down to your belly. The deer is delicious. He looks at Lotta and she obviously feels the same. Her eyes close as she spoons in another mouthful, and without realizing, she loses a splatter of dark brown sauce down her shirt.

"So you found the cave," Esther says. She stands and casually strolls to a table made from pale timber. A knife is waiting there, which she picks up to begin carving slices from a misshapen loaf of soda bread.

Lotta nods and swallows, then wipes her sleeve across her mouth, still oblivious to the streak of stew on her front. "We saw drawings. People feasting, and dancing. With the Glimm. It was . . . peaceful. Not what we were taught."

Moss doesn't take his eyes from Esther's arm, the way it saws at the bread, like she's performing an amputation.

*Nobody from the village comes here*, Esther said. And now that they are inside, Moss can't help but wonder if that was meant as a warning, like the two skeletons at the gate. His eyes find Lotta's. She has stopped eating and puts her bowl, half finished, on the floor.

"Is everything all right?" asks Fern.

"Why is this place forbidden?" Lotta asks bluntly.

Fern and Esther exchange looks.

"I mean," Lotta goes on, "you could feed a lot of families here. Build houses. A different sort of a life."

Moss hears the wistfulness in her voice, and he's right there with her, imagining how different his life would have been if he had grown up here. Plentiful food, sun, shelter from the insistent wind and its biting cold. A school, the cave temple. A life alongside the Glimm, not in sacrifice to it.

"As you know," says Fern quietly, "this island is ruled by the Council, and this valley is no different."

"They put the bodies at the gate?" Moss asks.

"Of course they did!" says Esther. "You thought it was us?"

Moss shakes his head.

"This place is a remnant of what the island used to be. Now it is a protected place. And we are its guardians." Esther's voice deepens with something like pride.

"The Council knows you're here?" says Moss. Like Lotta, his appetite has diminished, and he sets his bowl down, but accepts the bread that Esther passes him.

"Of course it does, you stupid boy," she barks.

Moss pauses with the bread halfway to his mouth. His cheeks grow hot.

Lotta's face hardens. "Then you work for them."

"And you don't?" says Esther. "We know who you are, Lotta Salter. We know you tend the horses for the lottery. As I said, nobody lives outside the rule of the Council, not even the girl who survived the Glimm."

"But the cave told us that we could be living in harmony with the Glimm," says Moss. "It gave us hope." He glances at Lotta, who nods. Her eyes shine too bright in the firelight.

Esther's voice is gruff. "The Council doesn't want harmony. It wants control."

Lotta looks down at her stew. "Why you? How did you end up here?"

Fern doesn't speak at first; instead, she glances at Esther again. They silently communicate with each other, weighing how much to disclose. Moss wonders how much of what they're saying is the truth, and how much is shaped by the Council.

"We knew too much," says Esther finally. "Our families tended the Manor House's deer herd, going back generations, we were told. My father found the cave and threatened to tell the rest of the island what he saw here. That's when he suffered an 'accident.' We were exiled before we could pass the story on."

"The Judge told me the deer were hunted to extinction," says Lotta.

"Another of the Council's lies."

"How do you know me?" asks Lotta. "If you've been here all this time?"

"Word travels," says Esther. "There are others who know of this place. They come and collect the deer meat for the Council. But they don't know about the cave, and we don't tell them. They're given very strict instructions not to wander if they know what's good for them."

"But if more people knew," presses Lotta, "the Council would lose its power. You're complicit in the lottery if you don't tell them."

"Don't you think we've thought of that? But thanks to you, there are only horses at stake now. Not humans. It could be so much worse. We like our life here."

Esther reaches across the table and takes Fern's hand. Another look passes between them. Complicity, but also love.

"They exiled us," Fern continues. "We were told if we ever returned, we'd be executed. They let us live, barely. On one condition."

Esther takes over now, her voice hard and brittle.

"That we tend the deer. Cull them when needed. Supply meat for the Council table. Pretend we never saw what we saw in that cave. And stop those Council thugs finding it."

Lotta and Moss exchange glances.

Fern stands abruptly and begins gathering the bowls. "As long as we tend the deer and don't speak, they leave us alone. It's exile. But it's better than the alternative."

No one speaks for a while. The only sound is the snap and pop of the fire.

Later, Fern and Esther make them up a bed of blankets by the hearth. Fern presses extra deerskins into their arms. "You'll be warm here," she says, and there's nothing but kindness in it.

Esther and Fern retreat to their room. The wooden door clicks shut behind them.

As they lie curled up under deer pelts, side by side on the floor, Lotta whispers, "I feel like I could stay here forever, but there's something not quite right."

Moss reaches out and finds her hand.

"We have to tell folk what we've found here," she says, and squeezes Moss's fingers. "But how can we do that without hurting these good people?"

Moss squeezes back, wanting to find words of comfort, of wisdom, but his mouth is too tired to form them.

The fire crackles.

The deer hide is warm against his cheek.

The long-awaited darkness takes him.

# 26

ONLY FERN is there when they wake, offering them food for the journey home—dried meat, oatcakes, a flask of smoky and strong-smelling broth. She is disconcertingly quiet and barely makes eye contact. Lotta wonders if she regrets telling them so much.

"We'll keep your secret," she promises, and Moss backs her up with a nod.

The shadows on Fern's face are sharp in the morning light.

As they ready the horses, packing the food into Salty's saddlebags while he munches on a carrot, Moss stops moving and puts his head on Hannah's neck.

"Come on," says Lotta. "We don't have time for cuddles."

His head snaps back and he breathes sharply. "Are you thinking what I'm thinking?"

"I don't think I am, no," she says.

"We're just going to go back and hand Hannah over?"

"No, of course not. We're going to go back and tell everyone what we found here. They'll have to listen to us. We'll put an end to the sacrifice."

"But you just told Fern we would keep their secret. How can we do that and also tell people what we've found?"

"But they'll be safe from the Council if we stop them. The islanders won't let any harm come to them."

Moss stares at her, his mouth grim.

"What?" says Lotta.

"Don't get cocky, Lotta. I think you're overestimating your power in the village."

"I've got the Glimm on my side, remember?"

"Really? You're going to tell them that, and they'll all bow down to you? Is that really what you want?"

Lotta can feel the anger pulsing off him like heat. He's never turned on her so quickly. His usually pale face is flushed and his jaw tight.

"No, of course not," she says. "Who do you think I am?"

"Well, Lotta, I really don't know. I think you haven't thought this through and you're putting everyone in danger, starting with Hannah, and then Fern and Esther."

"What do you propose?"

"I've had one idea, at least." He puts his hand on Hannah's neck, into the soft cave under her mane. "Hannah is safe here. Let's leave her in this valley, with this herd. She's got everything she needs here. Food, water, shelter. Company."

"But what about you? Your family? You'll be without a horse."

"I don't want to risk taking her back and losing her anyway. At least this way she has a life, not a violent, horrible death. They'll have to choose another horse."

"Hopefully it won't get that far."

"Hopefully, but just in case. And we can come back and get her when things have settled down."

Lotta can see the anger subsiding in his face. "All right. I think that's an excellent idea." She finishes adjusting the straps on Salty's saddle.

"We should tell Fern and Esther," says Moss. "They can use her for their work. I trust them."

"You shouldn't," comes a voice behind them.

They turn to find Esther blocking the pen gate. Fern stands alongside, her arm hooked through her partner's. In the other she holds her bow, and the quiver of arrows is on her back. Esther grips her axe, and a large knife sits snug at her waist.

"You can't go," says Esther. Her face is harder than it appeared last night. Deep frown lines etch her forehead.

"Why not?" asks Lotta.

"We heard you," says Fern. "You can't do what you want to do without giving us up. We're under instructions to kill any unauthorized villagers who breach the gates."

Lotta can't help herself, though in her heart is a knot of dread. "So why didn't you last night?"

Moss steps in front of Lotta before she can react further and starts to move toward the women. Esther drops the axe and unsheathes her knife in seconds. She holds it in front of them. Fern unhooks her arm and takes a step back, readying her bow.

"But you wouldn't do that," Moss says, calmly holding his hands up, palms out. "You fed us. Gave us warmth and shelter."

"You know too much," says Esther. "If you tell anyone you stayed here, we're dead."

"We heard you planning to tell everyone what you found." Fern takes an arrow and positions it on her bow but keeps it pointed at the ground. Her face is still shadowed.

"We won't," Lotta says quickly. "We'll lie. We'll say we slept in the woods. Please—"

"You don't understand," says Fern. *"The Council always finds out."*

Esther nods firmly, not taking her eyes from them. "Your arrogance won't save us."

Lotta knows she's lost them. Desperately, she looks at Moss. He's thinking, hard.

"I wasn't quite honest with you last night," he says.

This grabs their interest. They forget about Lotta and switch their attention to him fully.

"I'm not from the village. I'm a hideling. You know what that means?"

Lotta is startled to hear him say the word. He never calls himself a hideling, and it sounds twisted in his voice. Wrong.

The silence expands as the women stare back at him. Then, slowly, they both nod. "You hid from the lottery."

"My *parents* hid me," he corrects. "I didn't ask to be hid."

Lotta's heart skips. *I didn't ask to be hid.* The exact words he said the night they met. It sounds different now. Not a boy full of shame, but a young man claiming his truth.

"Because of what my parents did, I've lived in exile my whole life, like you. First in a dark cellar, where I never saw the sun, then out on the moors. I were always told we wasn't good enough to be with people. And now I know that it were the Council that took that from me, not the Glimm. My family was trying to save my life, but they ended up giving me half a life instead. If the Council finds out I've been here, they'll kill me on the spot. Not only that—they'll destroy the exiles, the hidelings. I've already seen what they can do when they don't get what they want, when they want. They took Hannah."

He walks back a step to put his hand on her withers. She turns her head and nudges his back.

"They took her for the lottery and deliberately drew her number. She means everything to me. If I go back with her, she's dead. And after that, it'll be me, and my family. All the exiled families."

Lotta studies the women's faces as they listen. She detects a softening.

"What's your full name, boy?" asks Esther.

"Moss Smith. My father Jacob were the village blacksmith before he were sent away. They wouldn't let him work and I believe he died, broken, because of it. I should be his apprentice now." His voice wavers with emotion.

Lotta feels a chasm open up inside her. How little she knows of him and, she is ashamed to admit, how much she has never asked about.

"I didn't know that," she says in a small voice. "I'm sorry."

Moss shakes his head. "There hasn't exactly been time to sit down and chat."

"I knew him," says Esther.

"We both did," Fern confirms. "His father was our blacksmith. Jacob used to come with him and help with the horses. Always smiling, that wee boy was, do you remember, Esther?"

Esther nods. Her grip on the knife has loosened, and it now hangs in her hand at her side.

Lotta isn't sure where Moss is going with this, but it seems to be working. Anything she says could ruin his moment—but can he do it on his own?

"Please . . ." She opens her mouth to speak, not sure what she is going to say next.

"Be quiet, Lotta," says Moss. "I haven't finished."

Lotta closes her mouth, tamping down the surge of indignation. *Trust him*, she tells herself. *You don't have to always be in control.*

"I'm here because I wanted to save my horse. That's all. But in trying to save my horse, I've learned so much more. About the Council to start with, how they rigged the lottery. About the Glimm."

He glances at Lotta, but she widens her eyes at him to say *not that*. She doesn't know how they'll react if she tells them of her connection.

"About the island," says Moss. "How things used to be. About *you*." At these last two words he reaches his hand out toward them, and his voice softens to almost a whisper. This has the desired effect. The women look at each other and Esther returns her knife to its sheath.

Moss hasn't finished. "I owe it to my dead, broken father—that boy you knew—and to my family, to take this further."

Oh, he is *good.*

"I would like to do a deal with you," he says.

Esther narrows her eyes. "What kind of a deal?"

"I will leave Hannah here with you. She'll be safe here. You can put her to work. And in return we'll try our very best to conceal that you have helped us. If you never see me again, you'll know we've failed."

He looks at Lotta, who nods. "I promise that too."

"If we never see you again," says Fern, "then the next people we see could very well be the Council come to destroy us."

"That is a possibility," says Moss. "But I hope not."

A long silence stretches between them, before Esther speaks. "That is very . . . honest of you."

Fern touches Esther's arm, and for the first time they both turn away to address each other. Lotta could lunge for them now: She's younger, stronger; she could incapacitate them both. But she won't.

Fern's voice is barely more than a murmur, threaded with a note of pleading. Their faces are so close, so intimate. Moss is staring at them intently, trying to hear, and he flinches when Lotta takes his hand and squeezes. He recovers and squeezes back. This is the moment when all they have is hope.

Finally the couple turns around.

"Very well," says Esther.

"We've lived a good life here, really," says Fern. "We realize that not everybody has been so fortunate. We're willing to take the risk."

Lotta didn't realize how much tension she's been holding in her body. She collapses to her knees, still holding Moss's hand. He crouches beside her and puts his other hand on her back. "It's all right," he says softly. "It's going to be all right."

# 27

**THEY MOVE THROUGH** the trees, both of them on Salty's back, not speaking. Moss's tears are dry now, but he is hollowed out by the morning's events and can't think how he will find the strength for the homeward journey. Or what will happen to them when Lotta returns without Hannah. He allows himself to go limp, moving with the side-to-side motion of Salty's gait. Hannah seemed oblivious to his goodbyes—she was too busy rolling in the green field before getting up, shaking herself like a wet dog, and trotting off to join the herd.

It's the best place for her, but it hurts. He almost wishes he could stay too.

They have nearly cleared the tree line when a movement to their right catches his eye. Salty sees it too—he snorts and shies.

Lotta stiffens in front of Moss.

"What was that?" she says, her voice low.

"It's just a horse," says Moss, but even as the words leave his mouth, he sees the saddle and bridle and knows instantly: It's not from the herd. Before he can react, something grabs his arm and he's wrenched sideways, falling and hitting the ground with a hard jolt. Pain shoots through his shoulder just as he hears Lotta grunt as the air is knocked out of her.

His first thought is that the women have changed their minds, that they've come for them after all, but no. This is a *man* now standing over him, emitting the rancid smell of animal sweat. He bends his massive, meaty frame to leer in their faces. Moss stares into the familiar, off-kilter eye holes of a sackcloth mask. The man makes a low growl in his throat as Lotta scrambles to her feet.

"Got you, ya little buggers!" The voice is deep and unpleasant, muffled by the mask. Before either of them can move, he lunges for Lotta and closes both of his heavy hands around her neck, shaking her like a baby's rattle.

"Run, Moss!" Lotta chokes through a constricted throat, but Moss won't leave her.

He uses all his force to propel himself and slams into the man, good shoulder first. He must have surprised him—the man stumbles, though doesn't lose his grip on Lotta. The pair sprawls sideways onto the forest floor. Moss tries to pull the henchman off Lotta, closing his hands over a damp, fleshy bicep, but the man lets one fist go to lash out at Moss, catching him on the mouth and knocking him back. Lotta wastes no time—she fumbles behind her back for her satchel buckle, kicking out at him with a boot.

Beside them, Salty panics and also kicks out, catching the assailant on the side of the head. The man lets go of Lotta and clutches his ear, dazed. She jumps up, bringing her hand out from behind her back.

Her knife! She has her knife. Moss feels a rush of relief. Lotta holds it out in front of her, motioning for him to get behind her.

As Moss moves past him, the groaning man lunges, barreling him into Lotta. They all crash to the ground, rolling. The knife is knocked from Lotta's hand by the impact. Moss yelps as the man pushes off him to grab it, then brings it to his throat.

The metal is cold against Moss's neck. His heart beats so fast he thinks it'll scare away the birds. He's delirious.

"You pissy little hideling," the man hisses. "I should kill you." His spittle settles on Moss's lips and in his eyes, burning like poison.

"No!" says Lotta.

"Stay back, bitch!" He tightens his grip on Moss's shirt, pressing him into the rough ground. A stone beneath Moss's head digs in. "I've got my orders. This little bastard wasn't a part of them, but nobody will miss a hideling, let alone mourn him."

"If you kill him, I run," says Lotta.

The man looks at her, weighing his options.

"Run," says Moss weakly.

"Come here, then," says the thug. "It's you the Judge wants."

Moss's pulse beats against the blade. If it beats any harder, he'll end up slicing his own throat. He tries not to swallow and lies as still as he can.

"You're bleeding," says Lotta.

The man puts one hand to his ear. When he brings it away, sure enough, it has blood on it.

"Damn horse," he says. "It's next."

"I'm sure the Judge will be thrilled if you kill one of his prize geldings. His granddaughter's horse, no less."

"Bullshit," says the man. He shakes his head, and through the eyeholes, Moss sees his lids close. The kick to the head is working its magic.

"It's true," says Lotta.

The man doesn't say anything and doesn't react when Lotta jumps forward and pushes him, hard. Moss gasps when the blade slices his skin as it leaves his throat. He sits up, panting, in time to see Lotta astride the man, raising a rock in her fist, but she's not fast enough—he rolls her over and pulls the knife back as if he's planning to stab her right in the heart.

And, from nowhere, a *twang*, sharp and sudden.

An arrow buries itself in the man's shoulder.

The knife falls uselessly to the ground. He cries out in pain.

Then Esther is there, axe in hand, striking the butt of it hard across the masked man's temple. He crumples.

The clearing goes still. There's only the sound of Lotta panting, pushing the man off, and struggling to her feet. She nudges him with her toe, checking he really is out cold, then looks around wildly, as if suddenly remembering something. Her eyes find Moss, still sitting on the ground, dazed.

"You're bleeding!" She rushes to him.

Moss puts a hand to his throat and brings it away, palm red and sticky like jam. He tests the cut with his fingers. "I'm fine," he says. "Just a scratch." His head is pounding worse than on the sunniest of days.

Fern lowers her bow. Her hands are shaking. Esther stands over the man, who is groaning but staying down.

Lotta crouches beside him, still breathing hard. His face is still hidden behind the cloth mask. She reaches for it. Hesitates. Then yanks it up.

She stares at him. Moss moves to stand beside her.

"I know that face," he says. It's fleshy and red, with broken blood vessels over the cheeks and nose—the sign of a man who enjoys too many ales—and with swollen eyelids and cracked lips. His limp brown hair is plastered to his forehead with sweat.

"Stormy Pete," says Lotta. "But why?"

Esther sighs. "He's come for the meat, Lotta," she says. "Only now, it's not just deer he's been sent to carve up."

"He works for the Council," Fern adds.

Pete's face is flushed, contorted in pain, but there's no mistaking the bitter twist of his mouth, the storm-cloud eyes that open and lock on Lotta's.

"Found you," he spits, blood flecking his lip.

Lotta stares. "You followed us."

"Not especially. But the Council knew you was up to no good when you didn't come back with that horse. Told me to keep an eye out for you. As soon as I saw that broken lock, I thought to myself, 'Pete, old son, now's your chance to get that girl for good.' You've always been trouble, in't you?"

Moss steps toward him, tense. "Back off."

Lotta raises a hand to stop him. Her voice is low, even. "You hate me that much?"

Pete laughs, raw and bitter. "You think you're so special, just because the Glimm turned you away. Well, we're on to you. It were a mistake, nothing more. You should have died that day, and now the Glimm is punishing us all. He don't want horses no more. And nobody will miss you if I take you out right now. Restore the balance, like."

Lotta puts her hand on her heart, as though something burns in her chest. "You don't even know me. You've got no idea."

"I know enough." He tries to sit up, gritting his teeth against the pain in his head. "The whole island knows the truth about you. That you're an aberration. You're nothing."

Lotta leans in closer, her voice like ice. "The truth is much more dangerous than you know, Stormy Pete. That's why you're here bleeding in the dirt, and I'm still standing. And the Judge wants the horse, fool, not me dead."

"I'll say it were an accident," Pete growls.

Fern stands behind them, bow still half drawn. "We can't let him walk out of here."

"No," Lotta says, standing. Her voice shakes, but only a little. "We can't."

Moss feels the color drain from his face. "What are you saying? You're not planning to kill him? Lotta?"

Pete looks up at her, hate smoldering behind his bruised eyes. "You think you've got some grand destiny, don't you? But you're poison, even the Glimm knew it." Quick as a hare, he reaches into his boot. Moss sees a glimpse of metal, then Pete strikes in a wide arc. Lotta jumps back but the blade catches Fern in the legs, tearing her skirt. She cries out and falls to the ground.

Moss doesn't see what happens next. His vision swims, the pain in the back of his head flaring and blooming like an explosion. He closes his eyes.

When he opens them again, Lotta is beside Fern, tearing a strip off her skirt and pressing it against the wound in her leg. The bow lies on the ground.

Stormy Pete lies still, eyes glassy, mouth slack. The forest around them is quiet. Too quiet.

Esther steps back, blood on her knife, breathing hard. Fern watches her, trembling now, while Lotta looks away resolutely. No one speaks.

Moss stares. He can't seem to move his feet. There's a strange rushing in his ears, like a river trapped inside his skull.

One moment Pete was lunging, the next he was gone.

"Get your things," Esther says. "You need to leave."

Lotta stands and won't look at anyone. Without a word, she walks over to where Salty is cowering some distance away and brings him back to the horrible scene. The horse's nostrils twitch at the smell of blood; he shudders, ready to flee.

Moss stands beside Lotta, limbs frozen, face hot. "They—he was going to kill us," he whispers, as though he's trying to convince himself.

Lotta lets out a puff of air that could easily be a sob. She breathes in again. She can't seem to catch her breath. "I didn't want this," she says, barely a murmur.

"No one did," Fern says gently. But there's a hardness in her voice, beneath the sorrow.

"If that man had gone back to the village, we'd all be dead," says Esther firmly. "They might come looking for him, but at least we've bought you some time."

"Yes," says Lotta.

Fern glances at the body. "If they come asking, we'll say we caught him coming out of the cave. That he wasn't supposed to be here. That we were following orders."

Esther nods. "That's what the rules say."

Lotta stares at them. "You'd lie for us?"

"We'd lie for *ourselves*," says Esther. "The truth won't save anyone."

"Thank you," says Moss numbly. "We owe you our lives." He touches Lotta's arm. "Come on. We should go."

She nods. He gives her a leg up, then uses a log to climb up behind her.

"Wait," says Esther. "You forgot this." She holds up Lotta's knife.

Lotta just stares at it.

"It's clean," says Esther. "It was my knife that did it."

Lotta takes the knife and fumbles with her satchel and sheath, then they're riding away without another word. The faint scent of pine smoke from the cottage follows them out of the forest.

Soon they're at the gate, which stands open enough to let them through. Only once does Lotta speak, and even then, it's barely more than a whisper. "I didn't know it would feel like this."

Pete's cart sits empty, his horse loose in the forest somewhere.

Moss doesn't answer; he just puts his hands inside her coat as they ride through the gate to see the island spread before them.

# 28

**IT HITS HER** all at once: the weight of the sky, the sodden moor, the brown wash of land stretching wide and empty. There's nothing green here, nothing soft. The valley feels far behind, like a dream already half forgotten. The raging sea in the distance is rapidly disappearing under the rush of rain traveling up the island toward them.

There's nothing for it but to put their heads down and ride into it. As soon as the rain is overhead, there's no wind, just a steady, vertical downpour. The land is swallowed in the low cloud.

"Doesn't it make you want to stay in the valley? To make a life there?" Moss's voice is close, warm in her ear. He squeezes her waist and she puts a hand on his.

"It's getting late," she says. "If we keep going, we'll make it by nightfall."

They ride in silence, alone with their thoughts, as the rain drenches their hair and breaches their collars to run down their backs. Salty's going is slow and measured on the downhill; every step carries the threat of slipping. The air is filled only with the wet sound of his hooves on the path and the rain drumming on the river and its rocks.

Lotta never liked Stormy Pete—he was a nasty piece of work—but she never wanted him dead. Still, something tells her he was the one to start the rumors about her, the mutterings that spread through the market and the inn: the sick children, the two-headed lambs. Her fault. Did the Council put him up to it? The Judge, feeding him lines to repeat like scripture?

*He don't want horses no more.*

What would Stormy Pete know about the Glimm's desires? It can only have come from Judge Hawthorne. After all, the Judge is its disciple, its vessel on earth. Or so they were told. There was a time she would have believed anything the Judge said. Now she doubts she'll believe a word from that twisted mouth ever again.

"Lotta?" Moss's voice is gentle, as if he's not sure he should break the quiet. "You all right?"

She takes a deep breath and exhales, closing her eyes, bringing herself back to her body—back to Moss—and out of her head. Her hands are wet and stiff, burning with the cold. Her boots are heavy with water.

"Not really, Moss. What about you?"

"No." He shivers against her back. "Cold. More tired than I've ever been."

"It's the shock."

"Yeah," he says. Then: "Can we stop for a bit?"

She's about to protest, to say there's no point—that they either get wet and cold on the way home or they get wet and cold standing still—when he points across the moor. Emerging from the cloud, the stone shepherd's hut they passed on the way.

"There!" he says. "See it? There might be a fireplace, fuel. Dry blankets."

Lotta is doubtful but she steers Salty left. He picks his way over the path, avoiding the swelling bog.

The hut is just as she remembers: squat, with a low turf roof, and a flimsy wooden door warped by time and damp. Moss shoulders it open, and it sighs like an old woman. Inside, it smells of peat smoke, damp earth, and sheep, and something else, sharp, familiar, and not in a good way. But it's dry. Outside, there's a lean-to for Salty to shelter under, and a basin filled with fresh rainwater. Lotta picks some grass for him and finds the paper twist of oats that Fern must have slipped into the food package.

She calls out to Moss, who is still exploring inside. "Blankets?"

He pokes his head out, followed by a hand holding a blanket. It's pocked with holes, but dry. He sneezes.

Lotta rubs Salty down and leaves the blanket draped over his back. He seems happy enough.

Inside, the air is close, but the stone walls hold a different kind of silence than the moor—thick and still. There's no wood, but the hearth is intact, and a stack of peat sits beside it, along with a mug, plate, and spoon, and even a kettle and a jar of nettle tea.

Moss drops to his knees and begins to arrange the pieces of peat in a tower over straw like he's done it a hundred times. His hands tremble.

"Let me," Lotta says softly, kneeling beside him.

Together, they coax a flame from the flint she keeps in her satchel. It's a struggle—her hands are cold, his weaker than usual—but eventually, the straw catches. A dull glow begins to bloom in the darkness.

Under the smoke, that smell again. Is it the tea? She touches the kettle. Warm. Someone has been here. His acrid sweat still lingers in the air. The walls lean in, and she freezes, chokes on the peat smoke.

Stormy Pete.

All she can do is gasp Moss's name. He clasps her forearms, pulls her to the doorway and out into the fresh air. The day is darker than ever.

"The smoke takes some getting used to," he says. "I can put it out."

"No." She stops him. "It's not that. *He* was here." Her hand is on her chest, slowing her breathing. "Just stay here for a moment."

When her heart has slowed, and the cold becomes unbearable, they slip back inside and sit on a low bench, close but not touching. Just breathing. Dripping. Steaming slowly like two wet stones left out in the sun.

"This rain . . . ," says Moss.

"It couldn't have come at a worse time," says Lotta.

"Yes, but . . ."

He seems slow to order his thoughts, too tired to think.

"Is it you?" he says eventually. "Is it because of how you're feeling?"

His words hang like a small cloud in the dim room. Lotta hears the sizzle of the burning peat.

"I'm sorry," he says quickly. "I didn't mean it's your fault or—"

"It's fine," she says. She holds her hands out to the fire. The rain does seem to mirror how she feels inside, just as the storm on the night at the inn and the tidal wave seemed to be brought out by the pull of her anger. And who knows how many other times that she hasn't noticed?

"I think you might be right," she says. She watches the flickering light play across his face. "I don't think I've ever slowed down long enough to feel anything like this," she says. "Until now. But I don't know how to stop it. It's not like I can put a lid on my feelings like on a pot."

"Here." Moss stands up and takes her hands, pulling her to her feet. He starts to unbutton her coat, and she lets him. He hangs it from one of the hooks above the fire. "It'll dry faster this way."

They undress, only as much as they need to, arranging their boots and outer garments around the fire, adding more bricks of peat.

After a while, Moss leans his head against her shoulder and closes his eyes. "Feels like we've been running for years," he murmurs. "Like we've always been running."

Without thinking, she brushes a curl of wet hair from his forehead. His breathing changes rhythm.

They sit in silence, the sound of the rain muffled by the thick stone walls, their wet clothes steaming slightly in the firelight. She wants to speak, to say something about Stormy Pete, or Fern, or the way her throat still burns with what almost happened—how she almost lost him to Pete's knife—but the words won't come.

Instead, she hears herself say, small and brittle, "I'm sorry."

Moss lifts his head, his face close. "For what?"

"I don't know," she says, voice cracking. "For all of it. For dragging you into this. For Hannah. For Stormy Pete. For you and Fern getting hurt. I can't stop thinking—what if I'd just hidden Hannah like you asked? Pete wouldn't have followed us; I wouldn't have put Fern and Esther in danger. *You* in danger . . ."

Her voice fails her. Her chest tightens. The tears come fast and hard. The rain on the roof intensifies, thrumming the air around them.

Moss puts his arms around her and holds her close, solid and warm. Lotta leans into him like she's falling, an ache in her chest.

He strokes her back gently. "It couldn't have happened any other way," he whispers. "You saved me. You saved Hannah. You was brave."

"I don't feel brave," she says against his shoulder. "I just feel broken. I'm scared, Moss. I'm scared of what will happen when we go back. What if nobody listens?"

"You're not broken," he says, pulling back slightly to look at her. "You're still here. So am I. That means something."

Her face is wet and hot and aching. He gently brushes her tears away with his thumb. She lets him. His eyes are so dark, made darker by his pupils expanding in the gloomy room. His eyebrows are crooked with concern.

Then he leans in, and his lips find hers. She closes her eyes and lets it happen, slow and warm. Soft as butter, just as she'd imagined. She kisses him back, the tremble still in her lips, her hands finding the back of his neck, cool and damp.

When they part, she presses her forehead to his. Her breathing is slowing.

"Listen," he says. "The rain. It's getting softer."

Lotta nods, her face still close, her fingers threaded together on his neck.

"It's still cold," she says. "Let's lie down."

Without a word, Moss unhooks her hands, keeping hold of one. He stands unsteadily and pulls her the short distance to the shepherd's only bed—nothing but a mattress of straw, covered by a blanket. Lotta watches him wobble slightly on his feet, her body too tired to do anything but follow, her mind thick with everything they've been through. Moss lets go and lowers himself down. He turns to lie on his side, his body exhaling before he does. "Just for a minute," he mumbles.

Within seconds, his breathing is slow and deep.

Lotta covers him with the last blanket and realizes that she too has never felt such fatigue, deep in her bones. She sways on her feet for a second, then climbs onto the bed beside him. Straw pokes through the blanket and pricks her skin. She sinks so low that she can feel the hard floor against her shoulder, but she doesn't care. She reaches over and draws the blanket over her, molding herself to Moss's warm back, breathing in the scent of him: salt and smoke; a touch of blood.

"I'm glad you're here," she whispers, and closes her eyes.

# 29

**Moss rides in front,** guiding Salty along the path through air smelling of rain and earth that bites at his skin. The rain has stopped, and clouds still hang low, but they've thinned, shot through with a bruise of purple and gold. The sun will soon sink, and they'll be riding in the dark.

"We slept the whole afternoon away," Lotta says, voice rough. "I can't believe it." Her arms squeeze his waist and the warmth of her face presses into his back.

When the sky begins to fade, his eyes adjust quickly—the way they always have—picking out the safe lines, the rise and fall of the track, the silver of standing water. The moor hums under them, alive with frog song and the distant creak of unseen things shifting in the wet earth. They pass no one. The world feels emptied out.

When they reach the bend in the road where they saw the lights in the bog, Moss pulls Salty up.

"Listen," he says.

There's nothing but the popping of the bog and a light wind singing in their ears.

"You think she's out there?" he asks.

Lotta shifts behind him. "The lights are gone. I think she's gone too. Moved on to some other bog."

"Do you think we'll see her again?" He finds himself curious to know more about her, despite the chill he feels when he thinks of her sharp, green-tinged teeth, the way she watched him as though she knew all his secrets. He reckons she could tear him apart with those hands of hers.

"I'd almost guarantee it," says Lotta. "She'll make herself known when she's good and ready."

Moss shivers. They've been riding for hours now, with more distance to come. He taps Salty's sides with his heels and he lurches into a trot, then a canter.

Moss is suddenly homesick, thinking about Mam's turnip stew.

The hamlet is quiet when they arrive. The other blackhouses crouch like sleeping beasts in the dark. Moss is surprised to see a candle burning in the window of his home.

Lotta jerks awake with a startled gasp as he brings Salty to a standstill.

"We're here," he murmurs. "Home. My home."

She says nothing but slides off Salty's back, landing lightly. Moss follows.

"How late is it?" She rubs at her groggy face.

"It's nearly morning, I think."

She nods toward the window. "Are they expecting us?"

"I don't think so." He knows Mam. He knows she worries. The candle is a hopeful gesture. That he will return.

He leads Salty over to Hannah's lean-to, where a net is still stuffed with hay. Lotta sees to him while Moss approaches the house.

The door groans open and once inside, Moss instantly knows that Mam is awake. He feels her sharp breath of fear. Who knows what has happened since he left? For all she knows, he could be a masked thug come to murder her and Stone in their beds.

He calls out softly. "It's me, Mam."

"Moss?" The curtain to her bed flies open and her face is there in the red glow of the peat fire—wild-haired, pale, her cheekbones sharp. He goes to her, and she throws her arms around his neck, sobbing. "I thought you was dead," she says.

Then Stone is beside him, and Moss hooks his arm around his brother's neck, breathing the unwashed smell of him.

"We thought you was gone," Mam says into his shoulder. "Sadie said you went after Hannah, but then you didn't come back. We thought . . ."

"I know," he says. "I'm sorry."

"We thought you was a goner," finishes Stone.

"I'm here," he says. "I'm fine."

A sound comes from outside, a thump. Mam stiffens.

"Wait," says Moss. He extracts himself and steps outside. Lotta stands in the yard, her saddlebag over her shoulder. "Come in," he says.

When they reenter the house, Mam is up with another candle lit, stoking the fire. She is not surprised to see Lotta. "I'm making some tea," she says simply. "Sit down, both of you. You must be exhausted."

Lotta flops gratefully into a chair, and Moss follows suit. Mam pushes some bread toward them, and Moss tears a chunk off for each of them. He's glad for the way the chewing fills the silence. Mam's bread was always hard as leather.

Stone is still in Mam's bed, his eyes bright beads in the gloom, staring at Lotta. "Where's Hannah?" he says suddenly. "What'd you do with her?"

"She's safe, Stone," says Moss. "That's all you need to know."

Stone nods but looks unconvinced.

"What's the price, Mossy?" Mam looks intently from his face to Lotta's.

"Mrs. Smith." They're the first words Lotta has spoken. "I won't lie to you. There's a storm coming."

"Lotta—"

"We have to tell her, Moss. She's a part of this story too."

Moss relents with a nod. He reaches for Lotta's hand, which lies on the table next to the steaming mug of tea that Mam places before her. Mam stares at their joined hands for a moment, then looks away, her lips pressed together.

Together, while Stone listens wide-eyed, they start to tell Mam of what they have seen.

"Jenny's real?" Stone pipes up. "I *knew* it," he says, almost to himself.

They continue. They tell of the mountains, the forest. The cave. Not Stormy Pete, though. Moss can't bring himself to remember just yet.

"Stone," he says. "You can't tell anyone what we're saying now, you hear? It's too dangerous."

"Knowledge *is* danger," says Mam. "It's always been this way, here, in this place. This wretched place. Folk always look the other way."

"Well," says Lotta, "it's also powerful. The Council has controlled us with fear for too long. It doesn't have to be this way. We know things now. We can change them."

"We know too much, you mean." Mam drops her face into her hands. "The Council will react if you do anything. Hannah were just a warning. They won't stand to be challenged."

"Lotta can challenge them, Mam. She has the Glimm on her side."

"Don't," says Lotta. "We don't know that. I don't yet know what it means."

"But you won't let that stop you, will you, girl? I can see it in your eyes."

"No," she says. "I won't."

Mam sighs. "This is all my fault. If I hadn't gone to Temple that day, they wouldn't have taken Hannah, and we wouldn't be sitting here now."

Nobody rushes to contradict her.

"We've seen another way," says Moss. "We don't have to live like this. You taught me that."

"Glimm help us," says Mam ruefully. "But I'm proud of you both. And now you need to get some sleep. Lotta, love, you can have my bed. I won't be able to sleep anymore tonight, and look—" She gestures to the window, where the sky is starting to gray at the horizon. "You can get a couple of hours before the sun is up for good."

Later, after Stone has fallen asleep beside him, and Mam has stepped outside to see to the animals, Moss goes to Lotta, hesitating before pulling back the curtain. She lies on her side, her face cushioned by her hands, which are together as if in prayer. Awake.

"I guess I had enough sleep in the hut," she says.

"And on Salty," he grins.

She smiles back. How long is it since they both smiled?

"I can't sleep now. My stomach's churning, Moss. And my head." She shuffles back, making room for him. He lies down beside her and strokes the hair around her face.

"Me too," he says. "What are we going to do?"

"I have to go back alone, you know that, right? It has to look like I've come and gone by myself. You need to be kept out of this."

It's his stomach's turn to roil. "You can't do this alone."

"I won't be alone. I have my brother, my family. I even have Daphne and Roderick, if that's worth anything. And I hope it is."

"They won't go against their grandfather!"

"Maybe not," she says.

An image comes to him then. A tall figure, standing aloof in his house, not three feet from where they now lie. “Councillor Lewis,” says Moss.

Lotta’s eyebrows rise. “What of him?”

“He warned us about Hannah being taken. He all but told us the lottery is rigged.”

“He’s Daphne’s father,” says Lotta. “But not the Judge’s son. Her mother was Judge Hawthorne’s daughter. She died not long after Daphne was born.”

“I think he might be worth keeping an eye on,” says Moss. “What if he can help?”

Lotta nods but says nothing.

“I agree you should go back alone at first,” he says. “But I *will* find a way to help you. We’re too far in this together now. And once the Judge realizes you’ve lost Hannah . . . well, they could come for us again. We have to be prepared.”

“I won’t let that happen,” she says.

Moss leans in and she doesn’t move away. He brushes her forehead with his lips, and she sighs.

“Are you all right?” he asks.

She nods, then shakes her head. “No. But I don’t think that matters right now.”

Outside, a trilling carries toward them from the moor. “You hear that?” says Moss. “Skylark. It’s always such a hopeful sound, don’t you think?”

“I’m beginning to think that, yes.”

In the dark, behind their curtain, it suddenly feels safe enough to close their eyes and sleep, just for a short while.

# 30

**By the time** she arrives at the village outskirts, the sun is a white orb above her in the dull sky. The sound reaches her first, of music and laughter, shrieking and hollow banging. Another festival? So soon? Have they given up on Hannah and decided to hold the lottery again? A strange cheer hums through the air. Then the breeze shifts, and she smells it: sour eggs, honey, yeast, sweat.

An engagement. A blackening.

She rounds the bend and sees the cart wobbling its way down the high street toward her, drawn by a placid dun mare. The cart bed is thick with straw, and in it sit two figures barely visible beneath layers of flour and dark syrup. Villagers line the route, shouting mock insults and hurling handfuls of flour. The horse barely flinches as an egg explodes against its rump.

Lotta slips off Salty and pulls him into a shadowed alleyway, unnoticed by the villagers intent on their ritual. It's only when the cart jolts past that she sees the groom's face beneath the streaks of molasses.

Roderick.

His mouth is twisted into a grin too wide, his eyes flickering in constant vigilance, watching for projectiles, laughing too loudly. Beside him, his slight, pale-haired bride is slumped forward, her arms covering her face. She winces each time something hits her, even though it's just for show—the ritual is not about inflicting pain. It's hard to believe, but it is supposed to bring luck to a young couple. Now the mess clings to the girl like shame.

Lotta barely has time to ponder why a Councillor's son is taking part in a village ritual meant for bird hunters and farmers' daughters, not the island's elite, when she spots a figure on the other side of the road, staring intently at the couple.

Marten.

While revelers dance around him, he stands rigid as a wall, his mouth a grim line, one arm around a basket. As the cart rolls in front of him, he dips into the basket and pulls out an egg. He draws his arm back and hurls it with all his might. The effort turns his face to an ugly red mask.

The egg hits Roderick square in the nose. His smile vanishes and he turns his head to see where it came from, just as another egg smashes into the side of the girl's head. She cries out, clutching at her ear. Roddy jumps to his feet, wiping egg yolk from his eyes with one rough sackcloth sleeve. He snarls. His teeth are remarkably white against his sticky, eggy, molasses-covered face. He springs from the still-moving cart—the driver is oblivious to the conflict playing out behind him—and shoves Marten full in the chest.

Marten braces against the blow, standing his ground. The two young men glare at each other silently for a moment, then Marten lunges at Roddy and together they fall to the ground.

Meg, Roddy's betrothed, lets out a high-pitched scream and the driver pulls the horse to a halt.

Lotta can't see what happens next; the pair are suddenly engulfed by a crowd. Some people are jeering at them, others cheering. They came out for sport, and sport they shall have.

Leaving Salty standing in the alleyway, Lotta launches herself across the street, ducking a flying egg, and races through a cloud of flour that stings her eyes and lungs.

She elbows her way through the crowd, aware now that people have noticed her, have stopped to turn and stare.

"Marten!" He doesn't hear her. Or he does, and he doesn't care. He rolls on the ground with Roddy, aiming clumsy punches.

Lotta grabs Marten's collar and hauls backward. "Enough!"

His weight resists her, then gives. Roderick scrambles to his feet, panting and furious, his hair streaked with sticky flour.

Shouts of indignation rise from the crowd.

*get him out of here* *sssssssss*

*what's she doing here?* *he's ruined it*

*bloody Salters*

*always ruin things*

The two young men glare at each other, but Lotta notices something else: Roddy's eyes are red, tears starting to wash his cheeks.

Lotta tightens her grip on Marten's arm. "Come on."

He doesn't speak, but he lets her lead him, shoulders rigid, breathing fast. Behind them, Roddy is slapped on the back, helped back onto the cart. Mutterings follow them, buzzing like wasps.

In the alleyway, she sets her jaw as she collects Salty. Without speaking they continue through to the quiet lane beyond, away from the stares of the village and the sharp stench of the ritual. A cheer erupts behind them, muffled by the stone buildings around them.

Marten drags his feet; he seems dazed, disoriented. His eyebrow has split and blood smears across his temple, mixing with Roddy's muck, which has rubbed off on him.

Lotta can bear the silence no longer. "Well, aren't you going to say something?"

They stop in the middle of the empty lane. Salty rests his forehead against her back. The gesture feels oddly reassuring. He's exhausted. She needs to get him home to some comfort; instead, she's mollycoddling her big brother.

Marten wakes up. His head lifts and his shoulders go back. His eyes on her are finally focused. "Glimm, Lotta, where you been? Ma and Da are sick with worry."

"But not you? You got more important worries, I suppose."

He drops his face into his filthy hands, and lows like a bull. "Ah, shit, Lottie. I don't know what happened. Why'd he have to *parade* her around like that? They've never done it before, the Council's kin. Why now?"

His shoulders start to shake, and a guttural sob comes out. He closes his eyes and thumps the side of his face with a dirty, bloodied fist.

"Marten, stop!" Even as she speaks, Lotta sees a shadow ducking into a doorway, a curtain flicker in the cottage they passed. Eyes are everywhere. She never trusted anybody here, and nothing's changed. "Let's just get back to the stables. I'll tell you everything when we get there. And you can explain yourself."

Marten scrubs at his face with his palms and heaves a deep sigh. He is silent for a few seconds, trying to swallow his tears down. Then he nods and follows her.

---

The stable yard is deserted when they arrive. No sign of Gregory, or of Dougie. Lotta feels a stab of guilt at leaving him to care for the horses for days without her. She mixes up some hot mash for Salty and washes his filthy legs; days' worth of bog mud clings to him like a blanket.

Marten tends to his own wounds.

"Things have been bad since you left," he says. "Roddy and me—we're done. He won't even talk to me. Said I have to let him go and not make trouble. That he'll have to make trouble for me in return if I make a fuss."

Lotta grimaces. That's all they need.

Marten finishes washing his pulpy knuckles in a basin and throws the bloodied rag on the ground. He brings his fist to his face and turns it, inspecting the grazes.

"But that's not all." He looks up from his hands and meets her eye. "The new crops are full of blackening. Poison." He stops, presses a hand over his mouth. "Folk are scared. Proper scared. And the Judge, he's been saying it's because we turned our backs on the old ways. That we've angered the Glimm. That the horse running off and you running after were going to make things worse for us all. That we have to pay."

"He means me," Lotta says. "I have to pay."

Marten looks fearful suddenly, as if it's only just occurred to him. He nods. "You. And the horse. That sacrifice were meant to protect us. That's what they think. That you—what were the word he said? *Defiled* it."

How much should she tell him? It's clear that despite his now-swollen eye and his bloodied fists, he still cares for Roddy. And Roddy is Council.

"But *you* know that's not true. That the lottery was rigged. There's so much more to it."

Her head is thick with the images from the cave: the music, the dance, the harmony with the Glimm.

"We've lost something," she says softly, more to herself than to Marten. "Not just the old ways as the Judge talks of them, but something *much* older. The way we were meant to live here, with the land . . . with the Glimm."

Marten's hands drop to his sides. He's finally thinking about something other than himself. "What did you find out there?"

She shakes her head. "I can't say too much just yet. I have to think."

She takes a brush and runs it over Salty's neck. With every stroke, dried dirt rises like smoke in the close air. There's a burning behind her eyes as she looks at Marten.

"The Glimm . . . it's not punishing us. I don't think it's angry. But we've broken something. We've lost our place in the harmony of this land. The blight . . . the crops . . . everything. Maybe it's not a punishment at all, but a sign that we're out of tune with the land, like a song that's gone wrong."

Her hand tightens on the brush, and she feels a strange, aching resolve settle in her chest. "This isn't about turning back to the past. It's about healing it. Finding a new way forward. We've got to fix what's broken, Marten. And that starts with understanding what's truly wrong."

"What are you going to do?"

"I need to find the Glimm."

Marten looks at her, horrified. "But that's suicide, Lotta! The Glimm will tear you to pieces!"

"I don't believe it will," she says quietly.

"And where will you find it? It's like a ghost. Nobody ever sees it, except at sacrifice. You'd have to lure it somehow."

"I don't know," she admits. "But I have to try."

"There's something else," says Marten. "After he said that, about the old ways, Constance tried to talk. But nobody would let her. She knows something they're not letting on."

"Constance?" says Lotta. "But they always listen to her. She's like the mother of the island." After Jenny, she's the oldest person on the island. She's one of the few people who Lotta trusts. She remembers her gentle hands and kindness when Wolf was born.

"Where is the horse, anyway?" asks Marten.

"I lost her. Don't ask me how. I'll tell them it ran into the bog. That Jenny took it."

"Jenny? You really think folk will believe that? She's just a nursery rhyme to them." His stricken face betrays him. He never grew out of the stories. His voice drops to a whisper, as though Jenny herself might overhear. "You found her?"

"Ma told me to, remember?"

"I didn't think she were serious!"

Lotta stares at him, unsmiling. He's been so absorbed by his heartbreak he's not been paying any attention to anything.

"Jenny's not quite what we thought either. I can't explain right now. Go home, Marten. Tell them I'm fine. I'm going to fix things." She glances down, gathering her thoughts. "It's what I need to do now. I'll see you all at Temple tomorrow."

"What about me?" he asks, as if she can possibly give him what he needs. All she can think about now is a hot bath. "And Roddy? I still love him, Lottie, and I know he still loves me."

She surprises herself—and Marten—by pulling him into a hug.

"You've still got us," she murmurs. "You've got your family. And we're going to need you more than ever. Roddy can go to hell."

# 31

**CONSTANCE'S COTTAGE** is as plain as all the others in the village—whitewashed stone, a thatched roof, and small windows that barely let in any light—except for one difference. Her front door is painted a bright yellow, so it can always be found, even on the dullest day.

"Lotta!" The midwife's worn face puckers in surprise. Or shock. She pokes her head out and looks up and down the lane before grabbing Lotta's wrist and pulling her over the threshold.

Inside, the house smells of garlic and onions, wafting from the cauldron boiling above the fire. Sagging chairs are covered with blankets and colorful cushions.

"What happened to you, girl?" She gestures for Lotta to sit, so she does, while Constance shuffles to another chair and lowers herself painfully into it. "Not as spry as I once was," she says, half to herself. She folds her clean white hands on top of her rough skirt and fixes an expectant gaze on Lotta from under her white lace cap. "Well?"

Lotta shifts her weight to try to find a comfortable spot. "I went after the lottery horse," she says. Now is the chance to test her lie. "Jenny took her. In the bog. She lured her in."

Constance just stares at Lotta, taking it in. Her black eyes shine in the light from the fire.

"Do you think I'm stupid, girl?" she whispers, as if someone might be listening. "I birthed you, and I birthed your ma, and I can tell when one of my girls is lying."

Lotta's cheeks are suddenly hot. The old woman is right; Lotta's forgotten about her knack for spotting a fib.

"Well?" Constance says again.

Lotta sniffs and lifts her chin. "Jenny's real. I've seen her. I talked to her."

Constance's lips are pursed but moving, left to right, as though trying to stop any words escaping.

"The lights, in the bog. I saw them, too."

Constance finally lets out a sigh, like steam from a kettle. "Of course she's real," she says. "She's as real as you or me."

"And you know she was just a woman, same as you and me? The island changed her, made her something new. Those stories they tell, those rhymes they sing. They're all made up."

Constance's eyes dart around the room, before she appears to make up her mind and looks back at Lotta. "I know that." Her voice is choked, subdued in the gloom.

"So why do you let people go on believing she's always just been a monster?"

Constance sighs. "You wouldn't understand." She pushes herself up off the arms of her chair and teeters over to the soup pot. Lotta waits while the old woman stirs its contents. Finally, she turns around to look at her. "It's what Jenny would want. She wants to be left alone. She's part of the bog now. She could never return."

"You know her? You know her child was sacrificed. But what I can't understand is, how long ago? Because we haven't always done it, Constance, and I think you know that."

"Shhh!" Constance holds out a finger, too far away to push it across Lotta's lips. "You must be careful, Lotta; you don't know what you're dealing with."

"I do know, Constance. And I think you do too."

Constance wobbles on her feet and Lotta jumps up to grab her elbows, to stop her from a likely fall. "Come on." She guides the midwife over to her chair. She can feel her trembling in her hands.

"You're marked, girl." She allows Lotta to support her as she lowers herself into the chair with a small moan. "You need to be careful. The Council has made sure that every man, woman, and baby is against you right now. They won't listen to a word you say."

Lotta hesitates. *Marked.* Like the lottery horses.

But she needs to know. She kneels beside Constance, so their faces are close. "Tell me. About Jenny. Why the lies about her?"

"You've worked it out for yourself, girl. It wasn't so long ago. But if the villagers think Jenny's always been here, they'll think we have too."

Lotta blinks. Why would they not believe that? There are ancient stones with carvings on them. Barrows, filled with the bones of the ancestors. Paintings in caves.

"I know we have," she says. "I've been to the mountains, Constance! We've been here forever and so has the Glimm! Only we used to live in harmony with it. We didn't have to sacrifice children! Or horses!" A fire ignites in her gut.

"Shh," Constance says again, but this time it's not to stop Lotta from speaking, but to calm her with a cool hand on the wrist. Lotta takes a deep breath in through her nostrils and lowers her head to the old woman's skirts.

"What is happening?" Lotta whispers.

She feels Constance's fingers stroking her dirty hair, snagging on knots and pieces of straw. How long is it since she had a hot bath? The gesture is more comforting even than Moss's touch. She feels the momentous events of the last few days well up in her like a fountain, and then she is sobbing, crying hot, wet tears into the midwife's skirt.

She barely registers what happens next, as Constance leads her to a back room, where there's another fire, and on it an enormous cauldron—the huge pot that Constance keeps on the simmer for emergencies.

"I'm too stiff," she says as she picks up a bucket and gestures to Lotta to fill it from the cauldron and empty it into the waiting bath. Lotta obeys, filling and emptying again and again.

"Now cold," says Constance. There are other buckets, with cold water in them, and Lotta puts these in too.

Constance helps her undress and into the bath. The warm water is unlike anything she's ever felt before, caressing her, so light and thin compared to the last time she was enticed into the water. The bog. She ducks her whole head under.

It's quiet.

The heat wraps around her limbs, loosens the ache from her bones, and presses gently against her eyes. She exhales, and bubbles rise, a soft rattle against her ears. For a moment, it's just peace.

Then a ripple of memory.

Jenny. The bog.

The bathwater thickens into peat-dark blackness. Her body no longer feels light, but heavy with wet clothes and sodden boots. The lights flicker, just beyond her vision, low and patient.

She remembers the weight of Jenny's hands, cool and damp. The feeling of being pulled. How her body had obeyed, not out of fear, but belonging. Her skin hadn't felt the chill. The bog received her like a cradle.

Then the song, rising through her, from the mud and the dark and the very depths of the island itself. It had known her. Recognized something ancient curled inside her, the way roots find each other underground.

And then . . .

"Mammy?"

That voice. A child's voice. *Her* voice. Echoing through bog and memory. The rope at her waist. The salt wind in her mouth. A shiver of bone. Hazel's scream. The splash.

It all comes back in a single breath held too long.

She jerks upward from the bath, gasping.

"I'm here," says a voice, and there's a reassuring hand on her arm. Constance sits on a low stool beside her, a cake of soap and a knitted cloth in her hand. A candle burns low on another stool beside her.

"You've seen some things, I can tell," she says. "Look at these bruises. Who did this to you?"

Lotta, back now in the low-ceilinged room at the rear of the midwife's house, catches a glimpse of the darkening sky outside.

She shakes her head, and accepts the soap, begins to run it over her aching body. She can't tell Constance about Stormy Pete. Not yet.

"Here," Constance grabs the soap off her and lathers it up, making bubbles that she runs through Lotta's hair.

"I used to bathe you when you were just a babe, you know. Once when your ma got sick, so sick, and couldn't look after you. You came out screaming and thrashing when you were born like you were being chased by a monster. Poor Marten thought his ma had birthed a wild cat for a sister."

The unspoken hangs between them. The lottery. What happened to her. What she survived.

"I've watched you, you know." Constance continues rubbing at Lotta's scalp, making it tingle. "Holding the world at bay. That kind of thing takes its toll on a soul. Here."

She stops rubbing and hands Lotta the soap. Then she picks up a bucket and dips it into the now mushroom-colored water and pours it over Lotta's head. Lotta draws in her limbs, hugging her knees and hunching her shoulders against the watery assault.

"One more." Constance repeats the motion.

The world blurs for a moment before Lotta wipes the soapy water from her eyes in time to see Constance rubbing at her wrists from the effort.

"Thank you," says Lotta. "You must feel like all the islanders are your children."

"Sometimes." A look of sorrow comes over her. "It's why I'm grateful to you for what happened. With the Glimm. I don't think I could have borne another senseless death of a child. I felt each one, here." Her hand, roped with veins, with swollen, red knuckles, strokes her chest.

Lotta shivers. The water is too cold now. It makes her bold. "And yet, you let the Council feed them to the Glimm."

Constance's face shows no emotions as she stares at the candle's reflection in the window, but Lotta can tell that, behind her eyes, she is fighting them. As she's had to do for years.

"I was told it was necessary," she says finally.

"And would you have fed your own child to the Glimm, Constance, if you had one? Maybe you don't feel that way about the islanders after all." Lotta sees the words are wounding the old woman. Good. Let her suffer.

"I *did* have a daughter."

Lotta recoils. This, she was *not* expecting. "And was she sacrificed?"

Constance is quiet for a moment, as if losing herself in a memory. "No, but my granddaughter was. Her name was drawn in the lottery, and there wasn't a damn thing I could do about it." She pauses. When she speaks, she won't meet Lotta's eyes. "Freya was her name."

The bath is suddenly unbearably icy. For a moment, in the candlelight, the water appears to turn black, then back to dirty brown, and the cold penetrates to Lotta's bones. She grips the sides of the bath and hauls herself up, shivering. Constance offers her a blanket absently, still lost in thought, and a hand to help Lotta step down onto the cold slate floor. Lotta takes them both.

"I know that name," she says. "That was the name of Jenny's daughter."

"Yes."

"Are you telling me that Jenny is your *daughter*?"

The room spins. Jenny the witch. Jenny the bog hag. *Lock up your children. Don't whistle at night. She'll wear your skin like a coat.*

"Tilly was her name." The words seem to stick in her throat. She lets out a wheezy cough. "Matilda. Not Jenny."

Still she won't meet Lotta's eye.

"Tilly refused the rewards the Council offered her, and she tried to physically intervene in the ceremony. Her own husband rejected her. I tried to talk to her, but she was so far gone into her grief she didn't recognize me. She became a problem for the Council—a reminder to everyone of what a terrible toll the sacrifice could have on a family, so they banished her as a warning to others. Told everyone to forget her. The island took her. I thought she was dead—drowned in the bog—until the rumors started about her, about a creature that haunted the moors. The Council indulged it. And nobody tried to defy them after that."

"Until the hidelings," says Lotta.

"Until the hidelings," Constance agrees. "And look what happened to them."

Lotta thinks of Jenny, her body one with the peat. The grief and loneliness she's had to endure.

"Constance," she says. "Do you believe the Glimm required sacrifice?"

Constance pauses, thinking.

"I did at first. But I hated it, and I wanted it to stop. And now I'm not so sure that it was ever needed."

"But the Council respects you, doesn't it? Why couldn't they listen to you and stop sending children to their death?"

Now she looks up, eyes sharp. "You don't understand. Judge

Hawthorne's father, and his father before him, were powerful men. And what would happen to all those new babies being born, if I was done away with?"

"Constance." Lotta senses the truth hovering around the old woman like the lights in the bog. "You have to tell me."

It's the midwife's turn for tears now. She wrings the knitted cloth over and over, water running down her sleeves and onto her skirt.

Lotta takes it off her and drops it into the bath. "Come on, we need to get warm."

They move back into the sitting room and Constance sits while Lotta, still clutching the blanket around her, puts more peat and sticks on the fire. Then she settles back in her chair and waits.

Constance stares into the flames, her hands trembling slightly as they stroke her damp skirt. The room feels tiny, with the fire's crackle the only sound between them.

"The thing you need to know, Lotta my love, is that the island wasn't always like this."

"I know that," says Lotta. "I told you."

"Let me speak!"

Lotta flinches at the fierce tone. She nods.

"The island has been inhabited for thousands of years. That is true. But not by us. Not by us. The original inhabitants fled years ago. Possibly hundreds of years. I am not from here, Lotta. I was brought here, by Judge Hawthorne the elder—our Judge's grandfather—when our Judge and I were just children, much younger than you, some eighty years ago. He put together a group of around fifty followers—criminals and outcasts many of them, though I didn't know it at the time—and loaded them onto a boat. Brought them here, thinking they could start fresh."

The weight of her words makes blood thrum in Lotta's ears. It's too much. She's going to be sick.

"Those fifty were the first to call themselves the island's people,"

Constance continues. "They created our history, our lore. But they didn't come to build a community where everyone is equal. They came to hide from a world that had turned against them for their beliefs. And to make sure their secrets stayed buried."

It all makes so much sense.

"There'd been rumors of an island where the inhabitants lived in peace and harmony with a creature that could only be described as a god, such was its power. The people had left long ago, driven out most likely by the same people who burned the forests to the ground. Those original survivors brought back stories that passed into myth. But Judge Hawthorne believed the Glimm was real, and he convinced others to join him. To worship. We lived in a place where there was only one invisible God, and to worship anything else was blasphemy. But he didn't care what the world believed. He wanted to go to a place where his god could be seen. Where his faith wouldn't be blasphemous. Where he could answer to no person or society. And most importantly, where he had absolute power. He set out to find the Glimm."

Constance pauses, her eyes reflecting the firelight. Lotta sits still, not daring to move, waiting for the next piece of the tale to fall.

"The maps of the world said, 'Here be monsters,' but Hawthorne saw it differently. He believed he could start a new life here. Away from everyone. Away from the laws and the God of the outside world. A place where *he* could be the king."

Lotta leans forward, giving the midwife a hard stare. Hiding her true feelings. "I can't believe all this, Constance. How could you have kept this from everybody for so long?"

"I didn't know any better, child. I followed my parents to a better life."

She continues talking, and Lotta listens. They brought livestock with them, but found there were already herds of deer, goats, and sheep, which had been roaming wild for who knows how long. At first the information Lotta is hearing is like a crushing weight on her shoulders. But gradually, the weight lifts. She realizes what this is, what

Constance is imparting: It's knowledge. And knowledge is power.

"Why are you telling me all this now?" she asks.

Constance sighs, for perhaps the hundredth time. "Because I'm tired, and I'm ill. I can't keep it in any longer. The Council has us believing there is nothing out there but monsters waiting to crush any boats we've built. That this island is the whole inhabited world. And I'm scared, Lotta. I'm scared that they're going to bring back the killings."

"But why the sacrifice?" *This is it*, she thinks.

Constance doesn't speak for a long time. The fire crackles, and Lotta can hear her own ragged breath, waiting.

Finally, the old woman says, almost too softly to hear: "Because the Glimm saved us once."

Lotta blinks. "Saved?"

Constance nods, slowly. "When we first came, we were starving. Lost. The voyage had wrecked half our stores. We didn't understand the land, not really. Some of the first winters—Glimm help us—we nearly died. Then one of us went missing. A child. There weren't many of us then. He vanished into the bog. And that spring . . . the sun came. The river ran full of fish. Deer came down from the mountains. The barley took root. The men said it was a miracle. The Judge said it was the Glimm."

She pauses, eyes glassy. Her voice trembles.

"So the next time food ran low again . . . another child died. Of sickness this time."

"No," Lotta whispers.

"And when that worked too, they built a story around it. A system. A rite. The Judge said it was ancient. That we were just continuing what the first people must've done. But he had no proof, Lotta. No proof at all. Just results. And fear. Of course, the Council's children were never included."

Constance wipes her nose on her sleeve.

“But that wasn’t all,” she continues, voice tightening. “People had started grumbling. Fighting. Some wanted to leave, others questioned the Judge’s authority. But after the first official sacrifice, that stopped. They saw the Glimm for the first time. Fear made them obedient. Grief made them quiet. The ritual didn’t just bring food, Lotta. It brought order.”

“But why does everybody think the sacrifice has been going on since the beginning of time?” asks Lotta. She is shaken to her core by Constance’s confession; yet somehow, she’s not surprised by it.

“The Council needed to ground it in ancient tradition and fear so that future islanders wouldn’t question it. They invented stories about what would happen if a child wasn’t sacrificed. They didn’t have to stretch the truth too much. Every three years brought a cycle of decay that was broken each time the Glimm appeared and took the child offered. I believed it, and so did my parents. The Judge and I are the last living people who came on that boat. We’re the only ones who know the truth.”

“So, what, they made a covenant? A pact?”

“Yes. All the original settlers agreed to lie. To tell the next generation that we had always been here. It didn’t take long. A desperate act became tradition. Then tradition became lore. And soon, the fear of breaking the pattern became more powerful than the truth ever could be. We’d seen the evidence with our own eyes. That the Glimm wanted children. Or so we thought. Until . . .”

“Until I came along.”

“It was a relief, Lotta, truly. Except the horses were killed yearly, just to be safe.”

Lotta can barely breathe. “But what if the Glimm never wanted it? What if there’s another way? A better way? That doesn’t just keep us alive, but helps us to really thrive?”

Constance’s voice is barely audible. “Then we’ve been doing something terrible for nigh on seventy years . . . for no reason at all.”

"I've been to the Black Mountains, Constance. Do you know what's there? It's how the whole island could be, if we did things right."

"I don't, and I don't care to know." Constance's eyes shine in the gloom. "If you're right, child, I fear it will break me."

# 32

**Lotta stumbles home** in the dark, dazed, back to the Manor House and her tiny rooms above the stables. By now, with Salty in the stable, Dougie will realize she has returned, and he's probably alerted Gregory, who has probably alerted the whole house. Let them. Her head and heart are so heavy with everything she's learned—about Jenny and Constance, a ship on the ocean—that she cares little for what else can happen tonight. But most of all she can't stop thinking about all those children. All those little lives, lost.

All that grief.

And beneath it all, the Glimm. The island hums under her feet with its pain.

She wishes Moss were here. Just to put his arms around her and tell her that everything will be all right. She could never have known, even a week ago, that meeting him would upend her life so. That she would ever consider having feelings for *anyone*, let alone a hideling.

No, not a hideling. An exile.

Something needs to change.

Inside the stable, she lights a lantern. Salty senses her near and nickers softly. She hangs the lantern on a hook and lets herself into his stall. He accepts the piece of carrot she offers and lets her run her fingers through his mane, which has been recently brushed. Not by her.

She makes soft wordless noises to him. A tune that forms in her throat. Without Hannah, the Council will choose another horse. If they want to punish her, they will choose Salty.

Lotta leans her forehead against his and breathes him in: the hay, the sweat, the warm, grassy musk of his coat. It reminds her of Hazel. A smell like innocence. Like safety. It makes her chest ache.

"I can't protect you," she whispers. "Not from them."

Salty flicks an ear. His body is steady and sure against hers.

Footsteps crunch in the yard outside. Light moves through the stable door.

Lotta steps back, hand on the latch of the stall, heart thudding.

"Lotta?" comes a voice. Cautious, uncertain. "It's me."

She lets out a slow breath. "In here, Daphne."

Lotta straightens up as Daphne steps into the stable, a shawl pulled tight around her shoulders. Her hair is loose, as though she's come from bed, the blond curls darkened by mist. Her eyes flick to Salty, then to Lotta herself, taking in the still-damp hair, the red eyes, the ruined boots.

"I saw the light," she says. "I thought maybe you were a ghost."

Lotta manages a weak smile. "Not yet."

Daphne takes a few tentative steps forward, the clip of her dainty boots muffled by straw. Then she crosses the space between them and throws her arms around Lotta, catching her off guard. The hug is rough, urgent. She smells of lavender and clean skin, the kind that never attracts muck and sweat. Lotta's suddenly grateful for Constance's bath, and the clean shirt she gave her.

"Roddy told me you were back," Daphne whispers against her

shoulder. "I thought you'd gone for good. Dead, or taken, or—"

"I know."

Daphne pulls back and looks into her eyes, searching. "They said you'd run away. That you'd taken that lottery horse and vanished onto the moors with a boy. That you weren't ever coming back. But I *knew* you wouldn't just leave me."

"I didn't. Where would I go?"

Daphne pulls her shawl tighter. "Where is it? The horse."

Lotta doesn't answer.

"And the boy? Who was he?"

"You wouldn't understand." She's not going to give Moss up, not to anyone.

Daphne shakes her head. "You think you've saved that horse," she says, "but you've just condemned another. The sacrifice will still go ahead. It doesn't matter which horse it is, really. You can't stop it from happening."

The words land like a stone in Lotta's stomach.

She turns to Salty, running a hand down his warm neck. "I know."

Daphne's eyes linger on Salty, the way they always did when Lotta rode him. "Have you seen Marten?"

"Yes," says Lotta. "At the blackening. Why was Roddy of all people having a blackening?"

"It was Papa's idea," sniffs Daphne. "He said it would make the villagers feel more warmly toward him. You know. So he's one of them. His betrothed, Meg—she was a villager once, remember? Imagine giving up your daughter like that, for a cow and a few goats!"

"Of course," Lotta says. "But why does your father suddenly want a Councillor's son to be a part of the village? You've always set yourselves apart. I thought that was the point."

"I know," says Daphne. "I thought it was daft. Then Roddy came back stinking and crying. He said Marten attacked him. Did you know?"

"I was there. I pulled Marten off him."

"What was that all about?"

"Daphne, you know perfectly well what that was about." Lotta casts her a stern look. "He's hurting."

Daphne shrugs. "He knew what he was letting himself in for. He can't expect to be with a Councillor's son. Roddy was only with him for a bit of fun."

"Can't expect it even now that Roddy's mixing with the plain folk?" Lotta makes her voice light, with a small chuckle she doesn't feel.

"You can laugh all you want, but that's right. Not even then. You must know that. Anyway, it was a disaster. I don't think they'll try that again. Poor Meg's covered in bruises. Who knew eggs could hurt so much? I don't think Marten was the only one pelting them too hard."

Lotta turns and gestures toward Salty. "Do you still want him?"

Daphne stops smiling. "What do you mean?"

"You can have him. I don't need him anymore. I've done all the training I can with him. He's perfect for you now." She has sapped all care from her voice, drawing on her old self.

Daphne's eyes narrow. "He's not actually yours to give, you know. I could have taken him anytime, but I saw how much he meant to you. Oh, you tried to hide it, I know. Have you even given him a name yet?"

"I have, actually. Wolf named him. Salty."

Daphne can't help herself; she lets out a laugh. Unlike Lotta's, it's bright in the darkened stall. She's still the carefree girl who doesn't have to think about much.

"That's a name for a stubby island pony, not a fine Council horse. I'll call him something else."

Lotta looks away. None of this is easy. It's just a name.

"Suit yourself," she says, landing a swift, nonchalant pat on Salty's rump. "It's for his own protection. You said yourself that they'll just take another horse for the sacrifice. And if they're out to punish me for losing that other horse, they'll take the one that matters to me the most. But if he's yours, they won't dare."

"That's not right."

"Nothing about this is right." Lotta runs her hand along Salty's flank, feeling the warmth of him, memorizing it. "He doesn't deserve to be caught up in this."

Daphne watches her. "Caught up in what?" Her voice is skeptical, as though thinking to herself *There she goes again.* "The lottery?"

"The lottery is rigged, you know that, don't you?"

Daphne snorts. "What do you mean, rigged?"

"They use it as punishment. The Council."

"Be very careful what you say next." Daphne's voice has taken on a menacing tone. It stops Lotta in her tracks. What is she thinking? Daphne is Council.

"Forget it," says Lotta. "Just take Salty. Tell everyone he's yours. Just don't say I asked you to. Please."

Daphne's expression is stony, but she nods. "Fine. I'll have him. Just until it's safe." The corners of her mouth betray her with a tiny smile.

"Thank you."

Daphne steps forward and strokes Salty's face gently. Lotta watches her for a moment, the ease of her touch, her clean, smooth hands with unbroken nails, the way the horse responds. It feels like a small betrayal. But necessary.

"Be careful, Lotta. Something's brewing. The Judge was furious when he heard that Marten was causing trouble. It's a good thing Marten already quit, or he'd be out of a job for certain. And I think you're caught up in it all too. The villagers are still gossiping about you. There was talk of sending someone out to bring you back."

Lotta stiffens. "But they didn't need to do that in the end, did they? Here I am."

"No," says Daphne. "I guess not. But I'm worried about what my grandfather will do. They say the Glimm is unhappy. And they all think you're the one who's caused it, somehow."

Lotta meets her gaze. "Do you think that too?"

Daphne sighs. "I'm not stupid enough to pick a side in public."

"But in private?"

"In private," Daphne says, after a pause, "I'm taking your damn horse. And hoping I don't regret it."

Lotta half smiles. "You won't. He likes you."

"I'm not you, though," Daphne mutters.

"I'll ask to see the Judge tomorrow," says Lotta. "I'll tell him I lost the horse and he'll have to pick another. It can't be Salty if you're out riding him."

"It's Temple tomorrow, remember? The whole town will be there. It's the day before the sacrifice."

"Of course," says Lotta.

"Be careful."

"I will."

Daphne unlatches the stall door and backs out. "This doesn't mean we're friends, you know."

"Glimm forbid."

And then she's gone. Lotta examines her hands. They're covered in small cuts, with dirt embedded in them. Her nails will never be clean again. She doesn't care. She throws her arms around Salty's neck and buries her face in his mane one last time.

# 33

**MOSS'S BACK ACHES.** He's hauled baskets full of peat back to the house in the moonlight. Without Hannah, he had better get used to it. A streak of light signals the start of the day as he stacks his last load.

"Moss, love," his mother calls from the doorway. "Come and get your porridge."

"It's light soon," he says, "and there's no clouds. I should keep going."

Mam looks as though she's about to reply, when she cocks her head. Hoofbeats drift over the moor, coming their way. Is it Lotta? Returning so soon? His stomach lifts at the thought of seeing her. He looks down at his filthy hands, his sweat-soaked shirt . . . but she has seen him at his worst. There are more important things at stake than hygiene.

He couldn't stop thinking about her yesterday, imagining the worst—Lotta imprisoned, punished, paraded through the streets—and Mam had to stop him from running after her when she left.

"She knows what she's doing," Mam said. "She got the measure of the village far more than you. You'll just blunder in there and ruin things."

Moss's jaw tightened. If only Mam had seen him, out on the moors, acting against all the fears she'd brought him up with, she wouldn't underestimate him. But he knew she was right. Better to stay and wait for the call.

He drops the empty basket, ready for whatever comes next.

But it's not her.

It's a young man with ruddy cheeks and hair cut close to his skull. He's riding a Council horse, a fiery black gelding billowing steam from its nostrils in the crisp morning air.

He hauls on the reins and the horse skids to a halt on stiff legs, tossing its head.

"Smiths! You're to report to the Temple with the rest of the townsfolk at noon. The Judge got an important announcement to make and everyone on the island needs to hear it. Even you." He screws his face up and spits on the ground as if the very act of speaking to them tastes foul.

A fist of fear grips Moss's gut. Mam clutches his arm, her sharp nails digging in.

The man has barely rested a beat before he hauls on the reins again, turning the horse's head back in the direction of Sadie's.

"Everyone?" calls Moss. "All the exiled folk, too?" He's hoping Sadie and the others might be spared from whatever is coming.

"They been told," the man yells. "Every man, woman, and child. Hidelings. Everyone!" Then he's galloping away.

"Oh, Moss, this can't be good," says Mam. She backs into the house, finds a chair with her outstretched hand, and sits, all while keeping an eye on his face.

Moss follows her in.

"Who were that?" Stone appears at the door, ruddy-faced and puffing.

"Someone from the village. We've been summoned to Temple."

Stone's face lights up, but when he sees his mother's downcast expression, he frowns. "I thought that's what you wanted, Mam. For us to be welcome at Temple. In't that what everything we've done's for? Hannah and the like?"

Mam and Moss exchange glances.

"We don't trust the Council, Stone," says Moss. "They've got teeth. Everything comes at a price, with them."

"What if they're punishing us for Hannah running away?" says Mam.

"Then why'd they need everyone to come?" says Moss. "The whole bleedin' island?"

"A public shaming?" Her face twists in anguish. The crease between her eyebrows deepens. "Stone, love, go outside and feed the chooks, will you? Moss and I need to talk."

Stone's face is grim, but he doesn't argue. Once he's gone, Mam turns back to Moss. Her voice drops to a whisper. "What if they want to bring back the child sacrifice? You *know* the hidelings will be the first to go. They'll want Stone. Or one of the other young ones."

Moss slumps in his chair. "So what do we do?"

Mam holds her head up. "We put on our best clothes. We walk over to Sadie's, and we all get in the cart and go to Temple. We show them that we belong there."

Moss groans. "Mam, we don't belong there, and we don't *want* to belong there. Trust me."

"You want to make changes, Moss? You and Lotta? This is your chance."

Moss's gut churns. But she is right. It's now or never.

# 34

"Lotta! Open up!"

The man's voice, followed by a loud thudding that rattles the door, jerks her awake. She blinks, adrift, then sees the small table and single chair, candle stubs burnt right down, the thin green curtain letting in a smudge of morning light. She's home. As much as a room above a stable can be called home. And she has slept too late.

The chill air reminds her that she collapsed into bed last night without lighting the fire. Instead, she shivered, fully clothed, under her blanket until she fell asleep.

"Lottie, please!"

*Ma.*

She jumps out of bed and crosses the room in one stride. The key grinds in the lock. She wasn't taking any chances last night with uninvited visitors.

Her parents' anxious faces greet her. Shona falls forward into the room and wraps her in a tight embrace. "Oh, thank Glimm," she says. "We thought you was dead."

Old habits take over; Lotta stands stiffly but doesn't recoil, at least.

"It's Marten, love," says her father. "They've taken him."

"Arrested!" cries her mother. "For attacking a Councillor's son!"

"Roddy? But surely he wouldn't have him arrested!"

"Well, it's either him, or Lewis, or one of the others. Those nasty men with sacks for faces took him."

"Where've they taken him?" It wasn't too many days ago that Marten was one of those faceless thugs. How much has changed, so quickly. She pulls on her jacket and picks up her boots. "And how did you get in?"

"The little boy let us in the gate. He's down there now with that girl, getting that gray horse of yours ready."

Dougie. She'll have to remember to thank him somehow.

Downstairs, Dougie is mucking out a stall in the empty stables.

"You decide to come back, did ya?" He puts aside the broom. His small face is smudged and set in a grimace. He looks older, sterner than the nervous boy she knows.

"Dougie—"

"Well, you're too late. I've done saddled all the horses and they've all ridden out, the whole family. Daphne were late. Didn't expect her to want the gray. Silver, she called him. They've gone to the village. There's a town meeting in the Temple."

"I'm sorry, I—"

"Don't matter." He sniffs. "I can manage on my own. Have done for days. Maybe they should make *me* head groom."

Is he turning against her now as well? Sweet Dougie?

"Come on." Shona tugs at her sleeve. "We've got the cart."

"But Marten," she says, and turns to Dougie, who has resumed sweeping violently, as though the straw and horse dung itself has betrayed him. "Did you see anything, Dougie? Do you know where they took him?"

He just shakes his head, concentrating on the task at hand like it's the most important job in the world.

Lotta allows herself to be led away. Outside the gate, Dobby, the sturdy dun gelding, stands with the Salters' cart; inside it, a small figure jumps up and down.

"Lottie!" Wolf climbs down and runs at her. She picks him up and holds him tight.

"They took Marten," he cries. "Men came."

"I know, darling," she says. "We're going to the Temple to find out what they've done with him."

∞

As they leave through the gate, two men in masks approach them on horses. Lotta recognizes the horses from the Judge's own herd.

"Lotta Salter," says one, forcing his voice down, unnaturally deep. "We're to escort you to Temple. Make sure you don't run off again."

Lotta can't help herself. "Hark at you, Ash Carter, trying to make your voice all dark and mysterious." She laughs, laying on extra scorn.

The boy says nothing, but his stocky companion snorts.

"Don't think I don't know it's you under there, Eddie; I can tell by your freckled hands. You look ridiculous. Everybody's laughing at you, you know."

That does the trick. Eddie rips his mask off. His face is hot underneath, with sweat dampening his temples. His thin eyebrows press down in annoyance, and he stares straight ahead, his blocky jaw set.

"See?" says Lotta. "Isn't that better?"

Her mother lays a warning hand on her arm but says nothing. Wolf has a blanket pressed to his face to stop himself laughing.

At the Temple, the Councillors and their families are gathered off to one side. There's no sign of the Judge, who will be inside, getting his robes on. Lotta sees Daphne, still on Salty, who is nervous in the crowd—he tosses his head uncontrollably. Daphne jerks on the reins, which only makes it worse.

*Get off him*, thinks Lotta. *Lead him away to a quiet spot.*

Too late. Daphne raises her riding whip and brings it down hard on Salty's rump, once, twice. Salty kicks out in fear, striking one of the other horses. Finally, Daphne, red-faced and close to tears, dismounts and leads Salty away to tether him by himself.

Lotta feels like crying herself. What was she thinking, leaving Salty in Daphne's care? It's too late now.

"Oi," says Eddie, grabbing Lotta's arm. "In there, *now.*"

Lotta shakes him off.

"There's no need for that, young man," says Lotta's father. "Can't you see she's going with you?"

Inside, the Temple is packed. Lotta's family manage to persuade a dour farmer and his family to move along to let them in, but when Lotta tries to join them, Eddie's hand is back on her arm. He's replaced his mask as well.

"Not you," he says. "You're coming with us. You got some explaining to do." He marches her up toward the front, then shoves her roughly into a pew, three rows from the platform. Daphne passes her on the way to the very front and shoots her a disappointed, quizzical look.

*I could do the same to you*, thinks Lotta.

She turns to look down the aisle, just in time for an unexpected sight: Moss enters the Temple, along with his mother and brother, and other people she hasn't seen before, including a girl who blends into the shadows behind Moss. Exiles. They shuffle nervously into the very back row, herded like livestock.

What are they doing here? Nobody is throwing them out, so they must have been summoned. It should give her hope; instead, it gives her a bad feeling.

Moss is finally wearing a jacket that fits, his hair brushed flat. The sight of him stirs something tender and aching in her. When his eyes find hers, they say it all. He's bewildered to be here, among villagers who barely tolerate his kind. But he's here. For her.

A murmur rises from the back pews, low and disbelieving. The villagers have spotted the exiles too. The murmurs sharpen into angry grumbles, then shouts, as three village men stand and loom over the newcomers.

Before the moment can erupt, Councillor Lewis rises from his seat on the platform. He strides down the aisle, his black coat flaring behind him, radiating control.

"They have been commanded to attend," he barks. "Sit down, all of you!"

The villagers mutter some more but do as they're told.

Just before Lotta turns back, she catches someone staring at her. It's Rona, Stormy Pete's wife. Lotta's stomach flips and her face throbs with sudden heat. She turns quickly, sure that Rona has seen right into her.

She doesn't have time to dwell on the thought; at that moment the Judge emerges from behind the altar, robed in heavy black embroidered with silver thread that glitters like frost. His muttonchops are neatly combed. His blue irises are stark against the red-veined whites of his eyes.

He steps onto the pulpit. The carved stone Glimm has always given him such authority; now that Lotta knows the truth, it mocks him. A farce.

"May the light of the Glimm fall upon you, good people of Brack."

The answer comes weakly. *"And upon you, as bright as the sun."*

The Judge's face falters—he was not expecting such a lack of gusto—but then hardens. "I call upon Lotta Salter to take the platform."

Lotta's fists tighten involuntarily. Butcher John, Eddie's father, shoves her in the ribs with one elbow, connecting with one of her many bruises. "You heard him, girl," he hisses.

A blast of nausea shoots through her. Clutching her side, she rises slowly. The hush in the Temple is unbearable. She feels all eyes on her as she ascends the stone steps. The Judge points her to the podium at the opposite end of the platform.

She mounts it and turns to face the congregation. She searches the crowd for her family. Her mother and father are seated where she left them, stiff and pale. Wolf sits between them, legs swinging, eyes wide. When he sees her, he lifts a hand, but no one else moves. Marten is nowhere to be seen. Where is he?

A murmur breaks out as people whisper to each other behind their hands, including Daphne and her friends. Roderick sits rigid, staring at her. His face is unreadable, apart from his purple, swollen eye and the cut on the bridge of his nose.

The Judge raises a hand. The crowd quiets.

"People of the Glimm," he says, voice echoing. "You've heard the rumors. The sacrifice horse is gone."

A low gasp, followed by mutters. Lotta's spine straightens.

The Judge turns to her. "Lotta Salter. You were the last to see the animal. Tell us what happened."

Her mouth is dry. The sea of faces before her is curious and suspicious. The stench of sweat pricks her nose—the smell of fear.

Her throat is suddenly murky. She coughs. "I went after it," she says. "But it had a head start. I chased it for two days." She looks at the Judge. "I know how important the horse was. I did everything I could. But you know those moors. You know how boggy they are. There's a reason we don't go that way."

Louder murmurs.

"I found the horse eventually. It had got lost in the bog. It wasn't alone."

She is met with silence. Anticipation.

She speaks up, and her voice cuts through the air, clear and certain. "Jenny Green took it."

There's a collective gasp from the congregation, laced with mutters of skepticism and disbelief.

"She's real?" someone cries.

"Jenny from the rhymes?"

"She's just a story!"

"She lured the horse into the bog," Lotta continues. "I tried to stop her. But it was like the land itself pulled it down. I think . . . I think she was trying to send a message."

The room erupts. Some are laughing, some shouting. A few are crying.

A woman's voice from the back. It's fish-faced Rona. "Jenny is trying to stop the sacrifice. She's *trying* to anger the Glimm!"

"But why?" shouts another.

"Revenge!" someone calls.

The Judge raises his hand again. The room calms. But before he can speak, Rona stands up.

"Lotta, tell me, did you see my Pete? Only he went looking for you, and he hasn't come home. You don't think . . . ?"

The Judge clamps his mouth shut, watching Lotta closely, waiting to hear what she'll say. Lotta hesitates. One wrong word, and it could all fall apart. She could easily say she saw Pete go into the bog—it would take care of all her problems. But it might stretch credibility just too far.

"I'm sorry, Rona," she says. "I don't know where he is." Not a lie. But not quite the truth.

Rona nods, a mixture of fear and relief on her face, and sits.

"Very well," says the Judge. "Then the sacrifice has been taken from us. Not by theft, nor by treason, but by the island itself."

"By Jenny!" a man barks out.

The children in the congregation shrink closer to their mothers.

"Choose another horse!" yells Butcher John. "Take *her* horse! That gray one she's always riding."

The Judge ignores him.

"Good people of Brack, it's clear that a horse will no longer satisfy the Glimm. This winter has been the harshest we've had in a lifetime. Only last week we heard testimony from you all of how hard your lives have become."

*Because of the Council*, thinks Lotta. *Not because of the Glimm.*

"That is why the Council has convened. A new offering must be made. One worthy of restoring balance."

Lotta's breath catches.

He won't.

He can't.

"There will be no need for a new lottery," the Judge says. "The Glimm has already chosen. A number was selected. A child has been called."

Lotta feels the world rumble beneath her feet. She grips the podium to stay upright. Others in the Temple have noticed—their eyes search the floor, uneasy.

"No," she whispers.

The Judge's voice rings out. "The number was thirty-two. Wolf Salter. Chosen by the Glimm. The sacrifice will take place at dawn."

# 35

**Rows ahead of Moss,** a woman screams. The sound is terrifying. Beside him, his mother grabs his hand, and that of his brother, and squeezes with all her might. Her eyes are tightly closed, tears pushed from their corners.

"Thank Glimm," she whispers.

"Mam!" says Moss. "How can you say that? It's Lotta's brother."

And Hannah's lottery number.

He stands up, shaking the hand off. All around him is chaos. Villagers are on their feet. Some of them are crying, clinging to their children, while others are whistling and clapping. Through it all, he sees Lotta sway at the podium, blinking. Then she leans forward and addresses the Judge at the top of her lungs.

"You're lying! This isn't the Glimm's will, this is *yours*!"

The Judge looks around for his thugs and gestures with his head for them to come and deal with her. Lotta turns her voice to the room.

"They've been lying to you!" she shouts. "For years! The Glimm doesn't want children, it wants music!"

Moss moves farther up the aisle as some people quieten to listen to her, but others shout insults that jumble together in the charged air.

*shut it, Lotta Salter* *what if she's right?*

*music?* *making excuses to save her brother*

*should've been you* *crazy*

*too old* *don't listen to her*

Lotta tries again. "You're being manipulated! It doesn't *want* human sacrifice."

"Lotta Salter." The Judge points at her. "If you continue to blaspheme in our Temple, you will be imprisoned alongside your brother!"

Lotta is undeterred. It's as though she has nothing left to lose. "You're feeding the Glimm your cruelty and calling it faith! You think this will fix your island? It won't! It won't!"

By now, the members of the Council are on their feet, looking alarmed. As he reaches the front, Moss makes eye contact with Lewis; the Councillor looks quickly away. Lotta looks like she might expire. She bends over, clutching her chest, her face red and glistening with sweat.

Moss reaches her before the thugs do. He stands behind her and puts both hands on her arms, gently pulling her back from the podium. Lotta is stiff, her gaze fixed on something in the crowd. Moss looks, and he sees her family—her mother, father, and little Wolf—huddled together, shaking and weeping. Her mother turns her face toward Lotta and silently mouths, *We told you.* Her eyes betray her disappointment and regret.

"Mamma—" Lotta whimpers. But her family stand and turn their backs on her, elbowing their way through the crowd to reach the doors.

Moss spots an old woman, white hair flying around her face, stooping in front of the Judge with her arms folded. Beneath the tumultuous noise, he hears her speak.

"It's time to end this now, Samuel. We've got to tell the truth."

As quick as lightning, the Judge redirects the thugs that are poised to grab Lotta and murmurs a new command. They swerve on the platform and scoop the old woman up like she's a nest of tiny bird bones. They carry her swiftly into the back room of the Temple, gone before anyone even notices. She didn't fight, but Moss saw her tears—saw her brittle hands curl into fists.

"Constance," whispers Lotta. She sounds defeated.

Moss gives her a gentle shake. "Come on," he says. "We need to get out of here."

As they move down off the stage, Lotta is seemingly in a trance. Her eyes are glazed over, and she is so pale that every freckle on her face stands out. She puts one heavy foot in front of the other. But as they're about to reach the exit, strong hands grab Moss's arms and throw him aside. He crashes painfully against a pew, ribs jarring, and gives a yelp.

It's not him the henchmen are after. Together they lift Lotta, all the fight gone from her, and carry her back toward the platform, while the Judge looks on, hands behind his back, nodding his smug head. Moss tries to follow, but bodies block his way—whether intentionally or not, he's unsure. By the time he stumbles to the platform again, Lotta has gone.

The Judge now stands with the other Councillors, all except Lewis, who's now in a huddle with his two blond children. The girl is crying. The boy looks miserable too, with downcast eyes and his usually proud Council shoulders slumped.

The other Councillors nod at each other, smiling, satisfied. They barely look at Moss, as if he is so far beneath them that he's invisible. *Good,* thinks Moss. *Let them underestimate me.*

Outside, Moss searches for Lotta's family to tell them what has happened, but they are nowhere to be seen. He's alert to the scornful looks the villagers are giving him as they drift away from the Temple.

"Moss." He feels a hand on his arm and turns to find Mam and Stone. "Come on, we're leaving." She has her shawl pulled tightly to her body. In the clean village square, she looks frailer than ever.

"They took her," says Moss. "Lotta."

Mam's hand flies to her mouth. "What will they do to her?"

"I don't know," he says truthfully. "But it can't be good. She tried to tell them." His voice cracks. "They wouldn't listen."

Stone leans into Mam and she puts a protective arm around his shoulder. Moss can tell she is still thinking about what could have happened, how it could have easily been Stone.

"What can we do?" she asks.

A soft voice pipes up beside him. "I can help, whatever it is."

Mam jumps. "Sadie, love! Don't sneak up on people like that."

"I weren't *sneaking*," Sadie says. "It's not my fault you wasn't paying attention."

Moss takes in Sadie's small, bony stature, her mouse-brown hair and gray smock, with boots too big for her. "I'm not sure how you can help. But thanks."

"Don't forget I'm a ghost," she says. "You can use me."

Moss ponders this. The only thing he can think to do is find out where the Council is hiding Lotta and find some way to free her.

Sadie nods toward the cart pulled by Pumpkin, where others from the hamlet sit, watching.

"They're all waiting for you. They want to have a meeting about what's just happened. About what it means for us."

"Tell them I'm staying."

Sadie nods and slips away to deliver the message.

"Be careful, Moss," Mam says. "What you're doing . . . it's reckless.

But it's also brave. I'm proud of you." She kisses him on the cheek and, taking Stone's hand, walks slowly back to the cart. Stone twists around to look at him and Moss gives him a reassuring wave. He was surprised when Mam had to lift herself on her toes for her lips to meet his cheek. How much has he grown since she last showed her tenderness this way?

Sadie skips back to him. "I'm staying too, though Da was none too pleased. What you thinking?"

"I'm thinking that if Mam hadn't gone to Temple that day and asked to be let back in, Hannah wouldn't have been taken, and we wouldn't be in this strife. But she only went on account of me. After I met Lotta, I went home sour as old milk about being hid. About being exiled. This is all my fault."

"Maybe," says Sadie. "It don't mean you was wrong."

"Weren't I? I didn't know how good I had it, really. This village life isn't all it's cracked up to be."

Sadie smiles. "I could have told you that for nothing, Moss Smith. In't you noticed how we all work together? It's the best way to survive. Some of us are good at cutting peat, some are good at weaving cloth. Some have tatties, some have milk. Some have a horse, some don't. It works. We all help each other. These villagers . . . none of them trusts another. They seem to hate each other."

They sit on the steps of the now deserted and locked Temple. There, Moss begins to speak. He tells Sadie everything that happened on their journey north.

After he has finished, Sadie whistles, low and long. "I knew things weren't right. Did you see how they carried off that old woman like a cloud on the wind? The midwife? I bet she's got some true stories to tell that they don't want to get out."

"And it's too late to ask her now."

"Do you remember the fish at the lottery?" asks Sadie. "Lotta's plan is working. Just now, didn't you see? The villagers are divided; I could tell. It started with the fish. You can see in folks' eyes they don't trust the Council no more. Especially not the ones with little ones, not now. They thought they was safe."

"They don't trust Lotta neither," Moss points out.

"Not yet, maybe. But if we can bring them proof of what she's been saying, they'll have to believe it."

"We need Lotta," says Moss. "And her brother. I didn't see him at all."

"Is there anyone else who can help? Someone close to the Council?"

Moss remembers the tense looks on the faces of the Lewis family. Lotta told him she and her brother were close to the two children, though she didn't trust them completely. Then there is Councillor Lewis himself. There's something about him that Moss can't put his finger on.

He dares to feel a sliver of hope.

"There might be," he says. A plan is forming in his mind—one that just might work.

# 36

*A* **HUM.** *A* **MELODY.** *Washing through her unconsciousness. It's close. It's—*

The smell wakes her. The stench of sweat and stale alcohol. A pinching pain grips her neck from sleeping at an awkward angle. She opens her eyes and waits for them to adjust to the dim room, lit from a single, unseen lantern that casts a faint, flickering light on the rough stone wall.

*Wolf.*

She groans. Her head pounds with a deep, echoing ache.

Whatever her head is resting on—the only soft thing on this bed which otherwise feels like bare boards beneath her—shifts, and the aches flare as her pulse leaps in response. A choking sound erupts into the room; it takes a moment for her to realize it's come from her own throat.

"Lottie?" A soft voice, followed by a cool hand on her forehead. "It's me."

*Marten.*

Lotta pulls herself stiffly to a sitting position and turns her head to look at him.

"Thank Glimm," he says and embraces her in a tight, malodorous hug. "I thought you was a goner. They gave you quite a knock, I think."

"Do they not have any soap at this inn?" she asks over his shoulder.

"Nice to see you too!" He pulls back to look at her.

It's only then that she sees he's also injured. His right eye is swollen almost shut, the skin around it tight and purple.

"What happened?" she says.

"Those bastards arrested me," says Marten. "For assaulting Roddy. I can't believe he betrayed me like this."

Lotta puts a hand on his arm. "I don't think it was Roddy. I think word got to the Judge."

He is silent for a moment, eyes darting between hers. Then he smacks his hand to his forehead.

"I *did* go to the inn after you left to see Constance. Had too many ales while those villagers burned holes in my back with their eyes. I'm not even sure how I got home. But I do remember getting into a bust-up with some of them over what happened."

Lotta tenses. "Did you tell anyone about what I said?"

Marten hangs his head. "I don't remember. I think I might have told them that the lottery were rigged. That my sister knows the truth."

"Marten!" She leans her head back against the wall, closes her eyes to the pain it causes. "How could you?"

"I'm sorry. I'm *so* sorry. I know I'm always disappointing you."

All she can see in her mind is Wolf. The terrified look on his face when her mother screamed and clutched him to her. She wants the stone floor to open so she can fall into a black, cavernous hole and never come out.

It's clear to her now: The Judge always intended for her to end up here with her brother.

Lotta takes a deep breath and opens her eyes again, staring at the glow from the lantern, which hovers around the corner, just out of sight. It's only now that she sees the bars. They're in a cage. As if they're farm animals.

She stands on shaking legs. "The Judge is sending a message to our family. And he must've wanted you out of the way for Temple today." She takes a few steps to stand at the bars. The lantern comes into view in a passageway with no windows in sight. She wonders if they're underground.

A damp, salty breeze stirs.

"Why are *you* here?" asks Marten.

She hasn't told him yet. She grips the bar to steady herself, then turns and shuffles back. Tears press against her throat.

"It's all gone so wrong," she says. She leans forward and puts her face in her hands. A sob escapes. How can she tell him?

His cool hand is on her back. "What is it? What's happened?"

She takes a deep breath. "It's Wolf. They're taking Wolf. They're sacrificing him to the Glimm at dawn."

Marten jumps to his feet.

"What?"

He leaps to the bars with one stride. "Oi!" He screams into the passageway. "Let us out of here, you bastards!" He turns to her, and even in the low light, she can see how his eyes burn. "And you're just telling me now? Glimm's sake! We're wasting time. How did this happen?"

Lotta curls further in on herself. It happened because she let it.

"It's my fault," she says into her hands. "If I hadn't tried to help Moss, and tried to find Jenny, they would've given Hannah to the Glimm and everything would be the way it was before."

Marten snorts. "This is *not* the time to feel sorry for yourself. What's done is done. That horse were only part of it. You'd have sniffed out their corruption anyway."

He kneels on the ground in front of her. He takes her hands from her face and grips them, staring into her stinging eyes.

"I've been blind. Mooning over Roddy, instead of helping you. And now Wolf—all of us—are paying the price. Where's your precious Glimm now, Lottie? Can't you call it? Tell it not to take Wolf?"

The Glimm. There was something . . . just before she woke up.

She sits up, senses alert. "How long was I out?"

"I don't know. At least a couple of hours."

She tries to think. They had thrown her into a room by herself at the back of the Temple, where she had sat for at least an hour, crying. It was a bare, windowless room used for storing furniture, although it may have had a different use at one time—painted, in large lettering along the wall: MAY THE LIGHT OF THE GLIMM FALL UPON US, AS BRIGHT AS THE SUN.

On the opposite wall, more words, though a phrase she didn't recognize: WE REMEMBER SO THAT THEY MAY FORGET.

A chill had rippled down her spine at the sight of it. Constance's story came flooding back—the voyage, the pact, the deliberate erasure of truth. How the Council had engineered the forgetting of the islanders' true history. She saw it clearly now: This was a place once meant for covert meetings, not storage. But the truth it held had been hidden in plain sight.

When they'd finally opened the door, she'd hurled a chair at Tommy Carter, catching him off guard. As he'd thrown his meaty arms up to protect himself, she'd bolted, only to be brought down by a vicious knock to the back of the head.

Who knows how long she was out before they brought her here?

Now there comes a sound, winnowing up the passageway. Low, booming.

"Can you hear that?" she asks.

Marten nods. "It's been coming and going."

"It's the sound near the cliffs. We must be under the Manor House." She touches the wall beside her. Damp.

Another sound, shivering beneath it. Humming. A faint hint of a musical note.

"What can you hear?" she asks.

"A hollow kind of crashing noise, like a big drum."

"And a musical note? Like a hum?"

Marten stares at her, head cocked. Listening. He shakes his head.

Lotta stands and moves to the bars of the cage again. The booming has subsided, but the humming lingers, quiet but persistent. "Now?"

Marten shakes his head. "Nothing."

Lotta grips the bars and closes her eyes. A warmth builds in her chest, spreading outward like hot water through her veins. Three notes gather inside her and rise, one by one, from her throat.

The humming stops.

Marten stands beside her, staring. His pale face is shocked.

Then up from the depths, through the earth; barreling up the stone passageway: the same three notes.

She's found the Glimm.

And the Glimm is singing back to her.

# 37

**THE HOURS DRIFT BY,** and with each one, the knot in Lotta's stomach grows bigger and heavier. Every now and then, Marten grips the bars and yells until he is hoarse. But still nobody comes. They have no food, no water, and only a bucket in the corner to relieve themselves.

Lotta drifts in and out of consciousness, trying to keep track of time. But with no windows, there is no way of telling if it is night or day.

Still she feels it: The Glimm is near. It hovers at the edge of her senses, cradling her in the dark. And so she does the only thing she can.

She pleads for mercy.

She pleads silently with the whole of herself, standing before the Glimm in her mind and begging it to spare her brother.

And then, at last: Heavy footsteps echo down the stone passageway.

A fresh glow spills into view, brighter than the lantern that's been left burning, and with it, dancing shadows approach.

Lotta stands, pulse racing. Marten was quicker; he already clutches the bars of the gate. There's no mistaking the silhouette, like a roosting buzzard, of the Judge. He is flanked by four enforcers carrying flaming torches, and he locks eyes with Lotta as soon as he is close enough. Trailing behind, with his own lantern, is Councillor Lewis, who will not meet her gaze at all.

"Let us out!" says Lotta. "This is wrong, and you know it!" She cocks her elbows at her sides, fists balled.

One of the enforcers lunges at Marten, who reels back. The thug laughs and another slaps him on the back.

"Is that really necessary?" asks the Judge. "Get behind me, before I put you in there with them." He pulls a great black key from his coat pocket and waves it at them.

The men shuffle back, eyes on each other. The Judge returns the key, leather strap dangling from his pocket like a rat's tail.

"You've trained them well in the art of hate, Judge Hawthorne," says Marten.

The Judge cocks his head. "You Salters. You've had such an easy existence. Well, no more." He leans close enough that Lotta can see the white ring that rims his blue iris. "You've caused quite a mess, Lotta Salter. Broken rules. Broken trust. Stirred up the muck at the bottom of the pond."

"Is that what this is?" Marten snaps. "A pond? You mean a stinking bog."

The Judge barely spares him a glance. "You might have been useful once, Master Salter. Shame about your weakness for drink and dramatics."

"I know where you've come from," says Lotta, feeling strangely calm. "And I know you invented the sacrifice for your own power."

"It was not *I* who initiated the sacrifice. It's a long tradition. How do you think we've survived so long in this inhospitable place? The Glimm thrived for *years* on the life force of children, and everyone understood what they gained by making the sacrifice. You got lucky, and now everyone is paying the price. Horses were never going to satisfy it for long."

"The Glimm won't do your bidding this time," says Lotta.

The Judge chuckles. "Oh, I think it will."

"You know what I said in the Temple is true. You've seen the cave. You know the stories there."

At the mention of the cave, the Judge takes a step closer.

"You met the guardians of the forest, I expect?"

*Careful.* Her cheeks burn. "I saw no guardians. Just two skeletons at the gates, trying to scare people away from the truth."

The Judge turns this over in his head. "I don't know what it is that you think you know."

"That we haven't been here forever. It's only been a couple of generations. Your grandfather made up the lore himself. The Council has been sponging off the villagers ever since."

Beside her, Marten's breath catches.

"I suppose you heard all this from the midwife," sneers the Judge. "Such a shame. We were friends once, when we were small. The only two children on such a long voyage. Her loyalty has served her well."

"What have you done with her?" asks Lotta, suddenly fearful for the old woman.

"You don't have to worry about her," says the Judge. "She's in no danger where she is."

Lotta switches tack. "Councillor Lewis," she says. "You *know* this is wrong. You have the power to change this."

Lewis is about to speak when the Judge turns and throws such a withering look at his son-in-law that he changes his mind and says nothing. He looks away, back the way they have come, his fingers twisting the ring on his right hand.

"I know you've been lying to everyone, Judge Hawthorne. You have no special connection to the Glimm. It doesn't tell you *anything*. You've rigged every lottery to punish people who have stood up to you."

"And who else have you been talking to?"

Lotta tries not to look directly at Lewis, but she senses him stiffen behind Hawthorne.

“So, you’re not denying it, Judge Hawthorne?” Lotta turns her gaze to the four enforcers, catching their eyes shining inside their mismatched mask holes. “Are you hearing all this, lads?”

They shift uneasily, exchange glances.

The Judge’s smugness slips.

“Enough talking. You should have kept your mouth shut and your head down, girl, and your brother may have been spared. It’s a pity—you’ve been very good with my horses. But I daresay that boy you’ve been training will make a suitable replacement.”

He turns away. With one hand he ushers the enforcers to continue on their way, then starts to move after them. “We have preparations to make. I’ll deal with you later.” He eyes them sideways, then strides away.

Lotta yells after him. “You claim to know the will of the Glimm, but you know nothing!”

The Judge’s step doesn’t falter. Lewis follows, but he gives Lotta a final glance. She sees something in his face. Sympathy. Remorse.

The procession moves deeper into the tunnel, their torchlight bouncing across the curved ceiling, the Judge’s words hanging in the air.

*I’ll deal with you later.*

Before long, the humming rises again—this time a raw, keening sound. A faint green light flares on the walls of the tunnel.

Then silence.

Lotta feels the color drain from her face. “Did you hear it that time?” she whispers.

Marten nods, bewilderment all over his face. “What *is* that?”

“It’s the Glimm. It’s in pain.” The words land like a weight in her chest.

“They’ve got it, haven’t they?”

Lotta stares down the tunnel, trying to make out anything at all, but it’s quiet and dark. “They’ve been *keeping* it here,” she murmurs. “How could I have missed it? All this time, it was right under my feet.”

"But how?" says Marten. "You can't contain something like that. The Glimm's all-powerful, Lottie. It's always judged us. No wonder it's punishing us all. And they was blaming *you*!"

"It's not punishing us, remember? I told you yesterday. It's calling us. We're the ones who broke our harmony with it. It's so connected with the island that the island's just responding to its pain. It doesn't *want* sacrifice."

"But why does the Glimm take the children, then?" he asks. "I just know Wolf is in danger. I can feel it in my bones. Can't you?"

Lotta closes her eyes. Yes. She feels it too. "How long have they kept it here? Maybe they starve it. Mistreat it."

"Lottie," begins Marten. "What did you mean when you told the Judge you knew where he'd come from? He talked about a voyage. What voyage?"

Lotta stays at the gate, arms knotted through the bars. Vigilant. She hasn't told Constance's story to anyone yet; she hasn't had the chance. She tried to tell her parents this morning on the way to Temple, but she couldn't because of Ash bloody Carter and Eddie, the butcher's son, riding so close. She recounts it all now, to Marten: the ship; the dying children and the supposed rewards. The islanders' pact. Their fear.

Their forgetting.

"We don't need to fear the Glimm. It's the Council we need to fear. And if they've really kept it . . . prisoner for this long, then it's no wonder the island—and everything that lives here—feels like it's dying. When the Glimm is sick, the island is sick. They've *made* the island sick, just to hold on to power."

Marten is quiet in the dim light. Lotta places a weary hand on his arm and squeezes.

"He said it feeds off the life force of children," he says eventually. His voice is strained with fatigue.

"That may be true, if that's all it's offered. If it's starving. But it's not necessary. I've seen another way."

There's a thud from nearby, then footsteps wending their way up the passage from below. Marten and Lotta take up their positions again, at the bars, but the footsteps don't slow this time. The six men stride purposefully past, eyes ahead. Only one turns, and Lotta recognizes the bulky but youthful frame—Tommy Carter, who loved her as a child, and possibly loves her still. His eyes are wide beneath the mask, and he gives an almost imperceptible nod.

A nod that says: *I've heard the truth.*

Hope rises in her chest. Word is spreading. Maybe, just maybe, the Council's grip is slipping.

# 38

**MINUTES GO BY.**

"Can you feel it still?" asks Marten.

Lotta shakes her head. "Not close, no."

"They've taken it to the saltings." He sits down hard on the bench and puts his face in his hands.

"Maybe," she says. "It might be time." She sits close beside him and leans in while he wraps his wiry arms around her. His smell doesn't bother her anymore. It's comforting, more than anything. She recalls Wolf's smell of milk and honey, the quickening of his impatient body as she held him.

She buries her face further into Marten's chest.

"Somebody's coming." Marten pushes her gently away and goes to the bars again.

Lotta hears it too. Light, patting footsteps. Not the heavy boots of the Judge's men.

Then, a slight figure appears in the passageway, no more than a shadow. A tiny girl, her features swallowed in the gloom.

"Found you!" she whispers. She turns to look behind her and beckons frantically, her flapping hand a blur.

And then, two more figures. A man and a woman. The woman carries a lantern and holds it up in front of her. For a moment, Lotta is blinded, and brings her arm up to her face.

"Thank Glimm, Lottie, we found you!" *Daphne.* Can it be possible?

Lotta lowers her arm as her eyes adjust to the new light. Standing beside Daphne, the person she least expected to see, and the one she finds she's happiest to see—Moss. She's surprised by the warmth that rises in her chest. Having him here feels unexpectedly *right.* The way his eyes lift to meet hers, full of quiet concern, makes her heartbeat steady.

"Are you all right?" His eyebrows crinkle. "Are you hurt?" His hands reach through the bars and she lurches forward to grab them, not quite believing they are real. But here are his hands, rough and warm, holding hers tight.

"Yes! Yes, I'm fine!" Tears of relief press at her eyes. "What time is it?"

"It's nearly dawn," says Daphne.

Lotta looks at her properly for the first time. Her blond curls lie loose on her shoulders. She wears a shawl over her simplest dress, and heavier boots than usual.

"Oh, Lottie!" Daphne cries, and bursts into sobs. "I'm so sorry! I had no idea this was going to happen. Any of it! You have to believe me."

Lotta feels a flicker of irritation. She can't afford to indulge anyone's guilt right now, least of all Daphne's. She pulls away from Moss, focusing back on the task at hand. "Never mind that now. Can you get us out?"

The smudge of a girl steps forward, grinning mischievously. "Tada!" She holds out a key with a thin leather strap. "Swiped it from that mean old man as he passed. Never even saw me."

"How did you all get here?" She looks Moss up and down. He's changed into dark clothes and a piece of familiar sacking sticks out of his pocket.

"It was Daphne," he says. "She helped."

"There's no time," says Daphne. "Give me that."

She takes the key from the girl and inserts it into the lock. The door swings open.

"You little beauty!" Marten rushes forward and lifts Daphne from her feet with an embrace. Daphne squeaks in surprise.

Moss takes Lotta in his arms. "I was so worried," he says into her neck. She can feel him inhaling her. She does the same. Sweat. Wool. And faintly beneath it: peat smoke. His chest is warm against hers.

Marten grabs Daphne's hand, and she lets him. "Roddy . . . Does he know I'm here?" The hope and fragility in his voice are dual pins in Lotta's heart.

"He does. But he has to be so careful, Marten. He's riding with our grandfather to the ceremony. It was easy for me to disappear. It wasn't easy for him. He's going to be the next Judge. I'm sorry."

Marten nods numbly, but Lotta has questions. Did he *want* to help or was that a convenient excuse not to? Will he give them away? The uncertainty gnaws at her, but she sees the silent resolve in Marten's jaw and says nothing.

"We should go," says Moss.

"Is the way clear?" asks Marten.

"It should be," says Daphne. "They've gone for now." She starts to move back the way they came.

"Wait," says Lotta. "I need to know what's down there."

"There isn't time!" Daphne protests.

"I'll be quick!"

She grabs the lantern from Daphne, who resists. "You can't go down there!"

Lotta stares into her friend's anxious face. Then she can't help herself. She holds the lantern handle tighter and pushes Daphne away.

Daphne judders back a step, puts an arm out to steady herself, shocked.

Lotta turns and runs.

The farther she goes down the passage, the tangier the air becomes—full of salt and damp. The booming sound rolls up a narrow stairwell, with steps chiseled into stone. At the bottom, she turns a corner and gasps as the passage gives way to a wide-open space with a soaring ceiling, lit by torches left by the Judge's men. It immediately reminds her of the cave in the mountains, but for the constant, surging sound of the sea.

In the darkness, a huge shape moves gently up and down, creaking and groaning with the sound of labored breathing.

Has she found it? Has she found the Glimm?

Running footsteps behind her make her turn. Her breath makes clouds in the damp air, lit by the light of the lantern. A single torch burns by the entrance to the passageway. Marten lifts it off the wall and comes toward her. As he gets nearer, his face grows still. Lotta turns and together they hold up their lights to see the creature before them.

"Be careful!" Daphne's voice comes from the entrance. "The water's deep!"

Lotta glances at her feet. She is standing dangerously close to the sheer drop—not on the bare rock she expects, but flagstones, neatly placed. She looks up and tries to decipher just what she is looking at. A huge wooden structure, floating on the water, tipping with the current this way and that. Giant vertical beams reach up into the darkness above, intersecting with more beams crossed horizontally. As it tosses, it strains against thick iron chains that creak and ring with every swell, tethering it in place.

"What is it?" Moss stands beside her now, his face frozen with awe.

"It's a ship," says Daphne, appearing at their shoulders.

Lotta turns to her, horrified. "You *knew* about this?"

"Of course I knew about it. The Judge is my grandfather. He wouldn't keep it a secret from me."

"But how could you hide something so big, for so long?" Marten is pacing along the flagstone now, trying to see it from all available angles.

"We're under the cliffs," says Daphne. "Nobody is allowed near them, remember? Not even bird hunters."

As if in answer, black shapes catch Lotta's eye, wheeling in the night outside the cave. There must be thousands of nesting birds out there. The ground is splattered white with their droppings.

"So you know everything," says Lotta. It's not a question; she never should have trusted her.

"I don't know what you mean by *everything*," says Daphne. "I know that we have a ship. I know that we can leave the island. Why, what do you know?"

"I told you the lottery is rigged. Do you believe me now?"

Daphne's lips press together. She doesn't reply.

*We don't have time for this*, thinks Lotta.

"What's the booming sound we hear?" she asks instead. "The humming, near the cliffs. Under the moors."

"I don't know about under the moors, but the booming is from the sea tunnels." Daphne gestures to the far end of the cavern. "There's a whole network of them, under the island. At high tide they fill with water. Sometimes the surge is quite violent."

It wasn't just a ship Lotta heard here. She spins on her heels and marches toward the back of the cave. All around her are shapes: barrels, crates made of wood, coils of rope.

"Stop!" says Daphne. "Look outside!"

Lotta stops and turns. A straight line of gray light, barely a whisper, lies far out to sea.

"Lotta," calls Marten. His voice is shrill, desperate. "We need to go. *Now.*"

"Just one more minute," she says, and within seconds she has reached the far end of the cavern. Underfoot, the ground becomes unsteady, as though she's walking on a pebble beach, or the loose shingle of the mountain path. Something crunches under her boots. At her feet, white bones glow in the light from her lantern. She takes a shocked step back and teeters on the uneven surface.

In the flickering glow of a nearby torch, something catches her eye, looming and swaying, like a creature half human. She recognizes the pale branches of deer antlers—there must be hundreds of them—piled high like a macabre sculpture. And behind it, on a rocky outcrop, stands a cage. An empty cage, large enough to hold a monster.

# 39

THE JOURNEY back through the tunnels is a blur. Lotta stumbles more than once; Moss's firm hands on her waist steady her. Part of her wants to stop, to try to think about what she found: a cage, big enough for the Glimm. An open gate, a sea-filled tunnel leading away under the island. A thick chain, secured to the rock face.

In the cave, she had shouted at Daphne, trying to make sense of it, trying to get some answers from her, but it was useless. Daphne was oblivious. She was clearly as shocked as they all were, pale with fatigue, and close to giving up on them.

So Lotta closed her mouth and pushed the idea of the Glimm, imprisoned—possibly tortured—from her mind.

At the end of the final passage, a wooden door opens to a narrow staircase. Daphne stops and turns to Lotta. "I know you don't believe it, but I want to help. I'm so sorry." Her hands find Lotta's wrists and close around them. "I had no idea this was coming—and that it would be Wolfie, of all children."

Lotta stands stiff, impenetrable. She says nothing.

Her silence clearly unsettles Daphne, who withdraws her hands and instead clutches her throat. "Is there anything else I can do? Anything at all?"

Lotta glares at her. "Can you tell them to call it off?"

Daphne's eyes grow wide. "They won't listen to me, you know that."

Lotta feels a hand on her shoulder.

"You've done what you can," says Marten. "We're grateful, aren't we, Lottie? We just need to keep moving."

Lotta nods, a creeping shame rising. "What if I told you the sacrifice isn't necessary, that there's another way?"

"She don't get it," Sadie pipes up.

Daphne shoots her a poisoned look. "Then I would listen. Here." She hands Lotta a piece of sacking. "You all need to wear these, in case we run into any servants skulking around. They'll just think you're my grandfather's enforcers on your way to put the boot in somewhere. They've been trained to avert their eyes."

Lotta does as she's told. The eye holes in the sackcloth are rough, uneven, one higher than the other, throwing everything off-kilter. It makes her feel unsteady in the world. It smells of chaff and hay and her nose begins to itch immediately.

Marten puts on his mask and Lotta shudders. He's indistinguishable from a Council thug. Moss sneezes inside his mask; he doesn't quite carry it off.

She nods toward Sadie, taking in her tiny frame and the dress she wears. "What about her? She'll never pass. At least I'm wearing trousers."

"Oh, don't you worry about me," says Sadie. "I can slip in with you and nobody will ever know I'm there. Trust me."

After the girl's trick with the keys, Lotta believes her.

"What's up here?" She taps on the door that stands ajar at the bottom of the stairs.

“It’s my grandfather’s library,” says Daphne. “We just need to get up there, then we can get out of the house without being seen. This place is full of hidden staircases so the servants don’t run headlong into people while carrying dirty linen and cleaning things—and Glimm knows what else.”

As they climb the staircase, it seems unending. The air is close and hot, all five of them tight together, trying to tread softly. Daphne explains that it goes up two floors of the house and that they’ll have to go back down another set of stairs once they get there.

At last they reach the library, and cool, fresh air. It’s smaller than Lotta remembers. But here are the heavy crimson curtains; here is the intricately patterned rug under their feet. She realizes now that none of it could have come from the island: the rug, the curtains, the books lining the shelves. These must have been brought here, long ago, from the Council’s place of origin. There is no way to make these things from the materials available on the island. She glances at Daphne, thinking of the richness of her usual clothes, and a strange new thought rises. Could these have come from elsewhere too? The Council families always looked so refined: better tailored, cleaner somehow. But surely not. Daphne’s clothes look new, not eighty years old.

Moss sneezes again. He claws at the string tied around his neck before ripping the mask off. He takes a deep breath through his nose. “I can’t do it anymore,” he says, panting. “Sorry.”

Daphne is already making for the door, but Lotta hesitates. If they were going to find proof to convince the islanders of the Council’s lies, it would surely be here. Constance spoke of a pact—a signed covenant. Could it be here, in the cabinets and bookcases that line the walls with cupboards and drawers? She hovers at the huge desk that dominates the center of the room. A strong smell of beeswax and smoke lingers around it.

Lotta quickly pulls open drawer after drawer: ink wells, pens, chalk, blank sheets of rough paper.

"Lottie!" Marten's voice is full of frustration. "Come *on*!"

Her fingers close over a book. For a moment there's a spark of hope, but when she opens it, she finds only lists: dates, names, items. The most recent reads:

*Jackson, Blankets*

*Shilling, Eggs*

She recognizes it now: a ledger. A log of everything the poor, starving villagers have handed over week after week for the Council's comfort. She feels a fresh surge of anger and closes the drawer too loudly.

"Lottie!" whispers Daphne, wide-eyed. She puts a shushing finger to her lips before putting her eye to the crack in the doorway.

Lotta joins the rest of them, who are staring at her in disbelief.

"I just wanted to find proof." Her voice betrays her weariness.

"The way is clear," says Daphne.

They follow her out to the dark corridor and into what looks at first like a cupboard. The stairs open at the bottom into another corridor.

Moss, with mask back on, moans and rubs at the spot where his nose must be. Through the holes, his eyes are glassy. "I don't know how much longer I can keep this on," he mumbles. "I'll be sneezing all the way through the house."

"We need to go quickly and quietly, then," says Daphne. They move past a staircase from the servants' rooms ("That leads up to the dining room," says Daphne) to stand at the door to the kitchen, which Lotta has passed through countless times before.

She'll never be welcomed into its warmth again.

"Walk with purpose behind me," says Daphne. "Like you've every right to be here."

They hear bustling from inside—pots banging and footsteps on slate floor. Murmured voices.

"Now!" Daphne opens the door decisively and strides through the kitchen. Lotta follows. With her trousers and boots, she knows she can pass as a man. But Daphne was right: She only receives one curious glance from a young scullery maid in a too-tight brown smock who turns away, alarmed, as though willing them to pass quickly. Everybody else in the kitchen keeps a self-conscious back turned.

Moss sneezes again.

Within seconds they're out the other side with the door closed behind them.

"Too easy," whispers Sadie gleefully.

"What now?" says Moss.

"Stables," says Lotta.

The back door to the kitchen opens out onto the stable yard, which is empty and quiet in the silvery morning light.

"The sun will be up soon," says Marten. "We need horses."

Inside the stables, most of the stalls are empty. Of course. The Council has ridden down to join the procession from the village to the saltings. Lotta runs down the line of them, looking over each door into stall after empty stall. Just as she is about to growl in despair, a small head pops out from the last one.

*Dougie.*

"Miss Lewis said you'd be coming and I should get him ready," he says. "I waited just in case."

Lotta casts a grateful look at Daphne, who stands wringing her hands at the stable entrance. Then she throws the stall door open and her arms around the stable boy.

Salty, tacked up with saddle and bridle, nickers softly.

"Thank you, Dougie," she says. "What would I do without you?"

He says nothing, but nods with a tight, proud smile beneath welling eyes.

"We need four more horses. Just bridles will do. Can you take the others to the field and grab them?"

Dougie nods and scrambles away to the tack room. Lotta leads Salty toward the outer doors, barking orders. Marten has her satchel—and her knife. He carries a small axe.

"What are you doing with that?" she asks.

He grimaces. "Just in case. What if we have to kill it? To save Wolf?"

"It can't come to that," she says. "That could destroy the island. Kill us all."

Marten nods and tucks the axe into his belt, then follows Dougie out to the paddock, Daphne trailing behind.

Moss appears by Lotta's side. "You should go ahead. Don't wait for us. We're using precious time." He looks exhausted.

Lotta mounts Salty. "Come with me, then. I need you." She reaches down and braces her arm for Moss to hook onto and swing himself up behind her.

Salty's shoes clatter on the cobbles of the stable yard. Sadie is at the gate. She heaves it open as Lotta squeezes Salty's sides with all the urgency coursing through her.

"Hold on!" she calls.

With Moss's arms tight around her waist and Salty quivering with excitement beneath her, Lotta guides the horse out into the open air, where a blustery wind greets them. She wills it to help them reach the saltings in time.

# 40

A **BLANKET** of black clouds presses low as they race toward the salt marshes—down the Manor House road, past the village turn, and across the stretch of farmland bruised by the harsh winter. An uneasy light is spreading across the land, but the sun has not yet appeared.

Lotta leans low over Salty's neck, her hands slipping on the reins as the heat rising from his coat slicks her hands with sweat. His mane lashes her face.

"There!" Moss's voice is nearly stolen by the wind. Ahead of them, lights: a ring of torches in the distance, where the land flattens out.

They've made it here already. Lotta tries not to picture the procession—the one she now remembers she took herself, riding on Hazel. She recalls the vibrations that wracked her body: nerves, but also excitement for what was to come. The flaming torches and the twirling minstrels. Masks of sackcloth and wool. The crown of blackthorn that pricked her scalp, her hands cold and stiff on Hazel's mane. Her father and mother, walking beside her. They hid their fears well.

Salty stumbles on the rough road, his hooves skidding over a patch of broken stone. Moss lurches sideways with a grunt, nearly pulling Lotta from the saddle.

"Whoa, Salty," Lotta murmurs, reining him in. Her voice is gentle, but her heart pounds. She's pushed him too hard with two riders and a brutal pace. He's not a sturdy island pony; he's fast and clever but not built for this kind of burden. She needs to remember that. She needs him strong for whatever comes next.

The air sharpens with salt. The wind slices across her cheeks, full of warning. She feels the now-familiar pull of the saltings. A humming that travels up through Salty's legs from the earth and into her spine, binding the three of them.

The Glimm is close. Does it feel her as well?

"Sorry." Moss adjusts his seat behind her, bringing her back to the moment.

"Can you feel it?" she asks. "It's close."

Moss sniffs the charged air. "I can feel *something*."

And then: music.

Not the Glimm, not the song of the saltings, but musicians with pounding drums, lilting bone flutes, a fiddle.

As they draw nearer, she sees beyond the crowd huddled in the wind by the shore. The standing stone. The tide is swirling across the flats, filling the deep channels and the shallow crevices, running over the reeds that catch the salt—the ones that, in another bay, her family have tended for hundreds of years to aid the production of salt crystals.

*No.* Not *hundreds* of years. Eighty years.

She grabs Salty's mane to steady herself as the world tilts. Everything she knows is a lie.

On the eastern horizon, the first ray of weak sun cuts through, lining the dark clouds with gold. A great cheer rises from the crowd. And that is when she sees him, his slim form draped in a white robe, caught in the light.

*Wolf.*

The man carrying him across the channel toward the standing stone is not her father—the back is too broad—and he holds Wolf high in his arms as the incoming tide swirls around his chest. Wolf appears limp, his chin resting on the man's shoulder. He is blindfolded.

Above the chaotic music, another sound cuts through: Wolf's terrified wailing. It slices into her like a scythe, and her body reacts as if it's been struck. Her throat feels suddenly raw, and she does something she has never done before. She kicks Salty in the sides. He lurches into a gallop again. As they approach the crowd, Lotta slows Salty to canter a wide arc around it. Faces turn. Reverent, smiling faces fall. Some of them blush furiously, caught out in their shame.

As she makes her presence known, she's hit by a startling truth.

She has never been to a sacrifice before. Not as a witness. She had forgotten her own. And the scene before her isn't too far removed from those depicted on the walls of the mountain cave. Folk hold ribbons on sticks; children wave them over their heads without a care. A fire burns nearby. Couples with crowns of green leaves leap over it, hands clasped and bound with ribbon, shrieking and stumbling, picking themselves up in a tangle of limbs. There is music and dancing.

The islanders are so achingly close to understanding what the Glimm wants, what it *needs*. But in the center, like a hovering black storm cloud, stands the Council. Solemn, robed, eyes watchful. Henchmen in sack masks stand nearby clutching weapons: an axe; a long stick, whittled to a vicious point; a hunting knife.

They have twisted the ceremony of the ancient civilization and turned it into something monstrous.

Another thing—the crowd is much smaller than it should be. Could some of the villagers have stayed away in protest? She can only hope.

Those who remain are not in harmony. While some revel, others hold each other tenderly, as if bruised. Jemima the baker stands with her sweet, simple son Reggie pressed to her side. Stormy Pete's wife, Rona, stands apart, eyes downcast, hugging herself.

And then there are the others—men like Butcher John and Farmer Evans—standing tall at the edges, watching with hunger as the man across the saltings begins to tie Wolf to the standing stone.

They want this.

They've been slowly poisoned to believe that sacrifice is inevitable and necessary, the answer to all their woes.

Lotta brings Salty to a standstill between the crowd and the water. Salty throws his head up, snorting, his sides heaving. The music ebbs and falls away.

Judge Hawthorne glares at her, his clean-shaven jaw jutted in naked loathing.

"You have to stop this!" Lotta yells. "You're making a huge mistake!"

The Judge shakes his head. With one hand, he signals to the enforcers closest to him. They start to move, but a clear voice rings out: "Let her speak!"

This is met with a few jeers, but they too fall away when a gust of wind careens across the crowd. Salty shies as a hat cartwheels toward him, his hooves stomping wetly on the damp ground, making a sucking sound. The thugs hesitate.

She can see it now: the doubt, the guilt, the hunger for change flickering like sparks among the crowd. Some eyes turn to her. Some flinch. Some hold her gaze.

Hawthorne sneers and steps to one side, revealing two figures behind him. Her parents. Standing with their bodies bowed, they shiver together in the cold wind in too few clothes. Their hands are bound with rope and tied together.

Still they won't look at her. Broken.

She wants to run to them, but she has to keep a level head.

"Lottie!" Wolf's faint voice carries across the marsh and into her soul. Her mother hears it too and folds further into herself. Allen meets Lotta's gaze and she fears that he blames her.

The two henchmen lurch toward her again, gripping their weapons. Salty throws his head up and backs away. Lotta turns him in a circle and he kicks out at the closest thug. Across the water, Wolf is impossibly small against the standing stone. In the rising sun, its shadow stretches out like an accusing finger.

"Music!" shouts the Judge, not taking his eyes off Lotta.

Of course. He understands the Glimm needs music. He is summoning it. But before the minstrels can start up again, the villagers turn at the sound of ragged hoofbeats approaching from the north. Marten and Daphne gallop bareback on shaggy island ponies—the fastest of the herd. Marten is bent forward, elbows out; Daphne's hair flows behind her.

Trailing them, Sadie and Dougie ride double on a smaller chestnut—Dougie's favorite. And behind them—a horse-drawn cart accompanied by riders on black ponies.

Moss has been quiet until now, a solid rock behind Lotta, giving her unspoken confidence. Now he gasps.

"It's Mam! It's all of them." He starts to dismount.

"Be careful," she says. But the Judge isn't interested in Moss; he has barely registered his presence.

Only Lewis turns to watch Moss go. He and Roderick have had their heads together since Daphne appeared. Roddy stands stiff in his black robes, his face pinched. His neckcloth looks more noose than decoration. His hands flutter at his throat, trying to loosen it.

The music has wheezed back to life, but the two horses carrying Marten and Daphne are upon them, foaming at the mouth, rumps slick with sweat. The sound of their restless hooves in mud nearly drowns out the flutes.

"Daphne," calls Lewis. "Get down from there please."

"No, Father," she says.

The music stops again. Biddy Jackson gapes at Daphne and says something to her husband, who looks at her askance. The other villagers don't seem to know what to do: Some stare in disbelief; others treat it like some kind of spectacle, staged for their entertainment.

The Judge goes red in the face. Spit forms at the corners of his mouth.

"Salters! Leave now or you will find yourselves in shackles like your parents. You will *not* disturb this ritual if you value your lives and theirs!"

Marten's face is stony, the bruised eye bloodshot and half closed. Roderick stares at him, aghast. Then he takes a tentative step forward. Lewis's arm snakes out to stop him, but Roddy shakes him off, resolute now, and strides with purpose to stand before Marten's horse.

His gaze drops to the axe, still hanging at Marten's belt. He puts a hand on the horse's rein.

"Let go," says Lotta, her voice low.

Roddy obeys. "I'm sorry," he says to Marten. "It wasn't me who had you arrested. You have to believe me."

Marten says nothing but his chest trembles with fast, shallow breaths. He is torn, hurt—Lotta can see it all over his face.

"Roddy." Daphne slides off her horse. "We have to stop this."

*"Roderick Lewis!"* The Judge storms forward, seizes Roddy's arm, and starts to drag him back. "Remember where your loyalties lie!"

Roddy stumbles, then finds his feet. He wrenches his arm from his grandfather's grip, shrugging off his robe in the process. It falls into the mud. Quick as a mouse, a child darts forward and scoops it up and away, holding it high like a streaming banner.

"Enough!" Finally Councillor Lewis speaks. "Judge Hawthorne, you will not manhandle my children."

The Judge turns his fury on him. "Remember your place, Amos," he growls. "Where you came from."

A thrill runs through the crowd. Nobody ever speaks of Lewis's origins: an ordinary village child, adopted into the Lewis family so Hawthorne's daughter could marry someone other than a blood relative.

The Council has always presented a united front. These cracks are a curiosity. A diversion. Behind Hawthorne and Lewis, bull-faced Stirling and a glowering Councillor Gray—who holds the wrist of his daughter Meg, now weeping gently—exchange words without taking their eyes off the action.

Daphne runs forward and throws her arms around her father's waist. She looks up into his face, eyes pleading. Her hair is tangled from the wind, her cloak streaked with mud. The Judge looks at her with disgust.

"Papa," she says. "You have to do something."

"Yes, Amos." A new voice—a woman's—carries over the crowd. "You got it in your power to release that child."

Lotta's mother finally comes to life. She raises her head long enough to look around, to squirm and test the ropes around her wrist. But some of the villagers bristle. Butcher John and Farmer Evans and others form a wall against the approaching newcomers, but when they spot the knives and axes they are carrying, they swiftly part.

Lotta's chest swells. Moss and Sadie are with them. Moss murmurs something scathing to the butcher, who drops his gaze and twists his mouth. The exiled families mingle with the villagers while Moss and his mother come closer. Proud, unafraid.

With one glance from the Judge, three henchmen step forward, weapons ready. The last one hangs back. He looks between the Judge and Lotta. Hawthorne has not yet noticed; he is too fixated on Moss's mother, ready to have her cut down without a thought.

Suddenly, Tommy Carter tears off his mask. His head is damp with sweat, his cheeks pink and shining. His eyes appeal to Lotta. *Am I doing the right thing?*

Lotta nods at him.

The boy lifts his voice to the crowd. “I can’t do this anymore! I can’t do the Council’s dirty work. We need to let the boy go.”

The Judge spins around and strikes Tommy across the face with the back of his hand. The sound cracks through the air and the boy stumbles, but it’s too late. The villagers are already erupting, shouting over one another, *at* one another. Hawthorne has lost their attention.

A flicker of movement catches Lotta’s eye. Out of the marsh, a man lurches toward the crowd, clothes dripping wet. He stops to catch his breath, shivering, and for a moment his eyes meet hers. Then he blinks and darts his gaze away. Farmer Jack is usually a harmless man, but one who is indebted to the Council, willing to do anything to keep favors. Lotta feels a stab of pity.

Out on the island, Wolf slumps against the stone, no longer crying. His stillness is somehow worse than the wailing.

Lotta’s blood surges. Now is the time to act.

Salty senses her rising pulse; he trembles as she gathers up the reins. She scans the crowd. Moss is with his mother, who’s speaking urgently to Lewis, hands gesturing. The Councillor bows his head to hear over the roar, frowning and nodding.

Moss catches her eye, sees the panic in her face, and pushes his way back through the now surging crowd.

“What can we do?” His eyes are wide and urgent.

“I need you, *now*,” she says. Salty is already straining to move.

Moss doesn’t hesitate. He takes her arm and swings up behind her again, casting a final look back at his mother to check she is safe.

“Hold on,” says Lotta.

While the crowd—including the Council—is distracted by the newcomers, Lotta does what she needs to do. She wheels Salty around and heads for the water. But as she approaches, the air shifts. Not a wind, but a steady, beating pulse that drives into her body.

Moss grunts in surprise. Shouts rise from the crowd.

*Something's happening!*

*Enjoy the show!* *Someone save the boy!*

*It's starting!*

The earth vibrates beneath them. The surface of the water shirrs and darkens. At the stone, Wolf has straightened up. His face is awry, twisted in terror. Lotta knows how he feels. She *remembers*.

And just as she did, all those years ago, he lets out a word. "Mammy?"

The Glimm is here.

# 41

Moss grips Lotta around the waist as Salty surges toward the marsh. His stomach clenches against the unsettling vibrations thrumming in the air. He knows she's hurtling them headlong into danger, but he resists the instinct to throw himself to the ground. He trusts her, and he knows this is the right thing to do. To save Wolf, and to let Lotta face the Glimm at last.

What he hasn't told her is that at his back is the knife his mother gave him, sheathed to his belt. Just in case.

Salty is slowed by the pull of the wet earth, his steps sinking.

Behind them, two of Hawthorne's men shout at them to stop, trying to follow on ragged ponies far better suited to the terrain, but they too are slowed by the mud.

Lotta calls out to Wolf as they come to a halt at the edge of the channel. "Don't be afraid, Wolfie! I'm coming!"

But even as she finishes speaking, the silt-heavy water starts to churn. It glows with a faint green light as tendrils of luminescence swirl and spiral. A musical hum rises from the surface like voices in harmony. The wind dies away completely.

In the channel, a long undulating shape appears with light for blood.

It reaches the point where the tip of the standing stone casts its weak shadow on the water, and then it surfaces.

It's more monstrous than Moss had ever imagined. Its head is the shape of a horse's, with ears and jaw in the same place, but here the similarities end. Fine scales, iridescent and slick, cover its body. And under its skin: flickering, pulsing forks of lightning for veins. Its mouth is wide, with dripping rows of spiny teeth. Dirty water runs off its impossibly long neck as it rises from the channel. But then it hits Moss: not the neck—it's the whole body, just as he's seen depicted in the cave and in the archways of the Temple. Its fine legs on its serpent body curl and twist like vines, ready to wrap around its prey.

As it moves, a sound like the snapping of bones fills the still air.

The horses behind them have long since bolted. One of the riders has fallen and is clawing his way back through the mud, driven by terror.

The creature shimmers before them, as though not entirely solid, but half flesh and half flickering, blue-green light.

"What will you do?" Moss hears the high-pitched panic in his own voice.

Lotta doesn't reply. Instead, she turns Salty back toward the shore, where the villagers have stopped arguing and stand frozen, watching.

At first Moss thinks she is running away, and he is ashamed of the relief he feels. But then she turns Salty again, facing the Glimm.

She digs her heels into Salty's sides, urging him into a fast canter. The horse heads straight to the channel, blinded by love and loyalty to his mistress. He reaches the edge and leaps.

For a moment, they are flying. The Glimm locks its burning gaze on them.

Then they land, and Salty stumbles under the weight of two riders. Moss slips off and hits solid ground, which knocks the air out of him.

Lotta holds on and steadies herself. Salty quickly recovers to stand firm.

"Lottie?" Wolf's head turns this way and that.

"I'm here, Wolfie. We're going to get you free now."

She nods at Moss—she's seen the knife at his belt. "Get him to safety," she says.

"What are you going to do?" asks Moss, his heart pumping so hard his chest aches. He draws the knife and holds it in front of him.

Lotta doesn't answer. She turns her back on them and rides closer to the Glimm.

Like a cat spying a bird, the creature spots Wolf, and the stuttering sound that escapes its throat freezes Moss's blood. It sways and puts its writhing legs on the ground. As it moves closer, Moss can see how emaciated it is. Its skull is visible beneath taut skin, eyes sunk into deep cavities. Its stare on Wolf is the same as the starving dogs left to scavenge on the moor when the villagers have no meat left to feed them.

Moss doesn't want to see what it will do next. He turns to Wolf. The boy is so small against the rock, nearly lost in its shadow. A terrible thought comes to him: *He's not big enough to satisfy that giant hunger.*

"Wolf." He pushes aside the thought and tries to make his words as low and calm as possible. "I'm Moss. I'm a friend of your sister's. We're going to get you out of here."

The boy turns to his voice.

The creature emits a high hissing sound. Moss dares to turn, just as it rises up again. Lotta shouts. "It's me you want!"

The Glimm finally shifts its stare to her, and in that moment, its face changes. Moss doesn't know how, but its wild hunger gives way to something almost human. Confusion flickers in its deep-set eyes.

Does it know her? Does it remember?

All at once, the air is thick with . . . emotion. Moss feels an even greater tightening in his chest—the same feeling he had when he thought he was going to lose Hannah. By the look on Lotta's face, she feels it too. But in the face of danger, before this creature, she has closed her eyes, her brow pinched.

Then she begins to sing.

Her voice rises, soft but steady—a song that moves through the air like a thread of light. No words, just an aching melody.

The Glimm hesitates, its sharp teeth parting slightly as the sound washes over it. Its harsh breathing slows; the flickering light along its body pulses in time with Lotta's melody.

Moss seizes the moment and turns back to Wolf.

He saws at the rope binding Wolf's waist, wrists trembling so hard he nearly drops the knife. "I'm going to leave your blindfold on, all right? And I don't want you to pull it off when your hands are free."

Wolf nods just as the rope frays, separates, and falls onto the ground.

Lotta's hands are bloodless on Salty's reins. The horse is transfixed as though hypnotized by the song—or by the sight of the glowing monster.

Because it *is* a monster, isn't it? It's the kind of creature to stalk children's dreams, not the benevolent god he's been brought up to believe in. No wonder the villagers are terrified of it—and of the Council, who has claimed to know its will.

"Get going, Moss!" Lotta breaks the song off and brings Moss back to the urgency of the task at hand.

"I've got you," he says gently to Wolf.

The Glimm lets out a grumble, and Lotta picks up the melody again. The glow from the creature's body ripples over the water.

Moss puts the knife back in its sheath, hoping he won't need it, and picks the boy up. He's light and warm.

"Lottie," the boy moans. His fingers twitch at his blindfold.

"Leave it on, please," says Moss. "It's what Lotta wants. She's fine. You don't have to worry about her." Moss dares to stop briefly to take another glance at Lotta—who has the Glimm locked in some kind of trance, swaying slightly—then carries Wolf to the edge of the water.

He hesitates.

The water still glows with an unearthly light. The tide is all the way in now, the channel much wider. Moss never learned to swim, not really. He still feels the panic of the first time he was in the small lake near the hamlet and his feet lost touch with the bottom. He had the overwhelming sense that something waited beneath the surface to pull him under. In his panic he'd thrashed around, which only made him sink and gulp mouthfuls of water, until his father had pulled him out by his collar. He's never gone so deep again.

He looks at Lotta, facing this huge creature, and he understands that she has trusted him with the most precious thing she knows.

He can't fail her. He takes one step into the water. His boot sinks into mud and gets stuck immediately. He grunts, nearly losing his balance, and manages to wrench it free.

No boots, then.

He sets Wolf down with a reassuring murmur, to quickly unlace and remove his boots.

"We can do this, little man."

Then he hears a voice, calling his name.

He looks up.

Across the water, at the edge of the marsh, the villagers are clustered in groups, watching. The air is completely still—even the gulls have disappeared. But coming toward him: Mam.

She half runs, half stumbles through the reeds. Her boots sink into the sucking mud with every step, but she doesn't stop. Her hair has come loose and her dress is streaked with dirt. Her face is gray and grim, but she's looking straight at him.

"You can do it," she says. "I'm coming to help."

He blinks. "What?"

"I said I'm coming with you. To help carry him."

"No, Mam, it's not safe—"

But she's already bending to take off her boots, just as he had. She wades into the glowing water before he can protest, skirts heavy with mud, arms outstretched. He hasn't seen her like this since he was small, when she'd waded into a storm to fetch a half-drowned lamb. Her body is a shadow in the bright water.

"Mam, stop!" The fierceness of his voice makes her pause. "I don't need your help anymore. I can do this."

She nods and crosses her arms tightly over her chest. Waiting.

Moss picks up Wolf and wades into the water. It's bitterly cold, quickly rising past his knees, then thighs. Wolf rests his head on Moss's shoulder, so still that he might be asleep. Or unconscious. But as the boy's body makes contact with the tide, he moans and grips Moss's neck tighter.

Moss hisses as the cold reaches his stomach, but he continues, each step dragging, every breath short. The light from the Glimm ripples over the surface.

Then the ground vanishes beneath his feet.

Moss gasps, instincts screaming. The weight of Wolf in his arms pushes them both under, and suddenly he's that boy again, choking on dirty lake water. Only this water is heavy with salt. It burns his throat.

Something brushes his legs, wraps around his ankle. He squirms with horror.

Then his feet touch the bottom, and he pushes off with all his determination. The seaweed—or whatever it was—falls away. As they resurface, Wolf cries out, and his chest heaves with a wracking cough.

"You're all right," Moss murmurs as his legs thrum beneath him, keeping them afloat. "I got you. Put both arms around my neck."

Wolf does as he is told, and Moss moves him around so the boy is on his back.

From the bank, Mam's voice carries over the water. "Swim, Moss! You can do it!"

He kicks, his arms flailing at first, but then he finds a rhythm, using both of his hands—free now—to push through the water. He is swimming—not well, but well enough. His mother watches, satisfied.

"You're doing it," she calls. "I never taught you to swim properly. You were too afraid. I'm sorry."

The words lodge deep in his chest.

Then his knees bump the bottom. Mam meets him, and together they haul Wolf out of the water, up onto the soft earth beyond the channel. Moss collapses beside him, soaked and shaking, but safe.

From here, they can see it all.

Lotta and Salty, tiny beneath the monstrous shape of the Glimm. The creature has unfurled to its full height, casting a ghostlight over the villagers, who are rooted in place. Lotta's voice carries across the saltings, bold, sure, and melodic.

And then, the Glimm opens its mouth wide.

And it sings back to her.

# 42

**THE SONG IS GIVING** the Glimm life; Lotta can feel it. It binds them together, thread by thread.

She slips down from Salty's back, placing a reassuring hand on his neck before creeping toward the creature, careful not to startle it. The Glimm bows its massive head—so close she feels its hot breath on her face again, thick with the scent of the moors and the marsh. The island thrums beneath her boots, fed by the Glimm's energy.

Then it turns, and she understands what it wants. While it continues to knit their harmonies together, it offers her its back. She climbs on, near its head. It is hot under her, the skin rough and with sharp hooks, keeping her from slipping as it begins to move, away from the standing stone, away from Salty, who paws the ground and tries to call her back.

Wolf is safe now. That's the most important thing. Moss and his mother hold him as they slump, exhausted, on the marsh, and she knows he's in good hands. Already, Marten charges toward them, axe in hand. Behind him, her parents have shaken off their severed ropes and move more slowly. Her father limps, stopping every few steps to rest before forging on. But they are free, the whole family.

The Glimm glides through the channel with her astride, lifting her above the water. On the far side, she alights, keeping one hand on it, feeling its light fill her body.

The villagers are starting to panic. Some remain frozen, locked in place like standing stones. Others turn to run, their screams weaving through the song.

She lets her melody fall away from her lips.

"Show them," she urges.

The Glimm turns its heavy head to her, blinks its deep-set eyes once. Then it faces the islanders.

The song becomes a rising crescendo.

It swells and envelops them all, stopping the fleeing villagers in their tracks. The saltings disappear. Lotta's mind is flooded with images. The cave paintings are brought to life: villagers singing and dancing with the Glimm, feasting beneath the stars; an island verdant and abundant, with forests of fruit and rivers teeming with fish. Joy trickles through her like warm water.

Then, a ship. Her pulse speeds in terror as new arrivals sweep through the island with weapons, dragging women by the arm back to the ship, setting fire to the forest, which burns and burns and burns.

Islanders flee to the mountains in despair, filling barrows with bodies of the dead as they go.

Lotta stumbles under the weight of their grief, every last soul. She cries out, doubled over, hands pressed to the earth as if she could steady herself against the tide of sorrow.

The last of the island's first people leave from the northern tip, slipping silently on a rough-hewn boat into the mist.

Silence. Lotta hears sobs and cries from the present, but her sight is filled only with emptiness.

The Glimm, alone, roams the barren landscape, howling at the loss of its kin.

Then . . . a glimmer of hope. New people arrive.

But instead of greeting the Glimm, they fear it. They build a Temple to it, but when it approaches them, they turn and run. A child drowns, lost in a bog. Its life force leeches into the earth, and the creature feeds on it—not by will, but by desperate instinct.

Soon, men in black come to find it; hope sings in its heart once more. But they come with weapons, with torches. They overpower it, chain it, pierce its skin with daggers, trying to make it bleed light.

They imprison it deep below the cliffs. Feeding it deer, but keeping it hungry, so the island sickens alongside it.

And then: the children.

Every last one of them parades in front of her eyes. A girl with a cheek scratched by the blackthorn crown. A boy holding a doll made from scraps of cloth and straw. Another with a limp, one leg shorter than the other. Villagers' faces, terrified by the sight of their children being taken, more terrified by what will happen if they are not.

A Judge with changing faces, inflicting pain.

Lotta sees it now, cowering in the underground cage, its solid back leg bound by a chain so tight it cuts into its flesh. Its eyes full of pain.

Then a wash of shame so strong she wants to dive deep into the salt marsh.

But the shame does not belong to her.

It is the Glimm's. The shame it feels every time it takes a child, because the children are keeping it alive—keeping the island from shriveling up and sinking into the sea—and it wishes it was not so.

The Glimm only wants music, connection: to draw its strength from their love, not from their fear.

Horses are not enough. That much, at least, is true.

With a final, mournful note, the song ends.

More silence, but for the sound of weeping.

Lotta looks around at her family, at Moss and his mother. They stand now, holding each other. She beckons them. A gesture that says *Don't be afraid.*

A cry cuts across the still air. "How *could* you?"

Then more.

*They've lied all this time*

*Those children*

*Those deaths*

*All for nothing*

*We trusted you*

*No more*

*No more*

*No more*

Lotta starts to walk toward the villagers, where they stand, accusing the Judge and the Council of deceiving them all. Lewis has his arms around Daphne and Roddy. Daphne's face is buried in his chest. The other Councillors are on their knees. Only the Judge stands, defiant.

The Glimm doesn't move. It tries to shimmy forward, but something is stopping it. It turns its head to look behind, and that's when Lotta sees it: the iron chain wrapped around its tail, held in place by a dorsal fin. Even from here she can see the old metal, slick with silt, cutting into the creature's swollen, infected flesh. The chain runs back into the channel, and, presumably, all the way to the underground tunnels. At the base of the fin is a lock the size of Lotta's fist.

"I will help you," she promises. The Glimm bows its head.

Her family reaches her, and they embrace. Her mother strokes her face and stares into her eyes. She's haunted by what she has seen, by what she has been through, but Lotta sees light there. Hope. Wolf squeezes her legs tightly and she lifts him up. She buries her face in his hair, which still, somehow, smells of milk.

Moss hangs back. She holds out her hand and he takes it. She kisses him on the cheek.

"Thank you," she whispers.

Together they walk the last distance to the shore to join the rest of the islanders, while the Glimm waits.

The enforcers' masks are off. She sees not only Tommy, but Ash Carter, Eddie the butcher's son, two more she hadn't recognized but now sees are sturdy farmers' sons. Once, Marten would have been there too. They surround the Council, weapons drawn.

Lotta walks up to them, shoulders back, head high.

"Let them go," she says to Tommy, and nods at the Lewis family. He steps aside and they back away from the rest of the Council. Daphne's eyes meet Lotta's. Her face is hollow, streaked with dirt—all the lightness gone. For now.

As Roddy emerges, Marten runs forward and they share a long embrace, murmuring in each other's ears. Councillor Gray looks on, appalled, while his daughter Meg stares at the ground, exuding relief rather than sorrow. Farmer Jack takes advantage of the moment to boldly step past his enforcer son and take her hand, pulling her away from the Council, back where she belongs.

Lotta turns to the Judge. "It's over now, Judge Hawthorne."

The man spits on the ground in front of her.

Lotta laughs, which only agitates him further.

"What do you think will happen now, girl? Do you think you can *replace* me? Do you think these people will listen to a girl who consorts with monsters?"

Lotta sighs. "Monsters? I thought you worshipped the Glimm as a god. Isn't this how we washed up here in the first place?"

"My grandfather thought so, but he soon discovered what we all know. It's just an animal with a few tricks. It's no all-powerful deity. The island needs a strong leader to keep order. This lot would have died off without my family. And now you think you can rule over them?" He gestures at the villagers who gather, pale and shocked, around them.

"I almost feel sorry for you," says Lotta. "Almost. Things don't have to bend to your narrow view of the world. We can build a new way. No more Council. No more sacrifices. We can all work together."

"What," says the Judge. "Even the cowardly hidelings? I see you have become quite fond of them. The villagers will never accept them after what they did."

Lotta looks over to where Sadie and her family stand by their cart. Moss's mother has joined them, with her arms around Moss's brother, whose face is wet with tears still.

"They've survived what you never could. I think they might teach us all how to live better. Together."

The villagers exchange wary glances, but nobody steps forward in dispute. A few nod slowly. A ripple of agreement moves through the crowd.

The Judge opens his mouth to say more, but a sudden shift in the light makes him stop.

A cold, musty wind stirs the marsh, carrying a papery rustle, like reeds disturbed. A low moan—part weather, part human—draws every eye toward it.

Something is moving.

From the dark shallows, a shape begins to rise.

A woman, limbs all angles, caked in glistening mud, hair straggling like kelp, crawls naked from the water.

A halo of lights follows her: tiny orbs, like fireflies, flickering in soft rhythm. Their luminescence pulses in time with the Glimm's own faint glow, as if answering it.

"Jenny," whispers Moss beside her. He and Lotta are the only ones not panicking at the sight. Gasps ripple through the villagers and Council alike. Someone screams.

*Bog hag!*

*It's her—it's Jenny!*

*She took the horse* *she'll take the children!*

"Don't be afraid!" calls Lotta. Trusting eyes turn to her. Others grab their children and run.

But Jenny doesn't stop. She walks on two feet now, hunched and slow, moving toward them with solemn purpose. The Glimm watches her, unmoving, from the shallows. Jenny's eyes are fixed not on Lotta, or the Glimm, or even the crowd.

Only the Judge.

The crowd stumbles back, clearing a path for her.

The Judge glares at her as she gets closer. "Witch," he spits. "Hag. Abomination. You should never have returned."

Jenny keeps walking.

"Do you remember me, Judge Hawthorne?" Her voice is low, almost tender. "Do you remember what you took from me? My daughter?"

A sigh runs around the villagers. Other mothers. Other daughters, lost.

The Judge sneers. "It wasn't me," he says. "It was my father."

Jenny draws beside Lotta and shrugs. "The Judge with three faces. You are all one in the eyes of the island. Of the Glimm."

She turns to Lotta.

"Hello, child."

Lotta hears gasps of disbelief around her. She nods at Jenny respectfully.

"You should be dead," the Judge growls. "Drowned in the bog. You're a ghost."

"I am, in a way," she says softly.

And then, without warning, she's on him. She lunges forward and grabs his face between muddy hands. He cowers, barely managing to keep his feet. Then she plants a kiss—almost tender—on his mouth while one hand reaches into his coat.

The Judge shudders and shrieks, but she doesn't hurt him. When she pulls away and lets him go, with something grasped in her taloned fist, he stumbles and falls on his backside, face gaunt as death. He seems smaller somehow. Diminished.

She turns and walks away. As she passes Lotta, she presses the cold object into her hand.

A key. Lotta turns its weight over in her hand, then runs to the Glimm. She holds the key up to show it; the creature closes its eyes in a slow blink of consent. She moves to its tail, finds the rusted lock, and inserts the key. It opens with a slow, grinding click. The chain falls away to lie like a cold serpent in the mud.

The Glimm is free.

It lifts its head.

Its luminescence intensifies, spreading in veins of light beneath its skin, across its fins, its flanks, its eyes. The light passes outward: into the marsh, the reeds, the shallow pools. Into Jenny.

She steps forward, eyes closed, lips stretched back over sharp teeth in what might be a smile. They come together. The Glimm winds around her in a spiral of light. She leans into it. Their bodies shimmer. Where they touch, the air ripples.

Then it draws her into the water without a struggle and slips away.

As the last of Jenny's silhouette is swallowed beneath the glowing surface, the marsh erupts.

A black mist spirals upward and spreads out across the land. Inside it, the bog lights grow and take on human form—dozens of small figures. Lost children. Their faces are pale and hollow, bodies fluid and formless apart from a scratched face, a limp, a ragged doll.

The villagers stand, transfixed.

The Judge tries to back away, but the enforcers hold him. The children wend their way toward him.

He throws up an arm, a useless protection.

They fall on him like a wave, a storm of light and shadow. He thrashes, tries to claw his way free, but small hands grasp him by the arms, push at his back, force his legs to move.

They pull him, push him, toward the water.

Lotta and the other islanders watch him go.

His scream is the last sound before a deep, peaceful silence.

Behind them, a lone flute pipes up. One by one, the villagers begin to sing.

*Oh, sing me a song of the saltings*
*Where all of our power lies*
*Where he'll come each year, on the first day of spring,*
*To show his love for us all*

# EPILOGUE

**"THERE'S A HORSE,"** says Lotta, pointing straight above them.

"Can't see it," says Moss. "Only a waterfall, there, see?"

"You're not looking properly. There! Its ears . . . Oh, never mind, the wind's taken it."

The clouds drift across the early evening sky, streaked with the colors of blooming foxgloves and gorse flower. The stone altar is still warm on their backs after the hot day, making Lotta feel pleasantly drowsy.

"Would anyone miss us if we just stayed here the night?"

"We could count the stars," says Moss.

In the distance, beyond the stone circle, through the trees, the sound of hammering intensifies, then stops altogether. Soon after, a clanging bell starts up.

Moss sighs beside her. "That's my shift starting, then. Race you!"

She's already on her feet before he's pushed himself upright.

Salty and Hannah lift their heads from the rich grass inside the circle, their jaws still working greedily. The crunch of their chewing is drowned out by the racket of birds settling for the night.

Lotta swings onto Salty's back in seconds, but she decides to wait for Moss to scramble up Hannah's extra height.

"I don't know why you bother," she calls to him, laughing. "Hannah will never outrun Salty! But let's see you try!"

Moss whoops behind her as they break into a fast canter along the wide forest road. They pass new cottages, still smelling of freshly sawn timber. Sadie's brother looks up from where he's chopping wood outside to wave as they go by.

The smell of roasting meat greets them as they burst into open space. Esther and Fern work the spit over the fire, wiping sweat from their brows. Lotta's mother is in the vast shared vegetable patch with Wolf, gathering green leaves in a basket. Wolf jumps up and down when he sees them, but his shout is lost to the sound of hoofbeats.

The new clean-smelling house stands tall and its frame is almost complete, built around a sturdy stone chimney. Inside, someone is humming. Councillor Lewis emerges from the shadowed doorway, hammer in hand. He nods at Moss, then at Lotta.

"I heard the bell," says Moss, sliding off Hannah's back. "I'm here."

His mother squeezes out from behind Lewis, elbowing him playfully in the ribs. "Move, Amos!" Sawdust speckles her hair.

Moss watches them together, and Lotta knows he's still not comfortable welcoming a Councillor into their home—never mind that he and Heather were childhood friends. More than friends, perhaps. Time will tell.

"Where do you need me?" asks Moss, stepping forward to take the hammer from Lewis.

But Lewis holds it aloft and smiles.

"No work for you tonight, young Smith," says Lewis. "There's a feast. Your mam and I have washed the potatoes and Stone's churning the butter."

"With those twig arms?" Moss snorts.

"*You* can make yourself useful by hooking Hannah up to the cart and taking everything down to the circle," says Heather, pushing him in the chest, making him smile.

"You too, Lotta." Lewis dips his head. "If that's all right with you."

Lotta smiles. "Of course."

She's glad that her family has come up from the marsh, but she feels her older brother's absence like a lost tooth—small, but enough to make her feel incomplete. "How are Marten and Roddy getting on? I miss him."

Lewis raises his eyebrows. "Roddy and Daphne will never leave the Manor House," he says, not unkindly. "They still think it's their birthright."

Lotta shrugs. "Maybe it is. But that doesn't mean Marten should stay there forever."

She holds a hand out in a flourish, as if offering Lewis the scene before them—the nearly finished house, the cooking smoke through the trees, the laughter drifting from the vegetable patch. Everything his children, and her brother, are missing.

He knows.

The feast in the stone circle is in full swing by the time the moon comes up. Lanterns hang from trees, glowing amber and blue. The altar is crowded with food: baskets of bread, platters of roasted chicken and venison, plates of greens, bowls of foraged berries swimming in honey. The smell of it all makes Lotta's stomach pang with hunger, and her heart swell with the bounty of it all. An offering, yes, but not to the Glimm—to the people who live here. Who have worked the land and gained a feast in return.

Moss's mother beckons him over to the fire, and soon he's turning potatoes in the coals, his face lit gold by the flames. Lewis joins him, handing him the blacksmith's hammer with a wink. "For tomorrow," he says. "We've almost finished the forge."

Moss looks down at it, weighing the handle in his hand.

"You'll teach me?" he says quietly.

"If you want to learn," says Lewis. "I know a bit. We could always use a blacksmith."

Lotta puts her hand on Moss's warm back, and he leans into it, turning to smile with possibility in his eyes.

She finds Wolf and Stone tucked under a bench, their mouths stained with berries, their eyes bright. "Are you eating all the berries?" she asks. "Will I need to go and pick some more?"

Wolf crawls out and hugs her. "Will the Glimm come?" he asks.

"We'll see," she says, ruffling his hair. "It'll come when it's ready."

Later, after the fire has burned low and the younger children have been carried off to bed, Lotta and Moss slip away and climb the side of the mountain with more berries as an excuse. They have no basket.

From up here they can see the sea off the northern end of the island, and beyond it, the wall of mist. The moon is high above, carving a silver path into the ocean. Below, the valley is still, but the sound of music still lingers in the air. The new hamlet nestles into the land like it's always been there—homes with smoke drifting from the chimneys, gardens of flowers and herbs, animals bedded down for the night. The wind carries the scent of gorse and earth and, surprisingly, so far up, salt. It makes her feel at home here.

She puts one hand on the ground. Yes, she still feels it.

Moss sits beside her, arm around her shoulders, keeping her warm. "When are your folks going back down?"

"Tomorrow. Da can't leave the salt farm for long," she says. "It's all he's ever known. It's in his blood. In his bones."

"And yours?"

Lotta doesn't answer right away. Her mind slips back to the cave, the paintings in it. The baskets of salt. The Glimm's song of the saltings—the one that haunted her dreams and her body—felt like it had come from deep time. From her body's ancestral memory of the island. Before language, even.

"I think it is," she says eventually. "Do you think it's possible that we're descended from them? The ones who first lived here?"

"I don't know," he says. "Maybe. Why do you ask?"

"The Glimm's song felt like something ancient that I *knew*," she says. "I can't believe that we've only been here such a short time."

"Just because the Council isn't from here, doesn't mean we're not. The stories of the Glimm had to come from somewhere. From someone."

A horse whinnies down below, cutting through the night air.

"What do you think is out there?" Moss asks, nodding toward the ocean. "Do you believe the stories? That the sea's full of monsters?"

"Maybe," Lotta says. "Or maybe that's what they told us, so we'd never leave."

Moss takes his arm away from her shoulders and lies back on the grass. "There's a ship in the cave," he says to the stars above.

"There is." Lotta joins him. The stars are clouds and sparkling dust motes.

"There must be books in the library—ones that tell you how to sail it."

"I'm sure," says Lotta. "And I think there are people on the Council who know, even if they pretend not to."

Moss exhales slowly. "So we could go, one day. To find out."

"Maybe."

They sit in silence for a long time, until Moss rolls over and plants his warm lips on hers. He tastes of ginger wine and berries. She wouldn't care if she never left, if she stayed here like this, in this moment.

When Moss lifts his face his breath catches. "Look."

She sits up. Far below, down the mountain pass, a glow begins to rise. Faint at first, like the shimmer of heat on stone, then growing clearer, brighter. A soft, turquoise pulse, like breath.

Moss leans forward. "Do you see that?"

Lotta's heart quickens. "Yes."

The music below gets louder.

The light drifts closer, slow and sure, like something remembering its way home.

ACKNOWLEDGMENTS

THIS NOVEL WAS WRITTEN in a bit of a fever dream fed by folklore, films, books, conversations, locations, history, and a lot of meanderings through the unconscious.

While the landscape and culture of Brack are fictional, I was lucky enough in 2024 to visit the Outer Hebrides and St. Kilda in Scotland, which helped me to imagine the physicality of the landscape and life on an isolated, barren island with moors and bogs and salt marshes and ancient standing stones—and to imagine an alternative history (or possible future).

Thanks very much to the following people there, who made my stay such a joy and who shared stories so generously, including Elaine and Richard at Galson Farm Guest House and Christina at the Bunker, both on Lewis, and Richard and Karen at Dirascal Cottage Annex on Scalpay. Thanks, too, to Angus at Kilda Cruises for one of the best days of my life, and to Seumas of Sea Harris, who made sure I got a seat when it was touch and go. The wonderful Shannon at Tràigh Mhòr

Pony Trekking took me across the Lewis moors on a beautiful black Shire X called Hannah, who of course snuck her way into the book.

Thanks to Robin Robertson (whose poem "Leaving St. Kilda" was one of the things that piqued my interest in the place) for allowing me to quote from your poem "Before the Donnachaidh Falls," from the collection of new Scottish folktales, *Grimoire* (Picador, 2020).

I couldn't have done it without the support of my wonderful agent, Gaia Banks, and my commissioning editors: Jenny Hellen at Allen & Unwin New Zealand, Bella Pearson and Hannah Featherstone at Guppy Books, and Karen Wojtyla at Margaret K. McElderry Books. Thank you all for your belief and trust in me, your patience, and your excellent, probing feedback.

Thanks to Emma Neale for your thoughtful editing and your lovely, gentle encouragement.

Thanks to the Frank Sargeson Trust—it was an honor to be a 2025 Frank Sargeson Fellow. It came at a crucial time and enabled me to finish this book undistracted.

Thanks to friends and helpers: Zoe Roland and Al Crawford for giving me such a moody, windswept place to write when I needed to get away; Erin Harrington and Jonathan King for your folk horror knowledge and assistance; and Steve and Belinda Hamlin for answering my vet-related questions and for good conversations.

Thanks to fellow writers who offered encouragement when I thought I might drown: Rachael Craw, Tania Roxborogh, Claire Mabey, and Leonie Agnew.

Finally, thanks to my family, who had to put up with my mental absence and quirky work habits throughout the writing of this book. I dedicate *Song of the Saltings* to my younger sister, Harriet Elworthy, who is a champion of children's books and a true horse girl.